Zanita

A novel in the world of Tricia Barr's Fireheart Series

B.J. Priester

Zanita is a work of fiction. Names, places, and incidents were born in the author's imagination. Any resemblance to real persons or events is coincidental.

ISBN: 1534605592
ISBN 13: 9781534605596
Library of Congress Control Number: 2016909683
CreateSpace Independent Publishing Platform
North Charleston, South Carolina

www.triciabarr.com
www.FANgirlblog.com
facebook.com/FireheartSeries
twitter.com/fangirlcantina
twitter.com/RedPenofLex

FOREWORD

T he seeds of the story ideas that became *Zanita* had their origins in the early stages of the character development for Daemyn, Utara, and Vespa in my novel *Wynde*, the first book in the Fireheart Series. Through countless hours of collaboration in brainstorming, creating, writing, and editing that novel, B.J. and I always kept in mind the planned future tales in my burgeoning storytelling world. From the beginning we envisioned *Zanita* as a novel he would write about the earliest adventures of Daemyn and Utara, building backstory and making connections forward, while I progressed onward with Vespa's journey in the principal Fireheart Series stories.

Over time, the development of *Zanita* drew on many sources of inspiration, including our respective backgrounds in engineering and law, the march of advancing technology in our world, lessons drawn from history and from the stories that have provided aspirational and cautionary guideposts for our storytelling, and even my experiences in a Barr family excursion to the African savannah. Now those initial seeds have bloomed into a tale I hope will bring you as much enjoyment in reading as we had creating it.

~ Tricia Barr

For Jaina and Jag, the beginning but not the end

DRAMATIS PERSONAE

Wynde Industries
Daemyn Wynde; Fith team Airspar pilot, venturist (male)
Elsa Ovella; chief of security (female)
Reiton Holtspring; business manager, venturist (male)

Prime Diplomatic Service
Utara Fireheart; counselor - Blonkas (female)
Aidan Stone; counselor - Blonkas (male)
Koster Fireheart; bureau chief - Durnow, Utara's father (male)

Friends & Family
J'ni Acai; wildlife conservation scientist (female)
Tracelea Chal; Aladarian Guard officer (female)

Rustle Tames; venturist (male)
Celia Lancer; venturist (female)
Sage Gaiser; venturist (female)

Sai Kuron; engineer, Daemyn's father (male)
Ripi Wynde; architect, Daemyn's mother (female)
Jasiri Berl; activist, Utara's mother (female)

Dom Farrier; Fith team Airspar coach (male)
Kaye; Fith team Airspar pilot (female)
Sayal; Fith team Airspar pilot (female)
Birk; Fith team Airspar pilot (male)

People of Prime

Marx Monson; corporate intelligence - Grandell Motors (male)

Birto Hybollo; senior agent - Prime Intelligence Service (male)

Kirkland Oggust; code hacker (male)

Allyton Granitine; reporter (female)

CROSSING LINES

"I don't care what the odds say. I never bet against Daemyn Wynde."

Jaret Dayelle, Airspar racing analyst, Nightly Sports Express

ONE

...*Solar Towers Airspar Track, Hyj-gon*

The engines wailed. The wind howled. The acceleration forced Daemyn Wynde back in the seat. The airblade rocketed along a straight line. The only one he would have in the otherwise circuitous path necessary to maximize his opportunities in the anchor leg of the match's second phase.

Solar Towers, the premiere racing venue in Hyj-gon, was the most difficult track on the planet. Its soaring spires, arching skyways, rotating solar panels, and significant variations in altitude combined to test the very limits of a pilot's skill.

He decelerated hard, his torso straining against the harness. Fingers crushing the yoke, teeth clenched, Daemyn tipped the blade on its wing and swung into a breath-stealing turn around one of the spires.

The roar of the crowd in the grandstand overwhelmed the shriek of his engines. The Fith Manufacturing-sponsored team had been Hyj-gon's best for over two decades. Daemyn had been the best pilot on Fith's team for the last four seasons. Whenever his blade passed by one of the many spectator areas on the course, it drew the biggest cheers. He had fans all across Prime, earned at least some applause at nearly every track, but nowhere else was like this. Not even close.

A quick glance at the heads-up display confirmed that the opposing pilot was still a few seconds behind relative to Daemyn's pace. Flying the anchor leg for the Grandell Motors team, Ritzer was an exceptional flyer. But the man was no match for Daemyn Wynde at Solar Towers. Born and raised here, he had visited the course hundreds of times as a pedestrian or spectator. The minutes of flying it as a competitor he savored above any other experience in his career.

Daemyn ignored the heads-up and simply flew. His airblade responded effortlessly to the controls. As always, his teammates Birk, Sayal, and Kaye had done their jobs in the first three legs. His task was to fly his best during the anchor leg, to put the second phase entirely out of reach – and give Fith a clear advantage over GM heading into the third phase.

His airblade soared cleanly through the center of a glimmering bright red gate hovering in the air. He tipped the blade on its port wing and whipped around another tower – descending just enough to put him right at the midpoint of the cobalt blue gate halfway through his turn. Once past the tower he yanked the yoke with both hands, climbing sharply toward another pair of gates.

He came over the top of the skyway upside down, his transparent canopy exposed to the thousands of spectators a few dozen meters below. The nose of his airblade pierced the meter-wide hologram in the center of the green gate, generating a dazzling sparkle of emerald light. The crowd cheered another deafening chorus of approval. Airspar had been born in Hyj-gon, and its people still embraced the sport like no other culture on Prime.

Daemyn flipped the blade around its central axis and came in perfectly level, right-side up, to swoop underneath the second skyway and through the green gate levitating a meter below its underside. He climbed again, rising over the skyways, and swung around. He banked to port, then starboard, then port again to weave through a closely set trio of spires. Each turn whipped him through an orange gate, and then he shoved the yoke and plunged toward his next set of targets.

Kaye's voice crackled in his headset. *"HUD."*

Daemyn spared a glance at the heads-up display – and his eyes widened.

Somehow Ritzer had missed one of the blue gates between two spires along the GM pilot's path. When Daemyn and his three teammates had planned their routes in the minutes before the start of the second phase, they had simply written off that high-value gate as GM's, just as Ritzer's team would have conceded some of them to Fith.

But if that target was still in play... It changed the calculus entirely.

Before he made an irreversible decision, Daemyn took one more second to review the data on the heads-up. Boomers and phaseshots. Smokers and flares. Speeders and twisters. His teammates had accumulated the combination of defensive and offensive utilities they had planned together. The intended remainder of Daemyn's anchor leg would complete their plan with Fith holding a utilities advantage likely – barring one of them succumbing to an error even bigger than the one Ritzer had made – to put the third phase out of reach for GM. If he stole that additional blue gate, though, it would be over before it started.

Only one more item of data mattered: the countdown timer on Ritzer's progress through the course. Once one pilot crossed the finish line, the tally sensors on all of the remaining gates would instantly deactivate. After his mistake, Ritzer hadn't tried to circle back for the blue gate, but had continued onward to get as much of the rest as he could on his weaving path to toward the finish line. It was the safe call. The right call, in the eyes of almost every Airspar pilot.

Daemyn Wynde, though, was one of the best pilots in the sport. Maybe *the* best, depending on who you asked.

In this situation, the best pilot in Airspar wouldn't make the safe call. The best pilot would steal the blue gate and put the match out of reach *now*.

Daemyn yanked his airblade into a sharp, screeching turn.

Another voice sounded in his headset. Fith's coach, Dom Farrier. *"I hope you know what you're doing."*

Daemyn didn't reply. The engines screeched. The acceleration expelled the air from his lungs. The airblade groaned. The yoke vibrated in his hands. He sliced across the course, weaving among the towers.

The overheating alarm blared from the console and the warning indicator flashed on the heads-up. Even with the wind hurtling through the intakes, the coolant system for the artronium engines couldn't keep up. Not at this speed. Not for long.

He swooped above one skyway, dove below another, and put the blade on a direct line for the blue gate ahead. His eyes flicked to the Ritzer countdown – three seconds – then the overheating warning – ten seconds. Daemyn held his path.

Two-point-nine seconds later the airblade charged through the blue gate, Daemyn slammed forward in the harness as he abruptly reduced engine speed, and the crowd erupted in a cheer like he hadn't heard in years.

～◯

...Blonkas, Rocco Administrative Region

Insects buzzed in the still air. The wide street, bordered on both sides by three-story rowhouses, remained clear. Barely past dawn, the sun low in the eastern sky, the neighborhood was quiet.

Gazing at the empty tents, the unused lounging chairs, and the other makeshift outdoor sleeping places the residents had set up at the bases of the rowhouses' walls, Utara Fireheart smiled. For the first time in six days, last night the power had stayed on. Without it, sleeping outside was the only tolerable option. When the air chillers were running, nobody passed up the chance for a good night's sleep in their beds.

Last night's luxury, though, preceded an inevitable power shutdown during the worst heat of this coming afternoon. It wouldn't take long for the residents to reemerge where, impossible as it seemed, the temperature was actually cooler. Six months into her assignment here, Utara was starting to think the intermittent, unreliable power was worse than simply having no power at all. No one could ever adjust to anything with everything constantly in flux.

"Quiet morning in Evostown," said the familiar voice of Aidan Stone, closing the front door of the adjacent rowhouse behind him.

"For once."

His long legs took him down the six steps in two bounds. He paced over and joined Utara sitting on the stairs to her building. "The plan's still on?"

"Last I heard, yes." She checked her comdee. "So far, so good."

He slapped his palms on his knees. "All right, then. I'll start rounding them up."

Less than an hour later, Utara and Aidan led a motley band of residents down the street. Some grandparents, some parents, and a handful of workers who didn't have to report until the afternoon shifts. Most of the children had been shuffled off to school, but a few of the older toddlers tagged along for lack of anything better to do. Although the neighborhood had earned its name for the large numbers of Aquarians who'd picked this area of the city as their home when Blonkas had opened for residential occupancy a quarter century ago, now Evostown had a significant number of Aladarians and Faytans, too. Their clothes spanned all the colors of the rainbow and more.

Every adult carried a large, empty canister. For now the transpariplast containers dangled from hands or sat tucked under arms. On the return walk, filled to the brim with water, they would be hefted in two arms even by the strongest individuals.

Utara didn't want to think about what would happen if the promised tankers didn't arrive in the square.

Hurrying a few quick steps to catch up to her side, Lucia, mother of four, apparently had the same worry. "You're sure they'll come?"

Utara gave a big, reassuring smile. "They will."

"We do our best to keep our storage tank full when the power is on," Lucia said. "But it will make me feel better to have a little extra on hand, just in case."

"I know. Me too."

Lucia took one hand off her empty canister and touched Utara's arm. "Thank you for carrying a share. Both of you."

"It's our job. All the same, you're welcome."

Lucia nodded and dropped back to walk with her father and a cousin. Aidan finished talking to Mazee, one of Evostown's trusted elders, and glanced her way. Seeing her unoccupied, he strode over to join her.

Canister swinging back and forth in one hand, he asked, "How's Lucia?"

"Grateful for the help."

"I bet."

"At least we're doing something." Utara kicked a small rock in the street, sending it tumbling away at high speed. Aidan raised a brow at her. "Anything is better than filling out forms by hand in triplicate to file weekly status reports. Especially when they contain exactly the same requests for urgent material assistance as the previous six weeks."

"Terminal inputs at least go faster. But that requires power to operate them."

"Right."

"Any update from the tankers?"

She checked her comdee again. "No. But they promised to let me know promptly if they had to cancel, so I'll count this as a good sign."

"Wish I had your confidence," Aidan said. "But maybe today fortune will finally go our way a little bit."

"It will," she promised herself as much as her colleague.

A few minutes later the group arrived in the square. Even though it wasn't hot yet, out of habit everyone took up positions in the shade under the trees. The tankers might arrive any time in the next hour, so they settled in to wait. The children played while the adults conversed. A few of the older men gathered around a small portable audiocaster tuned to the day's Airspar match. Listening to sporting races half a world away probably wasn't the best use of rechargeable energy cells, but at their age no one had the heart to deny them their one guilty pleasure.

Aidan sat down next to Utara on one of the benches. "They all could use a couple of smooth days right now."

"Yes, they could." She forced herself to not check the comdee. "A little stability would really help ease the tension."

"And cut down on the rumors."

"That too."

Her two-year mandatory service-term with the Aladarian Guard had convinced Utara more than ever that force and violence created more problems than they solved. She had joined the Prime Diplomatic Service because it was the best chance for her to pursue peaceful solutions. For now, only a few years into her career, that meant helping keep a struggling city from deteriorating into anarchy. Whatever the best intentions and analyses of the bureaucrats and social planners decades ago, it simply took longer than a generation and a half for a centuries-old nomadic culture to reinvent itself for urban residency. Modes of living took time to adapt, and the old ways were even slower to change. The PDS would have faced a major challenge in assisting the residents regardless, but the increasingly severe failings of the city's critical infrastructures only compounded the difficulties ten-fold.

"By the way," Aidan said. "I had an idea about how we might –"

The motorized roar at first sounded like an overload from the Airspar audio, but it only took a second for everyone's eyes to draw upward instead. Coming in low, not far above the rooftops, the security drone sped toward the city wall a hundred meters beyond the square. About three times the size of a vulture, the drone had its gun barrels deployed.

Before anyone could say anything, more engine roars split the air. Three additional drones chased after the first, one after the other in a line.

"What's going on?" Mazee asked.

Utara watched the drones disappear over the wall in the distance. Moments later came an unmistakable sound – the staccato, rolling growl of the drones' rapid-fire guns.

"Probably some wildlife that got too close," Aidan said loudly, so everyone in the group could hear. "Scaring them back before they reach the fences."

Utara hoped he was right. But she doubted it. One drone would be enough to chase off anything but a herd of hephagaunts. Occasionally a team of poachers might accidentally get within range of the city, but she'd never heard of more than two drones going after them. Four drones at once, fully a third of the external security subdivision's arsenal, wasn't good. Not at all.

Her comdee chirped. She checked its screen, praying her next words wouldn't involve telling all the residents to run. Instead she found a simple, one-line message that the water's arrival was imminent. For now, that was the best possible news. Hopefully the power would come on at some point tonight so she could check the latest briefing from the public safety division.

"The tankers!" someone shouted. "They're here!"

Utara looked over and confirmed it for herself. So did most of the others. Amid the bustle of gathering up their canisters to form a line, the drones were forgotten. The release of pent-up anxiety from the residents was palpable.

Grinning, she turned to Aidan. "Told you."

...Vartan Corp. research & development facility, suburbs of Kisko

In the darkest hour of night, he slid through the shadows as easily as a ghost. So well did he keep himself concealed, he might as well have been one.

The microfilament bodysuit absorbed light on the visible and infrared spectrums rather than reflecting it, more than enough to keep him invisible to the handful of security cams on the facility's perimeter. It would fool the human guards, too, if they'd been here, but they had passed by on their patrol six minutes earlier and would not return this way for nearly an hour. The weave of synthetic fibers in the soles of his shoes muffled his steps sufficiently to avoid triggering the audio sensors. His electronics, carried in a heavy case strapped to his belt at the small of his back, were shielded by a combination of a thin layer of humiin alloy and a micro-jammer. Although the detection technology Vartan Corporation had installed was far from inferior, his tech was better.

The best that money could buy, in fact. The higher-ups at Grandell Motors were more than capable of making any number of poor decisions in recent years, but cost-cutting in the corporate intelligence division was not one of them. In moments like this, the expenditures were worth every dract. He doubted that even the operatives of the Prime Intelligence Service had gear like this, not in a time of slashed budgets and blind optimism of a peaceful planetary future. Someday he would earn his way out of the greedy, mercenary world of corporate espionage and fulfill the calling to protect Prime and its people. Until then, though, he had a job to do. And every mission he completed successfully put him that much closer to his goal.

Tonight, success was inevitable. The tech helped make things easier, certainly, but mostly he struck with the advantage of superior information and analysis. He knew exactly where he was going, and precisely what he needed to do at each stage of his plan. He had studied the specifications of this facility in more detail than anyone in Vartan's security department ever had. Tonight they had already lost, because he had beaten them before he'd arrived.

With a long stride he arrived at the rear door of the three-story building toward the southwestern edge of the facility. He swung the carrycase around to his front, opened its cover, and withdrew a slender wire. Touching it to the bottom of the door's keypad, he waited. Three seconds later the panel flashed green. His gloved hand opened the door and he slipped inside. The emergency-exit stairwell was unlocked, as safety-code regulations required, and he bounded his way to the second floor.

The main corridor itself had no cams to monitor its length, but several of the individual room doors did. An odd decision, to be sure, but not the strangest security measure he'd ever encountered. He traversed his predetermined course along the hallway. First along one wall, then a diagonal across to the other, then back, then across once more, like the current in a mountain stream riding from eddy to eddy between the boulders.

He reached his destination – one of the doors without a cam. Again the wire from the handheld code-hacker gave him access in seconds. Shutting the door behind him, he appraised the room. He didn't need to risk activating the lums; the night-vision goggles provided plenty of visibility.

Yes, this was definitely the room assigned to the engineers working to develop high-density transpariplast. For Vartan Corporation it was a low priority; it would provide incremental benefit to the deep-sea research submersibles they built for universities and exploratory venturists, which provided only a small segment of their annual revenues. What Vartan hadn't yet figured out – and Grandell Motors had – was that the technology would radically reduce the cost of several key components across millions of vehicles Grandell built or repaired every year.

Even if Grandell had been inclined to license the technology from Vartan – which they weren't – that would only be possible after Vartan finished successfully developing it. Which, apparently, they were in no rush to do. Grandell, on the other hand, was prepared to invest the engineer-hours and financing to get it done. In moments like these, the corporate intelligence division more than paid for itself.

In a matter of minutes the data from the workstations was downloaded to his portable datadrives. Securing them in his carrycase, he returned to the door. For an instant he hesitated, wondering if he'd heard footsteps in the corridor beyond. But it was nothing. He opened the door and retraced his steps.

Honestly, his escape hardly qualified as subterfuge. He was back through the corridor, down the stairs, and out the door in no time. The cams and sensors on the grounds were as easy to defeat on the way out as the way in, and he had slipped out beneath the eastern perimeter fence less than seventeen minutes after he'd entered.

That left him only four cams to avoid – two on the street, one on a bank, and the last guarding the gate to a private residence – before he reached the city park. Amid the darkness cast by the wide canopies of limbs in the towering trees and the dimmest illumination of the stars in a cloud-dabbled sky, he didn't bother to chart a hidden course from trunk to trunk. He simply jogged across the grounds until he emerged at the other side, pausing beneath a soaring elm.

He retrieved the comdee from his carrycase and sent the innocuous text message to the other member of corporate intelligence who'd accompanied him to Kisko. HOW'S THE TEAM? He was within his predicted window for extraction, so Dana Bristow was already charting a meandering course on the streets from their hotel to the park, ready for the signal to pick him up and head straight to their waiting shuttlecraft. A hopeless Airspar fanatic, no doubt she had been listening to the match the entire time.

Moments later came the answer. LOSING TO FITH. SHIGGERS.

Idly he wondered if the slur was meant for the Fith team, or Grandell's own. Frankly he didn't care one way or the other. But he pretended to, because it was expected.

His thumb reached to reply – just as the black Grandell Motors two-seater swung its way to the edge of the road in front of him. The door opened of its own accord as he strolled out from behind the elm, and easily he slid into the seat.

"We're stinking it up," she grumbled, answering the question he would have asked. "You have it?"

"I do."

Bristow nodded. "Nobody on the roads this time of night. We'll be in the air in twenty. Back in the Valley before dawn."

"Perfect."

Patting his carrycase, for the first time tonight Marx Monson smiled.

TWO

...Solar Towers Airspar Track

It would be a tough shot.

The current target in his sights was a sphere of light at the pinnacle of one of the spires. The stationary location helped, at least. The difficulty came from the sphere's constantly shifting size: about six meters in diameter at its widest extension, two meters at the smallest. Anything other than a dead-center hit would have to be timed perfectly, or run the risk of missing the sphere and scoring no points.

With the number of easier opportunities that invariably arose over the course of the third phase, Daemyn probably wouldn't have bothered in an ordinary match. Even with the high point total earned with a hit, wise strategy counseled against wasting a shot from a limited arsenal on a low chance of success.

Thanks to his steal of the blue gate in the final seconds of the second phase, though, the match against Grandell Motors already was a full-on rout. Fith would win even if he failed to score another point in this phase – and with his utilities far from depleted, there was no way that was going to happen.

But they had a lot more at stake than the entry in the win/loss column. His airblade had crashed in the first match of the season after an opposing pilot's wing had clipped a skybridge and the debris had shredded one of Daemyn's engines. Even though he'd pushed himself to the limit to recover from his injuries and get cleared to fly again, he'd missed nearly half the season by the time he'd rejoined his teammates in competition. By then all of the Airspar commentators and analysts, in the media and among the fans alike, had declared it impossible for Fith to make the championships. Daemyn was determined to prove them wrong. After the results of the previous match

Fith had climbed to tenth place in the standings. In points, they were well within striking distance of overtaking Yoshigura for eighth – the final qualifying spot in the upcoming Airspar championships – and rising to seventh wasn't out of the question. Although the greatest single factor in the standings algorithm was wins and losses, total points scored and margin of victory both also had significant weight. If they trounced GM badly enough, the combined effect on their rating would be considerable.

Drawing closer, Daemyn swung his airblade around a spire and watched the pattern of the sphere's expansion and contraction one more time. He weaved around the last intervening spire, lined up the targeting reticule on his heads-up display, flicked a thumb-switch on the yoke, and squeezed the trigger.

With a loud *thwap* and a burst of smoke, the speeder utility fired from the launch tube under his port wing. Trailing propellant exhaust, it rocketed ahead at full speed on a straight line. Although the globe of light was shrinking as it approached, Daemyn's aim had been good enough – the speeder passed within a meter of the sphere's center, setting off a dazzling display of sparkling lights as the target recognized his hit.

He whipped the airblade into a barrel-roll and cut back across the course. The icons on his heads-up showed Sayal in the lead heavy blade hanging back near Fith's primary stationary goal, the easiest place for GM to score points – if they could get past the variety of defensive utilities at her disposal. Birk flew a bit further out in the second heavy, driving off GM's second light before it could fire any of its offensive utilities. Kaye raced Fith's second light toward a pair of targets at the far end of the course, while GM's second heavy sped to intercept her. For the moment, that left Daemyn to deal with Ritzer in the lead light and Nevald in the lead heavy.

"*Want some cover?*" Sayal asked.

Quickly he considered the target icons on the heads-up. The other heavy's pursuit of Kaye had left one of the rotating rings exposed.

"Not this pass," he told her. "One of them may try for the goal instead of me."

"*Copy.*"

Daemyn pushed the throttle to maximum. He dipped under a skyway and swerved around the wide lower segment of one of the towers. A glance at the heads-up confirmed Nevald heading his way, with Ritzer not far behind. Daemyn slowed, gaining altitude to line up for his run at the ring.

The console beeped, alerting him that Nevald had reached firing range. The running tally in his head told him that the heavy blade had exhausted its supply of boomers. Nevald likely would try a flare. Daemyn took a long, focused look at the path ahead of him, then knocked his chin toggle.

The eyeshades dropped into place a second before Nevald fired the flare. Daemyn didn't blink or close his eyes. The eyeshades did their job, dimming the incandescent trail of the flare enough that Daemyn's gaze never had to waver from the ring in the distance. Speeding toward the spires, he knocked the chin toggle and flicked his thumb to switch over to twisters.

By the time he reached the first spire, the eyeshades were gone. He tipped the airblade on its port wing, fired, and swung around. A second later he was tipped on the starboard wing, firing again and swooping back. The next second he banked to port again, fired the third twister, and leveled out as he rounded the last spire.

Three wiggling lines snaked their way toward the ring. About eight meters across, it made a full rotation every two seconds. The first twister sailed cleanly through the circle. The second impacted against the thick metal of ring, exploding in a brilliant ball of incinerating propellant. The detonation of the utility didn't affect the ring in the slightest, though; it continued its rotation unabated, just in time to allow the third twister to zip through along nearly the identical line as the first.

Daemyn didn't bother checking the heads-up's updated score. He looked only for Nevald and Ritzer, and wasn't surprised where he found them. With Birk drawn off, Nevald was making a desperate run toward the primary goal, hoping to get something past Sayal in a duel of heavies before the match clock expired. Ritzer had read the course the same way Daemyn had – the rotating ring was the best undefended target.

He toggled Sayal's comm back on. "I'll block Ritzer?"

"Copy. I'm good on Nevald."

Cutting beneath a skyway, Daemyn surged toward the oncoming GM light. His own light had been armed almost exclusively with the offensive utilities, but he did have one pair of phaseshots loaded. Keeping Ritzer from scoring on the ring was as good an opportunity as any to use them.

To time the shot right, Ritzer would need a fairly straight path at the ring. But from his direction of approach, there were too many towers in the way; he'd have to cut through the lane with the skyways.

Daemyn swung a wide turn around a pair of adjacent spires, then headed on a perpendicular trajectory to Ritzer's approach. As he and Ritzer rapidly converged, Daemyn aimed his targeting reticule at nothing in particular in the distance – along a line that would send the phaseshots right through Ritzer's line of sight if he came over the top of the skyway. Squeezing the trigger, Daemyn shoved the yoke and swung his airblade to a lower altitude – about four meters lower than where Ritzer would be if he flew under the skyway instead. Now he had guaranteed Ritzer bad aim whichever flight path he chose; either way, the phaseshots or the proximity alarm would keep him distracted.

He didn't even bother to check which way Ritzer went. A thoroughly thwarted Nevald was heading back his way, but Daemyn was already swooping around in the direction of GM's stationary goal. He still had five speeders left to fire, even if all he could do was shoot them in a last-ditch utility dump at the goal. He had less than two minutes left in the match. That was just enough to time to finish running up the score.

...Blonkas

Sawing with the serrated edge of her knife at the sturdy shell of the turanoot, Utara savored the rare moment of relative tranquility in Evostown. No one pounding on the door with an anxious question or frightening bit of gossip. No parents fearful for what the coming months might bring for their children. No beeping comdee heralding an urgent comm or worrisome text alert. The slower, water-laden trek back to their homes had left everyone exhausted; most of the residents now rested in the shade, hidden from the sweltering sun. Utara and Aidan had made sure to walk separately among the group, allowing them to talk to many different residents on the way. For once, nothing of immediate urgency had presented itself in those conversations.

For a few minutes, at least, they had time to simply sit and eat. Once she got the fruit's shell cracked open, anyway.

While Utara sawed away, Aidan pursued a more direct route toward the turanoot's tender, juicy interior. With one hand he steadied the irregularly shaped orb on the table. With the other he raised his knife over his head – then slammed it down, driving the tip deep into the fruit. He adjusted the turanoot slightly, then wrenched his fist and forearm downward to the table, bringing the blade of the knife with them on a vicious slice through the fruit. Setting down the knife, he hefted the turanoot in two hands. A firm yank, a soft *fwap!*, and he triumphantly set down the severed halves of the fruit on the table before him.

He grinned at her. "Want me to split yours?"

Sawing and shaking her head, she said, "No. I've got it."

"If you insist."

He took his time slicing up the squishy innards of the turanoot while he waited for her to open hers. It didn't take her that much longer, fortunately. As soon as she started cutting her fruit into bite-sized morsels, he popped the first of his into his mouth.

"Has anyone replied about the drones?" she asked.

Chewing, he shook his head.

"Not to me, either." She didn't like the delay; it was a tactic their PDS superiors had begun using more frequently lately. So she focused on the positive. "Word seems to be getting around that some of the rumors about the other neighborhoods aren't actually true."

He nodded. "Definitely. Hasto was really fired up the other day. Absolutely convinced that Rockville is getting power all day and night, and that it's because it's mostly Terrans there. Now he's come around that what I'd heard from Tyku is worth believing."

Utara had only met their fellow junior diplomat once, but Aidan had known him since their years together at Hillside Conservatory. "Berta said something very similar to me. So did Ronii."

"That's good. The more mothers who think that way, the better."

"Yes. If people can't trust that power and water are being shared equitably throughout the city, things will only get worse."

He held up a finger, poised to say something, but had to reach for his water and take a long drink first. "You're still hearing rumors about the other Future Cities, though, right?"

"A little. Not any new ones today, only repeats of the ones from the last few weeks."

"Same for me."

She took another bite, then a long drink from her water. "Why?"

He frowned. "Just a feeling. The anxiety seems to be shifting direction. Instead of projecting their fears on other neighborhoods in Blonkas, they're redirecting to the other cities."

"I could certainly see that happening." Utara ate another bite, thinking. The most common rumors didn't make a lot of sense – that Durnow, located in a considerably drier climate than Blonkas where agriculture was more difficult, was hoarding overstock of grain and fruit, or that Tagron, on the coastline where the continent's largest river emptied into the ocean, had a major shortage of water – but rumors rarely did. "The more impersonal the target, the easier it is to aim your outrage at them."

"Right."

"Except the one about Luppitan."

"That some people are leaving the city entirely, going to live on the savannah?" Aidan shook his head. "That's suicide. Nobody's that desperate."

"That's just it, though."

"Hmm?" Mid-chew, he motioned for her to explain.

"All the other rumors come from a fear of, well, abandonment. That they'll be left to die while the others get to survive. This one, it's something different. That Blonkas actually has it better, that things are worse some-where else."

He gazed across the room, lost in thought. "I hadn't considered it that way. But you're right. It's not about anger. It's about..."

When his words hung in the air, she said, "Hopelessness."

"Yes."

Utara didn't know what else to say, so for a few minutes they sat in silence and finished off the rest of their respective turanoots. When she finished, she carried her two half-shells to the trash and dropped them in. When she started to walk back to the table to get Aidan's, he waved her off.

With a smooth flick of his wrist he lobbed a shell half into the air, sending it on a perfect arc from his hand into the trash bin. A second toss plopped the other half in too.

He pushed back his chair and stood. "I promised Mazee I'd show him how to repair the insulation that keeps the condensation off their generator today, and I'm already late."

"I'm going to make some comms."

"To anyone in particular?"

"Friends and contacts in some of the other Future Cities."

He stared at her. "You're going to make the trek into the field office now?"

Normally she'd agree about avoiding the lengthy excursion across Blonkas in the worst heat of the day, but intercity communications would be considerably faster and easier on a compupod. "Tonight won't be good for reaching people, and it shouldn't wait until tomorrow."

"You're sure?"

"I am. See you when I get back?"

He was already out the door, but he leaned back and peeked his head past the door frame so he could reply. "Where else would I go?"

...Midland Savannahs Wildlife Sanctuary

As it did every day, dawn brought movement. The winds tickling the long grasses and the tops of the trees. The birds flitting about, snatching insects. A lone rhynohog, snuffling in the dirt. The vultures circling high above, performing their grim surveillance for any leftovers the nighttime predators might have abandoned.

Today, it also meant the zeraffe herd awoke and resumed another hours-long burst of progress in their migration. First, though, they would drink. Eating would come later, to refuel their bodies after the surge across the savannah. To survive that trek they needed plenty of hydration, and this slender river – the same one at which they'd made a nightly stop for count-less zeraffe generations – was the perfect source.

Atop the nearest rise, standing on the hood of her parked truck, J'ni Acai watched the black-and-white mammals jostle and bellow in preparation for their journey. The individual animals were different, of course, but the conglomerated mass of flesh and slender legs and long necks looked the same as it always did. A few heads popped skyward to keep watch for predators, stretched to full height a meter above the ground. Most of the zeraffes, though, kept on drinking. She wasn't sure how many times she'd witnessed the spectacle growing up – the count was long lost, as anyone's would be, in the hazy memories of young childhood – but this year was the fifth occasion she had made her way to this spot to actually study the majestic herd with the observational perspective of a scientist. On the one hand, that meant she could no longer just stand and watch; she was constantly catching details, spotting subtleties, and making mental notes. On the other hand, none of it detracted in the slightest from the natural beauty before her.

She had another six months, maybe longer, before her advisor back at Rampart would expect to see a draft of her dissertation on the role of the zeraffe migration in the savannah's ecology. Considering she was well underway in writing it, J'ni wasn't worried. She had plenty of time. She'd probably –

Kinana. With the advantage of height and distance, J'ni saw it a split-second before the zeraffes did.

Powered by its massive hind legs, the merciless feline had sprung from its hiding place in the low shrubbery of the copse. It cleared nearly fifteen meters in the air. A few of the zeraffes, heads held high, caught the motion. The kinana's paws hit the ground once, just for an instant. By the time the zeraffes had started their first warbling bellows of alarm, the second leap had brought the predator down on the back of one of their older, slower compatriots.

The herd's reaction looked choreographed. Zeraffes bolted away from the impact point in all directions, putting distance between themselves and the threat. No retaliation, no rescue; only flight. As if on cue, one bite from the kinana snapped its victim's spinal cord and punctured several key arteries. Teeth still buried in flesh, the kinana rode the body of the dying zeraffe to the ground. While the herd reformed in a single mass thirty meters away, a plume of dust rose from the riverbank.

The kinana began to eat. Keeping its distance, with a few more of its members on guard for another attack, the herd wended its way back to the river. The zeraffes had a long day ahead. They could sacrifice one of their number, but not their consumption of water. So they drank. J'ni wondered if they mourned.

"Circle of life," she said to herself.

Something else caught her attention, and she raised her eyes to the sky. Far ahead a single towering line of smoke – a bright red flare, the color of children's candy – rocketed toward the heavens. J'ni bounded down from the hood, swung up into the seat, and started the truck.

She considered it while she drove. Urgent, but not an emergency. After much insistence on J'ni's part, Urttu finally had agreed last year to accept a comdee with a satellite connection. The chieftain of the Turtu clan, though, had only used it once – when quickly obtaining medicine from J'ni had been the only way to save a young child's life. For anything else he always used the flares, and let J'ni make her way to the nomads' current location when she could. The bright red one, though, meant Urttu thought it was very important.

She accelerated, pushing the truck to go faster than it should on the dirt road. Really, calling it a road was generous. For most of its length it was little more than two parallel lines worn into the ground, with fits and starts of flora between them and the grasses growing to their usual height on either side. She rode out every bump and bounce, and didn't slow down.

J'ni cut the engine fifty meters from the camp so it wouldn't startle the herd of phanters. Whatever Urttu was dealing with, he didn't need to have to wrangle a stampede on top of it. She hopped from the truck and started walking. The nomads had seen the dust plume from her truck, of course, and two men were striding briskly out to greet her. One was Urttu; the younger one she didn't recognize.

"It is good to see you," Urttu said when they met halfway.

"And you, as well," she replied, offering the old man a respectful bow. He never hesitated to use the nomad's ancestral language with her, because she spoke it fluently. No doubt that was why Urttu and his clan always sought out her help, rather than anyone else's.

"This is my nephew's son, Baxxol of the Ippela."

The boy was smiling, so she smiled back. "I am Acai."

The boy nodded. "One of the rangers."

Technically she wasn't. The scientists like J'ni had privileges to move throughout the wildlife sanctuary and weapons for self-defense, but they had no law enforcement authority. To the nomads, though, it was a distinction without a difference. J'ni had electronic tech, modern weapons, and lived in a fixed dwelling.

Anxiety on his face, Urttu prompted, "Go on. Tell her."

"A visitor from the Kurpietals spoke of seeing a new clan on the plains on his way to reach us. We thought he was telling stories. But then two days ago, one of our scouts saw them for himself. My father sent three more to confirm it."

J'ni frowned. It didn't make any sense. "A new clan?"

The boy looked equally disconcerted. "A group of people. Traveling together. They have a few trucks, like yours, but most are walking. And they have no phanters."

"No phanters?"

"That was why we didn't talk to them. They're *axchay.*"

The word didn't have a direct translation, but the closest meaning was *from the city*, carrying with it a connotation of strangeness and alienation. J'ni looked to Urttu. This time of year the Kurpietals would be even further away than the Ippela. Two hundred fifty kilometers, maybe more. That was most of the way to Luppitan. "Why come all the way here to tell me?"

The boy hesitated, and the chieftain said, "My nephew knows I trust you, and there is no one else for them to tell. The rangers there are gone."

The hair on the back of J'ni's neck stood on end. Whatever was happening to the north, something was very, very wrong.

To the boy she said, "Thank you. And thank your father for me." She bowed again to Urttu. "I have to go."

The old man valued tradition deeply, but the sadness in his eyes told her he took no offense. Not this time. "You must."

J'ni reached out and patted the boy's shoulder, then turned and ran toward her truck.

THREE

...Fith Hangar, Solar Towers Airspar Track

"**W**ynde!"

Continuing to run his gloved hand along the leading edge of the air-blade's wing, Daemyn acted as though he hadn't heard Farrier's shriek from across the hangar. The coach would know better, of course, and that would only make him angrier. Which was fine with Daemyn; the more furious Dom got, the sooner he'd storm off in a pique and leave Daemyn alone.

No such luck yet, though. "Wynde!"

Slowly and deliberately, Daemyn turned away from the airblade. "Is something wrong, Coach?"

"Yes!"

"What's that?"

"You know exactly what it is!"

"I do?"

Farrier stopped in front of him, fists clenched. "Don't play innocent with me. We've talked about this. Repeatedly."

Calmly, Daemyn tugged off his gloves one finger at a time. "That narrows it down, I admit. But you're going to have to be a little more specific."

"You crossed Ritzer's line."

"Oh, that." Daemyn tamped down the urge to grin. "Yes, I did."

"He almost crashed."

"No, he didn't. Be reasonable."

Farrier glared. "You'd already flown past, of course you couldn't have seen. It'll be plain enough in the footage reviews."

"Really?"

"Yes, really."

Daemyn shrugged. "I expect better of him."

Farrier waggled a finger. "That's not good enough, and you know it."

"Of course it is." Daemyn made sure the coach was looking him in the eyes. "If he can't handle a quick intersecting pass, he shouldn't be out there on the course in the first place."

Farrier had enough experience with Airspar, and was enough of a perfectionist in his expectations for his own team, that he couldn't argue that point. "Don't change the subject. You shouldn't have crossed his line."

"Was it a penalty?"

It was a rhetorical question, but the coach answered it anyway. "No."

"Well, then until they change the rules, it's a legal maneuver. We won the race fair and square. Isn't that what matters?"

"It's not that simple."

"Why not? If Grandell has an inferior pilot on their squad, how is that Fith's problem? Anyone else's problem, either, for that matter?"

Probably because Daemyn was refusing to concede, Farrier was seething. "The future of our sport is at stake now, Daemyn. We all have a role to play in saving it."

"By losing our shot at the championships?"

"That's not what I mean, and you know it."

Daemyn shook his head. "Airspar is popular because it's exciting. Take the excitement away, and the fans will stop caring. That'll kill the future of our sport faster than anything else."

"I wouldn't be so sure about that." Farrier took a step closer. "One exposé on brain damage was practically all it took to end boxing. Abuse of enhancers shut down farball across the planet in less than a year. Even martia isn't what it used to be. It doesn't take much to get the politicians meddling these days – especially when it's something as popular as Airspar is."

"Its popularity is exactly why we're a long way from anything like that happening."

"You really think so? Exciting is one thing; fireballs on live broadcasts are something else. We can't risk all of Airspar over your ego."

"They're not going to abolish Airspar over a few crossed lines now and then in the heat of a match."

"It's not about the crossed line!"

"What is it about, then?"

Farrier sighed, and some of his fury left with it. "After all the races you missed this season, I'd think it would be obvious."

"You said yourself it was a freak accident. Nothing anybody could've done to prevent it."

"That's true in your case, yes."

"And in spite of everything, we're almost in the championships again. Why are we arguing? We should be celebrating our win, and getting ready to qualify into the championships at Torrini Atolls."

"This climb up the standings, Daemyn, it's some of the best racing this team has ever done. That *any* team has ever done. None of it will matter if our inability to assure pilot safety gets the whole sport shut down."

"Ritzer didn't crash."

"You got lucky! If he had? On this track? He'd be dead."

"Oh, come on. It's not —"

"How many more crashes, Daemyn? How many more dead pilots do you think it will take before New Romas steps in? Give me a number."

"It isn't an all-or-nothing choice, Coach." Daemyn caught sight of Reiton Holtspring headed their way, striding purposely across the hangar deck. Idly he wondered whether his agent, business manager, and friend was more worried about reining in Dom's temper or Daemyn's unerring willingness to test it. Probably both. "The blades are getting safer all the time. Ejection seats are quicker. We're only just starting to understand the potential to use AIs to override the pilot to prevent —"

"Even if you're right," Farrier said, "timing is everything. If it takes too long to develop the right tech, to get measures in place, and we have another disaster? Then all of your brilliant ideas will be meaningless, because Airspar won't exist."

"If we compromise the integrity of the sport out of fear of what some cowardly politicians might do, we don't deserve to have it exist, anyway."

"Gentlemen," Reiton said, arriving to join them. "I trust I'm not interrupting anything too acrimonious?"

Daemyn flashed a smile. "We were just discussing how I crossed Ritzer's line."

"Indeed." Farrier waggled a finger again. "We'll take this up another time, after you've seen the footage and have had a chance to realize just how precarious of a position you put us all in."

"All right." Daemyn's reply lacked sincerity. Reiton shot him a warning glance.

"You can be as frustrated as you like about what I said," Farrier offered with equal insincerity, "as long as you don't do it again."

"You know I can't promise that, Coach."

"It wasn't a request."

Daemyn crossed his arms. "And if I do?"

"Daemyn..." So much for Reiton staying out of it.

Farrier glared. "Don't push me, Wynde."

"Or what?" He uncrossed his arms and spread them out to encompass the entire Fith hangar. "You have three championship titles with me on your team."

And without Daemyn, zero trophies. Reiton coughed audibly and ran his hand through his hair. With a finger and his thumb tucked aside, the gesture used three fingers. A reminder to Daemyn – they had a plan. A three-part plan to free them from having to rely on Fith or any other sponsors or financers ever again. A plan that wasn't ready to implement. Not quite yet.

"I have to get to the media room and talk about the race." Daemyn made his voice genuine and, if not exactly humble, at least the slightest bit conciliatory. "I'll think about what you said, and I promise to watch the footage carefully to see what you're talking about."

Farrier accepted the truce with a nod. "Later, then."

"Later." After the coach had walked away, Daemyn turned to Reiton. "Meet you back at the office?"

"Sounds good." His friend grinned. "Try to remember to be nicer to the reporters than you were to poor Dom just now."

"Of course." Daemyn smiled. "You know me. All charisma and charm."

...*Prime Diplomatic Service Field Office, Blonkas*

Hurrying toward the enormous glass doors, Utara was glad she had remembered the cycle of transit shutdowns correctly. With the air circulation fans offline and the midday sun beating down as fiercely as out on the savannah, it was insufferably hot in central Blonkas. Even traversing the few blocks from the monorail station to the main Ministry building had her sweating. Walking all the way here from Evostown... She didn't even want to think about it.

The doors slid open as she topped the grand staircase. The *whoosh* of chilled air sent the hair on her arms standing on end. She bounded inside to let the doors slide shut behind her. A few people were milling around in the lobby, clearly waiting for others to arrive to join them, but the entry checkpoint itself was empty. Focused on appraising the residents and reaching for her PDS identification badge where she'd tucked it into her pocket, she almost didn't hear the guard at the entry checkpoint discreetly call out to her.

"Counselor Fireheart?"

She looked up. "Yes, Oscar?"

The guard waved her forward reassuringly. "Come on through."

Utara strode quickly toward him. "Thank you."

She passed through the checkpoint and the scanner beeped to validate that she carried nothing dangerous. The old man smiled. "Be sure you remember to get out the badge after you've settled into the office." Oscar winked at her. "Some of my colleagues on the later shifts are more sticklers for following rules."

Utara smiled back. "I will. Thanks again."

She knew these hallways well. After a quick stop in the privy to tidy herself up, she made her way through the other Cultural Ministry offices until she reached the PDS field office toward the back. Danya the administrative assistant, the amiable Aquarian who had shepherded two decades' worth of junior counselors and service-term designees through their assignments to the Future City, kept her comm headset on while she gave Utara a gigantic wave in greeting like she always did. Only one of the other counselors was in the office today – no doubt the rest were dealing with all manner of distress in the city just as Utara was – so she had her pick of the shared offices to use.

Within minutes she was seated at the desk with an active compupod and a large pitcher of chilled water. She drank two full glasses while reading her messages and the PDS briefings and quickly catching up on the media summaries from the day's events elsewhere on Prime. None of the Blonkas status reports, even from the external security subdivision, made any mention of the drone incident this morning. She scribbled a note to check on it after she finished her comms. Right now, though, it was time to get down to business, to achieve the goal she had set out for herself in coming here.

She tapped the icon for the PDS directory. The red dot next to her immediate supervisor's name marked him as unavailable. A quick check of his viewable daily calendar confirmed that although he was in Tagron today, he was booked for the rest of the day. So was his boss, an official at PDS headquarters in New Romas. Given the mind-numbing levels of bureaucracy in the capital, they probably had a long-distance meeting with each other. Utara wouldn't be thwarted so easily, though. Among the eleven other Future Cities, several of the other senior counselors knew her well and even a couple of the envoys would remember her enough to take her comm.

Just as Utara about to select the most familiar name on the senior counselor list, the dot beside the name at the very top of the directory toggled from red to green. Foson Solaris. The Deputy Minister in charge of the entire PDS. Her fingers hesitated. She remembered her father's advice: that adapting to circumstances as they changed was a crucial skill for succeeding as a diplomat. Her original plan could wait a few minutes longer. It would be a bold move for a counselor in her third year of PDS service to take a matter straight to one of the second-ranked officials in the entire Cultural Ministry. And yet...

Utara hit the icon and waited. Worst case she'd get sent to his voice messages. She could disconnect, leave no message, and everyone would assume she'd commed his line by accident. Things like that happened all the time with the less-than-helpful way the directory was organized.

The compupod trilled and the transmission connected. A few seconds later, Solaris's face filled the screen. "Good afternoon, Counselor Fireheart."

It was early morning in New Romas. Solaris was legendary for knowing what time it was anywhere on the planet. "Deputy Minister," Utara said. "I apologize for disturbing the start of your day."

The bronze-skinned Aladarian reached for a steaming mug and took a sip. "No need. You would not contact me lightly."

That was true, and even this comm would be viewed by many as a breach of protocol. But Utara had to try. "I've reviewed the latest briefings, and I fear they do not convey the full extent of the dire situation here in Blonkas. Given the sources of our problems, I imagine the situation is similarly distressed in the other Future Cities, as well."

Solaris took another long sip, then set down the mug. "Tell me what you're experiencing."

"The biggest danger is the shortage of power. To conserve, different geographic zones or consumption sectors are turned off at different times. Residential areas can be without light at night, or without cooling in the day. Without reliable refrigeration, no one risks buying perishable foods anymore. Entire lines of the monorails are out of service for hours at a time, and people are unable to get to work or make it home. When the air circulation fans are offline in the city center, the temperature rises far too rapidly."

"And the water supply?"

"Still uncontaminated," Utara replied. She didn't add *at least so far*, but she didn't have to. "But rationing has been instituted. Only necessary usages are permitted, and even then people are beginning to worry that one day they'll wake up and discover that access to clean water will be as unreliable as the power."

"The Cities were not designed to function in this manner," the minister said, his eyes drawn to something away from his compupod screen.

"Not for extended periods of time, no," Utara said. "The population might be able to make do if it were just one problem. But power and water both is... very difficult. Word is already spreading from the agricultural workers that the locally grown food supply is in danger, and the deliveries from beyond Loorriri have been unreliable for years, at least at prices most people can afford. Everyone knows that food rationing is the next step. If all three backbone necessities are compromised..."

"Yes." Solaris ran a hand through the graying hair on his head. "You're right that the information we're receiving at the higher levels in the Ministry does not reflect a reality on the ground in Loorriri nearly that dire. I will make an immediate effort to ensure that we obtain full and accurate assessments from Blonkas and all of the other Future Cities without delay."

"How long will that take?" she asked expectantly.

"Six to eight weeks to make initial findings, most likely, followed by a review board to determine the best approach for taking action."

Utara blinked. The contrast between his latest remark and the rest of what he'd said took her a second to process. "Surely there must be something you can do in the meantime?"

For a moment the minister closed his eyes. Then he opened them again and held her gaze across the thousands of miles between their compupod screens. "My PDS discretionary funds were exhausted months ago. The Cultural Ministry is currently operating over budget, much to the chagrin of the Prime Minister, and we're facing a reduction in our budgeted allocations of at least ten percent for the next fiscal year. Even if the CM and I could prioritize the situation on Loorriri to the very top at the Ministry level – which would be a challenge even in the best years – I doubt anything close to the resources you'd need would be forthcoming."

"I understand." Utara tried not to let the horror show on her face. "Thank you for your time, Deputy Minister. I'm sorry to have troubled you."

"No, Counselor," he said, leaning forward. "Thank you. I will see what I can do, and making a start on taking action today is far better than if it had taken weeks or months for this information to reach me. But for now, I'm afraid the Future Cities are on their own."

"Many blessings," Utara offered.

"Many blessings to you," Solaris replied in turn, and it sounded entirely genuine. "Give your father my regards."

"I will," Utara said, and held her smile until Solaris ended the comm from his side.

For a while she sat at the desk, trying to avoid the overpowering sensation of helplessness clawing at her. She stared at the map of Prime on the wall, wondering how it was that the rest of the planet could so easily turn a blind eye to the suffering of Loorriri and its people. Then inspiration struck and Utara had a new idea.

Maybe Blonkas couldn't count on New Romas to do anything quickly, but they weren't the only ones who might be able to help.

~⌒⊃

...*Grandell Motors Corporate Intelligence Division, Grandell Valley*

"What am I missing?"

Ordinarily, Monson tended to agree with those who viewed talking to oneself as annoying to others at best, symptomatic of underlying mental unwellness at worst. Sometimes, though, speaking frustrations aloud was the best way to expel them from the mind, to move on toward clearer and cleaner thinking.

Unfortunately, he'd tried that several times already this morning to no avail. It wasn't helping.

"Idiot."

And then, just like that, it did. He'd meant the insult to refer to himself, but his brain had connected it to the data collected on the three wide screens before him.

"Of course."

If things weren't making sense, it was probably because *they didn't.*

It was a simple mistake to make, after all. Boynton Logistics Dynamics was a massive corporation, with a headquarters sprawled across half of Port Vulcania and manufacturing and research-and-development facilities on three continents. It had corporate leadership with decades of experience, a board of directors with leading economists and scholars, and several significant shareholders unafraid to make their voices heard at annual meetings. Boynton was exactly the kind of organization that could be expected to act rationally in response to economic incentives and shifting business conditions. Monson had spent the morning trying to figure out how to make the information he had gathered add up to a sensible corporate strategy.

Now he understood. It didn't add up because Boynton was deliberately spreading misinformation, both publicly and off the record. No doubt much of the information was still true, or at least within the usual boundaries of self-important bragging and reassuring platitudes. But some of it was affirmatively untrue. And Boynton – or some segment of its fairly senior leadership – was counting on nobody figuring it out until whatever mess they were dealing with could be either cleaned up or covered up.

If Monson had discovered their ploy, though, it was only a matter of time before others did, as well. Boynton was playing a dangerous game, one they were bound to lose.

Idiots, indeed.

Just as the realization had shifted his view on Boynton as a corporate entity, so too it spun all the data on his screens into a whole new perspective. Which were the truths, and which were the lies? Before the data had been like a set of tiles, with Monson seeking to form the mosaic. Now each tile had two sides – truth and falsehood – and creating the correct mosaic was considerably more complicated. Which tiles to flip over, and which to leave unturned? Where to begin? Yet the puzzle that had seemed so inexplicable suddenly had become solvable.

Certain information unquestionably was accurate. Much of Boynton's reported revenues he had verified through independent sources. Their contracts with various Ministries in New Romas were public records. The existence and basic specifications of the various artificial intelligences providing logistical, administrative, and humanitarian management services to the Future Cities on the Loorriri continent had been the subject of legislative hearings, media reporting, and public displays of their abilities. Given their nature, a range of less significant details of Boynton's operations also seemed unlikely to be deceptive. Publicly, Boynton was insisting that its corporate financials were stable and secure, and not without evidence to support those assertions. Monson's investigations, though, had raised several red flags.

One of them kept drawing his eye back to the left-hand screen. Boynton had won the contracts for the AIs as the lowest bidder, saving the government millions compared to the other companies. The deal was still plenty lucrative, however, exceeding many revenue lines from Boynton's other divisions, and practically enough by itself to support the entire AI division.

Yet a few months earlier he had encountered a former employee of the company – a man telling a different version of events inside Boynton. He had claimed that instead of thriving, the AI division was failing. Budgets had been cut and projects eliminated. Numerous individuals, from hardware engineers to software coders, had been unceremoniously laid off. At the time, Monson had discounted the tale as the ranting hyperbole of a disgruntled ex-employee probably justifiably fired for some manner of workplace misconduct. Still, the man had been willing to sell Monson a datadrive full of technical data on Boynton's security measures for a surprisingly reasonable price.

Tiles already were flipping over in his mind's eye, forming the start of a new mosaic of the state of Boynton Logistics Dynamics. Others tiles wobbled in equipoise, ready to fall in either direction. Plenty of dracts remained in Monson's monthly discretionary fund to pay handsomely for the right information. The first step would be to find out what else the ex-Boynton man knew.

Monson sat forward in his chair, fingers ready on the compupod. His eagerness had returned, because now he finally understood the situation he faced. The game was afoot, and all that remained was determining how to proceed. Monson was going to win.

He always did.

FOUR

...Midland Savannahs Wildlife Sanctuary

The scorching sun was high in the cloudless midday sky when J'ni's eyes, constantly scanning the horizon, caught sight of the ragged dust plume that had to be the mysterious new arrivals on the savannah. She estimated their distance from the expressway and decided she could continue on it for at least another fifteen minutes.

One of the few paved roads in the wildlife sanctuary, the expressway was the only reason she had been able to cover the distance this quickly. Built at the same time as the Future Cities, it began at Durnow, capital of the Zanita Administrative Region, passed by the outskirts of Agoelo, one of the few longstanding permanent settlements on the savannah, and continued on to Luppitan, capital of the Lupya Administrative Region. Only the rangers and scientists used the expressway with any regularity; government officials and corporate types travelling between Luppitan and Durnow always flew, and the nomads didn't use motorized vehicles. The guard at the border checkpoint had recognized her truck from a distance, and she'd barely had to slow down for him to wave her through. J'ni's was probably the first face he'd seen today.

Not that the politicians' borders mattered out here. The savannah had existed for millennia. So had the flora and fauna, and the symbiosis of the ecosystem. The winds and rains, the migrations and mating patterns, the predators and prey – they obeyed no boundaries. The wildlife sanctuary spanned several Administrative Regions, and politicians had given it a name – Midland Savannahs – guaranteed to offend no constituency. On the ground, though, no one called this place that. They called it by its name in the nomad's language, the one the politicians had ignorantly appropriated for one of their ARs. It was the name J'ni called this place too. *Zanita*.

The nomads and their phanters were newcomers by comparison – perhaps four dozen centuries, if the anthropologists and archaeologists had done their analysis correctly – but they lived with the land and the animals, respecting nature. The other humans to come to the Loorriri continent in the recent centuries hadn't done so, and they'd paid the price. Every few generations the people elsewhere on Prime forgot the lessons of their predecessors and decided that Loorriri was ripe for plunder – its gemstones and metals, timber and coal, exotic plants and wildlife with medicinal uses or supposedly magical powers. Every time the interlopers had failed, succumbing to a combination of the animals, the weather, and each other. The ones that didn't die had either returned to wherever they'd come from or assimilated into the local non-nomadic populations in settlements like Agoelo.

The Future Cities, at least, weren't motivated by a desire to strip the land for profit. Bringing higher education, science and technology, and modern medicine to the people of Loorriri wasn't a bad idea. In fact, it was a good one. J'ni had lived both ways – her childhood on the savannah and her young adulthood at boarding school and Rampart – and that meant she saw the pros and cons better than almost anyone. Even Urttu, a chieftain on the traditionalist end of the spectrum, recognized the positive role access to at least some tech and medicines could play in the lives of his people. But a good idea with poor implementation sometimes ended up worse off than a bad idea. J'ni was starting to fear that was exactly what the Future Cities had become.

She turned off the expressway and sped down a dirt road in the direction of the dust plume. She was about to give up on finding an easy path to cut perpendicular from the road toward the plume when she came to the swale and thin stream flowing at its zenith. It made sense; they would need water. J'ni turned off the road and drove along the upper slope of the swale. It was bumpy, but not as bad as she'd expected.

Rounding a bend in the swale and the grove of trees at its point, she found them. Around a hundred people. Men, women, and children. Some of the adults had rifles. Five trucks loaded with supplies, including food, water tanks, fuel tanks, and a noticeable number of vehicle-sized batteries. Their trek hadn't been too spontaneous, then, if they'd taken the time to gather this much before they left. But the group looked pretty haggard, so the journey had been taking its toll.

J'ni blared her truck's horn as she pulled it to a stop. Three times. Loudly.

One of their sentries saw her, waved, and started walking toward her. J'ni stepped down from the truck and strode out to meet him.

"Acai," she said, extending her arm.

He locked his forearm with hers. "Keron. You're one of the rangers?"

"I'm from further south, down near Durnow," she said, hoping her non-answer worked. If she was reading the situation right, though, these people would be as clueless about the status of the individuals working in the wild-life sanctuary as Urttu and his kin.

He nodded. "We haven't seen any up here."

"They got recalled to Luppitan?"

He shrugged. "Maybe? We don't know. But they were having some problems with the animals in the preserve before we left, so it would make sense."

It did. "How long ago was that?"

Keron thought about it for a moment. "A little over a week now, I guess. It's been... rougher than we expected."

J'ni kept her face impassive, making sure she didn't give away how stupid his last statement sounded. "Why did you leave? I've been to Luppitan. It's –"

"Not what you remember." He shook his head. "Not anymore."

"What changed?"

"Everything. They're rationing water, both for drinking and other uses. The stores are still selling, but they're limiting how much food you can buy at one time, too. To prevent hoarding, or so they say. People are getting desperate. Stealing, robbing... It's not safe."

No matter what Keron and his fellows believed, life on the savannah was considerably more dangerous. The nomads had generations' worth of knowledge and wisdom for surviving the savannah's terrain, weather, and wildlife. The refugees had none of that. Rifles wouldn't help them hunt if they had no idea where to look, nor help defend them from the predators they'd never see coming. Without sturdy shelter or knowing where to hide, the first major storm would devastate them. But J'ni had no resources to spare, and they had far too much to learn for her to possibly teach them.

J'ni glanced at the sky. She could stay a few hours; then she would have to leave to make sure she got as far as Agoelo before nightfall. She would do what she could until then. After that, the refugees would have to face the consequences of their choices on their own.

A group of middle-aged individuals, three men and two women, had started walking in their direction. "Is that your leadership team?" When Keron nodded, she said, "All right. Let's talk to them. I'll see if I can pass along some advice that might help."

<hr/>

...Media Briefing Room, Solar Towers Airspar Track

It should have been impossible, and yet the questions somehow managed to become even more inane the longer Daemyn's session with the media persisted. But he kept the smile on his face, the gleam in his eyes, his hands crossed neatly on the table in front of him, and pretended that the questions and the answers really mattered. Sometimes he wondered if he had a future in acting when his racing days were over – until he remembered how much more money he could make as a venturist instead. That thought was enough to ensure his grin was entirely genuine.

"What do you think of your chances to qualify for the championships?"

"Well," he said, "I'd rather have qualified already, to be honest." He waited for the predictable chuckles of the assembled reports to fade. "Winning today on our home track, getting up to ninth – that was important, obviously. Looking ahead, we always fly well at Torrini Atolls. With the last match to go, I'd say our chances are pretty good."

"Which other team do see as your biggest challenge?"

"Reddy." Another round of chuckles; Reddy Motors was currently in first place. "Grandell has a solid team this year. We'd be foolish not to watch our backs for them."

"Any truth to the rumors of tension between you and Coach Farrier?"

Daemyn raised a brow. "What did he say when you asked him?"

All the reporters laughed. The latest questioner replied, "He said he wouldn't dignify rumors with a response."

"See?" Daemyn tapped a single finger against his temple. "He and I are thinking on exactly the same frequency."

Another group chuckle, and then the questions continued. Daemyn compelled himself to tolerate another fifteen minutes. He thanked the reporters, tossed a wave to the cameras, and hurried off the dais and out the rear door of the briefing room into the dimly lit corridor beyond.

Elsa Ovella was waiting for him. Her long legs easily matched his stride down the narrow hallway. "That went well."

"Doesn't it always?"

"Let's call it *usually*."

"That hurts." They turned down an intersecting corridor, heading toward the landing platforms. He popped his comdee off his belt, tapped a three-digit code on its screen, and put it back. "Any updates of note?"

"Not today." In addition to serving as Daemyn's personal bodyguard, Elsa led the corporate intelligence division of Wynde Industries. Lately counter-espionage had been her primary focus, but a number of other matters, including several potential threats to Daemyn's personal safety from Airspar fans of dubious mental soundness, also kept her attention. "One of our men in the field is supposed to check in with an update tomorrow, though."

Daemyn knew better than to ask which operative it was, or which rival he was spying on. "Works for me."

They emerged into the bright sun of the landing platform. Daemyn raised a hand to shield his eyes, took a second to get his bearings, and strode off toward his personal shuttlecraft. He only got a few steps before the thumping of running feet started.

"Daemyn Wynde!" One of the men jogging toward him was carrying a vidcam. The other shouted, "Is it true you're dating Corin Rockreikes?"

The only thing more absurd than the questions from the Airspar reporters was the questions from the trashmags. This one was particularly ludicrous. He and Corin barely managed professional courtesy at mandatory multi-team public appearances. Friendship, much less romance, was hilariously improbable.

Snapping his comdee off his belt, he forced a smile. "What gave you that idea?"

"A source told us —"

The trashmag scum got a little too close and wound up with Elsa in his face, towering over him. Daemyn was not a small man, and Elsa outmatched him, too. The physique — and glare — of a retired PARTE soldier only compounded the effect. No one took Elsa Ovella anything less than deadly seriously.

While she backed the two men off, Daemyn quickly checked the comdee screen. ENGINES READY. He tapped a button, signaling the ship to lower the ramp. Keeping the comdee in his hand, he walked briskly toward the ship. Elsa would follow.

"You didn't deny it!" the trashmag shouter called after him.

Daemyn squashed the urge to make an obscene gesture. Instead he checked the screen. HOT LAUNCH? 1 = YES. 2 = NO. Despite his annoyance, Daemyn couldn't help but smile. He had used those same codes with *WyndeStalker* for at least the last six months, yet the insistently precise AI reminded him every time. He tapped *2*.

He glanced back over his shoulder and yelled, "I didn't not confirm it, either!"

Let them figure that one out for a while. A few bounding strides later, he and Elsa were up the ramp and into the ship. In the cockpit, Daemyn slid into the pilot's seat and strapped in. Out of habit, Elsa took the seat directly behind his, even tough Reiton wasn't here and the co-pilot's seat was empty. Takeoff went effortlessly too.

Only a few seconds into flight, though, *Stalker* flashed a message across the heads-up display on the front viewport. PURSUIT. Among the various icons for nearby flying vehicles, two small ones turned from green to red.

"You've got to be kidding me."

Elsa had seen the message too. "They don't give up easily, I'll give them that. Two hoverbikes, about twenty meters back and closing."

"I see them," Daemyn said, reaching for the console. "I'm going to shoot them down."

Elsa chuckled. "No, you won't."

"Why not?"

"Because you can't race – or run Wynde Industries – if you're serving prison time for murder."

He scowled. "Good point. I'll just shoot *at* them."

"Or attempted murder."

"Some boomers and flares in their general direction, then."

"Or installation of illegal weaponry on a civilian vessel."

"It's Airspar tech," Daemyn insisted. He swerved *Stalker* around a cargo carrier, but the hoverbikes kept up. "We're still in track airspace."

"Would you rather compete for a championship or argue the legal technicalities and technological specifications to the courts?"

"I hate you."

"I know."

"You always take away my fun."

"Only sometimes," Elsa said. "I wouldn't be very good at my job if it didn't also include protecting you from yourself."

She was right about that, even if he was never going to admit it to her. Of course, she already knew both of those facts were true. It was one of the reasons he could always count on her. Daemyn had a very limited number of people he could trust absolutely, and Elsa was one of them.

"Fine, you win," he said, reaching for the switch for the afterburners. "But I assume you have no objection if I manage to lose them between here and WI?"

"Air traffic infractions I can live with."

"Excellent."

He didn't bother asking if she'd strapped in. She knew better. The acceleration flung them back in their seats for a moment, and then *WyndeStalker* left the hoverbikes and their obnoxious riders hopelessly behind.

...Blonkas

Utara's good fortune on her trek to the PDS field office had not repeated itself for her return journey. She had arrived at the monorail station to discover an unscheduled shutdown of the closest line back to Evostown. Half an hour later she caught the northwesterly bound train that covered half the distance westward without putting her too far northward. The rest of the way, though, she'd had to walk. No small task on an ordinary day, but a daunting prospect indeed on a sweltering afternoon like today.

On the plus side, the quickest route from her monorail exit station to Evostown was to cut across the nature preserve that bisected the western side of the city. The first segment of her hike had taken her through the aviary. The trees had provided much-appreciated shade, and the sights and songs of the hundreds of avians never failed to make her smile. By the time she'd reached the open expanse of the grasslands section, Utara's spirits had been much better.

The soaring skybridge above the rolling grasses exposed her to the relentless sun, but it also offered a picturesque, unobstructed view of the natural beauty below. Maintaining her pace in her hike along the bridge, Utara kept her eyes peeled for rare animals she almost never had the chance to see anymore.

A trio of zeraffes galloped together, racing, playing, reveling in the breeze. At the end of a stream a rhynohog dug into the muddy soil, seeking worms for its afternoon snack. A mother ulapod and her young trundled toward a different bed of wildflowers to munch. Atop a low rise, a lone tigre lay stretched to full extension, as if to absorb every last possible centimeter of the sun's warming rays. The great cat kept its head raised, ears darting back and forth like miniature sensor dishes, but made not even a hint of a move toward claiming any prey.

For all she looked, though, Utara could not catch sight of the other, even more deadly feline predator in this section of the preserve: the kinana. Hunted by poachers practically to the point of extinction, seeing one in the wild was even rarer than catching a glimpse of the breeding pairs maintained in the preserves in each of the Future Cities. Today was not her lucky day – to see a kinana, or for anything else.

The last segment before she left the preserve, at least, was one that never failed to make her smile. As usual, the scarlet baboons filled the air with hoots, shrieks, and cries in a hilarious melodic cacophony. Tempted as she was to stop and listen, she couldn't afford the delay.

Weaving her way through her shortcuts along streets and cutting down alleys, she arrived back at Evostown when the sun was finally starting to get low enough in the sky that the air would begin to cool. Aidan was tossing a ball with some of the younger children; even small moments like that helped distract from the turmoil around them. When he saw Utara coming he caught the ball, stepped over to one of the older girls, handed it to her, and gave her a reassuring pat on the shoulder before striding away from the children to reach Utara.

He wiped his brow on his bare forearm. "Any luck?"

"Not what we were hoping."

Quickly she recapped what she'd learned from the briefings and her conversation with Solaris. The information she'd heard in her comms with counselors in several of the other Future Cities hadn't been any better. The rumors weren't accurate, but the truth wouldn't be reassuring to the residents of Blonkas by any stretch, either

"Can't say I'm surprised. Unfortunately."

"I know."

"Were you able to find out anything about those drones? What they were after?"

"Not a thing. Either nobody knows, or those who do aren't talking."

Aidan scowled. "I don't like it."

"Neither do I." Utara forced a smile. "But I have an idea for helping Evostown, and maybe a lot more people, too."

He walked into the shade cast by one of the rowhouses. He paused, then gave up and leaned back against the wall. "Let's hear it."

"I'm taking vacation time —"

"Ha!" He didn't bother trying to conceal his ensuing belly-laugh, which by all appearances was entirely genuine. He held up a finger, taking a moment to compose himself. "Happy? You got me. Now, tell me the real idea."

"I'm going to use some of my vacation time —"

"Since when do you —"

Her stare silenced him. She waited an extra second to make sure he was suitably chastened, then continued. "To personally impress upon some of our leaders the urgent need for support and resources here. Even some small improvements in quality of life could make a big difference. Maybe I can't get the power plants funded, but keeping the water running and some reliable shipments of food would really help."

"It sure would." He blew out a long sigh. "But if New Romas isn't, who's in a position to help?"

"The cultural governors."

Aiden grinned broadly, but he clenched his fists and barely managed not to laugh aloud again. "There are a lot of them, Utara. And most of them are just as broke as New Romas, if not worse."

"I realize that." She tried not to scowl at him, and failed. "I already have several in mind to talk to first. I'll start with the ones that have strong economic growth, and some others that have deep ties to Loorriri. We only need a few. Even one or two, if they contribute enough."

"They already complain about the tax revenues they have to contribute to New Romas. I doubt they'll be interested in sending money here instead, where it'll only be wasted by another bankrupt government agency in a slightly different way."

"That's why I'm not going to ask for funding." She stopped herself from letting the words rush out. "With humanitarian relief they can send direct aid. It might be excess from food stockpiles they didn't use up during the storm season, or equipment that's outdated for them but much better than we have here, or technicians to help make repairs."

"Even humanitarian relief costs money, Utara."

"I know. But we have to do something."

"We are. We're making the residents' lives better every day. One family at a time."

"And that part's important. I realize that." She caught herself, and took a deep breath. "Our daily routines are only triage, helping Evostown manage one day after the next. If that's all we ever do, though, we're not achieving any results that actually change the situation in the neighborhood, much less all of Blonkas, for the better in the long term. Improving their lives on the margins isn't good enough. We should be making a difference. That's what the PDS is supposed to do."

Aidan sighed. "I suppose you're right." He gestured around them. "What do we have to lose at this point, right?"

"Exactly. I know someone will step up. Their sense of responsibility will be too strong. Even if it takes me a couple of weeks to find the right ones."

He shook his head, grinning to himself. "Well, then I guess it's not such a bad thing you've got all that unused vacation time banked up."

"See? I told you it's a good plan."

"Something like that." He pushed off the wall, heading back into the sunlit street. "When will you leave?"

"Tomorrow."

FIVE

...The Birdsong restaurant, City of Buneen, Hyj-gon

Looking out into the enormous arboretum, the narrow terrace upon which they sat gave the appearance of hanging suspended in midair dozens of meters above the lush flora below. The gentle artificial breeze carried the sweet aromas of the flowers to their noses. Only the invisible energy barrier kept the multitude of vibrantly colored songbirds from darting down to the table to steal morsels from their plates; the chirps and cries of their melodies reached their ears just fine, though, creating the illusion of immersion in nature amid the heart of Hyj-gon's industrial capital.

In the heart of the arboretum sat a simple shrine, encircled by the slender flames of dozens of lit candles. It memorialized the massive firestorm nearly a quarter century ago that had swept across the plains before ravaging Karagashi, whose uninhabited ruins were slowly crumbling back into the soil less than a hundred kilometers away. Daemyn and his parents had boarded one of the last rooftop evacuation flights before the tornadic conflagration had consumed the city. Tens of thousands of other Faytans had not been so fortunate. The family rarely spoke of the event and its aftermath any more, but all three of them honored the opportunity to pay their respects to the dead, and their memories.

The center of the burnished bronze table separated along a trio of seams, opening to allow the next course of their meal to rise into place before them. Steam rolled off the precisely sliced cubes of meat, with diced cheeses and vegetables arranged artistically around the rim of the large circular serving dish.

The two men waited for Ripi Wynde to go first. She speared a pork cube with the slender longfork and drew it to her plate. She glanced to Daemyn. "Have you thought any more about my suggestion?"

He and his father reached for a pair of salmon cubes simultaneously. "Which one, specifically?"

She grinned at him mischievously. "That now that you're thirty, it's time for you to find a nice young –"

"Dear..." The disapproving glower on Sai Kuron's face didn't match the light-heartedness of the admonishment in his tone.

Daemyn stifled a chuckle before it escaped his lips. Lately it seemed that he and his father disagreed on almost everything. But this was the one topic where they remained inveterate allies – their mutual belief that he didn't need his mother meddling in his personal life.

"No, it's all right." His knife easily cut the cube into several smaller pieces. "Actually, I have been thinking about that suggestion."

His mother's expression immediately grew suspicious. "You have?"

"Yes. And I've decided that I don't agree. At least not yet."

His father chortled. "See?" he said, emphasizing the point by skewering a piece of salmon with his knife. "That's what you get for asking."

Ripi was undaunted. "Not even Corin Rockreikes?"

"What about her?"

"They said you're dating."

Daemyn glared. "*Who* said?"

His mother waved her fork in the air like a conductor's baton. "I don't remember. One of those reporters. It was the other day on –"

"I've told you before, Mother," he said, not sure whether to be maddeningly frustrated or fatalistically amused. "Don't believe everything you see in the trashmags."

"So you're not dating her?"

"No."

She leaned forward and whispered, "We can keep a secret."

Daemyn bent toward her, responding in an equally hushed tone. "We're … not dating." He laughed at his mother's disapproving pout. "We're hardly on speaking terms, much less friendly."

"That's too bad."

46

From the corner of the terrace the serving robot lifted off from its perch, a decanter of water on one side and wine on the other. It hovered to the table, refilling Daemyn's glass and then Sai's. For a few minutes they ate in silence, relishing the taste of the cuisine and the peaceful environs of the arboretum.

Naturally, his father ruined the moment. "How do you think your company will look on the ledgers this quarter?" What he meant was, *When are you going to give up these foolish diversions and start planning for a real career?*

Daemyn used his longfork to stab two slices of cheese. "I'm meeting with Reiton Holtspring later today. The marzite battery is outpacing projections, and I've seen solid numbers on the nav-sensor and acceleration booster, as well."

His father gave a noncommittal grunt, but for once didn't actually comment on the unstated admission that Daemyn's corporation still wouldn't be making a profit.

"We have a design in the works that's the most promising so far. Once we demonstrate how effective it is in an airblade, it won't just be other Airspar teams who will be clamoring to buy it."

"Good for you, dear," his mother said unconvincingly.

Daemyn popped some food into his mouth. The innovations in R&D at Wynde Industries weren't limited in application to Airspar; the technology would make personal vehicles and many other types of aircraft faster, safer, and more fuel-efficient. But they'd been over this countless times before, and he had no interest in making yet another futile attempt to get them to understand.

His father reached for some more vegetables. "You won't be able to trade on the popularity of Airspar indefinitely, either. Another crash like that could —"

"Sai!"

He offered a half-apologetic shrug to his wife. "Even a full career has its limits. When your face isn't on the broadcasts every week for the races, things will change. That's all I'm trying to say."

"Not all change is for the worse," Daemyn said.

"That's true." His mother smiled. "Such as my *suggestion*."

His father laughed and Daemyn smiled. He accepted her point with a nod.

Fortunately, the mirthful moment ended this latest venture into the long-fruitless line of discussion. Besides, his father's apprehensiveness wasn't really so much about the popularity of Airspar as a sport as the fact that Daemyn had named his company Wynde Industries. Daemyn could recite all of his father's points by rote. Fame was fleeting. Even if he remained famous after his racing career ended, the public could turn on a celebrity in an instant, suddenly shunning someone they previously had revered. If Daemyn Wynde himself ever lost favor, it would destroy Wynde Industries the brand right along with his personal wealth. An impersonal corporate name, not associated with any individual's rise or fall, was the safer and more reliable choice.

But Daemyn knew better. His mother had worked for nearly three decades at the most prestigious architecture firm in Hyj-gon. She had designed some of the most artistic and recognizable buildings and skyways on all of Prime. And yet she would never reap the acclaim for her work. To the Primean public they were simply visually memorable structures generated from some faceless corporate entity. Daemyn was not going to let that happen to him. When Wynde Industries succeeded, everyone would remember the name – and the face.

His parents would understand eventually. Or at least, he had to believe that. To them, he was a skilled engineer wasting his formative career years racing airblades and puttering in his money-pit of a company. To Daemyn, none of it was a waste. Someday they would see why.

Someday, all of Prime would see.

...Durnow, Zanita Administrative Region

Sitting on a bench in the plaza stretching out in front of the intercontinental transportation hub, her travel bag tucked between her feet, Utara couldn't help but see her surroundings as a microcosm of everything about Loorriri and the problems the continent now faced. When its construction had been started decades ago, the facility's design, both functionally and artistically, would have made it one of finest in the world for its time. Would have, if it had ever been fully built out as intended. But for reasons Utara could easily imagine – budget overruns, expenditure reductions, taxation revenues lower than estimated, and perhaps others lost to the forgotten memories of history – the dream of its planners had never become a reality.

The plaza was a weak imitation of its intended glory. Many of the massive stone tiles on its surface were cracked or gouged. Most of the trees were long since dead and gone, and all of the planters and flowerpots were empty. The majestic fountain had not spouted in years, leaving only a bizarrely out of place Aquarian sculpture amid the dusty savannah and Terran architecture.

The transportation hub had fared no better. From the outside, the imposing building gave the impression of a stolid, impregnable fortress. The paint had long since faded or peeled away, but the structure itself showed no weakness. Inside, however, was another matter. Walking through its spacious, mostly vacant corridors after arriving here on the shuttle flight from Blonkas, Utara had been struck by how lonely the hollow building seemed. What had been imagined as a grand portal between Loorriri and the rest of Prime was today an unremarkable facility hardly capable of capturing the fancy of even a small child, much less the few world travelers who passed through.

The sight of her parents hurrying toward her across the stone was a welcome change to her thoughts. Content to leave her bag briefly unattended amid the deserted plaza, Utara bounded from the bench and rushed to greet them. The three of them shared a long, firm embrace before stepping apart.

Koster Fireheart reached out a finger and tucked a stray lock behind Utara's ear. "You still haven't cut your hair."

"I haven't had time," she insisted, reflexively reaching behind her head to check the tie-back holding the ponytail in place.

"Well, I've always liked it longer anyway," her mother said. Jasiri Berl touched her on the arm. "It's wonderful to see you, even if it's only for an hour."

Utara nodded. She hadn't seen them in months, and didn't know how much longer it would be before she would be able to make time away from Blonkas again. Her eyes kept wandering back to her father's hair, trying to determine if he really had gone grayer or if she was imagining things. "I'll try not to talk PDS the whole time."

"With you two?" Her mother laughed, a wonderfully joyous sound as ever. "That's hopeless. I accept it."

"Excellent," Koster said, wrapping an arm around his wife. "Then we won't have to feel bad about monopolizing the topic of conversation."

"Before I forget," Utara said, "Foson Solaris sends his regards."

Her father raised a brow. "You talked to him?"

"Briefly." In her message telling them what time she'd be waiting at the hub between shuttle flights, she hadn't mentioned that part. So she explained it quickly. "That's when I decided the cultural governors were my best chance."

Koster frowned in thought. "I'm not sure they'll be in much better position to assist fiscally than New Romas, but it's more likely than trying to squeeze water from a boulder in the Ministry bureaucracy."

"Thanks." If anyone would know that, it was her father. He easily could have risen through the upper echelons of the Prime Diplomatic Service to become the Deputy Minister years ago. Maybe even won election as Cultural Minister if he'd wanted it. But just over a quarter-century ago he had made a different choice – to stay in Durnow rather than return to New Romas, where so many of his friends and family lived, to marry Jasiri and build a life, have a family, with her here. "Speaking of boulders, the Red Rock Aladarians are my first stop."

Her father smiled approvingly. "They've had an affinity for Loorriri since the second didamon rush. Many of their kin still live here."

"That was my thinking, too," Utara said. "I talked to other counselors in Luppitan and Tagron. I figured I couldn't do better than asking you about the situation in Durnow."

Koster nodded. He'd only gone a few sentences into his update, though, when his comdee trilled. "Sorry," he said. "Give me a moment."

While he turned away and spoke into the device in a hushed voice, Jasiri leaned in closer to Utara. She smiled and shook her head. "There's always something urgent that requires his attention. Some days I wonder if he's holding this city together simply by his own sheer willpower. I don't know how they'd manage if he ever retired."

Utara wasn't ready to think about the notion of her father retiring. Not that he didn't deserve it; she simply didn't like facing the reality of his age. "Well, don't let him give you any ideas. You're a long way off from that yourself."

Her mother laughed. "Thanks for reminding me." She leaned even closer, whispering almost conspiratorially. "How's Aidan?"

"Uh, good." What an odd question. "As far as I know."

"You're not worried about leaving him behind in Blonkas right now?"

Utara doubted she was keeping the confusion off her face. "No. He has a good handle on everything. He'll be fine."

Before Jasiri could say anything more, Koster rejoined them. "Sorry about that. Now, where was I? Oh yes, the power grid. In the last few weeks..."

Utara listened carefully, committing as many details as she could to memory. Most of the problems in Durnow were the same ones facing Blonkas, which certainly helped make the information easier to remember. Fortunately, the situation in Durnow was considerably more stable than Blonkas. Perhaps that meant some of the other Future Cities would be better off than Utara had feared, too. On the other hand, the fact that so many of the Future Cities seemed to be suffering breakdowns in the same core systems only made the overall prospects for improving their circumstances that much more distressing to consider.

When he finished Utara said, "All right. Enough business. How are my cousins doing?"

When Jasiri began to regale Utara with the latest updates on her sister's three teenaged children and her brother's young son, her face lit up. Watching his wife, Koster beamed. Utara found herself smiling too, and made sure to savor every single second of the moment.

...Grandell Motors campus, Grandell Valley

Monson tore the remaining clump of bread in thirds and tossed one of the pieces out into the lake. It plopped atop the water, sending small circular ripples outward. He waited. By his count the fastest fish strike had taken three seconds, the longest eleven seconds.

Apparently the fish were as ambivalent about the cafeteria's offerings as its human customer.

A splash signaled the morsel's disappearance just as Dana Bristow's "hey" carried down the gentle slope to his ears. Monson lobbed the pair of remaining tidbits into the lake, then turned and met her halfway up the grassy incline.

"Thought I might find you here," she said.

He nodded. In recent weeks the lakeside had become his favorite place to think, away from compupods and datascreens. Perhaps he was becoming a bit too predictable, though. "Anything of note from the patent office?"

"Not even off the record." Her skills weren't in question; rather, the object of her inquiries, Fith, had become an exceedingly dull rival of late. "Their R&D on the next-gen spaceworthy engines must be going even slower than I predicted."

"Or they're playing the odds waiting to disclose whatever they've come up with, if they think they have something no one else is close to."

Gazing out over the lake, she considered it for a moment. "Possible. Unlike them, but possible."

"Nothing on Wynde Industries either, I assume?"

"Two more filings related to the marzite battery, and one related to the housing used to connect it to an engine."

He couldn't help the chuckle that escaped his lips. "Sometimes I think Daemyn Wynde does this to mock me."

Smiling, Bristow met his eyes. "Considering he doesn't even know you exist, I highly doubt that's the case."

"Just because it's implausible doesn't mean it's untrue."

"You've got me there."

"There's still tension on the racing team?"

"I could tell you that without spying on them. But yes. Farrier can't stand him, and the feeling is mutual."

"They won't fire him? Or arrange a trade?"

She shook her head. "Hyj-gon's native son, and probably the biggest name in their favorite cultural pastime? Not a chance. Farrier would get fired first."

Monson frowned and glanced away to watch the birds swooping above the placid surface of the lake. "He's up to something with Wynde Industries. I can feel it. This doesn't make sense, not with so many weeks out of competition. I know the way his brain works – every minute he wasn't rehabbing his injury, he'd have been working in his labs. He's too good an engineer to come up empty after all that time. A man with that many secrets, and who goes to such lengths to protect them, is hiding something significant. And not just from Fith."

"I agree with you on that much. Fith isn't who he'd be worried about. As long as he keeps winning them races, they're content to tolerate his endorsement deals and his pet projects at his little company on the side. They don't see him as a threat."

"Well, they should."

"Should we?" The tone in her voice drew his gaze back to her.

Their eyes met. "Fith, GM, everyone. I've studied him enough to know the kind of man he is."

"This almost sounds personal, more than objective analysis."

"No. But I devote the most attention to the most significant risk factors."

"If you say so. Tell me, Marx – what kind of man is Daemyn Wynde?"

"The swagger of the Airspar jockey, the charm in front of the cameras, the engineer striving to bring the high-tech progress of Airspar to the masses? It's all a feint, a diversion. Every match, every segment, he flies to win. Ruthless and uncompromising. Unstoppable. A man like that doesn't just play to win in Airspar. That's how he lives every aspect of his life."

Bristow canted her head. "You think he'll run for office?"

"I doubt it. The abrasiveness that shows at times – that part, at least, is real. He'd never be able to consistently play nice long enough to win an election."

"What does he want, then?"

Monson looked out over the lake again. "Money. Influence. Power." He drew in a breath, and let it out. "Everything."

SIX

...Blonkas

When he heard his comdee beeping again, Aidan couldn't help the "oh, shig" that passed his lips. Holding the wooden beam in place while Hasto pounded two more nails, he said, "Sorry. Finish up and then I'll check that." A nail clenched between his teeth, Hasto nodded and put the one in his fingers up to the right spot on the wood.

Aidan held his raised arm steady and wondered what the comm could possibly be this time. The first comm had been right after midday. The power had been out in Rockville for nearly forty-eight hours, and Tyku had been checking about the status in Evostown. The power hadn't come back here either, but for Aidan and the residents of this neighborhood, that meant only a little more than twenty-four hours – not long enough for anyone here to have started worrying about it not coming back on relatively soon, just like its irregular off-and-on cycles had done for the last few months. The next two comms had been other PDS counselors in the city, also inquiring about lack of power for longer than a full day. Aidan hadn't said anything to the residents, of course, but three was a pattern. He could only hope this fourth comm wasn't someone letting him know the power was out in all of Blonkas. If the grid went down entirely... Well, with as dilapidated as it was, he wasn't sure they'd ever get it back running again.

Hasto finished pounding in the nails and Aidan let go of the beam. Hasto appraised their work and gave a firm nod. "Thank you."

"You're welcome," Aidan said. He gave the smaller man a pat on the shoulder, then strode over to where his comdee rested on the window ledge, recharging its solar-powered battery cell in the blazing sun.

The name on the screen wasn't one he'd been expecting. He looked for a voice message but didn't see one, so he tapped the icon to comm her back.

Danya answered almost immediately – and completely skipped her usual effervescent greetings. "Aidan, what do your commitments look like the rest of the day?"

"Nothing important. I can easily cancel or reschedule."

"Good." She paused. "Is our conversation secure?"

Aidan's breath caught. With his comdee held up to his ear, her words wouldn't be overheard. "Confirmed."

"Thank you. Come to the city-wide EOC as quickly as you can."

If the PDS counselors were being summoned to the Emergency Operations Center, then the situation in the city was more unstable than he'd thought. "Understood. I'll be there."

"Many blessings, Aidan," Danya said, the only usual thing about their conversation.

She ended the comm from her end before he could respond in kind.

...Wynde Industries, Fenwei City, Hyj-gon

The conference room's windows stretched floor to ceiling the entire length of the room. Atop one of the soaring towers, the view gave a panoramic perspective on Fenwei City's many spires, landing platforms, and elegant walkways. Air traffic zipped along the designated routes at multiple altitudes, weaving thin lines around the glimmering metal buildings. Far in the distance, many kilometers away across the rolling plains, a thunderstorm was brewing. In Fenwei City, the sun shone brightly.

Standing at the window, he kept his eyes on the blooming white columns and their thunderheads. Often as invisible as the air itself, Fayti's power was indomitable when she chose to display it. Someday, Daemyn Wynde would be as powerful and feared as the storm. But that day was not here yet.

Step one in the plan was to take Wynde Industries from a small company that everyone viewed as an idle hobby of an Airspar racer into a major player in Primean manufacturing and technology. With that achieved, they could finance almost any project or investment they wanted. Step two would push WI to the next level – sponsoring their own Airspar team, with the WI brand flying in every race. That was the point of no return. Some teams might tolerate a racer owning a business on the side, but none of them would hire him again if he launched his own team and failed. Step three, the end game, was Daemyn's ultimate dream. The money, resources, and Airspar team to accomplish what he'd always wanted: to design and build airblades. And not just any blades. The best blades in the world. Getting there, though, would take more patience. Probably a lot of it.

He heard the footsteps approaching and turned to face his friend. Reiton slid into the seat facing the windows at the end of the table. While Reiton readied his compupod, Daemyn took the chair across from him. For now he put the storm of the future from his mind and focused on the present.

Reiton looked up. "Ready?"

"Shoot."

The table was solid crystal, clear as ice. On its flat surface before Daemyn a brilliantly colored graph blossomed. Each line indicated a different revenue stream, some for Wynde Industries, others for Daemyn personally. For a moment the graph remained the same, and then each line extended to indicate growth in the previous quarter.

Daemyn let out a low whistle.

Reiton chuckled. "The investments?"

"I'm impressed."

"So am I." The main chart shrank to ten percent of its size, temporarily replaced by an equally multi-colored itemized chart. "Some of it is due to the overall improvement in the securities and equities markets, but –"

"Even with all the instability in New Romas and the budgets?"

"Yes. Analysts are predicting that the Prime Minister will have to seek additional approvals for outsourcing certain functions to private entities."

Daemyn nodded. It would save the government millions – and boost the profits of the corporations in sectors that won the contracts. "And the rest?"

"Wise choices by Celia. She picked a lot of winners, and very few losers."

"No kidding. If she worked for me, I'd give her a bonus. But she doesn't, so she'll just have to keep her massive fee."

Reiton laughed. "She'll live."

The investments chart vanished and another, showing income from Daemyn's endorsement contracts, splashed onto the smooth crystal to replace it. Although the overall amount had only increased slightly, this was by far the single biggest current revenue stream in his budget. "We only added the one new deal with Worty ElectroTech this quarter," Reiton reminded him. "I'd wondered if your crash might reduce interest, but it hasn't hurt you. We're holding steady on all the others."

"Anything up for renewal?"

"Not until the third quarter. They look to be done deals to continue, but I still want you to get face time with all of them in advance of the contracts."

"Understood." Daemyn flicked a finger, dismissing the chart. "How am I doing on personal expenses?"

"Under budget again." The next chart compared this quarter with the previous seven. "In fact, it's hardly changed in two years. You make it very easy on me when you don't spend money on anything."

Daemyn chuckled. It wasn't so far from the truth, though. He had kept the same apartment from six years ago, even though he could afford a far nicer one – or a penthouse suite – by now. Unlike some of his Airspar rivals, he only owned the one home; he didn't see a need for any others, not with his parents and WI both here in Hyj-gon too. He didn't spend lavishly on food or clothes. His vacations weren't cheap, but he didn't have time for more than one vacation a year and he always tied it somehow into his efforts to expand Wynde Industries. And while he was constantly upgrading *WyndeStalker*, there was only so much money a man could spend on a single shuttlecraft. Staying under budget wasn't difficult when there were so few things he enjoyed spending money on.

"If you're bored doing the accounting," he said, "I'll start spending more."

Reiton ignored him. "Which leaves Wynde Industries. A net loss, of course, but well within the targeted parameters."

The next chart broke down the corporation's revenue and expenses by division. Management and Operations both incurred expenses, but they had stayed within budget. When credited with the present and expected future value of their successes – in both espionage and counter-espionage – as offsets against their expenses, corporate intelligence displayed as a net positive for the quarter. Every product actually on the market was turning a profit, some by a wider margin than others, which put Production in the positive, as well.

One line caught Daemyn's attention. "The marzite battery is way ahead of projections, isn't it?"

"Definitely."

"Any ideas why?"

Reiton shrugged. "Only theories for now. My team is researching the sales trends and running regressions for various factors to see if we can tease it out."

"Best guess?"

"It's more closely associated with Airspar than the others. People like the idea that they're using the same vehicle battery as a famous racer uses."

Daemyn drummed his fingers on the table. "Well, that's certainly an interesting bit of information to consider further if the analysis vets out."

"Yes."

Which left R&D as the only division sharply in the negative. Enough to put the entire corporation in the negative for the quarter, in fact. But as Reiton had said, expenditures had remained within the goals they had set. And the goals were all in service of their long-term plan. In the short run, yes, R&D was losing money – but it was an investment no different than the securities their friend Celia Lancer managed or the time and effort he spent cultivating his public persona to yield those lucrative endorsement contracts. Over time, the payoff from R&D would dwarf everything else. They just had to be patient.

"All right," Daemyn said. "Let's see it with the projections for Project Lariat."

Reiton's chart flashed onto the table. The worst-case scenario put WI marginally profitable overall. The average-expected scenario was successful, but moderately so. The best-case scenario was... astronomical. If that course came to pass, practically overnight WI would be one of the most profitable companies on Prime.

Daemyn slapped his open palm down on the table. "Look at that!"

Reiton was smiling too, but he kept his voice measured. "It's the best possible outcome. All of the pieces have to fall into place and even then we'd still need a little bit of luck. Which isn't to say the expected outcome is bad. But it's not, well, *that*."

Daemyn nodded. "I know. Don't worry, I won't do anything stupid."

The reassuring reply never came. Instead Reiton's gaze had returned to his compupod. The man never stopped tinkering with his numbers, much like Daemyn with his projects down in the lab.

"Or maybe I will," Daemyn said, "if that's what it takes to get your attention."

"Oh, I heard you the first time."

"Then we're in agreement."

"On the avoidance of ill-advised decisions? Yes."

Daemyn pushed back from his chair, stood up, and paced back to the window. The thunderstorm was moving south, perpendicular to the city. During their meeting it had only grown taller, grayer, and more powerful.

"We're almost there," he said to Reiton, keeping his eyes on the thunderheads.

"I agree."

He turned back to his friend. "If we can move that average-expected up fifteen percent, maybe twenty, I think we can start seriously looking at step one."

Reiton nodded. "I'll run the numbers and see what it would take to get there."

"Take your time." Daemyn looked out the window again, his eyes drawn once more to the storm lashing the plains. "I'll try to figure out how we can get into that best-case column instead. If we hit that, we're all the way to step two in one strike."

"*If* we hit it," Reiton said. "I'd love to get there as much as you would. But once we do, they'll come after us. The other teams, the other sponsors... It'll make Airspar competition look like child's play."

Daemyn glanced back, grinning. "That's fine. I've beaten them all before. I'll beat them again." He crossed to the door. "Anything else on your list?"

Reiton didn't even glance at the transi. "The logo."

"What about it?"

"As in, we don't have one yet. And WI needs one. And if you don't make a decision soon, I'm going to pick a logo for you."

Daemyn laughed. "Right. I'll get to that shortly."

"That's what you said after my last three reminders."

"I will this time. I promise."

He looked over his shoulder to see Reiton nod, then surged out into the corridor and bounded toward the lab.

...Durnow

Punctual as ever, Utara had bid farewell to her parents an hour ago and hurried back into the transportation hub to ensure she had enough time to spare before the shuttle would begin boarding for the flight to Magentolia. Naturally that meant the departure was now delayed for an indeterminate amount of time. The grumpy man at the counter insisted the shuttle would leave at some point later today, but Utara was becoming less convinced the longer she and the other passengers waited without any updates.

At least she had fully charged her PDS compupod and could get some work done while she waited. She had started by drafting notes on the key points she should make to each of the cultural governors on her itinerary. She wasn't satisfied yet, but she'd made a good start. The general notes, though, already had triggered several ideas for specific points to emphasize to the Red Rock Aladarians. They were the first meeting, currently scheduled for early morning the day after tomorrow. Quickly she added those ideas to her notes before she lost track of them.

She had barely finished when the compupod chimed to indicate an incoming comm. Utara tapped the icon. Expecting it might be Aidan, she let out a small "oh!" when she realized who it was instead. She reached into her bag for the earbud; no one was sitting near her in the departure lounge, but there was no reason anyone but her needed to hear the other end of the conversation. Tucking it into her ear, she tapped again to accept the transmission and waited for the image of her old friend to appear on the screen.

"I saw your message when I got back," J'ni Acai said. The wall behind her revealed she was at her home out in the wildlife sanctuary. "I guess you're delayed."

"It's Durnow," Utara said, smiling. "Of course we are."

J'ni smiled too. "That's why I thought it was worth a try to catch you."

"Everything's still going well with the research and the breeding program?" They had spoken a week ago, chatting for hours like old times. Utara had more important questions to ask, but there was always time to be a good friend.

"It is." As usual, J'ni got right down to business. "There's something in the air, it seems. If I hadn't found your message, I would've commed you."

In her message, Utara had explained the purpose of her travels beyond Loorriri, but had deliberately avoided mentioning any specifics about the problems in Blonkas or the exact nature of the subject she'd said she wanted to ask J'ni about. If her friend had a similar impetus for reaching out to her... "That doesn't sound good."

"It's not. But you should go first."

"Yesterday morning Aidan and I happened to be over in one of the squares near the wall, helping some residents from Evostown pick up from a water tanker. We saw a flock of four vultures on the prowl."

J'ni sat back in her chair. "Security drones? Did they open fire outside the city?"

"Yes, and yes."

"How close?"

"They were squawking pretty loudly. We could all hear them."

"And no one in Blonkas would tell you what they were shooting at."

"Correct." If the topic hadn't been so serious, Utara would have smiled. This kind of conversation was surprisingly easy when you knew the other person as well as she and J'ni knew each other. "Any ideas?"

Her old friend released a long, slow sigh. "With four of them? You probably already figured out it's not animals."

"That had been my thought, yes."

"I agree. Anything that roams in packs or herds wouldn't take more than two drones to scare off, and even the toughest kinanas or caimans couldn't stand up against two drones, either. So sending four, it has to be a human threat. A heavily armed human threat, presumably."

That was exactly what Utara had been afraid of. "Poachers?"

J'ni put her elbows on her desk and ran her hands through her hair. "Hard to imagine. I've never heard of them banding together in groups larger than a few people. And not the nomads. They don't have that kind of weaponry, and they'd have no interest in coming to the city regardless."

"Who, then?"

"I have a theory. But first, let me tell you why I was going to comm you."

For several minutes, J'ni told Utara about her experiences the previous day: the flare from the nomad chieftain Urttu and what she had learned from their meeting, finding the refugees on the savannah, and what they had told her about the rapidly deteriorating situation in Luppitan.

Utara took a moment to let it all sink in. "You think it's desperation?"

"You mean refugees from one city trying to force their way into another?"

"Maybe?"

"I doubt it." J'ni idly tapped her fingers on the desk. "The refugees I saw, they got so desperate they wanted *out*. Anyone else in their shoes, from Luppitan or anywhere else – trading one Future City for another doesn't seem like the kind of solution they'd be looking for."

"When you put it like that... Yes. So your theory is?"

"The outlaws, all the various types, have been laying low the last few years. The rangers have been more aggressive, and prospecting, robbing tourists, and the rest just haven't been profitable lately they way they used to be. The only reason most of them have managed to escape capture is by staying on the run in small groups, never enough to attract attention or warrant major intervention."

"Like the poachers."

"Yes. But poachers are only interested in very specific animals for very specific reasons. For them, one or two big scores covers them for a year or more. The outlaws, they'll take whatever they can get. Targets of opportunity. The bigger and richer the better, though. No limits for them. Not like the poachers."

Utara nodded. They could strike against the refugees, but robbing them wouldn't yield much. Striking a Future City, though, would prove very lucrative indeed – but only if they could attack, plunder, and get away with it. Utara knew her history, from Prime as a whole to Loorriri in particular. Raiders at the gates were a threat as ancient as human civilization itself. The outlaws would have the necessary heavy weapons, but they'd also need large numbers and leadership.

"Have you seen or heard any indications of an... organization forming?"

"No. But now I'm certainly going to try to find out."

"Let me know what you find. I'll pass along anything I can learn, too."

J'ni nodded. Neither of them felt like talking more, not after these revelations, so they said quick farewells and ended the comm.

Utara took out the earbud and returned it to her bag. For a long moment she simply sat, staring at her compupod screen. She needed to get back to her preparation notes. But the sinking dread in the pit of her stomach wouldn't go away.

～

...Emergency Operations Center, Blonkas

The attendees were mostly who Aidan had expected. The entire PDS supervisory team in Blonkas, as well as all of the counselors. Numerous high-level employees from the city bureaucracy, including the power, water, sanitation, public safety, public health, and transportation divisions. The city's Deputy Mayor for Operations, Tarzo Lanche, stood at the front of the sloping auditorium, ready to lead the briefing. Although one representative from the law enforcement subdivision of public safety was present, the external security subdivision was conspicuously absent.

"Thank you, everyone, for coming on short notice," Lanche said. "I apologize for disrupting your important obligations elsewhere in Blonkas, but there is critical information to share, and I believe this is the most efficient way to ensure all of you have the most up-to-date, most accurate information possible."

Tyku leaned over to Aidan and whispered. "Also to ensure no one else hears it."

"No kidding," he whispered back.

Lanche tapped a button on his compupod, and the screen behind him displayed a bar graph with varied column heights and associated trendlines. "You're all well aware of the difficulties we've had with maintaining reliable power. Despite many pleas from our power division through all of the appropriate channels, including the Cultural Minister and our representatives in the Lower Assembly, we have been unable to obtain either the parts we need to make repairs or the funding to purchase them on the open market."

Aidan made a mental note to contact Utara at some point tonight. Although her plan was to focus on the cultural governors, it would still help her to know not to waste her time with the offices in the Lower Assembly.

"Two days ago, we experienced a complete failure of one of the three primary reactors. The repair efforts were unsuccessful, and it appears that no amount of work short of replacement will suffice." Lanche tapped his pod, displaying a new chart. "Our first duty must be keeping the two remaining reactors functioning. Given their similar tenuous state of disrepair, each must spend a considerable portion of the day running at minimal output levels. Consequently, for the foreseeable future we must operate the city on the assumption that the power supply will be approximately twenty-five percent of rated baseline."

Beside him, Tyku let out a sharp hiss. Aidan knew what was coming next, too.

"Essential services must remain operational, most importantly water delivery and water quality functions." Lanche switched to the next chart, which showed the priority order of which Operations divisions would receive power first. "You will see the respective expected allocation of power to each division listed here."

Lanche paused, giving everyone time to read the chart. Aidan didn't bother looking at the top of the list. His eyes went right to the bottom, where he found exactly what he was looking for. Power for ordinary residential use was deemed non-essential, which meant the allocation for all of the dwellings in Evostown, Rockville, and the other neighborhoods was zero.

"Question," said one of the bureaucrats from the public health division. When Lanche acknowledged her she said, "I don't understand. How can some of those upper lines, third and fourth down in particular, be getting more than the healing centers and center-city air circulation fans combined?"

"As you know," Lanche told the entire auditorium, "the artificial intelligence which runs our logistics management is one of the few technologies here in Blonkas that is actually new and top-of-the-line. Although maximizing the human welfare of the residents of Blonkas is its highest protocol, sometimes reducing power to certain uses poses a greater overall risk compared to other, seemingly more directly beneficial uses. We see the outputs of those risk-reward calculations indicated on the chart."

The algorithms of the AI, not human judgment, would determine just how miserable daily life in Blonkas got. After that, Aidan could only bring himself to half-listen to the rest of the briefing. His mind was already scrambling to think of ways to help the residents of Evostown adapt to life in the rowhouses without power – and ways to keep panic from taking hold. In hindsight, a few of those hole-pocked walls he had helped repair might have proven useful for ventilation.

When the briefing ended he spent a few minutes talking with his PDS colleagues, but unlike their usual camaraderie this time the fretful conversations did nothing to improve his mood. Most of his peers were too focused on the ramifications of the power shutdowns to talk about anything else. Tyku hadn't heard anything about the threat to the city that had required the simultaneous deployment of four security drones, nor had the three counselors from other neighborhoods Aidan managed to be able to ask. They weren't even aware of the incident, much less the explanation behind it. For a security matter that significant, somebody should have heard something by now.

So he gave up on finding answers and went outside, letting the late-afternoon sun warm his face. It was going to be a long walk back to Evostown.

SEVEN

Bent over his console, eyes fixed to readings for the engine's speed output and fuel efficiency, Daemyn asked, "How's it look?"

"Steady, and within parameters."

"By what margin?"

A pause. "Wide. Forty percent or more for the last... nine minutes."

"Excellent." Until now, overheating had been the perpetual problem with the design. "I think we finally have it calibrated."

The response was a noncommittal grunt.

Daemyn looked to the other man. "You think we're sacrificing too much speed?"

"No." He chuckled. "Just my pessimism showing through. That's all."

Daemyn smiled. Marty Filson had been an aeronautical engineer since Daemyn's parents were in diapers. He had worked on all manner of aircraft and spacecraft engines over the years, but airblades had always been his favorite. Retired from Fith for nearly a decade, Filson couldn't stay away from a workshop no matter how hard he tried. It had been a long time, though, since anyone had made a real breakthrough in airblade engine design – more than the marginal upgrades and small design tweaks that cropped up at the start of each Airspar season. The prospect of accomplishing that with Project Lariat had been more than enough to keep Filson in an exclusive consulting arrangement with Wynde Industries for the past ten months. And the prospect of having his name forever associated with the revolutionary engine design ensured Filson's complete discretion with the company's trade secrets. In fact, Filson's obsession with the design's secrecy probably exceeded Daemyn's. Which was saying something.

"All right," Daemyn said. "My readings look good, too. Testing session complete."

"Copy that."

Together the two men executed the protocol to wind down the test in an orderly progression that created the lowest possible risk to the engine's stability. Ten minutes later the engine's roar was silent and all the data was secured on Daemyn's compupod. They tapped a few buttons to power down the consoles, then headed for the door.

Filson went first down the stairs from the oversight booth into the expansive laboratory bay. Daemyn never looked at the steps beneath his feet. He kept his eyes on the single engine mounted on struts in the center of the otherwise empty floor – peering closely, inspecting for any signs of damage or wear, focusing on every centimeter of the glittering metal. Filson paused at the base of the stairs, and they walked side by side toward the engine.

"So," Filson said, pacing a perimeter around the struts for the close-up visual inspection. "The other engines. I can have the adjustments made by tomorrow."

"That soon?"

The old man winked. "Let's call it close-of-business tomorrow."

"Works for me."

Filson ran a hand along the curving edge of the engine's front section. "They're all close. We've been honing in on these parameters for weeks."

Daemyn nodded. "And how long to test them?"

"All of them? At least a week, I imagine." Filson gazed off toward the far wall of the lab bay, the same expression he always wore while running calculations in his head. "Six or seven per day, probably. Eight if we're lucky. Swapping out one engine for the next in here takes the most time. The actual testing to confirm conformance won't take long."

"Assuming the calibrations are correct, of course."

"Ha!" Filson waggled a finger. "I'm the pessimistic one, Wynde. Remember that."

"Yes, sir." Daemyn took two long strides back from the engine and appraised it. "That schedule works well. I wouldn't have time to make any decisions until after Torrini Atolls at the earliest, regardless."

Walking over to reach his side, Filson gave him an overly dramatic suspicious look. "Are you thinking what I think you're thinking?"

"I think so." Daemyn took a deep breath. "Assuming all the engines pass conformance, go ahead and select two you think are most representative and have Bakerton mount them on a blade."

"You're sure?"

"Yes."

"So." Filson leaned to the side, looking at something on the engine's underside. "Where are we going to fly?"

That was the million-dract question, indeed. The only test track with enough secrecy to prevent public view of a flight belonged to the Unified Forces — and the military wasn't about to allow a civilian, no matter how famous an Airspar racer he might be, to bring proprietary corporate tech there. Anywhere else on the planet, they had to assume the test flight would be observed. Maybe they would get lucky — but Daemyn wasn't going to count on it.

"Naper Peak should be quiet this time of year."

Filson shrugged. "At least it's close."

"Exactly." Wynde Industries owned a transport large enough to fully enclose the blade for the jaunt to and from the track at the base of Hyj-gon's northern mountain range. The test flight itself would be all they would expose.

"And what will you say if someone manages a viscap or a vid, and we get questions about the tech?"

"I'll tell them the truth," Daemyn said, and his answer came out more confidently than he'd expected. But he meant every bit of it. "That Wynde Industries has developed the first self-contained, closed-system airblade engine."

...Magentolia

The dark hues of the polished stone and burnished wood in Judicar Magmar's office suite gave the impression of entering a cave. Utara pushed away the sensation of the walls closing in around her and concentrated on the key points of the presentation she would be making to the leader of the Red Rock Aladarians. She had reviewed them enough times that she didn't need to review her notes. Instead she sat in the chair, ticking through the list in her mind.

Finally the administrative assistant ushered her inside the governor's formal office. The middle-aged man rose from his desk to greet her. Utara was surprised at how mundane his attire was, considering the significance of his position. For a few minutes they exchanged the obligatory formalities and pleasantries. Then Magmar strode back around his desk to the high-backed chair, and indicated Utara should take one of the low seats opposite him. She waited for him to settle into his chair, then sat down too.

"My assistant provided the executive summary you sent ahead, Counselor Fireheart, which I've read," he said, leaning forward to brace his elbows on the desk. "What would be most helpful for me, to start, is a bit more detail on what Loorriri and the Future Cities are currently facing. As you can imagine, the media for all intents and purposes ignores the existence of the continent completely, and the briefs from New Romas are sparse on updates, at best. Nothing even close in value to the personal observations of a PDS emissary charged with helping ensure their stability."

"I understand, Judicar, certainly," Utara said. She began by quickly explaining that she was serving in Blonkas and had learned about conditions in the other cities from contacts of hers and Aidan's, as well as her father. "Each of the Future Cities is facing significant difficulty, but not in the same way. The problems arise from the circumstances present in their respective locations. For example, the greatest problem in Blonkas is the failure of one of the main reactors, which creates substantial shortages of power. Although the climate supports sustainable agriculture for the city, the lack of power poses a threat that the water purification facilities will fall offline, too. Durnow, on the other hand, was built on the banks of the Kyetalle River. Its water supply is reliable, but the nearby land is nutrient-poor, so agriculture has proven very challenging and the locally produced food supply is constantly on the edge of collapse."

Magmar nodded grimly. He asked few more questions about the cities, and Utara did her best to answer them. Then he took his elbows off the desk and sat back in his chair. "And, at your own personal expense and vacation leave, you've traveled all this way to seek assistance for the people of the Future Cities because the local governments are falling short in their ability to close the gap."

"Essentially, yes. I wish it were otherwise."

"I thought the artificial intelligences were meant to remedy much of the budgetary pressure in funding the operations of the cities?"

"For New Romas, that's been true," Utara said. "A substantial number of the positions for bureaucrats, technical advisors, security forces, and the like have been able to be eliminated since the AIs have been in place. But the money that was saved wasn't reallocated to other functions in Loorriri such as updating infrastructure. When they were built, the Future Cities had a twenty-year design-life in the engineering and technological planning. We're well past that now in each city, by more than a decade in Durnow and several of the others. Without doubt, the innocent residents are bearing the impact."

"I can't say I'm surprised, unfortunately." Magmar reached out a hand and idly ran a finger along the edge of his desk. "Some of the minerals we mine here have great value in interstellar trade. For many years, that meant our people had the benefit of a revenue stream that many other regions did not. Recently, though, New Romas has been insisting on higher and higher *management fees* for their role in negotiating the trade agreements with our alien partners. If Prime's economy overall were faring better, we might be able to make up the difference in other ways. But the tax revenue for my government has declined even more steeply than for New Romas."

"That's why I'm hoping we might be able to find some way to render in-kind assistance instead of direct financial support," Utara reminded him. She had emphasized that idea in her executive summary.

"What did you have in mind?"

"I fulfilled my service term in the Aladarian Guard, so I'm familiar with the level of technical expertise and scientific talent among its members. And the Red Rock Aladarians have long been very influential in its leadership." Utara sat forward in her chair. "It has been years since the Guard was deployed for security purposes on Prime itself, and even the space crews run training maneuvers and make the occasional rescue. We are blessed to be a planet at peace. If we explain the situation in Loorriri, surely members of the Guard would volunteer to render humanitarian assistance in the Future Cities rather than sit on their hands for military missions that will not come."

For a long moment Magmar sat unmoving, silent. He clasped his hands before him. "A noble suggestion. I will share it with my advisors, and if they agree, I will share it with the Guard Council. I pledge that we will give it our most serious consideration."

"Thank you," Utara said, and meant it. "That's all I can ask."

"I should advise you, though, not to get your hopes up too greatly. While Loorriri has its fair share of residents of Aladarian descent, many of my fellow leaders in the Aladarian community do not view them as truly our kin. The people of Loorriri have been there too long, mingled too much with the indigenous clans and others who came to the continent to make their homes. In the minds of many in the rest of Prime, Loorriri's cultures are their own. Separate and apart from ours."

"They worship the same gods," Utara insisted. The words spilled out. "The Aladarians in Blonkas speak the same prayers, observe the same holidays and celebrate the same feasts. They're no different than –"

"I know," Magmar said, holding up a gentle palm. "The Aladarians in Loorriri are no more dissimilar from the Aladarians of Red Rock than the ones of the Fernal Peaks. You do not have to convince me. Sadly, others do not share our cultural insight, and it is persuading them that will be the greatest challenge to making headway with your proposal."

Utara nodded. "I appreciate your honesty."

He tipped his head. "I wish you the all the best, Counselor Fireheart, in your mission to help your people. In your place, I would do the same. May Aladare shine his grace upon your success."

...Blonkas

The shouting grew louder and angrier. Aidan broke into a jog. Whatever the current topic of the disagreement was, he had to do something to calm emotions quickly. If the rest of the residents saw their elders lose their cool, all bets were off.

Not that he blamed them. Like the other Future Cities across Loorriri, Blonkas had been built with the promise of the modern technology and comfortable urban environment enjoyed by most of the rest of Prime. Sustaining that living standard, though, required significant quantities of constant power. If the lack of power endured too long, the entire human ecosystem of the city would collapse. Blonkas hadn't reached that point yet, but it loomed on the time horizon. And everyone, even those who didn't understand the science or the engineering of how the city functioned, knew it.

Aidan rounded the corner to find Mazee and several of the other elders arguing with a group of younger men, Hasto included. He'd only raised his voice a few times since coming Evostown, and he did it again now. "What's the problem, my friends?"

For just a moment a startled look passed across Mazee's eyes. No doubt in reaction both to the volume of Aidan's voice and the lack of any deferential honorifics in the greeting. Indicating the group of elders with a gesture he replied, "We are advising patience. Although it falls on ears that do not hear."

Aidan turned to Hasto and the younger men. "And why is that?"

One of them, Roturo, took a step toward him. "Because their eyes do not see, and their brains do not think."

Deliberately stern, Aidan raised a brow. Never before had he heard such disrespect directed toward the elders. Disdain for the bureaucrats in Blonkas or the government in New Romas, sure, but not for their own neighbors and kin. He matched the other man's step forward and stood tall, for once not hesitating to remind everyone in both groups of men just how big Aidan's advantage in height and muscle really was. "That's unfair, Roturo, and you know it. The situation is very difficult for everyone right now, and it has no easy answers."

"Roturo speaks the truth," Hasto declared, and other young men added their support with words and gestures too.

"They want us to sit here, doing nothing, letting our families suffer," Roturo said, fists clenching. "The answers are not easy, I admit. But that is all the more reason we must to do everything we can to *look* for them."

"A reasonable idea – in principle." Aidan took a long step forward, putting himself between the elders and the young men. The briefing at the EOC had been only two days ago, and it was hard to believe his friends had become this tense with each other in that short amount of time. "Clearly none of us are in any position to actually turn the power back on, or build our own generator for Evostown, yes?"

Both groups nodded. If he could start them from common ground, maybe he had a chance to defuse this. "And we can at least agree that the rumors about Rockville are false? That the rest of Blonkas shares the same power situation as ours?"

Again both groups conceded to him. Between Aidan's PDS contacts and their own infrequent comdee conversations with friends elsewhere in Blonkas, even the most skeptical of the young men had come around. That was progress compared to the last few weeks, at least.

"All right," Aidan said calmly, "this is a start. For now, what we face in Blonkas is what it is. And that –" He spread an arm to encompass the elders, offering them the best smile he could muster. "– strongly supports doing everything we can to guide our friends and neighbors to have patience." Before anyone could interrupt, he spread his other arm to the young men and smiled at them, too. "And yet we need not helplessly accept our fate, either. The people of Prime have a long tradition of changing the course of events with our deeds, do we not?"

"In the right time, in the right way," Mazee interjected. "History also shows us many examples of fanciful notions and fruitless plans which end in failure and tragedy."

"As well as tragedies from doing nothing," Hasto insisted, "where suffering could have been prevented by taking action, by fighting back."

"Wise words from both, can we agree?" Aidan kept his arms spread wide and the smile on his face. "Our challenge is to examine our options and make the right choice, for our people, in our situation, here today. And as I said, the answer is not easy."

He paused, waiting to see if anyone spoke up to argue. When they didn't, he pressed on. He faced Hasto, Roturo, and their friends. "If action is the course you think is best, and we cannot simply relocate from Evostown to somewhere else in Blonkas to find power there, what do you have in mind?"

"Leave," Roturo said, firmly but a little too quickly.

Aidan lowered his arms. To avoid making any confrontational or dismissive gesture, he clasped his hands behind his back. "To go where?"

"Luppitan, Durnow, wherever we can," Hasto replied.

"Everyone from Evostown?"

"Of course," Roturo said. "We can't leave people behind to suffer, or worse."

"Even if we assume they have fully functioning reactors, which we do not know," Aidan said, keeping his voice calm and level, "what if they do not have the resources – power, water, food, housing, and the rest – to support an addition to their population of that magnitude?"

Hasto didn't have the answer, but he did have his anger. "It can't be worse than here."

Aidan let that flawed logic slide for the moment. He had another, more important, point to make. "And how will you get there?"

"However we can," Roturo said, crossing his arms. The young man knew better than to suggest the shuttles that flew from Blonkas to other Future Cities. As the number of daily shuttles had been reduced over the past year, the number of open seats was limited and the price had become very expensive. The cost of chartering a single shuttle was out of reach for Evostown's residents, much less the number of flights that would be needed to transport everyone. "Even if it means walking."

So the rumors were spreading after all. And they were creating the worst kind of combination of fear and inspiration. "You're young and healthy," Aidan reminded Roturo, Hasto, and others. "With some luck, you might be able to pull it off. But your friends and families? The children, your grandparents? Do you really think they could?"

"Our ancestors lived out there for centuries," Hasto said, "long before these Future Cities were ever built. We can do it again. All of us."

"When we came to live in the city," Mazee said, "I was already a grown man. A father. Older than you are today. When I close my eyes, I can remember exactly what our clan's life in the wilds required. Whether we remain here in the city, or we leave its walls, the years will catch up with me soon enough. But I do not want my children, my grandchildren, to have to endure what I did in my youth. The hunger, the hunts, the dangers lurking around every bend of the river. The city has problems, yes. Life in the wilds is something none of you would ever want."

Roturo gave the elder a respectful nod. Then he said, "The wisdom of experience is worth hearing, always, but in the end each generation must make its own choices."

Aidan met Mazee's gaze, but he couldn't say what both of them were thinking. If the young men really did leave Blonkas, and take others with them, tragedy was guaranteed.

EIGHT

…*Wynde Industries*

His vision refused to dismiss its blurry gaze. His brain ached. His back protested against any further duration in the chair.

Blowing out his breath in a huff, Daemyn admitted that perhaps it was time to do something other than stare at the conformance testing data on the oversized screen connected to his compupod. He closed the file, sent the compupod into low-power mode, and rested his face in his hands. After a few long breaths he stood up, stretched his back, and marched out of his office.

He wasn't really heading anywhere in particular, but soon found himself standing outside the door to the corporate intelligence suite. As good a place as any to take a break.

Daemyn strode inside, greeted the three analysts working in their cubicles, and kept walking toward the back office. Elsa saw him coming and waved for him to enter.

Once the door was closed behind him, she set aside the transies she'd been holding in her hands. "Something on your mind?"

"Not especially." He gestured his hand in a circle, indicating his plan to pace around her office. "Anything entertaining?"

"Somebody apparently thinks you're working on some sort of major modification to the connection joints for airblade wings."

Corporate espionage aimed at the battery he would have anticipated. The nav-sensor or the acceleration booster, too, maybe. But connection joints wasn't a project WI was even working on. "Really?"

"Definitely. I picked up on the new line of inquiry a couple of weeks ago, but I couldn't pin it down. Yesterday I finally put the clues together."

Daemyn leaned forward to stretch, bracing his hands on the back of one of the chairs at the desk. "I wonder what information they're using to come to that conclusion."

"I wonder that too, but I haven't figured it out yet. If we crack it, I'll let you know."

"Any idea who it is?"

She shook her head. "I've ruled out GM, Fith, or Reddy. Beyond that, it could be anybody."

"Anybody who's bad at inferences."

She chuckled. "Right."

Pushing off the chair, he started pacing again. "Speaking of our friends at GM, they're still digging for intel on us?"

"Very diligently. Mostly that fellow Monson from their corporate intelligence."

"He's a persistent little rascal." Daemyn glanced through the transpariplast to the analysts working at their stations. "Were you able to find out anything more about him?"

Elsa leaned back in her chair. In the office's lighting, her cropped blonde hair and the sharp lines of her Polar Aquarian features made for a striking visage. "The identity is a swipe, no doubt about it. But it has to be one of the best I've ever seen. I've tried every angle, worked every trick, and come up with nothing."

"Impressive."

"Very. It's as if one day – *poof!* – he appeared spontaneously on the plains of Loorriri and walked into town."

Daemyn laughed. "Something out of a vid."

"A vid I'd be able to get the script for."

"Fair enough." Done pacing, he lowered himself into one of the chairs. "Well, whatever he's hiding, someday we'll figure out who he really is."

"Evos willing."

"In the meantime, let's file some more updates at the Patent Office. It'll throw him off the scent or drive him crazy. Either one I can live with."

She winked. "Will do."

"And what's your latest analysis on GM?"

"The deeper we dig, the worse it looks."

"How bad?"

She narrowed her eyes, considering her answer. "Not bankruptcy, I don't think, unless one of their lines has a major unanticipated failure. But revenues are down and R&D is struggling. They'll need a major new infusion of capital soon to keep the company stable."

He scratched an itch on his knee. "Bonds won't work."

"No. Their credit rating isn't strong enough."

"New investors on the private side?"

"Possibly." She sat forward, bracing her elbows on the desk, and held his gaze. "Or a major improvement in name recognition and brand reputation from a dramatic increase in the prominence of their Airspar team."

"If they get me, they'll win a championship or two."

"Exactly. And one of the most famous names in the sport constantly associated with them, instead of Fith, all across the media."

He mulled it over for a moment. "You think that's their play?"

"I do."

"That's... pretty desperate."

"I agree."

"I mean, it would probably work, but –"

She laughed. "Mighty humble of you, Daemyn."

"Well, it would."

She waved it off. "You did say *probably*."

"I did." He rose from the chair. "If that's their play – if they think my championship flying and my fame are enough to save their company – maybe I'm better positioned than I thought."

"To keep those assets right here for the benefit of WI?"

"If they're that valuable? Why shouldn't I?" He frowned, thinking. "Keep digging. The weaker they are, the stronger position we're in. But we need to be sure."

She took a breath. "There's one other thing."

Something in her voice made him shiver. "What?"

"I was about to bring it to you." She picked up the transies she'd been reading when he arrived. "We'd seen evidence of an intrusion from a hacker, but couldn't find any sign of where they'd been in our systems or what they'd done. I was beginning to think it was just ghost data. A misinterpretation."

"But it's not."

"No. Someone got in. How and when, we're not sure yet."

"What'd they do?"

"We've been over the systems thoroughly three times. No code viruses, no rewrites, no erasures. Nothing."

Daemyn knew where this was going, and he didn't like it one bit. "They took something."

She met his gaze. "The Project Lariat data. All of it."

"How is that possible?"

Besides the two of them and Reiton Holtspring, only four other WI employees even knew the designation Project Lariat, and two of those didn't know what it was. No physical documents existed. The digital files were encoded so that any duplicate would fully erase itself automatically within two minutes if it was accessed without first entering the appropriate nineteen digit passcode. And those files only existed in two places: Daemyn's compupod, and Marty Filson's. Even the best hack into WI's systems shouldn't have gained access to the compupods. But apparently someone had. Someone whose talent for hacking exceeded anything Daemyn had ever seen.

"I don't know," she said.

He held her gaze. "Find out."

Elsa's eyes narrowed, once more the PARTE soldier ready to strike and take down an opponent before they knew what hit them. "Oh, believe me. I will."

…Balcom Islands

The tiled stone terrace granted an expansive view of the rolling sea. The gentle crash of the waves on the rocks below provided a constant soothing rhythm to the background noise, pierced only by the occasional cry of a shorebird in pursuit of a meal. Enough clouds dotted the sky to keep the sun's light from becoming too bright. In the distance two massive water-bound shipping vessels headed outward toward open ocean.

"I must admit, my people are fortunate to not face such circumstances here." The High Magister of the archipelago's government had listened attentively to Utara's description of the problems facing the Future Cities, only interrupting to clarify specific details. "New Romas should be ashamed of what it has allowed to transpire in Loorriri."

"I wish I didn't have to agree." Utara doubted the elderly woman was baiting her, but she couldn't risk it. The Magister was one of the few prominent politicians on Prime known for consistently advocating for the election of the Prime Minister candidate she believed to be the best choice for the post, rather than basing her support on personal ties, cultural affiliation, or political favors. Unfortunately, her favored candidate had lost each of the last three PM elections. "And there is plenty of blame to go around, between our Prime Ministers, the Senate and the Assembly, and the Cultural Ministry. Even the PDS has not pressed the case as vigorously as perhaps it should have."

The Magister lifted a hand off the table in a reassuring gesture. "The cultural governors are not blameless by any means, either, Counselor. My peers tend to focus so deeply on their own, local problems that they pay no mind to what takes place on the rest of Prime, even the collateral consequences of their own actions."

Utara nodded.

For a moment the Magister seemed distracted, gazing out over the waves. Then she laughed lightly, almost to herself. "I am an old woman, Counselor Fireheart. Old enough to be your grandmother, I imagine."

"Oh," she said, offering her a sly smile, "you look far too young for that."

The Magister laughed again, louder this time. "The PDS has trained you well, young lady." She looked out to the sea again. "In my lifetime I have seen many changes on Prime. Some for the better, others for the worse. I was young then, and did not fully understand the ramifications, but I can recall when the Future Cities were first proposed for Loorriri. Such a grand and noble idea. With such promise." She turned to look at Utara. "For you, even growing up in the first of them, it must seem a part of distant history."

"In many ways, yes." After the endless Senate debates had concluded and the votes in favor of establishing the Future Cities finally had prevailed in the Lower Assembly, the implementation of the gargantuan program had been equally fraught. Yet somehow the final locations of each city had been selected, the designs finalized, and construction begun. Funding from New Romas had been plentiful at first, along with the wildly successful sale of bonds to a public initially eager to help improve the quality of life of their fellow Primeans – but it had not taken long for the entire enterprise to become over budget and behind schedule. The Cultural Ministry, charged with oversight and execution of the plan, had pressed onward relentlessly. The Future Cities had come online in phases over the span of a decade; the first ones, beginning with Durnow, had been settled before Utara was born, while the last had filled with residents when she was a young child. "But I've heard so many tales from my father over the years that sometimes it feels like I was there myself."

"Indeed." A bird cawed, and the Magister's eyes tracked its flight across the sky. "I would have backed him in a heartbeat had he ever run for CM. Perhaps even PM after that." She met Utara's eyes again. "But I cannot judge his choices any more than he would judge mine. Is he still in Durnow?"

"Yes." Although Koster Fireheart had assisted with the settlement and initiation of many of Loorriri's Future Cities, Durnow had been his focus and his home ever since he had met her mother there in the earliest weeks of its official opening to its new population. "I saw him before I departed."

The Magister smiled. She waved a hand to the ocean. "My children and grandchildren left our islands behind years ago." She chuckled to herself. "Perhaps one of these days I will travel to visit them, instead of insisting they come to me."

"To be fair," Utara offered, "you're probably a lot busier than they are."

"I am!" The old woman laughed heartily. "I like you, Counselor."

Utara tipped her head graciously.

Then Magister grew serious again. "Tell me your opinion. Your *honest* opinion." She paused, gathering her thoughts. "The promise of the Future Cities was to bring, shall we say, *progress* to the people of Loorriri. Not just education and medicine, but their overall quality of life. To end the wars over resources, the violence among factions simply seeking to eke out a meager existence from unwelcoming terrain, by bringing them all together in cities where everyone could share in its benefits. To allow the nomads to share in the bounty of Prime, instead of wandering the land with their phanters. Do you think we have accomplished our goal?"

Utara had anticipated the question. The Judicar of the Red Rock Aladarians hadn't asked it, but the Magister did. The reality was muddled somewhere among *Not as far as we should have* and *Yes, but* and *Mostly, except.* What she gave was her prepared answer. "I think the Future Cities have achieved many positive objectives, but they have not yet lived up to their potential."

"If New Romas and the rest of Prime deliver on our promises, our bold experiment can still succeed? Even now?"

"Yes. Absolutely." In that answer, at least, Utara had complete certainty.

"And if we do not?" The Magister sat back in her chair. Suddenly she looked frail and defeated, not the vibrant woman she had been just minutes ago. "If we fall short?"

She had asked for her honesty, so Utara sat forward in the chair and gave it to her. "I don't know. But that is why we must not allow it to happen. The people of Loorriri are counting on us, and I won't give up until we help them."

"I believe you, Counselor Fireheart." For a moment her smile was broad and genuine. "And I pray to Evos that you succeed."

"Thank you."

The Magister grew sad. "I have seen our culture in the Balcom Islands change over the decades. Much of the change I like, some of it I despise. But our culture endures, and it will for decades to come. If the Future Cities fail, however – if it occurs because Prime allows it to happen – then we will not only have ruined the lives of the individuals who suffer today, but also their entire culture long into the future. I never thought I would live to see a world in which the people of Loorriri would have been better off remaining gentle nomads and ruthless scavengers than in trusting their fellow Primeans to do right by them. But I fear that reality may come to pass."

Utara fought to keep her composure, and barely succeeded. "I won't let that happen," she said, forcing her voice to remain level. "No matter what I have to do."

Deep down inside, though, she feared exactly the same thing as the Magister.

...*Grandell Motors Corporate Intelligence Division*

The beeping comdee broke his concentration. For an instant, Monson considered ignoring it and resuming his analysis of the trends in the day's trading on the securities and commodities exchanges. Then he remembered who might be contacting him, and swiveled his chair away from the screens to the table behind him.

Hand poised in the air, it took him a moment to recognize which of the six comdees had chimed. He saw it, snatched it up, and checked the screen.

TEN MINUTES.

"Perfect."

Monson kept the comdee in his hand and swiveled back around to the screens. A quick tap dismissed the trading data and called up the executive summary of his rapidly expanding dossier on Boynton Logistics Dynamics. It only took a few seconds to bring his questions back to the fore of his mind.

When he'd followed up with his ex-Boynton contact, the man had mentioned that his friends among the remaining employees in the AI division had been complaining about the oppressive hours they'd needed to work recently. He hadn't known any specifics, but an offer of a substantial additional sum of dracts had – within mere hours – produced the name and contact information of a current Boynton employee willing to tell everything to Monson for a comparable sum.

Over the last five days, Monson had ripened both leads. One of his assets in Port Vulcania, a local investigator whom he had hired for various tasks a dozen times in the past, had kept the Boynton facilities under surreptitious observation and had confirmed the long hours being worked by the AI division employees. After an initial tentativeness from his new contact, their exchange of text messages – and a reasonable increase in the bounty Monson was offering for inside information – finally had produced an arrangement for the imminent voice comm.

On cue, the comdee chimed. Monson tapped the button on his desk. The privacy bubble swiftly dropped into place around him to ensure no ambient noise would give away his location – or his employer.

He triggered the comdee active. "The down-payment is posted?"

"It's here," a woman's voice said. *"As agreed."*

"The rest will follow when we're concluded," he assured her. "But I imagine your friend has vouched for my sincerity to you, as he did for yours to me."

"Yes."

"Excellent. Let's begin." Monson took one last glance at the notes he had prepared. "Clearly something is seriously amiss within the AI division. What's creating the untenable situation?"

"That's a good word for it." She huffed. *"We're supposed to be spending a quarter of our time, at most, on the Loorriri AIs. There's only twelve of them, they all run the same AI code, and the Future Cities were constructed from the same fundamental city plans so each of them operates city management services in essentially the same way. As compared to our various other AIs all around the world, which have a lot more variations in coding and many more differences in operational circumstances. But lately, we're basically dealing with Loorriri all the time, every day. The entire division."*

"That's unusual?"

"I've been here almost eight years. This is the worst, by far. On raw server usage alone, the Loorriri AIs are running at triple rated baseline. It's the highest I've ever seen, and it's getting worse every week. And of course management won't give us anything close to the level of personnel or resources we need to deal with this."

"What's going wrong with the AIs?"

"It's not a malfunction. Within the terms of their programming, they're operating as designed. They've simply been pressed, by circumstances on the ground over there, into much more extensive analytical performance than ever before."

Monson already had considered the possibility of something problematic with the Future Cities or their AIs, but hadn't been able to uncover anything of note. As usual, the media reports offered scant news on the continent. A speech from a Lower Assembly delegate on one day, a feature on the wildlife preservation scientists the next. A warning to prospective tourists that the equatorial rainy season was about to begin. A new video of a vicious tiger taking down a hapless winterbuck. But accounts of current events in the Future Cities, or developments in the daily lives of their people, were almost nowhere to be found. Even the few reporters who regularly covered Loorriri had filed nothing the least bit insightful. If anyone ought to know what was happening there, they would. Unless they were still unaware that the story existed in the first place? That seemed unlikely, but it was possible.

"What's happening in Loorriri?"

She paused for a moment. *"There's not a pattern. It's something different in every city. In one, it's water delivery. In another, power shortages. Or food supply, or an increase in crime. Each city's AI is adapting to its own situation."*

"This need for adaptation, it hasn't arisen before?"

"Not on the current scale, no. And certainly not in so many cities at the same time."

Monson suspected the answer to his next question, but he wanted to be certain. "The AIs in the different cities, they not only analyze separately, but collectively as well?"

"That's right. The AIs can't communicate directly, but each one is connected to the central management hub, from which they all access data, coding upgrades, and the like. That enables each AI to learn from the experiences of the others, both what to repeat and what to avoid."

"Very efficient," Monson said. "But without a pattern to their current situations, little ability exists to synergize across the cities."

"Exactly. Hence the exponential increase in total usage that we've been spending so much time dealing with."

"That makes sense." For a few more minutes Monson asked additional questions about Boynton's corporate hierarchy and employee morale, and she provided the relevant details. Until he gleaned more from other avenues of investigation, though, there wasn't much more he could learn for now. "This has been extremely helpful," he told her. "I would be more than willing to renew our arrangement at a future time, perhaps at some point in the weeks ahead, if you are interested."

"I am," she said. *"I wonder..."*

When she hesitated, he prodded, "Yes?"

"I know you won't say who you work for, and that's fine. I don't expect you to. But if by chance your employer is someone who's a competitor of Boynton, who might be looking for AI coders or the like, well, let's just say I'm not the only one here who'd be open to working somewhere else."

"I'll keep that in mind," Monson said. Grandell Motors did not have need of individuals with those skills, especially ones willing to spill trade secrets. But sometimes one contact was a perfect fit for another, or an asset could be paid in information rather than money. This latest mystery woman from Boynton Logistics Dynamics had more than proven her value to Monson. He would not make the mistake of dismissing that lightly. His mind already was spinning out dozens of angles for steering the situation to his advantage. "In the meantime, might I pass along a bit of advice, from years working for a company mismanaged much the same as yours?"

"I'm all ears."

"If you and your peers keep working harder, putting in more hours, warding off any major problems even if the smaller issues still emerge – if you continue doing that, management will never change anything. They don't care how much you suffer; they only care if the job gets done. And you're still doing it for them."

"I can't just quit. None of us could. We have families to support."

"Oh, I don't mean to suggest anything that extreme. But I think you should provide the same level of dedication, diligence, and commitment to Boynton that management is providing to you."

"And if something goes wrong because we're no longer putting in the extra effort to save their rear ends, maybe they'll finally start paying attention."

"Precisely." Monson smiled. "I will be in touch with you again."

"I'll await your signal," she said, and ended the comm.

NINE

...Occanan

Compared to the glittering modernity of Hyj-gon, the principality's well-worn stone streets and faded stucco buildings seemed practically quaint. The royal family knew how to throw a spectacular days-long party leading up to an Airspar race, though, so the fans were more than happy to ignore the aged infrastructure. No matter the inevitable cracks and blemishes of an ancient city, the track itself was immaculately maintained to ensure a thrilling match every time.

Walking on the uneven paving toward their destination, Daemyn paused at the low stone wall to look out over the sweeping vista. The city sloped downward to the sea, the evening sun sparkling across the rooftops in a brilliant patchwork of painted tiles. The placid ocean shimmered a brilliant cerulean. The small islands and slender natural obelisks pocking the expansive bay had made entry to the city by water treacherous for centuries – but created the perfect venue for an over-water Airspar course. Tomorrow Daemyn would be cutting over the waves and swooping over the islands in a race generated by the best course designers on Prime. Already hundreds of yachts and boats had laid anchor in the bay to stake out the best positions to watch the airblades. He would make sure they didn't leave Torrini Atolls disappointed, at least not from Fith's matches.

From behind he heard the stutter of feet on the paving stones. Half-turning, he saw what he'd expected – yet another trashmag snooper with a vidcam. Ordinarily, the ambiance in Occanan would have inspired a grotesquely comedic facial expression to ruin the vid. With everything on his mind today, though, the only reply Daemyn cared to give was an obscene gesture. Before he managed to lift his hand, Elsa surged two strides in the man's direction. The look on her face made clear her mood was even worse than Daemyn's. For a long second the snooper's eyes bugged out. Then he spun around and ran off as fast as he could.

Elsa headed off toward the restaurant. Daemyn and Reiton were laughing so hard they couldn't walk.

She stopped and glanced back at them. "What?"

"The... look... " Reiton held up a palm, gasping for air. "On... his face."

"Priceless," Daemyn said, finally getting his own mirth under control. "All right. Let's go. Dinner awaits."

They made it the rest of the way without further interruption from the trashmags, although Daemyn did stop once to sign autographs. Another party was arriving at the restaurant right when they were. It took Daemyn a second to realize who it was.

He offered a polite nod. "Corin."

Their eyes met. "Wynde."

Then the hostess was leading Rockreikes and her four associates into the dimly lit confines of the restaurant, and nothing more was said.

After they were out of earshot Reiton said, "Nice lady."

Daemyn shrugged and said, "Didn't really feel like having a conversation with her anyway."

Elsa's bemusement was written all over her face. Daemyn looked at her. "What?"

She shook her head. "It's amazing you don't have a girlfriend."

"Right?" Reiton chimed in.

Daemyn crossed his arms. "*That* is neither of your business."

The hostess returned. "If you'll follow me, please?"

They reached their table – a booth nestled in the recesses of the back corner of the seating area – and Reiton slid into the bench seat opposite Daemyn. Elsa moved to follow, keeping herself on the outside. Daemyn was about to slide onto his side when he thought he recognized the graying, middle-aged man seated at the adjacent booth. He held up a hand to his friends and leaned around the edge of the other booth.

The man smiled. "Master Wynde."

Daemyn smiled back. Fortunately, he'd been right. They'd only met in person once before, two years ago at another Airspar track on halfway across the planet. "Master Windwalker. How fares your fine institution?"

"Overall, we are doing well. Our racing team, however, could use some improvement." Windwalker gave a sly smile. "It is quite impressive to see you flying again so soon after that awful crash. Every pilot I know would have written off this season's championships. But not you, it seems."

Daemyn grinned. "Do I make it that obvious?"

"To those who pay attention, at least."

Interesting that the president of Kedu Academy had chosen to reveal himself to be among that group. "We'll make up more points in the standings tomorrow."

"I'm sure you will. I won't take up your time this evening with a big race looming, of course. When your season is concluded, hopefully many weeks from now, I would like to invite you to visit the grounds of the Academy, along with as many of your friends as would be interested in accompanying you. I believe Kedu and the venturists share many common ideas about Prime's future, and the opportunities it presents for the planet." Windwalker paused, holding Daemyn's gaze. "And for us."

Daemyn certainly hadn't been expecting that. But he kept the surprise off his face and nodded. "Certainly. I'm always interested in additional perspectives, and from like-minded individuals in particular."

"Excellent. We'll speak again soon." With a small gesture, Windwalker indicated Daemyn's booth. "Enjoy your meal, Master Wynde. The food here is exquisite."

"Thank you," Daemyn said. "You too."

Daemyn slid into the booth across from Reiton and Elsa. Holtspring looked at him curiously. "What was that about?"

"I'm... not sure." Daemyn tapped his fingers on the edge of the burnished wooden table. "Perhaps another potential ally."

Elsa raised a brow. "A professor? Really?"

Reiton shrugged. "I'm sure they're not *all* useless."

"We learned from some of the best," Daemyn reminded his friend. "You never know. Besides, it can't hurt to take a meeting." He turned to Elsa.

"Right now, though, we have other priorities. Where are we on the Project Lariat hack?"

~⌒~

...*Midland Savannahs Wildlife Sanctuary*

J'ni rubbed her palms together, scraping off the caked dirt. She'd done the best she could here, but it certainly didn't feel like enough.

Overhead a vulture cried. Helpless to vent her emotions any other way, J'ni bent down, snatched up a rock, and heaved it skyward. "Go! Get out of here!" Her aim hadn't been very good, but the avian and his remaining brethren took the hint all the same. They scattered in three directions, powerful wings beating to lift them into the soaring updrafts over the grasses.

Truth be told, she owed the vultures thanks. Without the swarm circling over this location – dozens of them, more than enough to catch her attention as a highly unusual sight on the savannah – she might never have found the bodies. Not that anything had been left but the bones by the time she'd arrived, between the silver jackal tracks on the ground and the vultures from the air. Even bones deserved a proper burial.

Standing beside her truck, J'ni considered her options. The ambush had been vicious and cruel. The armed attackers, at least twenty of them, had arrived on foot and struck from multiple angles at once. She saw no indications anyone had been able to fight back. The attackers had departed to the east, taking three of the refugee's trucks with them. The survivors had fled to the south. They'd probably been too afraid to return to bury the bodies. The outlaws hadn't bothered.

She could try to contact Utara, now that she had some direct substantiation of their concerns about the outlaw threat. But even if her friend somehow could manage to get the attention of the leadership in Luppitan or Durnow to take action against the outlaws, J'ni had no idea where to tell them to look. More likely, it wouldn't matter anyway. The Future Cities would simply increase their own perimeter patrols and leave the refugees and nomads to fend for themselves.

The survivors, though, might still have a chance if she got to them in time. They'd been on the move a day and a half at most, many of them on foot. In her truck, she ought to be able to catch up to them in hours.

She hopped in her truck, started the engine, and turned to follow the southerly path trodden into the savannah. Without any rain the last few days, the tracks were easy enough to follow. Onward she drove, each minute bringing more dread of what she might find. She tried not to think about it.

Barely an hour into her sojourn, she spotted another truck parked atop a ridgeline in the distance. It didn't belong to the refugees; theirs were new to the savannah, still only about two weeks removed from city life in Luppitan. This truck was dirty and worn, its paint long faded from the blazing sun. Like J'ni's.

Honking the horn once, she pulled to a stop a dozen meters away. With a deep breath she reached for the loaded pistol on the seat next to her. She stepped down from her truck, tucked the pistol in her belt at the small of her back, and started walking.

She topped the ridgeline to find a man and a woman walking up the slope to meet her. He was a tall and imposing Faytan, middle-aged, his skin tanned and weathered. She was tall too, a bronze-skinned Aladarian. The gear on their belts and strapped into their truck revealed clearly enough what they did to survive out here. Neither wore a weapon, at least not visibly, and they held their hands out and open.

When they drew close the man said, "Acai?"

She had never seen these two before, she was sure of it. But the poachers knew her – or had been in this part of the savannah long enough to make an educated guess who she was. She knew better than to bother asking their names and answered simply, "Yes."

The woman motioned a hand to the makeshift camp at the foot of the ridge. Some damaged tents, a few burnt-out campfires, two trucks – and no people. "They never had a chance, really."

"Definitely feline tracks," the man explained. "Three adults and two young. Had to be tigres. Too big for cheeters, and kinanas hunt alone."

"Cheeters wouldn't be that bold, either," J'ni said.

The man nodded. "We buried the bodies. What was left of them. Finished ... well, not long before you got here."

J'ni swallowed hard. "How many?"

The woman took a moment estimating on her fingers. "Twenty-five, probably. Not counting the ones that got dragged far off. We couldn't find those."

J'ni nodded. Potentially as many as forty captive refugees on the three stolen trucks. If any of them were still alive. Now she really did have to get word to Durnow at once, one way or another. "I appreciate what you did."

The poachers waited. Maybe they expected J'ni to threaten to call the rangers, or try to arrest them herself for their crimes against the sanctuary's wildlife. On some other day, she might have. Would have, probably. But not today.

"Many blessings," the man finally said, repeated by the woman quickly and quietly before the pair turned to walk back to their truck.

"Many blessings," J'ni said, and returned to her truck too.

She sat in the driver's seat and watched the other truck drive away across the savannah. Once they were gone she vented her rage and grief to the sun and the breeze, until she finally slumped back in the seat, spent, and cried.

...Balcom Islands

Utara looked at her list one more time.

No matter how long she stared at it, though, nothing changed. She already had visited the two cultural governors mostly likely to be sympathetic to the Future Cities' plight and had failed to garner even the smallest measure of actual, tangible support toward improving their conditions. Worse, it wasn't as simple as her pleas failing to persuade; the reality had been abundantly clear that no arguments she could muster – moral or emotional, political or financial – would be enough to change their minds. Whatever compassion they might feel for the suffering of the people of Loorriri was resoundingly overwhelmed by the need to attend to the struggles of their own people.

If her top two choices had fallen so far short, she couldn't imagine the other alternatives on the list going any better. Maybe her whole plan had been pointless from the start. Utara had used almost a week's vacation time already, with nothing to show for it. Maybe it would be better to return to Loorriri and do the best she could for Blonkas, as her father had done in Durnow for so many years.

The sound on the veepee was muted, but a rapid flickering of the images on the screen caught her attention in her peripheral vision. She glanced up to see another of the insufferably perpetual advertisements for Airspar. Utara had never been able to understand how so many Primeans could be so fixated on the reckless, pointless spectacle. But they were. By the millions.

"Of course!" she exclaimed to herself, practically startled by the sound of her own voice in the nearly silent hotel room.

People – politicians and cultural governors included – were obsessed with Airspar. She could use that her advantage.

Her father always said that the only way to truly reach people was to speak to them on terms they could understand in circumstances when they were open to listening. Many of the residents of the Future Cities loved Airspar just like the rest of Prime – and driving home that commonality amid the congregated camaraderie of a match would have an impact far beyond the abstractions of a financial discussion in a staid office. The environment of the match would create very different circumstances for listening, too – temporarily freed from the familiar pressures of daily politics, loosened by the thrill of the race, the politicians in attendance would be far more open-minded at the Airspar match than they would be for a meeting in their offices. Her hope swelled anew.

Occanan was an expensive place to visit, but she needed to take a gamble.

Utara sprang from her chair and started packing. She didn't have a moment to spare. The Airspar match at Torrini Atolls started tomorrow.

~⌒◡

...Blonkas

The sense of anticipation hung in the air like a great burst of static electricity waiting to discharge. With the children just home from school, people of all ages were gathered in the street between the rowhouses. Some sat; other stood. Everyone waited.

A few hours ago word had arrived over the dedicated notification frequency that power would be restored to Evostown in late afternoon. The automated message had advised that power might be active for as short as three hours and as long as six, but for the people here any amount of power was cause for rejoicing.

Aidan certainly understood why. So many things the residents took for granted had become painfully unavailable. Backup batteries could keep com-dees charged, but without visionpods and audiocasters Evostown felt severed from the city beyond the neighborhood, much less the rest of Prime. The incinerator that disposed of the neighborhood's trash was inoperable, and the accumulating refuse was emitting a foul stench that permeated the streets on the vagaries of the wind. The city's sanitation division vehicles also operated on batteries, leaving them non-functional without power to recharge and unable to assist with alternative methods of disposal. The water-delivery tankers had stopped coming too, which eliminated the option of maintaining any surplus supply of stored water. At least the pipes still flowed with clean water, and fortunately that was enough to sustain the minimum necessities of avoiding dehydration and maintaining functional privies. Uses for personal hygiene, though, had to be kept to the minimum, only adding to the overall feeling of unease and discomfort. A few hours of power to the neighborhood wouldn't cure all those ills, not by a long shot, but it certainly would provide a much-needed boost to the residents' spirits.

Loud laughing drew his attention. He glanced over to see Hasto, Roturo, and two of their friends sharing the moment of levity. The young men hadn't abandoned their ludicrous notions of leaving the city to trek across the land, but they'd at least kept their discussions to themselves and had avoided upsetting others the last few days. Maybe a turn for the better would convince them to see the situation more reasonably. Aidan could hope so, anyway.

"Listen!" someone shouted. Someone else yelled, "Hush!"

Within seconds an eerie silence fell over the street. The first hint of power was the low hum of the air chillers in the basement of each building reactivating. Then a soft *pop* as the nearest street lamp turned on. A moment later, the sound of an audiocaster.

Cheers erupted. Smiles and laughs, hugs and dancing. Some people rushed inside to turn on their air chillers and recharge their compupods. Others remained outside, enjoying the moment with family and friends.

For now, Aidan stayed seated on the front stoop of the rowhouse and watched. Every happy minute the residents experienced was a blessing. Some of them came up and thanked him; he didn't have the heart to tell them he'd played no role in their newfound good fortune. Really, though, they weren't thanking him personally anyway. Aidan was a proxy for the PDS and the government officials who led Blonkas – and who somehow had found a way to get the power back on. Silently he prayed to Tarah, beseeching her to give the people of Evostown as many hours of this happiness as they could possibly have today. He didn't even ask her for tomorrow, or the day after.

Lost in thought, he didn't know how long the power had been on when the nearly deafening emergency alert sirens began their shrill blare.

Aidan reacted on instinct. "Inside!" he shouted. "Everyone get inside!"

He bounded from the stoop and ran down the street, yelling and waving his arms as he went. Most of the residents needed little prodding, and raced for the doors to their rowhouses. A few of the younger children stood frozen in place; with a smile and a reassuring hand he pointed each one in the direction of their respective homes and guided them on their scampering ways. Glancing over his shoulder, he saw Hasto and Roturo assisting several of the older residents to climb the steps. By the time Aidan got back to his own rowhouse the two men had finished. They met him in the middle of the now-deserted street as the sirens' wail wound down.

"What's going on?" Hasto asked.

"This better not be somebody's sick idea of a good time to run a drill," Roturo added.

Aidan snatched his comdee off his belt and held it visible in his hand. "I will get answers as quickly as possible, and let you know."

Roturo accepted the pledge with a nod, and Hasto reached out and gripped Aidan's shoulder firmly for a moment. Then the two men ran off toward their homes and Aidan sprang up the steps to his.

He didn't sit down when he'd closed the door to his apartment behind him. He tapped the icon for the PDS field office and waited. That gave him long enough to realize that the power was still on. He strode over and turned on the visionpod. He toggled over to the city government's emergency alert channel. All he found was the city seal – and complete silence.

"You're connected, Aidan," came Danya's voice from the comdee. *"Hold for the conference line."* The transmission went mute before he could ask anything.

With a silent veepee and muted comdee, the next two minutes lasted an eternity. Finally the comdee beeped.

"Thank you for your patience, everyone," said the voice of Peitro Samuel, the senior PDS envoy in Blonkas. *"The sirens have activated citywide."*

Aidan's eyes shot back to the veepee, but it was still silent and bare.

"Earlier today," Samuel continued, *"the city government's leadership council authorized an emergency override of the determination by the logistics-management artificial intelligence as to the distribution of power. Several neighborhoods already have had periods with power, others have it now, and several more will receive it later tonight. Due to the reallocation of power to the residential neighborhoods, however, power previously allocated by the AI to other uses was no longer available for those purposes. The siren alert is due to an unforeseen consequence of those power cuts. The public safety division does not yet know the complete extent of the impacts, but they believed it was necessary to err on the side of caution until the situation is fully assessed."*

Someone on the conference line asked what Aidan was thinking. What all the PDS counselors on the line no doubt were thinking. *"How bad is it?"*

For a long, dreadful moment Samuel didn't reply.

The lums in Aidan's apartment flickered. The veepee fuzzed static before the city seal returned. Another flicker of the lums.

Then the power went out – and the sirens began to wail once more.

To himself Aidan said, "Bad."

TEN

...Occanan

Somehow Utara had pulled it off. She had managed to convince the over-worked, frazzled desk attendant into crediting her PDS travel voucher toward a seat on one of the last flights to the principality on the eve of the Airspar race, even though customers were offering to pay triple the usual fare to get aboard. Then she had found a hotel room on the outskirts of the city for a high but tolerable price. Worn from a long day of travel, she'd actually fallen asleep for the rest of the night and had awakened refreshed and ready to face her mission once more.

Walking at a deliberate pace through the crowd on the expansive stone plaza abutting the bay, Utara kept her eyes open for anyone worth talking to. If she could find one of the cultural governors or other politicians high on her list, so much the better – but she wouldn't limit herself to the list, either. The matches would last all day, so she had plenty of time to make her case to as many dignitaries as possible. Between the plaza, which spanned much of the length of the bay's shoreline, and the multiple enormous stone piers jutting out into the bay to provide even closer views of the airblades' flights, numerous opportunities for encounters with the people she sought would present themselves. In the meantime, before the racing began she had other options. Her first idea was the dazzling, expensive hotels frequented by the wealthy and powerful.

Even early in the morning the sun beat down, reflecting its heat from the stone paving. Occanan wasn't nearly as hot as Blonkas, of course, but the last thing Utara could afford was to let the temperature tire her too early. She hurried the last dozen meters to the nearest of her target hotels and slipped inside as a trio of tall Suterrans bounded out into the street.

She ambled through the spacious lobby, scanning the guests and marveling at the ornate furnishings and artwork that bedecked the high-ceilinged chamber. The hotel was undeniably impressive – definitely the kind of place most of the cultural governors would favor for a cross-planetary excursion. After about fifteen minutes, though, she'd had no luck spotting anyone noteworthy.

Right before she was ready to try another hotel, she caught sight of a short, rotund middle-aged man in expensive Faytan garb descending the wide staircase on the northern end of the room. Utara peered closer. It took her a second, but she recognized him as the deputy premier of Sansato, an Airspar-obsessed region near Hyj-gon. Trying not to make herself too obvious, she cut across the lobby in his direction.

Utara stepped around an elderly Aquarian couple and reached his side. Keeping her voice polite and calm to avoid startling him, she said, "Deputy Premier Mataki? I wonder if I might have a moment of your time?"

He turned to her, his expression skeptical. "Do I know you?"

"No, sir. We haven't met." She offered a respectful bow. "Counselor Utara Fireheart, Prime Diplomatic Service."

"Oh, PDS. That's lovely."

"It is?"

He grinned. "I'd feared you were a reporter."

Utara smiled back. "Not at all. I didn't realize they were so troublesome for you."

"They're troublesome for everyone, as far as I'm concerned." He shook his head, amused at himself. "Much as I might wish it were otherwise, Not-A-Reporter Fireheart, I'm forced to speculate that you didn't make my acquaintance simply due to my political stature, such as it is – but rather that you have some manner of PDS or government business you want to discuss with me."

"Yes, I do."

"Very well." Mataki pointed toward the main doors back out to the plaza. "I have a meeting roughly a kilometer from here. If you'll walk with me, we can discuss it on the way."

"I'd be delighted, Deputy Premier," she said, and matched his pace.

Unlike the Judicar and the High Magister, he hadn't already read her executive summary on the situation in Loorriri. After the practice from her discussions with the other two politicians, though, Utara found that laying out the issues for Mataki went a lot more smoothly than she'd expected. It took her only a couple of minutes to explain why she had come to Occanan and what she hoped to achieve.

"It's a disgrace that it's come to this," Mataki said. "The people should be able to trust that New Romas will do its job in providing stability and security – not make their lives worse."

"In many ways the job gets done well enough," Utara offered. "For most of Prime."

"That's true." He met her eyes. "But not for the residents of the Future Cities, as you see it?"

"No."

Mataki sighed. "You've turned to the cultural governors for help because our governments, for the most part, do far better at serving our people than New Romas does. But I'm afraid there's nothing I can offer to you, Counselor. The unfortunate truth is that Sansato might be closer to the kind of fiscal collapse you've seen in Loorriri than you realize."

Her surprise was real, and Utara didn't try to hide it. "I'm…"

Mataki dipped his gaze.

"How is that possible? Just last year Yoshigura had record profits, and –"

The deputy premier laughed, not so much bitterly as fatalistically. "Our companies have never been stronger, and tax revenue is increasing. We're one of the few places on Prime that's happening."

Which could only mean expenses were rising even faster. "You have costs you are unable to counterbalance?"

"Fayti has blessed the people of Sansato with health as well as wealth. We have more retirees than ever before, and they were promised pensions in earlier, more stable times. Our current generation of children is the largest in our history, too, and their expenses for education, wellness, and future-care accounts are only growing. With that combination, revenues simply cannot keep up."

Utara nodded. "What are you going to do?"

"We've already instituted the beginning stages of austerity measures. Each segment of the budget has been proportionally reduced. So far the extent has been small enough that most people haven't noticed. Soon, though, that will no longer be the case."

Utara didn't doubt his sincerity, but she had to make him see that the situation in Sansato wasn't nearly as grim as it seemed – and that conditions in Loorriri were far worse. She didn't need a lot from him. Only enough to make a difference. "What about the next-generation solar cells? From what I've read, they're able to produce ten times the power at a fraction of the cost of traditional reactors. And there is great promise in the wind combines, as well. With those technologies in place to improve efficiencies so dramatically, your energy expenses will plummet."

"In time, yes," Mataki conceded. "But for the foreseeable future, during the years it takes to phase them into our power grid, alternative fuels cannot solve the budget crisis we face."

"Sure they can," said a man's voice from right beside them. "You just have to take care to do the accounting properly."

First Utara and Mataki looked at each other. Then, simultaneously, they looked to the interloper. The corner of his mouth curled toward the beginning of a grin, but his eyes were deadly serious. "Sorry to intrude, but I couldn't help overhearing. New fuel technologies are something of a passion of mine."

Mataki grinned back. "Especially the Faytan ones, I expect."

"Naturally." The man turned to Utara. "I'm –"

"I know who you are," she said. The words came out a little more brusquely than she'd intended, but not by much. While it was true she wasn't much of an Airspar fan, he would have no way of knowing that. Everyone recognized the most famous names and faces: Corin Rockreikes, Drummond Keel, and –

"Daemyn Wynde," he stated, as if he preferred the introduction. "And you are?"

She stopped herself from saying *it's none of your business.* Like Mataki, Wynde was Faytan, but their familiarity seemed to run deeper than that. She didn't want to risk ticking off the deputy premier if the racer was a respected cultural peer, or even a friend. So she forced a polite smile and said, "Utara Fireheart."

"From the Prime Diplomatic Service."

She shouldn't have been surprised a championship-winning racer was so observant, but she was. The PDS logo on her shirt was barely two centimeters wide. "Yes, and I was discussing government business with the deputy premier."

"More specifically," Wynde said, "you were talking about alternative fuels and their budget impacts."

"We were," Mataki said before Utara could reply. "But some corporate-style clever accounting tricks won't resolve Sansato's deficits."

"Not a trick," Wynde insisted. "If I spend twenty this year and ten next year, it's a total of thirty and an average of fifteen. Short-term thinking focuses on the twenty and sees it as a problem. Long-term thinking sees the total and the average as more important, and views it as an opportunity."

"Venturist thinking, more specifically," Mataki said, flashing the racer a smirk. "For an individual, or a company owned by one, spending the twenty now and counting on the ten to show up and balance the ledger later may very well be a risk worth taking. The stakes are much higher for a governmental budget, and the risks must be managed accordingly. The decision-making factors are a lot more complicated."

"In their particulars, sure," Wynde conceded. "But the fundamental principle is sound. If I know that I have a surplus coming next year, there's nothing wrong with a deficit-spend this year. It evens out over the two-year window."

"It would, but only if the surplus actually materializes," Utara said. "Maybe corporate finances are a lot more predictable than government revenues; I wouldn't know. But I can assure you of this: even leaving aside the Treasury's continuing difficulties in New Romas, revenues and expenses for cultural region budgets are notoriously unstable from year to year. The principle may be sound, but reality isn't."

"Counselor Fireheart is right," Mataki said. "And believe me, the Premier is even more deeply entrenched in that mindset than her explanation of it."

"It's not only about the money," Wynde said.

Utara was about to redirect the conversation — *her* conversation with Mataki, until Wynde had hijacked it — back to the crisis in the Future Cities when she noticed the racer make a quick hand gesture to two people standing a little over two meters away. The tall, striking Polar Aquarian woman gave a tiny shrug before her eyes resumed scanning the crowd around them. The shorter, well-coiffed man in the immaculately tailored business suit nodded and shifted his weight to the other foot. Distracted and a bit curious, Utara lost her chance.

"Look at what's happened in Airspar since the switch to artronium," Wynde continued. "It's all a matter of open record, so I'm not sharing any trade secrets here. The public likes the artronium engines because the airblades are faster, so attendance and viewership are both at all-time record levels. For the teams, the expense for fuel has fallen through the floor. They're spending more dracts than ever on R&D, and the rapid improvements in blade tech speak for themselves."

"More money to spend on pilot salaries and bonuses, too," Utara noted.

"Yes, that's another upside," Wynde agreed, amiably ignoring her implication. "And there's more. Look around us here at Torrini Atolls. Before, the sky would get choked with exhaust no matter how hard they tried to keep the air moving. We'd be seeing a haze in the air already, just from the testing runs yesterday. Look out there today." He raised a hand, pointing to the brilliantly clear blue sky above the waters. "Nothing. The air quality at the tracks is remarkable now. It improves the races because it's easier on the engines and the pilots. It's better for the spectators, too, of course. While the budget impacts are very positive, it's the ecological benefit of artronium that has made the switch such a success."

Mataki took in the vista and said, "I can't argue with you on that."

"Yes, that's an improvement for Airspar," Utara said, "but most of the older-generation reactors in Sansato, like the ones in the Future Cities, are already zero-impact ecologically. While new technology would improve efficiency and reduce cost, it can't be justified by collateral benefits comparable to racing's switch to artronium."

Wynde paused, but she couldn't read the expression on his face. "That's probably right," he said, "but my overall point remains sound. The long-term benefits of the transition to alternative fuel sources dramatically overcomes the short-term expenditures to make it happen. A skilled accountant will be able to make that point, with the numbers, in a way that even your most recalcitrant politicians can't deny, Deputy Premier."

"Maybe in Hyj-gon," Mataki said. "In Sansato, it's not that simple. The infrastructure adjustments would be substantial."

Wynde's eyes darted over to Utara. Before she could say anything he told the other man, "Then don't start there. The infrastructure in the Future Cities is considerably newer, and won't require nearly as much adaptation. Our Faytan tech is good, and our companies are waiting for the right chance to prove it. With the government's support to ensure it's a sound investment – maybe even a tax deduction rather than a direct subsidy, if that'll make the budget bureaucrats happy – they'd rush to install it in Loorriri and let it demonstrate its value in actual use on the ground. Before you know it, your politicians would be begging you and the Premier to pay for it in all your cities in Sansato, as well."

Utara had to play back his words in her head to make sure she'd heard him right. What was going on? Why was he trying to help the Future Cities? There had to be something in it for him. But she had no idea what it could possibly be. Whatever his reasons, though, he was helping to make her case.

"Master Wynde is right," she told Mataki. "New power generators would be far easier to install in the Future Cities than elsewhere on Prime, and unreliable power has been one of the greatest challenges to the cities' success. The significantly increased yields from the new technology would allow us to tackle many of the other problems more effectively, as well. If we could get private firms to front some of the cost, that would make things happen even faster."

Mataki spread his hands wide. "Much like a team flying against Fith with you in the lead, Daemyn, I can see when I'm outmatched. When I return to Sansato, Counselor Fireheart, I'll propose your idea to the Premier. If we can present this as helping our local industry succeed, rather than a budget outlay from the government, it might have a chance of going somewhere." Before either of them could offer their thanks, Mataki pressed on. "Now if you'll excuse me, I'm about to be late for my meeting. Many blessings to you both."

With a few quick strides the deputy premier was gone. Utara looked up at Wynde. "Thank you."

He smiled. "I never turn down a chance to illuminate backward-thinking government officials on the benefits of following a venturist approach."

"Honestly, at this point I don't care what kind of ideology convinces him, as long as it does. The Future Cities need all the help they can get, sooner rather than later."

Wynde canted his head, seeming to look closely at her for the first time. "You're from Loorriri? Originally, I mean. Not just your PDS assignment."

"I grew up in Zanita." As soon as it left her mouth, Utara wondered why she'd told him that.

"I've only seen viscaps."

"Pictures don't do it justice."

"I don't doubt it. If I'm ever in the neighborhood, I'll look you up and you can give me a tour in return for the assist today."

"It's the least I can do. I'd be happy to show you around." It was a cheap pledge for Utara to make, considering the long odds against an Airspar celebrity bothering to set foot on Loorriri. She turned to go. "Good luck in —"

"Hey, listen," Wynde said. He waited for her to glance back at him. "On a ticket you bought on a government salary, I doubt you'll get a great view of the track."

"I haven't checked," she told him. It was truth, too.

"My friends came to watch me race today. Torrini Atolls is their favorite track." He waved over the two people he'd signaled earlier. "Out on the yacht is the best spot anywhere —"

"I appreciate the offer, but I really need to start finding more cultural governors to talk to."

"I'm not trying to flirt with you."

For a moment Utara thought maybe he sounded just a little bit too defensive in his last statement. She didn't know why that made her smile, but it did. "Oh, I believe you. I can tell you're all business, all the time."

"That he is." The man in the suit extended his hand. "Reiton Holtspring."

Utara gripped his forearm in the customary greeting. "Utara Fireheart."

Quickly Wynde leaned in and whispered something to Holtspring. "Sorry," he said to her when he finished. "But I have to get to the hangars. Coach Farrier will be excessively cranky if I'm late."

"Good luck today," she said.

Wynde nodded and strode off briskly. Slicing effortlessly through the crowd, the tall blonde matched his pace before overtaking him to lead the way.

Holtspring glanced after them, then looked back to Utara. "That was a bit abrupt. He's usually more polite."

Utara grinned. "Could have fooled me."

"Perhaps interrupting a politician's conversation isn't his finest moment," Holtspring conceded, offering a grin in return. "Speaking of which, it seems you have important matters to attend to."

"Yes. I'd better get back to work."

"In that case, I won't keep you. Many blessings, Counselor Fireheart."

"Many blessings."

He turned and headed into the crowd, strolling in the direction of one of the piers farther down the plaza. Utara scanned the people around her, looking for any prospects to approach. Still, something about Wynde's invitation kept tickling her mind. Government salaries. Government revenues, and budgets… The real money wasn't with the cultural governors. It was elsewhere. Such as, out on a venturist's yacht.

She found herself weaving between the pedestrians, hurrying after Holtspring. Quickly she caught up to him. Reaching his side she said, "Actually…"

ELEVEN

...Blonkas

The sirens had stopped by nightfall, when the notification frequency had brought word of a temporary citywide curfew. By mid-morning, though, the curfew still hadn't been lifted. It wasn't fear of arrest that kept the residents of Evostown indoors, but fear of whatever unknown danger had created the curfew order in the first place. Several of the elders had sent Aidan text messages asking what he knew, but they had not asked to meet, individually or in a group. Less trusting in the judgment of authority figures like the bureaucrats – especially now – and more confident in their own invincibility to walk the streets, Hasto and Roturo had demanded to speak to Aidan in person. At this point, the last thing he would have done was refuse them. That would only have made the situation worse for everyone.

Now the three men stood in Aidan's apartment. Nobody had any inclination to sit down. "The notifications didn't give a reason," Hasto said. "Which means it's something they don't want us to know."

Roturo nodded vigorously. "Have you heard anything?"

"Not much," Aidan said. "The emergency codes also don't refer to a specific kind of danger. The Future Cities have common codes for severe weather alerts, groundquakes, other kinds of natural disasters. Different ones for crime or looting, or buildings on fire, various types of manmade threats. These codes, though, are a general public safety warning."

"So they really are hiding the truth from you?" Hasto asked.

"Or," Aidan said, keeping his voice measured, "they never had reason before to create a code for the way things have gone wrong this time."

Roturo cursed, then braced his hands on the back of a chair. "If the power's out in the whole city, it could be out in the preserve, too. You think the animals got loose."

"We don't have a code for it in the system, and it would explain the need for a curfew even during the day."

Hasto considered it. "That does make sense."

"I guess it would explain the gunfire, too," Roturo conceded. "Too many people have been told about it from too many different friends who heard it themselves. It's not a rumor. It's happening out there."

"I believe you," Aidan assured him. He took a deep breath and gathered his thoughts. "If the animals really have escaped, we'll have evidence of that soon enough one way or the other. It won't take much longer for something to wander its way into Evostown."

"Unless they're faking the codes on the emergency frequency," Roturo pointed out. "There are people who listen in and know the codes. It could be something different, and they're trying to hide the truth as long as they can."

Aidan had considered that possibility, too. It was unlikely, but not impossible. "I think that would be more counterproductive than helpful overall. It might conceal things from the public for a little while, but in the meantime —"

The abrupt knock at the apartment door was loud and firm. "Hold on," Aidan told the two young men before walking over to the door. Unclenching his fists, he opened it.

The two law enforcement agents standing in the hallway wore body armor and helmets, but the faceplates were raised and their rifles were slung across their backs by the straps. "Aidan Stone?"

"That's me."

"We've been ordered to bring you to the EOC."

…Scarlet Envy, *moored in Occanan Bay*

The venturists' yacht was by far the largest waterbound vessel Utara had ever personally set foot on. She was pretty sure it was longer than the air shuttle that had flown her to Occanan. Its mass was so great it gave almost no hint of floating atop the waves; only the salty aroma of the sea and the cries of the shorebirds gave that away. Now anchored at a perfect vantage point in the bay, the engines had barely rumbled to propel them out here. The compulsory round of the Airspar match had already started, but her hosts weren't watching. At least not yet. Utara was starting to wonder.

"Only a few more minutes," Reiton Holtspring said, hurrying up to rejoin Utara on the wide lower deck. "They're finishing up."

Utara put on a smile. "It's all right. I've been using the time to perfect my arguments for why the Future Cities offer a good return on investment."

The words sounded a lot more confident than she felt. She had been aboard the yacht over an hour, but had only spoken to the other venturists for the quick minute it had taken Holtspring to make the introductions. After that Rustle Tames, Sage Gaiser, and Celia Lancer had gone upstairs to the smaller enclosed observation deck below the pilot's cabin. From the peeks she'd stolen in that direction, they appeared to be holding some kind of vid-cam conference. Holtspring had been back and forth several times, making sure Utara was comfortable and apologizing for the wait.

"I have no doubt." He glanced outward, momentarily distracted by a raucous, inexplicable cheer from the spectators on one of the nearby water-craft. "We really are here to watch Daemyn race, you know. Sage lined up this conference about a potential investment months ago, before we had the race schedule."

"And then Daemyn —" She forced herself to use his first name, since Holtspring was referring to his friends that way. "— added another business meeting to the itinerary on short notice, with no advance preparation."

"Well, yes." He chuckled. "Trust me, it's not the first time."

"I'll be sure to take full advantage of my accidental opportunity, then."

"As will we. Sometimes the biggest rewards arrive in unexpected ways."

"It would be helpful to know," she asked, "does one of you own an energy company, or an investment along those lines?"

"I wish," Holtspring said, laughing. "We don't. At least not yet."

"Daemyn seemed quite eager to talk to Deputy Premier Mataki about installing new Faytan technology in the Future Cities. I thought perhaps he saw a personal stake in it."

"Nothing that direct, no."

"Well, hopefully your meeting with me isn't disappointing compared to the conference. While I can justify how you'll make a profit in Loorriri, I imagine the rate of return may not measure up to other possibilities you may have access to."

He raised a brow at her. "I had you pegged as much more idealistic, Counselor Fireheart. Why else would you be out here in Occanan, trying to convince people to help the Future Cities, unless you believed they would be willing to do the right thing? And yet you seem awfully cynical about me and my friends."

"Everyone approaches life from their own perspective, and pursues the goals they value." She met his eyes and didn't waver. "Unless I'm very misinformed, the venturists are motivated by profit, not the public interest."

"I see." Holtspring paused. "And you think those two values are incompatible?"

"Not necessarily," she admitted. "But I can think of quite a few examples where a selfish pursuit of profit harmed the public interest a great deal."

"Fair enough. I could do the same. But consider where we are right now. This —" He gestured to the Torrini Atolls Airspar Track around them. "— is a perfect example of how pursuing the public interest in the wrong way can be counterproductive to economic responsibility, too."

"How's that?" It was a genuine question. She had a feeling he was eager to answer it.

"It's not your sector of the government, I know, but look at what New Romas has done to the sporting industries. In the name of athlete safety, and protecting from injury in the youth leagues, and even deterring children from having the *wrong* role models, whatever that means, they've essentially shut down any number of sports. If it were only the competitors and coaches affected, that would be one thing – but it's all the other jobs and incomes that derived from those sports, too. This one race, here at Torrini Atolls, generates enough tax revenue to fund the principality's operating budget for over a third of the year."

"I didn't know that."

"Most people don't. So imagine how much tax revenue New Romas would lose, all the local host sites of the different tracks would lose, if Airspar disappeared. Now multiply that by the number of sports they've already crushed." Holtspring shook his head. "I'm not saying their goals weren't admirable. But in a fiscal environment where the government is already running short on funds, the policies they adopted made everything worse. It's all very short-sighted. Which, unfortunately, is the way most politicians think and act."

"A lot of them, anyway." Utara couldn't dispute that, much as she wished things were different. Prime and its people deserved better. "As we agreed, though, short-sighted pursuit of profit can be just as damaging. To innocent people's jobs, to people's health, even the whole economy."

"Indeed." He had been occasionally glancing to the observation deck, and this time he gestured up a quick acknowledgement before returning his attention to her. "But the venturists, we're not short-sighted. A quick, gigantic short-term return here or there? Sure, I wouldn't turn it down, at least as long as it wouldn't undermine the overall strategy. True, enduring wealth, though? That only comes from long-term vision."

Utara found the obvious question on the tip of her tongue. She hesitated, then realized she had to ask it. Whatever the answer was, she'd know how to approach the pitch ahead – or whether she was wasting her time on this yacht, and should ask them to take her back to shore. "And you and your friends genuinely are interested in pursuing the right long-term vision for Loorriri?"

Holtspring smiled broadly and pointed a finger directly at her. "*That*," he said, "is exactly the right question to ask. I knew there was something I liked about you, Utara."

"Oh," she said, and felt the blush rising in her cheeks.

His eyes widened. Quickly he leaned in close, whispering in her ear. "Don't worry, it's not like that at all. You're not my type."

"Uh, thanks?" she whispered back. But the relief flooding through her also drained the heat from her face, and when she turned to greet the three venturists striding across the deck toward them, Utara had her composure fully restored.

"All right, everyone," Holtspring said. He quickly checked the large vee-pee screen filled with the live race updates. "We have about thirty minutes before Fith starts their run. That gives us plenty of time to discuss the Future Cities with our new friend here."

~~◯

...Emergency Operations Center, Blonkas

"The curfew is holding in most of the city," Peitro Samuel told the PDS counselors assembled in the small conference room off the hallway leading to the main briefing auditorium. As he spoke he pointed to the map on the display screen that consumed most of the far wall. "Evostown is quiet. Same for Arcadia and Doroon for the most part. Nothing the law-enforcement subdivision can't handle. It's Rockville where the concern lies, and where we've been asked to assist in calming the situation."

Samuel zoomed the map to focus on the single neighborhood. "Most of the cams are offline due to the power shutdowns, so we don't have much in the way of live feeds. But what EOC is hearing from the officials in the area, as well as some resident reports over the emergency frequencies, isn't good."

Tyku put a hand in the air. When Samuel acknowledged him he asked, "What's different there compared to the rest of the city?"

Aidan was wondering the same thing. Every neighborhood faced the same extreme uncertainty now troubling the entire city, and even the Terrans, who made up the substantial majority of Rockville's residents, had their share of agitators and instigators among them. Only something significant could have put the whole neighborhood in a state of upheaval bad enough to call in extra support from the PDS.

"Something knocked out the main water pipeline yesterday afternoon," Samuel said. "It may have been collateral damage from the bridge collapse caused by the ulapod stampede when they broke free, but that hasn't yet been determined with certainty. Regardless, the damage is severe and repairs will be lengthy."

Aidan shook his head. With tanker operations hindered by the under-supply of power, Rockville was facing an immediate – and, from the residents' perspective, indefinite – shortage of clean water. Combine that with no power, and daily life suddenly looked a lot less tolerable. His friends in Evostown wouldn't take well to that kind of news, either.

"Our assignment has two goals," Samuel continued. "First, to defuse the volatile situation in Rockville as much as possible. Don't lie to them; don't make promises the government won't be able to deliver. We need to reassure these people that they're not forgotten, and they'll be taken care of as fast and as best as possible. Second, we'll gather as much information there as we can. With the cams offline, eyes on the ground is our best chance to keep this manageable."

The senior envoy paused and looked around the conference room. "If you feel you need to stay in your designated neighborhoods to maintain calm there, I don't want to sacrifice that. But if you can spare a few hours to assist in Rockville, I can use as many volunteers as I can get."

Within moments a half-dozen counselors were offering to help. Aidan had put up his hand, too. "I don't know anyone there personally, and they won't know me. But I am Terran, and it might help to have as many of us as we can working the crowds. I'm in."

...Torrini Atolls Airspar Track, Occanan

"Everyone ready?" Birk asked, hustling up to join the Fith teammates gathered around the holographic track map displaying the designated route and maneuvers in the compulsory phase. The four of them had flown it together twice already in practice, the second time ending less than twenty minutes ago, but his unnecessary question was practically part of their preflight routine.

"Good for me," Kaye said.

"Me too," Sayal agreed.

When Daemyn didn't say anything, the other three looked at him. "What?" They continued to stare at him, so he added, "I'm ready. When am I not?"

Kaye peered at him suspiciously. Sayal shrugged. Once again reviewing the map, Birk didn't seem to care. They waited for him to finish. When he slapped his palms on the edge of the display table Sayal said, "Any new suggestions for the heavies after the last run?"

This was their usual method for assessing the compulsory phase on difficult courses, especially when Fith had drawn a fairly early spot in the order like they had today. The scores posted from the initial competitors set the tone for the remaining teams. Fith's two lights were capable of earning the very best scores on the board regardless of weather conditions and course design, and all the pilots at the track knew it. The closer the heavies could get to that potential, while also ensuring the four airblades remained synchronized in their execution of the phase, the greater the demoralizing impact would be on the other teams. So the pilots always looked for any little detail where a small tweak in technique could improve the heavies' performance and raise the team's score.

"Not from me," Daemyn said. He pointed to two locations on the route. "We definitely know those spots will be particularly tricky for you, but that'll be true for everyone in a heavy."

"Yep," said Birk, and Sayal nodded too. The two of them started chattering away about their strategy for addressing those maneuvers.

Daemyn's eyes traced over the map. Held in the air at waist level, his hands made tiny adjustments back and forth, already anticipating the turns and curves, climbs and dives, laid out among the islands, gates, and tower-markers that made up the compulsory phase at Torrini Atolls. It wasn't the hardest they'd seen this season, but it was still a difficult run. He could already tell the points where the weaker pilots – on the other teams, not any of his teammates – would struggle to stay in sync. Most of the light blades would be able to manage pretty well, though.

While his eyes and hands started through the map again, his mind kept replaying the latest update from Elsa. His greatest fears had been realized. The fact someone had hacked into WI's network and stolen data was bad enough; that they'd copied the specs and testing results for Project Lariat was the worst-case scenario. The whole thing still didn't make sense, though. Stealing the core trade secrets for several of WI's products would be extremely valuable to their competitors – or extremely harmful to Daemyn, if that was the goal. Yet the hacker had taken only the data on Project Lariat, by far the hardest to reproduce even with all the technical specifications and undeniably farther from launching into mass production than some of the other products in development. And the hacker had left WI's data behind, rather than erasing or corrupting it. Corporate espionage had automatically been their first assumption, but Elsa had said that the further she dug into the hack, the less anything along those lines was adding up. After reading her report, Daemyn agreed with her. The only thing worse than knowing he'd been hacked was that he had absolutely no idea why.

"Daemyn?"

He blinked. Then he realized Kaye had said something to him. "Hmm?"

She was eyeing him dubiously again. "I said, it's almost time to get to the cockpits."

"Right," he said. "I know."

She held his gaze. "Something the matter? You seem distracted."

"Not at all," he lied. "Just focused on the course."

"Good," Kaye said, clearly not convinced.

"Good," he replied, and forcibly propelled thoughts of anything but Airspar from his mind. He had a match to win.

TWELVE

…Scarlet Envy

"Why not?" Celia Lancer asked.

Reiton Holtspring laughed. "We already have enough critics, inside and outside the government. People who think we're trying to buy influence with New Romas to rig the laws in our favor. Who think we put profits above people. The last thing we need is to give them the ammunition to argue that we're *literally* trying to purchase a controlling stake in the Future Cities."

"That's not what we'd be doing," Lancer said. "I'm saying it should be a loan at a favorable interest rate, not an acquisition of any kind of ownership interest."

"Technically, sure," Sage Gaiser said. "But it's the perception that matters. If we're funding infrastructure improvement projects instead of the Treasury, people are going to see it as the venturists trying to substitute ourselves for the government."

"Exactly," Holtspring said.

"A much more indirect program, then," Utara said. Throughout their discussion, she had kept revisiting in her mind the basic challenge Wynde had laid out to Mataki back on the plaza: to take the long-term view of the venturists, not the short-term thinking that dominated in New Romas and the bureaucracies, by a willingness to account for all the benefits and costs, not only the dracts. "Not one that helps the government financially. Something that helps the residents directly instead. It might save the government money overall, but your outlay isn't going to them."

Holtspring smiled. Gaiser and Lancer looked at each other, then nodded.

Seated next to Utara in the circle of chairs set out on the deck, Rustle Tames hadn't said much so far. Now he put his nearly empty glass on the low

115

table and leaned forward. "I think I have an alternative that builds on Counselor Fireheart's idea, although it's about another option than the residents."

He waited for everyone's attention. "We've funded several major wilderness-area conservation initiatives the last several years. Utara mentioned the nature preserves built into each of the cities. What if we offered to make a donation – or even a loan, I suppose – to cover the costs of operating them while the government conducts the necessary infrastructure repairs? The money is still fungible and we're still providing the backing to make the repairs possible, but the perception is different."

Lancer nodded. "We're helping the animals, not end-running the government."

"This intrigues me," Gaiser said. Holtspring added, "Me too."

Utara took her string of hope and pulled on it. "The daily operation of the preserves is handled by the same AIs that perform the resource management for the residents, and the zoologists are local employees, not part of an agency in New Romas like the PDS counselors. That puts the preserves under a city's budget, meaning those funds could be reallocated locally to other uses if the preserve costs were covered. It wouldn't have to go back through New Romas, where it would run the risk of getting diverted to something else."

"I'm willing to pursue this angle and see if it's feasible," Tames said. He looked around the circle of venturists, and everyone nodded.

With the next set of compulsory runs about to begin, most of the group rose from their chairs and went to stand along the deck's railings. Lancer remained seated. "Most people don't see venturists as a solution to hopeless situations."

"With the right resources," Utara said, "no situation is hopeless."

Lancer leaned forward, bracing her elbows on her knees. "And that's why you're here?"

Utara had thought the five of them had listened intently when she'd explained the crisis in the Future Cities and her lack of success at obtaining relief from public officials. Maybe Lancer had been distracted. "Yes. I believe this is the best chance to help the Future Cities that I've found so far."

"Hmm."

Waiting, Utara expected the other woman to say more. When she didn't, Utara asked, "Have I offended you?"

"What?" Lancer blinked. "No, nothing of the sort. In fact, it seems I've misjudged you, Utara."

"How's that?"

Lancer smiled. "Most of the people who are this interested in Daemyn and his money are really after... well, something else."

"I didn't realize," Utara said, and meant it.

"Why would you?" Lancer sat up straight again. "On the other hand, I think you've judged your best chance correctly. Though I suspect you still haven't quite figured out why we're showing such interest in helping the Future Cities."

"It's not that I think you have bad motives." She considered what to say, and decided to meet Lancer's candor with her own. "But... you're venturists."

"We are. And you don't think we'd do anything for free. Even if it's the right thing to do, there'd have to be something in it for us."

"In the long term, there would have to be some way for you to profit."

"You're not wrong," Lancer said, entirely in a friendly way, and shrugged. "But this opportunity is only one of several potential investments we're considering, to go alongside the portfolio of investments we already hold. If you could see all the pieces at once, as we do, putting the puzzle together would make more sense."

"I'm sure." Utara wondered what other plans for Loorriri – and for Prime – the venturists were scheming about. "Nonetheless, you said yourself that this would appear to most as a hopeless situation."

"The odds of turning a profit, even over the long run, have to be part of the calculus. Many variables are out of our control. Certainly it's worth investigating thoroughly, including the size of the potential upside payoffs if the investment succeeds, too. Still, no matter how the numbers fall, the Future Cities would be a pretty risky gamble."

"To me," Utara said, "betting on humanity sounds like the best odds."

Lancer smiled again. "Maybe so."

"Hey, come on," Gaiser called to them from the railing. "It's starting."

"After you," Lancer said, and let Utara lead the way.

...Blonkas

Aidan couldn't ignore the stark fact that six PDS counselors had been transported to Rockville in an armored truck along with six law enforcement agents with the same body armor and rifles as the pair who'd picked him up this morning. Aidan was confident the senior envoy had told the counselors everything he could about what they'd find in Rockville, but even Peitro Samuel didn't have the full story.

The street was empty. At least this part of Rockville was still obeying the curfew. As soon as the counselors were out of the truck, though, the agents closed the doors and the truck accelerated away. *That* certainly didn't make Aidan feel any better, either.

The six of them gathered around the transi map of Rockville in Tyku's hands. About a dozen locations were marked. Tyku pointed to each one and explained what little information they had about why it had been flagged for attention. Then he pointed to a spot that wasn't marked.

"On the way," Tyku said, "Samuel commed me about a new report of a mob moving toward the pumping station here. You can't see the water lines on this map, but the pumping station supplies significant sectors adjacent to Rockville. Any interference with the station potentially would be very serious."

"Has the mob been confirmed?" Aidan asked.

"No," Tyku replied.

"But it was serious enough for them to comm you with an update."

"Right."

Aidan nodded. "Then we can't risk it. I'll go check it out." He leaned around to get a better look at the map. "Show me one more time exactly where I'm going."

...Torrini Atolls Airspar Track

Rocketing away from the Fith team's landing platform, Daemyn said, "Activate HUD." Two columns of data blossomed on the left side of the interior surface of his cockpit canopy; a single column appeared on the right side. He took once quick glance. "Narrow comparator listings to current opponent and Match Four winner only."

By the time he glanced back a few seconds later, the right-side display was no longer a full column of data, but rather three simple lines: Fith, CasTel, and Yoshigura. The only scores that mattered.

He tapped the comm button on the yoke. "Let's win this."

His three teammates acknowledged affirmatively. Farrier added, *"It looks like they're coming out in their usual formation..."* From the control booth, the coach paused while he watched the CasTel airblades zip away from their landing platform, too. *"Confirmed, they're starting in Romas-Two. That's the opening we wanted. Let's make the most of it."*

CasTel would expect Saxon-Four, the standard counter to Romas-Two. In an ordinary match, that would have been Fith's choice, as well. But today, too much was at stake. When Farrier had proposed countering with Whiskey-Nine instead, Daemyn and his teammates had immediately agreed. The spread-wide formation would leave them temporarily out of position defensively, almost certainly giving CasTel a quick score – but by going boldly on the offensive in the opening seconds of the phase, Fith would out-tally them significantly. If it took CasTel too long to realize their play, the early scoring might be enough for Fith to hold the lead through the entire phase.

"Copy that," Daemyn said, and tapped the line closed.

He swung his blade around, aiming the nose toward the north end of the track. One more time he ran through their final-phase strategy. With the cushion they'd acquired from CasTel's subpar flying in the compulsory phase and holding them even in utilities acquisition in the second phase, Fith could afford to take another big chance or two later, too. He just had to decide when and where.

Beep.

The blade rushed onward, the countdown sounding in his headset.

Beep.

Daemyn flexed his fingers on the yoke. He took a slow, measured breath.

Beep.

His eyes focused on the track ahead. The HUD became a fuzzy blur in his peripheral vision. A green blob to the left, and as long as it stayed that way he probably wouldn't look again. A thin squiggle to the right, where the scoring comparisons were about to start updating live.

Boooop.

The engines surged and Daemyn knew nothing but the airblade and its path through the sky. He swerved around a tower, climbing toward the clouds. Rather than Saxon-Four's move to intercept CasTel's lead light, he dove into the next turn. He flew low, hardly more than a few meters above the waves, leaving his teammates – and his opponents – to his south.

He checked the icons on the HUD. CasTel was still flying Romas-Two. They hadn't figured it out yet.

And now it was too late.

Daemyn wrenched the yoke toward him as hard as he could, pulling the blade into the steepest climb it could manage. He muscled the turn to starboard equally sharply, whipping the blade within two meters of an obelisk. He leveled out of the turn and cut back to port – with a clear, undefended path to Fith's goal for at least three seconds.

He mashed the trigger and held it, dumping utility after utility in a straight line toward the goal. At two-point-eight seconds he released the trigger and yanked the yoke into a vicious loop and barrel-roll that brought him clear before CasTel's heavy got there.

Banking around an island, he spared at glance at the right-side HUD.

Kaye, too, had scored more than he'd hoped.

"Yeah!" he shouted to no one but himself, and steered the blade back toward Fith's goal to regroup for their next onslaught.

...Blonkas

Several hundred people crowded the hillside. More than Aidan had expected. Mostly adults and some teenagers, mainly but not entirely Terrans, the swarm of men and women surged down the gradual slope toward the pumping station. They hollered and jostled, not a calm voice among them. He heard a few cheers from the front, but the shouts and cries dominated the air. They were angrier than he had expected, too.

Aidan used his size advantage to force his way through the crowd from the side. He needed to get to the front. It was his only chance. Amid the close quarters and the yelling, no one noticed his government-issue uniform or the PDS emblems on the sleeves of his shirt.

He glanced among the people as he pressed ahead. They carried the tools and makeshift supplies they intended to use to break into the facility and retrieve water. Hundreds of the same transpariplast canisters they used in Evostown. Axes and hammers, several ladders, and even a few blowtorches.

Another cheer rose, louder this time. Aidan pushed forward. Then he saw it.

From somewhere they had acquired a huge metal beam, perhaps seven or eight meters long, and they had lined it up to use as a battering ram to take down a section of the five-meter metal fence. A plan that ordinarily wouldn't have been workable when the fence was surging with electrical current to keep interlopers away – but the power was out, and the mob knew it.

Aidan shoved between two men and stepped into the gap in the crowd that had formed to make room for the group hefting the beam to maneuver. He strode closer to the beam. Raising his arms in the air, he shouted for the mob's attention. "I know you're angry and scared," he called out. "I am too. But this isn't the answer."

The response came in all manner of insults and curses. Aidan didn't have much time.

"Listen to me," he insisted as loud as he could, praying enough of the people could hear. "If you get in there, and you open the pipe – and I can see you're ready to do that – what are you going to do when you're done? How are you going to close off the pipe again?"

The anxious ripple in the crowd confirmed they hadn't thought through their plan that far ahead. Aidan stepped closer to the men carrying the beam. "If you don't, if it ends up leaking, that will only make the water shortages worse. For you, and for everyone else in Blonkas."

For a moment longer the mob rumbled. Then a man screamed, "It doesn't matter! Don't listen to him! We need water *now*!" Another man yelled, "He's right!" A woman added, "That's someone else's problem! My family needs water!"

One of the men carrying the beam, a Terran even taller and broader than Aidan, let go of the metal and spun toward him. Without a word, the man swung a punch. Aidan managed to duck at the last second, but that only gave his adversary time to knock him to the ground with a swift kick. The mob cheered.

From his seat in the dirt Aidan watched the beam smash into the fence.

...Scarlet Envy

"Utara?" Gently a hand touched her shoulder. "Is everything all right?"

She turned and gave Rustle Tames the best smile she could muster. She tapped her comdee to standby mode and lowered her hand. "It's probably nothing."

"There's no doubt they'll be thrilled by your news. It hasn't been that long. I'm sure they'll comm you back when they can."

"That's just it." Utara shook her head. "I haven't been able to even leave a message, much less talk to someone. It's like the signal isn't getting through. Not to anyone."

He frowned. "Maybe it's a problem with the PDS comm network?"

"I was able to reach the field office in Durnow. They didn't know anything." Utara took a breath to steady herself. "I tried through the residential network, but that didn't work, either."

"Well, there has to be some explanation. A whole city can't just go offline."

"Comdee connections to Loorriri are never the best anyway," Utara said. "If you can hold a vidcam conference, this ship must have powerful transmitters installed. Do you think I might be able to give those a try?"

"I can't imagine that would be a problem." Tames waved a hand to get the other venturists' attention. When Sage Gaiser looked over at him, he made a gesture Utara didn't understand. "I'll go up to the comm suite and see if I can get a signal through to Blonkas," he told her. "I'm sure it's only a technical malfunction of some sort. In the meantime, you should watch some more of the match."

"I'd prefer to join you, if that's all right."

"Of course." He put a hand on her arm. "We'll try for PDS first, but any connection will do."

"Thank you."

~⟲

...Torrini Atolls Airspar Track

"Birk, get over there," Daemyn barked.

"On it."

Daemyn dropped his airblade into a long, looping swerve around one of the small islands. Checking the heads-up, he confirmed his teammate's heavy racing to cut off the CasTel team's light before it got close enough to take a shot at Fith's goal.

Flying this much on the defensive wasn't going to be good enough, though. Simply defeating CasTel wouldn't accomplish their goal. To move up to eighth – to qualify for the championships – Fith needed to win by a much bigger margin than their current lead.

"Kaye, cover me," he said. "Let's make a run."

"Copy."

Daemyn came around the island and climbed to port. One of CasTel's heavies turned off its trajectory and rushed right for him.

He continued the ascent for a few seconds, then whipped the blade into a swift rolling turn that brought him around to head starboard toward the CasTel goal. The considerably less maneuverable heavy blade tried to keep up, but lost precious seconds of pursuit in the process. The other CasTel heavy, though, had zoomed around and lined up right in front of the goal, ready to cut him off.

From behind Kaye fired a flare, trying to distract the heavy on Daemyn's tail. The CasTel pilot dipped and readjusted, evading it easily. She fired another toward the heavy ahead, but its pilot dodged with hardly an effort, too.

"Loop back," she said. *"We've got time."*

One light against two heavies was about the worst mismatch a pilot could face in Airspar. The strategy book counseled Kaye's advice: loop back and try again. Improve the odds.

He glanced to the timer on the heads-up. Time wasn't running out, but it wasn't exactly on their side, either. He dove, swinging his blade around an island.

"I can do this," Daemyn insisted.

Speeding toward his target, Daemyn readied a pair of twisters. The chasing CasTel heavy swung wide and looped around a spire, lining up a shot. From above near the goal, the other heavy descended in a gradual dive, ready to fire if its teammate missed.

Daemyn arced his blade upward and aimed for the goal. From below starboard, the CasTel heavy blade loosed a boomer. So did the second heavy overhead.

Daemyn squeezed the trigger, firing the two twisters at the CasTel goal. He didn't bother to watch their path – he knew the shot was true. He banked away to port to dodge the descending boomer. It sailed past harmlessly.

Too late he realized he'd misjudged the shot from below. It hadn't been fired at him; it had been fired to where the other boomer has forced him to dodge. He slammed the yoke, pushing his blade into a dive.

The boomer didn't go off as close as it should have, but still Daemyn's airblade bucked viciously. For a moment he thought he would maintain control, but then his blade flipped upside down and began to plunge uncontrollably toward the waters of the bay. He seized the yoke, trying to overpower its frenetic jiggling.

"Come on," Daemyn growled into his cockpit.

Still the blade fell, its wings making a leisurely rotation. He yanked the yoke again while waters below rushed toward him.

At the last second the wings jerked, the engines kicked, and the plummeting airblade righted itself into a swooping arc that cleared the tops of the waves with barely a meter to spare.

Daemyn hissed a sigh of relief. The feeling didn't last.

An alarm blared on his console. In his headset Kaye said, *"It's your port wing. Bad. Not sure how much longer you'll be flyable."*

The readout on the heads-up confirmed her report. Even if he'd wanted to risk keeping the blade aloft, with this much damage the rules dictated an immediate return to the team's platform or the entire match would be forfeited.

Daemyn kept the blade low to the water, making sure he had control. He didn't bother to check the tally on the HUD. The points he'd scored no longer mattered – he wouldn't be scoring any more. With Fith reduced to one light blade for the remaining minutes of the third phase, CasTel would no doubt be able to score enough points to win the match outright. Fith's loss would guarantee they didn't qualify for the championships.

Just like that, his Airspar season was over.

~⌒

...Blonkas

Aidan stood on the hillside, watching the madness at the pumping station. A section of the fence was down, and the mob had opened several holes in one of the primary pipes leaving the station building. After some initial desperate jostling, the crowd had figured out a pattern for moving empty canisters closer to the pipe and cycling the full ones away. The alarms were blaring and the emergency lights were flashing, but the people simply ignored them. Every few minutes a loud, mechanical voice would bellow "You must leave the facility at once!" but the mob ignored that, too.

With the roar of the crowd he barely heard his comdee chiming. "Stone."

"Aidan," came a panicked voice. It sounded like Samuel, but he wasn't sure. *"You have to stop them. You have to get them out of the pumping station."*

"I can't," he said. "I did my best. But it's too late now."

"No, you don't understand. It's not just the pum—"

Aidan checked the comdee, but the transmission was still connected. "Are you there?"

The comdee fritzed with static. Then the voice returned. *"—en to me. Get them out of there before it's too late. I don't know how much longer we can keep —"*

The transmission cut off. Aidan tried to piece together what Samuel had been trying to tell him. He knew the main point, though: get the mob out of the pumping station. And that was the one thing he had no chance of achieving.

Again the mechanical voice bellowed the warning to leave the facility. The crowd of people didn't even seem to register it.

A few seconds later, Aidan heard the shriek of the engines in the sky. He looked up. Two security drones. One coming from the east, the other from the west.

He dove, pressing himself flat against the hillside, arms shielding his head. The clattering of the guns overcame the whine of the engines. The ground beneath him reverberated with dozens upon dozens of bullet impacts. A few people cried out in fear or agony, but most of them did not have time to scream.

The gunfire ceased abruptly. While the noise of the engines faded, Aidan raised his head. The drones soared overhead, curving into a mirrored pair of sharp loops to bring them around for a second pass.

Not that it mattered anymore. The ground at the pumping station was already covered with bodies and blood.

FREEFALL

"Available: Technical Specifications — Wynde Industries. Extremely Valuable. Serious Offers Only."

ShadowNet Upload 3411-8904-7762

THIRTEEN

...Fith Hangar, Torrini Atolls Airspar Track

"Amazing how fast they can pack it all up," Birk said.

The four airblades were no longer visible, each carefully sealed within a Fith Manufacturing shipping container. Two more, equally large containers held all of the team's equipment, tools, and gear. This time, though, their destination wasn't the next track on the Airspar schedule. Everything was headed back to Hyj-gon for repairs, adjustments, and upgrades during the few months before the first practices for next season would begin.

Sayal shook her head. "Those mechanics better not mess up too much with their tinkering. My blade is fine the way it is."

"Not a chance," Kaye said. "Making *improvements* is what they do."

"As long as the design engineers keep them in line, I guess," Sayal conceded.

"Good luck with that," Birk said. "Anyway, I'd better head out. My wife told me after the race that she has a big surprise for me at home. Something I'll like, but she won't say what. It's driving me *crazy*."

"Is she pregnant?" Kaye asked.

When Birk's eyes flew wide, Sayal patted him on the arm. "Probably just another kryli puppy."

Birk scowled. "That's not helping."

Daemyn extended a hand and the two men locked forearms. The only thing he could think of to say was, "Sorry."

"I mean, sure, it would've been nice," Birk said. "But it's been a long shot for months. I never thought we'd get so close."

To Daemyn, Sayal said, "Don't get hurt next season, and we'll be in the championships for sure, all right?"

"Right," Daemyn said.

Birk nodded, and offered a wave to the three of them. "See you soon."

"I told my parents I'd swing by on the way home," Sayal said after he'd gone. "Where are you headed?"

"My brother's taking me to see the Cathedral on the Mount," Kaye said. "I've always wanted to go."

Sayal looked at Daemyn. "And you?"

"You have to ask?"

Kaye harrumphed. "Promise me you'll stick your head outside Wynde Industries for at least a week."

"A whole week?" When she moved to slug him in the arm, Daemyn held up his hands. "You win. At least a week."

"Good."

They said their farewells, and the two women hurried away toward their respective personal shuttlecraft. That left Daemyn alone in the hangar.

Or not. Only after they'd taken off did he notice Farrier standing a few meters away, waiting patiently. Whatever else he thought of him, Daemyn had to give the coach credit for having the good judgment of not intruding into the teammates' parting. He took a breath and strode over to join the other man.

At first, Farrier simply kept looking at him.

"I thought I could pull it off," Daemyn said finally.

"Oh, you *could* have. Maybe. If everything broke your way. But you *didn't*."

"It was our best chance."

"No, actually. It wasn't."

Daemyn wanted to argue the point. Inhaling, he readied himself to start his rationalizations. But that was all they were. So he said, "Maybe you're right."

"Hmph." Farrier crossed his arms. "Think about that in the offseason."

"I will."

"Think about this, too." Farrier canted his head in the direction of Daemyn's departed teammates. "They'll be calling for a change. The fans. The reporters and commentators. Maybe even Fith, though on their own they have enough confidence in me to let me run this team my way. Unless they cave to the outside pressure. Which is possible."

"And?"

"And... Fith won't fire me, nor will they fire you. So which of the others do you want me to replace?"

"None. You know that."

"I do. But what if I don't have a choice?"

Daemyn sighed. "I don't know."

"Welcome to my world."

He met the coach's eyes. "I'm sorry."

Something in Farrier's stern expression softened, if only slightly. "So am I."

"I'll do better next season," Daemyn said, and meant it.

Farrier accepted the pledge with a nod. Then he said something Daemyn would never have expected. "Do you still want to be one of the greatest of all time? Is achieving that legacy still something that drives you?"

Daemyn had made that comment years ago, back in his first season under Farrier. Apparently the coach had remembered all this time. So Daemyn told him the truth. "Yes. It is."

"Your flying has never been better, Daemyn. And you might be able to improve your skills on the margins, here and there." Farrier held his gaze firmly. "If you really want to attain your goals, it's your judgment you need to work on. You take your talents and add wisdom – you'll be unbeatable."

Daemyn took a second to formulate his response. What he decided was to show Farrier the same respect he had just received. He extended his hand and said, "Thank you, Coach. For everything."

Farrier's face remained impassive, but he locked forearms with Daemyn. "Don't spend all your time off thinking about Airspar," the coach whispered. "Get away. Refresh and recharge. Come back ready to win the championship next season – with your head fully in the game."

"I will," Daemyn promised.

The men stepped back from one another. Farrier gave Daemyn one more tip of the head, then headed off across the hangar toward the exit on the far wall. Daemyn took a deep breath, turned, and started walking toward *WyndeStalker.*

Halfway there, Reiton Holtspring caught up to him. "How'd that go?"

"It was… different." Daemyn looked out the open mouth of hangar toward the shimmering blue waves of the ocean. "I have a lot to think about."

∽〇

…*Prime Diplomatic Service Loorriri Bureau Headquarters, Durnow*

"I still can't get through."

Utara squashed the momentary urge to fling the comdee across the room. She took a deep breath and set the useless device down on the table. Doing her best to put on a smile, she turned to face her father's desk.

For the moment he kept his back to her. One hand worked at the screen of his compupod, slowly and deliberately. A single finger hovering in the air then darting downward like a crane plunging for food in a stream, unsuccessfully, before returning to its poised position, ready to strike again. The other hand held his comdee to his ear; given the lack of words from him over the past two minutes, he apparently still anticipated a response from the person on the other end of the comm.

She waited. Finally he said, "I see. Well, I appreciate you checking on my behalf in any event. Many blessings."

He set down the comdee, tapped the pod screen one more time, and then spun in his chair to face outward across the desk in her direction.

"Well?" Utara said.

Koster raised a brow. "Comdee lines into Blonkas are down across the board, and most external communications have been severed, as well. Fortunately we still have a few backchannel ways of contacting the leadership at the EOC."

"The AI did this?"

"Initially, yes."

"Why?"

132

"That's a very good question." He used a kerchief to wipe the sweat from his brow. "We're still piecing together the bits of information we have, but it appears as though a mob formed in one of the neighborhoods to undertake a raid on a water pumping station. Part of the AI's function is to maintain the security of the public utilities, so it quickly assessed this mob as a threat. When it determined the people were using their comdees to organize and carry out the raid, it shut off the network."

A harsh response, but Utara could imagine many of the human public safety officials she knew making a similar decision under the circumstances. "Can't the EOC override it? Why are comms still out?"

"At this time, the government believes it is best to allow the communications embargo to remain in place."

Which government, Utara wondered, but he always chose his words carefully. Whatever was going on, he wasn't at liberty to say more, even to his daughter. "They'll have a shuttle going in soon. Standard protocol to reinforce emergency operations personnel in a crisis. PDS flight or otherwise, I need to make sure they let me aboard."

Her father gave her a regretful smile. "There's not going to be any shuttle for you to hop. Not today. Not any time soon."

"Ground transport, then? It'll take longer, but –"

"It's not just a comms embargo, Utara."

"I don't understand."

"Blonkas is locked down. No inbound travel is functional, civilian or government."

The Unified Forces would be necessary to execute that kind of order. Only once in their history had a Future City ever been locked down. That had been more than a decade ago when fears, ultimately proven unfounded, of a rapidly spreading outbreak of the highly contagious Torkuna virus had rippled within Luppitan. But the situation in Blonkas was no natural disaster or biological epidemic.

"It's for the best, for your sake," Koster said.

Of its own volition, the question formed on the tip of Utara's tongue. Though she had learned much already in her time in the PDS, she certainly did not yet possess his level of expertise in the intricacies of the inner workings of the thought processes of officials in Future Cities leadership, much less Primean politics writ large. Still, she knew she was right about this situation – there was only one reason for these actions.

So she asked him. "What are they hiding?"

"Information is sparse on that score, too. Blonkas EOC has been, I believe, deliberately cryptic."

"You're confident in the information that the AI assessed the mob as a security threat to the water supply?"

"I expect that will prove out to be accurate."

"And the threat arose quickly enough that the AI executed a sudden shutdown of the comdee network as a countermeasure."

"Yes. Even though, as options go, that would seem to be a fairly ineffective one. Presumably it ruled out better options as too slow."

Utara clenched her fists to stop her hands from shaking. "The only rapid-response security measure available in Blonkas is the drones."

Her father sighed, then said, "Unfortunately, I suspect that's exactly what happened. The AI would prioritize the welfare of the city and the security of the water supply over the well-being, even the lives, of a small number of violent individuals."

Utara released her fingers and asked the next, obvious question. "What about a larger number of people?"

"Let's pray," Koster said, "that we don't find out."

Utara nodded, but she knew the people of Evostown too well. With or without working comdees, they would learn the truth of what was happening in their city soon enough. And it wouldn't matter that the mob had created the volatile confrontation in the first place – the people of Blonkas would never accept their fellow city residents being slaughtered by the AI and its drones. The city leadership and the PDS needed to stabilize the situation in the city immediately.

"What about Durnow?" she asked. "We have the same AI as Blonkas."

"The same technology, yes," Koster said. "But every city is unique, and different computers manage each city separately."

"The AIs talk to each other on a network, though," Utara pointed out.

"They do."

She stopped her fingers from tapping on her knees. "So the Durnow AI probably knows more about what's going on in Blonkas than any person here does."

"That's likely, yes."

Utara looked her father in the eyes. "What does that mean?"

He held her gaze and said, "I don't know."

...Blonkas

It had been shortly before dawn when the armored transport had dropped off Aidan at the edge of Evostown and left him there without so much as a word from the law enforcement agents. Not that his PDS superiors had been any more talkative. No apology for the massacre at the pumping station. No word of thanks for his attempt to calm the mob, fruitless as it had been, or his efforts to tend to the wounded, which at least had been somewhat more successful in saving a number of lives. No debriefing at the healing center, no offer of transport to the EOC for further updates. Simply a ride home and a command to shelter in place and wait for further instructions.

With the power shut down, only the faintest glow of the moon had managed to make it through the thick clouds. Aidan had walked his way back to his apartment as much by memory as anything else. Though the bed awaited him in the other room, sleep was out of the question. Too many thoughts rattled around in his brain. How could he hope to articulate the extent of the danger to his friends in Evostown? What could he possibly say? He wished Utara were here. Then he would have someone to help him figure it out.

He couldn't have been home more than five minutes when the loud, insistent knocking at his front door began. Apparently he hadn't been the only one with a sleepless night, and his return had been noticed despite the darkness overpowering the streets. Aidan bounded to the door in a series of long strides.

"That's enough!" he barked through the door while he unlatched the locks.

The knocking stopped. He opened the door and found exactly who he'd expected. This time, Hasto and Roturo didn't ask for permission to enter.

He shut the door and latched one of the locks, then turned to face them. "Well?"

"Is it true?" Roturo demanded.

Aidan took a long, slow breath. He could only imagine the number of rumors that must be swirling in Evostown at this point, with the visionpods inoperable and the comdee network deactivated. "Which *it?*"

"Rockville."

"You'll have to be more specific."

Hasto took a step forward. "You were there when it happened, weren't you?"

Aidan held up his hands. The last thing he needed was the young men thinking he was deliberately evading their questions. "I was in Rockville, yes, as part of the team they sent to try to calm things down. But again, specific. What have you heard?"

For just a moment, the raging intensity dropped away from Roturo's face. "That a lot of people died."

Before Aidan could respond, Hasto said, "Did you see it?"

"I was there."

"Knarf it all to the Hells," Roturo said, almost under his breath.

"What are people saying?" Aidan asked.

"Around here, anyway," Hasto said, "the only thing most people have heard is that something happened in Rockville and a lot of people died."

"Died from getting shot," Roturo added.

"Right." Hasto started pacing around the small room. "A few of the really crazy folks are saying that soldiers shot them, but nobody really believes that. It's just... not possible. Soldiers wouldn't massacre other people like that. They just wouldn't. So, really... The only thing that makes any sense is the drones."

"Yes," Aidan said. He made a split-second decision to tell the truth and explain, rather than try to change the subject. "It was the drones. But —"

"Why?" Roturo's question came out practically as a wail. "Why would they do that?"

"There was a mob," Aidan replied, keeping his voice as collected as he could manage. "They smashed their way into one of the pumping stations."

"You heard that?" Hasto asked.

"No, I saw it."

Hasto nodded, and looked to Roturo. The other man nodded, too.

It was a small victory that they believed him, but it was something. "The alarms went off, and the warnings told them to leave. But they didn't."

"But killing them?" Hasto was pacing again. "For trying to get water?"

"I —"

"It's insane," Roturo said. "I mean, I understand about the water. Everyone has to get their fair chance, and it's not right for some people to try to steal more than what others get. But arrest them or put them in jail or something. It *killed* them."

"Murdered them," Hasto growled.

Aidan said the only thing he could. "I know."

"What are you going to do about it?" Roturo demanded.

"I don't think there's anything I can do."

"Not you personally," Hasto said. "You, the government."

Aidan blinked. It had been months since the residents of Evostown had thought of him that way, instead of as an individual trying to make a difference in their neighborhood. "I don't know. The people who oversee the —"

"Tell them to turn it off," Hasto spat.

"It's not like that. There's not just a switch. And besides, the —"

"Then at least tell that knarfing computer that it's not allowed to shoot people anymore," Roturo said.

"I'm sure they're trying. But —"

"No," Roturo said. "This is a city for people. The computer is supposed to make our lives better. That's how it works. They just need to tell it what to do."

Aidan paused to take a breath. "They will."

"Yeah," Hasto said. "And if it doesn't listen?"

"If it murders people for taking water," Roturo said, giving a grim chuckle, "maybe it'll just shoot the people trying to tell it what to do."

Aidan wondered that, too. If the AI really went rogue, what could anyone in Blonkas possibly do to stop it? "Until the managers get everything under control," he said, "the best way we can help Evostown is to do everything in our power to guarantee that nobody here gives the drones any reason to want to open fire on our streets. Right?"

The two young men looked at each other. They didn't say anything.

"I know it shouldn't be this way," Aidan told them. "But we have to manage the situation as best we can until the people who are able to fix this can do it."

"But if they don't fix it," Hasto insisted, "we can't just sit here and do nothing while everyone suffers."

Roturo clenched his fists. "We'll find a way to shoot them out of the sky if we have to. Drones don't get to kill anyone in Evostown."

"It won't come to that, because they'll fix it," Aidan said. "In the meantime, it's very important that you help me make sure Mazee and the others understand the plan."

Hasto and Roturo nodded, but there was no confidence in their faces. The three of them headed for the door. Deep down, though, Aidan knew the solution wasn't that simple. Not even close.

FOURTEEN

...Blonkas

The tallest building in Evostown rose a mere six stories high, but its position in the north-central section of the neighborhood provided a surprisingly good view of much of the rest of Blonkas. Yesterday Roturo had been the one to suggest setting up an observation perch on the roof. With no power for the veepees and the comdee network still offline, the only news – or rumors – that reached anyone in the city were those that travelled by foot. Now, at least, they could keep something of an eye on things.

Not that much of what they'd seen was particularly reassuring. Late last evening, shortly before dusk, a major fire had broken out somewhere in the far northeasterly area of Blonkas. They hadn't actually seen the flames from their rooftop post, but the towering plume of smoke was unmistakable rising into the sky. From lower down, though, like the third- and fourth-story residential windows, the smoke couldn't be seen. The winds sheering the plume out over the city walls had ensured it couldn't be smelled, either. Hasto had proposed they not tell anyone about the fire for now to avoid panicking their families and friends in Evostown, and Roturo had not hesitated to agree. The young men were coming to understand the burdens of leadership, and the tough decisions that sometimes came with it. Aidan had told them so, and that he was proud of them for their exercise of judgment, but the pair had accepted the compliment with only quiet, grim nods.

This morning the vista of the city was little better. The rising smoke in the northeast was gone, but the fire had been much too far away for them to see the extent of the damage. A thick haze hung over the distant rooftops, the heat and humidity no longer dissipated by the air-circulation fans in the city center.

Hasto pointed in that direction. "Is it supposed to be wobbling like that?"

The other two men looked over to follow the line of his extended finger. "I don't see it," Roturo said. "Which one?"

Aidan peered toward the soaring skyscrapers in the middle of downtown. "Start at the one with the pyramid top in the middle. Then go... four to the right from there."

Hasto mirrored the counting with the tip of his finger. "That's right."

"I found it," Roturo said.

The three of them appraised the building for nearly a minute. Finally Hasto said, "So? Is it just me or is that one wobbling?"

"Not a lot," Roturo said. He held up his palm flat in the air, perpendicular to his body, and angled his fingertips back and forth slightly. "But I think I see it, too."

"So do I," Aidan agreed.

"Is it supposed to do that?" Hasto asked him.

Aidan was no engineer. It was possible the absence of the circulation fans had altered the air patterns among the skyscrapers in a substantial way. He owed them better than a guess, though. "I've never seen it do that before."

"That's... not good," Roturo said.

Abruptly their attention was captured by a thundering bellow recognizable by anyone who'd ever visited the city's animal preserve. Except that the bellow was close. Far too close. The three of them ran to the southern end of the rooftop.

"Out of the street!" Aidan shouted.

"Move! Move!" Roturo yelled. Hasto gestured wildly and called down, "Run! Get out of the way! Run, now!"

Already startled by the enormous beast's trumpeting, the handful of pedestrians down on the street glanced upward in fright. Then the ground shook beneath their feet – so much that Aidan could see the effect of it from the roof. Without a second thought the people began to run for the doorways of the closest residences.

A few seconds later the hephagaunt barreled into view. A stampede of one, it charged down the street at a full run. Each stomp of its massive feet crunched a hole into the pavement. The animal raised its head and, still surging past them at top speed, bellowed again. The sound echoed off the walls, doubling the volume of the noise.

Then, as quickly as it had come into view, the hephagaunt was gone. They heard a few more stomps of its feet, and another bellow, before the concrete and brick of the neighborhood swallowed up the sounds.

Only to be replaced by another. Roturo asked it first. "What's that?"

The men rushed back to the northern edge of the rooftop. Hasto pointed. "There!"

The sight was unmistakable. Two or three neighborhoods to the north, security drones spiraled over the rooftops. From further away it might have resembled a band of four vultures circling over carrion, but they were close enough to see the reality clearly.

"What's going on?" Hasto asked.

Aidan shook his head. "I can't see anything. Only the drones."

For at least a minute they watched the drones continue their concentric flight pattern. Then, with the kind of precision only possible from computer control, the formation split into two flights. They arced outward in opposite directions, east and west, before simultaneously executing perfect switchbacks. The two pairs of drones raced toward one another, but not at their fastest speed. At their cruising speed.

As one, the drones opened fire at the same instant. Hasto gasped. Roturo clenched his hands on the ledge. Aidan stood still, watching. They couldn't see the targets, or the reason for the drones to gather and shoot.

But this was no pumping station riot like the one Aidan had witnessed three days earlier. This time it was a residential neighborhood. From the flight pattern, Aidan was pretty sure the drones weren't just firing at the streets, but into the buildings, too.

"Whatever we have to do," he said quietly. "We keep everything peaceful in Evostown. No matter how we have to keep people in line."

The two young men never took their eyes off the incessantly firing drones in the distance. But each of them made sure to nod.

...Emergency Operations Center, Durnow

"In my experience," Captain Valance had said to Utara a little over a year ago while managing his way through a sudden engine failure on the *Aladare's Pyre* during what should have been routine training maneuvers by the Aladarian Guard, "it's invariably true that the number and severity of the breaches of the bureaucrat's high-minded regulations is directly proportional to the extent of the emergency faced by the real people who actually have to solve Prime's problems."

The old man was avuncular and wise, and in her time serving under his command she'd learned he was almost always right. Which meant, right now, that the situation in the Durnow EOC was pretty bad. Terrible, actually.

For one thing, the doors to the secure command center were supposed to be kept shut at all times and only opened for individuals with appropriate credentials. Currently they were propped open by a pair of heavy desk chairs, and all sorts of people who shouldn't have had access were coming and going without so much as a raised eyebrow from the security guards. For her part Utara was wearing her official PDS badge, but it only rated her with clearance to government facilities in Blonkas, not any of the other Future Cities. Really, a position on the bureaucratic hierarchy as low as a junior counselor in the PDS had no business even being in this room during a major outbreak of citywide disorder. She kept expecting someone to insist on her making an unceremonious exit, but nobody seemed to notice she was even present, much less care enough to expel her. If Durnow's EOC managers weren't going to object that Utara shouldn't be here, then she certainly wasn't about to let them know.

The real heart of the problem, though, was the fact that the city's leaders weren't actually in charge. In a crisis of this magnitude, the mayor personally ought to be in command. If he couldn't be present, at a minimum one of the several deputy mayors could run the EOC in his place. Instead, though, those men and women stood to the side, talking idly among themselves – while her father stood perched at the podium console at the front of the sloping amphitheater. Admittedly Koster Fireheart was the most senior PDS official stationed on the entire continent, and he had been working in Durnow longer than any of the politicians had been part of the city's executive team. Nonetheless, the role of the PDS in the Future Cities was to help the residents, not lead the government. No matter how much they rightfully respected his decades-long commitment to Durnow, ceding authority to her father without any legal basis indicated the depth of the panic gripping the city's administrators.

While keeping an ear open to learn as much as she could from listening to the ongoing status reports, Utara tried to figure out how to get one of the operators away from a console long enough for her to repurpose it to send a set of messages she was already drafting in her head. So far, no one had become distracted enough for her to sneak past them to carry out her plan.

Utara stepped behind the chairs of two women intently focused on the workstations in front of them and scooted further toward the communications stations. She slid into the narrow aisle between the rows of consoles and hustled several rows toward the rear of the room, staying out of everyone's way as best she could. Once she got within earshot of the comms technicians she angled herself halfway into the closest row and stood off the shoulder of another tech. She gazed upward, pretending to scrutinize the data scrolling on the closest overhead display screen but really listening to the comms techs.

She caught names here and there, occasionally a word or two. But mostly it was an inaudible morass of shouting and gesturing. Right after she had decided to wait another minute before giving up, a shrill whistle split the din. Abruptly the room grew far quieter.

Her father lowered his fingers from his lips. From the podium console, he shouted up in Utara's general direction. "Comms! Status reports. Blonkas still out?"

"Affirmative," one of the techs shouted back.

"Luppitan?"

"Level Orange," another tech replied. The same threat level as Durnow was currently showing on the central screen behind Koster. "Word is out on the street that Blonkas is off the grid. Rumors are rampant. So far only isolated incidents of violence."

Koster nodded. "Any reactive measures noted from their AI?"

"Double the usual number of drones in the sky, but nothing else beyond that so far."

"Keep checking through all available channels," her father said. "Tagron up."

"Red across the board," replied a third tech.

Utara forced herself not to grab hold of the back of the chair in front of her. Blonkas' decline had been troublesome enough when she'd left. If other Future Cities were spiraling out of control, too, how much worse must it be in Blonkas, where events had started earlier? Aidan could handle himself no matter the circumstances, but no doubt he was missing a second PDS counselor to help with the residents of Evostown. After she got her messages sent, she would have to try to find another way to get back there. She took a deep breath to fight down her racing pulse and listened closely through the ambient murmur in the room, which was growing steadily louder again.

"Two neighborhoods essentially in a state of insurrection," the young woman continued. "Three pumping stations were attacked simultaneously. When drones flew overhead, improvised weapons were used to shoot down one of them."

A gasp echoed through the room. Koster remained impassive. "How did the AI respond?"

The comms tech hesitated, then said, "Unknown, sir."

"Because their AI dropped an embargo over them too?"

"No, sir. The feed was terminated. I'm trying to reconnect with their EOC currently."

"That's not good," Koster said. "We need to figure out what −"

The piercing wail of the alarm on the wall caused almost everyone in the room to flinch involuntarily. The accompanying red warning lights began to strobe, too. Koster yelled something to a manager three podiums away. A few seconds later the alarm cut off in mid-shriek. The strobing lights kept flashing.

"Status," Koster shouted to no one in particular. "What happened?"

"Comms are down," the first tech said.

"Which ones?"

"Ours," the tech said, standing up. He leaned side to side, checking the display screens of the adjacent workstations. "Everything. External communications embargoed, internal comdee networks deactivated."

Her father checked his podium. "We didn't give that order."

"Sir," bellowed another man from the left edge of the front row. "That's affirmative. It didn't originate in the EOC."

144

Koster turned to him. "The AI?"

"Pending a confirmation check..." The man held up a hand, one finger raised. "Got it. Confirmed, sir. Comms cutoff by the AI's own initiative."

For the first time in years, Utara heard her father curse.

She didn't disagree. Already she was moving toward the open doors at the back of the room. Whatever the rest of the status reports might be, they would be obsolete within minutes now that the comdee network was down. Worse, there wasn't anything else she could learn here – and with her plan blasted to pieces, nothing more she could do from the EOC, either.

Stepping around a pair of public safety officials hurrying inside the command center, Utara turned into the corridor and broke into a run. She knew where she had to go next, and she had to get there fast.

<hr />

...WyndeStalker

Turning over in the bed yet again, Daemyn finally decided to admit that he wasn't going to fall back asleep. At least he had been able to nod off for a few hours. Besides, less than an hour remained in the flight anyway.

He got up and headed for the galley. Elsa was immersed in reading when he stepped through the portal. Sometimes he wondered if she ever slept.

Daemyn settled into his usual spot. He stretched his legs out before him, set the compupod on the corner table, and leaned back against the padding of the curved seating bench. "Any luck?"

She didn't need him to be more specific to know exactly what he was worried about. "Yes and no."

"The good news first, then."

"We've confirmed the parameters of the hack. We've also verified that it was one intrusion on one day, via an *extremely* creative method of entry. And, of course, that entry point and several equivalents we identified have now been closed off."

"And the bad news?"

"Still no idea who it was."

"Any clues?"

"Not a one. We can't even tell what continent it was from."

Daemyn whistled. "Impressive. And frightening."

"Exactly."

The update made him a little less anxious, but not by much. After losing so many hours of sleep over it, the last thing he wanted was to think about it more. Extending his arm, he tapped the compupod's icon to activate the much larger visionpod on the far wall and display the pod's screen there. The veepee chimed, and a moment later the brilliant colors burst across the screen.

"Which first?" he asked Elsa. "Trashmags or Airspar?"

Seated upright ninety degrees around the table, she finally glanced up from her compupod on the table. "Trashmags will be more entertaining this time."

"Hmph."

"More entertaining *for me*."

"Very supportive. Thank you."

She was right, though. The Airspar coverage would only aggravate him. His fingers clenched thinking about it. So the maddening stupidity of the trashmags might loosen his spirit enough to get him through the racing reports.

He tapped another icon on the compupod, then clasped his hands behind his head and interlinked his fingers. The screen coalesced into the usual listing grid. "Wow. Only four today."

"Better be careful, Daemyn," she said. "You might be getting boring."

"I'll manage."

The first report was yet another gossip reporter claiming to have an insider source who confirmed a romantic relationship between Daemyn and Corin Rockreikes. The next two – different trashmags, but clearly sourced from the same tipster – claimed that Daemyn had been spotted at a hotel bar two nights ago, so inebriated that he had been nearly unable to stand.

"Did we even go to that place this time?"

Elsa shook her head. "Last year."

"I thought so."

The final entry was video, not text. When it began to play, Daemyn frowned. He recognized the reporter, but her specialty was vidstars and singers, not sports. Still, the algorithms that scanned the media for references to Daemyn rarely erred, and the public-relations team at Wynde Industries almost always caught the few mistakes that slipped through the computer. So he must have garnered a mention in her report somehow.

"Our first story tonight," the reporter said, "takes us to the troubled production of *Matadors of Rombovia*, where –"

Daemyn reached over to the compupod and dragged his finger along the lower edge of the vidbox. In a few second he'd advanced to the next segment.

"– interesting name has jumped to the head of the list. It's not her usual type of role, but sources tell me that Lyssa Shrine is now the leading contender for –"

He advanced the video further. While he did, Elsa said, "I like her."

"This reporter?"

"No. Shrine. She's a lot more talented than people give her credit for."

He shrugged. "If you say so."

The video resumed. "– refused to be more specific. But the director did have this to say. I quote, 'You know Daemyn Wynde, the Airspar champion? Like him. That build. The character's not a racer, obviously, but that's the physique I want.' So, there you have it, folks. Your next superspy looks like Hyj-gon's favorite pilot."

"Well," Daemyn said. "I'll admit I didn't see that coming."

Elsa was laughing.

"What?"

"The concept of you as a superspy," she said. "It's bizarre."

"Hey, I think I could pull it off."

"Keep telling yourself that, Daemyn."

He closed out the empty list. "Another day with no worrisome reports about me or WI. That's always a good thing."

"Yes. Although at this point I think you're probably due."

He'd been thinking the same thing. His list of unread messages appeared on the veepee. He scanned the names. "Nothing from Rustle."

"Hmm?"

"He said he'd let me know when he found out more about what's going on in Loorriri. Why the comms were down, and the difficulties in the Future Cities."

Elsa looked up from her pod. "Tames never forgets. If he hasn't sent you an update, it's because he doesn't have one."

"It's been three days. That can't be right."

"Apparently it is."

If it was true Rustle hadn't been able to learn anything, that was bad. Possibly very bad. Daemyn deactivated the veepee and tugged the compupod from the table into his lap. He called up the news feeds.

His regular settings showed hundreds upon hundreds of reports on Airspar. Over a dozen about the Fith team in the prior hour alone. Nearly thirty economic reports from Hyj-gon, and seven about lobbying and other political activity in New Romas on behalf of the province's interests. Even one report that briefly mentioned his mother in connection with the final completion of construction on a tower in Fenwei that she had designed several years ago.

Toggling away from the defaults, Daemyn quickly entered a new series of search parameters. Loorriri. The Future Cities, each one by name.

He tapped the icon. He waited.

Elsa asked, "What'd you find?"

"Nothing."

"Nothing useful?"

"No. Literally *nothing*. For the past... seven hours."

She paused. "That's unusual, don't you think?"

"I've never checked before," he admitted. "But it has to be out of the ordinary, doesn't it?"

"A whole continent gone off the grid? I'd certainly think so."

"Right." Daemyn stared at the podscreen. "Something's not right about this."

FIFTEEN

…Durnow

Utara kept to the side streets and back alleys as best she could. As hard as she prayed to Aladare that no major tragedy would befall her parents' city, the reality was clear. If a violent confrontation between the AI and an angry mob happened in Durnow, it would take place in one of the public squares or wide boulevards. And if one came, Utara had no means at her disposal to stop it.

She jammed that thought out of her mind and ran faster. The quicker pace was good, but now her slingbag was bouncing uncontrollably at her hip. She reached down and snatched the top handle, hefting the bag a little higher. It was awkward to run that way, but at least it was less distracting than the constant assault from the bag.

She slowed for a moment and turned down another narrow street. If she remembered the map in her head correctly, this one would cut her across this neighborhood and bring her within a few minute's sprint of her parents' home. With one hand holding up the slingbag and an eye kept on the mostly vacant sidewalk before her, Utara spared a glance or two at the buildings as she passed them.

The power was still on. That was important. The level of anxiety among the residents would surely increase without access to information from media networks or comdees, but the closer daily life stayed to normal, the better.

A corner café still served patrons, who ate their meals and sipped their drinks as if nothing was amiss. One man tapped in annoyance at his comdee, but the others hadn't even seemed to notice yet.

She heard a child's shout and her stomach plunged. Then she realized it was only a raucous holler from a ballgame in an alleyway, and forced the dread from her gut.

Onward she ran, all the while working out her next move. Her conversation with Foson Solaris had convinced her that the government in New Romas suffered from a longstanding lack of accurate information on the conditions in the Future Cities. The comms embargo over Blonkas was problematic for a lot of reasons, but especially for keeping accurate information unavailable. The one over Durnow was more troubling – because though she didn't have any evidence yet, Utara suspected that each of the other Future Cities was also embargoed now, probably at the same time Durnow was. Worst of all was the fact that the Tagron EOC had refused to give Durnow's EOC a full and accurate status report. It was bad enough that the AI was locking down communications in a desperate calculation at preventing panic and widespread disorder. If the human leaders of the Future Cities stooped to lying about what was happening on their watch, solving the crisis would be infinitely more difficult.

The only way to fix this was to make sure everyone knew the truth. The leaders in New Romas had to know. Once they understood – *really* comprehended – what was happening in Loorriri, they would not stand idly by and let their fellow Primeans suffer and die in agony.

Utara had to get word out. Even better, she had to get *proof* out. With a communications embargo in place, that only left her two options. One was to bypass the embargo, but she didn't have anything close to the code-hacking skills needed to do something like that, and she didn't know anyone who did. Which meant the other option was her only choice – getting outside the city and onto the savannah with a comms device strong enough to reach the rest of Prime.

Her father owned a pair of them. Even on an ordinary day he often carried one with him, and with the upheaval brewing in Durnow she was certain he'd have it with him now. The other would be at her parents' home. Utara needed to retrieve it and start making comms before things got too far out of control.

A distant shout ripped the air. Adult, male, and angry. Another. And another. Then more following in a rising, turbulent cacophony.

Utara suppressed the urge to look, to run in the direction of the shout, to find out what was going on. She had spent her career in the PDS so far making a difference in individual lives, even the lives of the residents in a whole neighborhood like Evostown. It was the best part of her job, and she was good at it, too. But right now, she had to put that impulse aside. The amount of lives at stake in the Future Cities was a number she couldn't let herself fathom.

The shouting hadn't let up. It was a few blocks away, from the sound of it, and growing farther behind her as Utara continued running.

A loud smash. She couldn't tell what had made the noise, but it was big and metal and it couldn't possibly be good.

Another smash. A roar of approval from a crowd.

The next *boom* was so violent Utara wondered if it was an explosive detonation rather than something falling over. She glanced over her shoulder long enough to look for fire or smoke, but didn't see any.

The crowd roared again, louder and fiercer. Another *boom*, this time definitely something exploding. The crowd cheered.

A second later, the only thing Utara could hear was the shrieking engines of security drones. They were coming in fast and way too low. Instinctively she looked up at the sound – and flinched at the sight of a drone passing so close to a rooftop she thought it would crash right into it. Then they were gone from sight, too fast for her to count how many. The engine noise dulled as the drones vanished behind the buildings along the street.

The eruption of their machineguns opening fire, though, was a sound Utara could hear as clearly as if she was standing right beneath them.

The drones fired for what seemed like forever. When the rattling staccato finally ended, Utara waited for the sound of screams.

She heard nothing.

Then she realized she was standing still on the sidewalk, rooted in place. She took a sharp breath, turned, and started running again.

...Blonkas

Striding toward their central meeting point where they checked in every hour to share updates, Aidan had much less of a sensation of dread than he'd felt in a long time. It was... nice. For once.

The last couple of hours had gone better than Aidan had expected. Once Hasto and Roturo had enlisted a few more of their friends to help the cause of keeping calm, they'd been able to spread the word quickly. It would have gone even faster if Utara had been here too; they could have used her trusted status among the mothers to share the information through their networks of friends and families, as well. Still, the men had managed pretty well on their own so far. Not that *the drones only shoot when provoked* was a particularly great message to have to deliver, but it gave the residents of Evostown something to hold onto. If they stayed inside and didn't cause trouble, they'd stay alive.

The real test had come an hour earlier, when water had stopped flowing from the pipes again. They had hurried to remind everyone that this was normal – the new normal, anyway – and right on schedule. Even without the electronic clocks, the angle of the sun in the sky confirmed that the same pattern was in place. Hours from now the water would come back on, just like it was supposed to. Not everyone was convinced, but enough of them were. That was the only thing that mattered.

Hasto was waiting for him under the tree. He caught sight of Aidan and called out, "Anything?"

Shaking his head visibly, he called back, "Not this time."

Hasto nodded. He glanced down another street and tossed a wave. A few seconds later Roturo emerged into view at a brisk jog.

"Didn't want to be late," the young man said between breaths.

Aidan patted him on the shoulder. "Anything to report?"

Huffing air, Roturo shook his head.

"I only heard one new thing," Hasto said. "That some of the people in Arcadia forced open the gates and left the city. But people seem to know it doesn't make much sense. If the drones are shooting people who cause trouble, wouldn't they have stopped the ones trying to get the gates open?"

Roturo nodded. "That's a good point."

"If that explanation keeps the residents here from worrying about it, that's fine with me for now," Aidan said. "We'll take every hour of peace in Evostown we can get."

A dull roar echoed down the street. The three men looked skyward in unison, but they saw nothing except the cloudless blue panorama. They waited, listening. The roar was definitely mechanical. Some form of aircraft engines – and much bigger than the drones. From the warbling pulse within the roar, multiple craft. The noise sounded like it was getting closer, but with the way the buildings made everything echo and reverberate, it was hard to tell.

"Up we go," Aidan said.

He started off in the direction of the building with their observation perch, but Hasto and Roturo weren't as patient. Aidan had to break into a run to keep up.

By the time they stepped out onto the sixth-story roof, the noise was definitely more distinct. Their first instinct was to look out over the city – but nothing was there. They turned, scanning the sky.

Hasto found it first. "There!"

Aidan recognized it immediately. "Unified Forces."

To the southwest, in the distance over the rolling hills beyond the city wall, hovered a flight of six Rapid Assault Craft. Powered by engines that adjusted rotation either to fly them forward or sustain a hover, the RACs were the aging but still common aircraft used to deploy strike forces from the military's elite commando units, the PARTEs.

"What are they waiting for?" Roturo asked.

"Probably trying to figure out what to do first," Hasto replied.

"Probably," Aidan agreed, although he had a feeling he was certain exactly what the PARTEs first target would be. If the AI's software wasn't following instructions the way it was supposed to, even the most sophisticated computers always had a vulnerability – the hardware. The idea had occurred to him, too. A bombing strike from the Air Branch was out of the question with the command center's proximity to so many innocent people. PARTE, though, had the expertise to insert into the facility and blow up the mainframes in a controlled detonation.

The question was, had the AI already figured out that plan, as well?

"Here they come," Roturo said.

Three RACs swooped in over the city wall in a single-file line and headed toward the city center. They hadn't come far before a higher-pitched wailing of smaller engines split the air from the other direction. Aidan turned over his shoulder to see a swarm of eight security drones racing toward the oncoming RACs.

The military craft split up. One continued straight toward the city center, while the other two swerved outward in opposite directions. A single drone peeled off to pursue the RAC on the left. The remaining drones split into two flights, one going after the central RAC and the other looping toward the one on the right.

The two groups of drones opened fire simultaneously.

"Oh, shig," Hasto said.

Shooting from multiple angles, coordinating their pattern of fire, the drones made quick work of the two RACs. The military craft did their best to return fire with their rockets and heavy guns, but the drones were too small and too fast – and too well organized. The bullets from the drones' machine-guns ripped into the RACs' wings, engines, and cockpits. The RAC on the right fell from the sky, careening into a building and exploding in a massive fireball. The other RAC dropped a few seconds later, erupting in a towering plume of flame a few blocks away from the first crash.

Enraptured with the devastating sight, Aidan had lost track of the third RAC and its lone pursuer. He found it quickly, though. Further ahead the RAC had looped away from the city center and was hovering above the wide roof of a low building. PARTE soldiers rappelled down from the craft to the roof. The solitary drone flew a slow, wide orbit around the site in a crisp circle a few blocks in diameter.

"What are they doing?" Roturo asked.

"They'll try to make it on foot," Aidan said.

"But the drones..." Hasto couldn't even finish the thought.

The moment the last of the PARTE was down on the building, the RAC swooped away from the rooftop. The single drone suddenly rocketed inward, heading straight toward it. The machineguns fired – but only briefly. Just long enough to eviscerate the craft's cockpit.

"Why'd they do that?" Hasto wondered aloud.

Aidan couldn't figure it out, either.

The RAC was still flying. The drone took up position right behind it, following the same flight path. Without any humans at the controls, the RAC flew at top speed on a straight course toward the other three RACs hovering beyond the city walls.

The three men turned and followed its path as it flew back over the city with the drone on its tail. The instant before the RAC reached the wall, it opened fire. Rockets. Heavy guns. Cannons. Every single weapon on the craft unloaded its full ferocity on the other three RACs.

They never stood a chance.

By the time the blazing light and deafening roar of the trio of gigantic explosions had faded away, the staccato bursts of the drones' machineguns were firing intermittently behind them, picking off the PARTE soldiers one by one.

...Millennium Grand Hotel, Port Vulcania

"Is all this sneaking around really necessary?"

Elsa glanced back at Daemyn and shrugged overdramatically. "Admittedly GM would be the one facing the massive fine for in-season contract tampering, not you. But you'd be in breach of your contract with Fith. They'd fire you. And the consequential damages in the event of a dismissal for cause would be..."

"A lot," Reiton supplied from behind him. "So keep sneaking."

"Fine, fine," Daemyn muttered. He kept the hat on his head, his neck bent low, and the long coat wrapped around him. A few moments later the trio emerged from the lift and strode quickly to the door of one of the hotel's luxury suites. Elsa snapped out a keycard from her palm, open the door, and ushered them into the suite's foyer.

"I'll wait here," she said. Daemyn and Reiton removed their hats and coats, which Elsa deposited on a chair. The two men checked their appearances in the wide mirror, then headed into the suite's sitting room.

Reese Garold, the chief executive officer of Grandell Motors, was waiting for them alone. The obligatory armlocks and greetings passed quickly; the men had met one another previously, and Garold's intermediary had made the purpose of the meeting clear when the invitation had been extended two days ago. The proposal had arisen so quickly, in fact, that they'd changed

WyndeStalker's itinerary to travel directly to Port Vulcania from Occanan before returning to Hyj-gon.

Garold took a seat on one sofa, while Daemyn and Reiton sat together on the one opposite him.

"So," Reiton said. "Let's get down to business. We know why you'd want to bring Daemyn aboard for your team – you've got two skilled heavy pilots and a very strong second light. What you've been missing is a top-notch lead light."

Garold didn't even try to play coy. He tipped his head, then said, "That's right. We think with Daemyn flying lead, we'd be an immediate championship contender. If not the favorite."

"We agree." Reiton leaned forward. "But Daemyn's winning now, and Fith's other pilots are all under contract for at least three more seasons. What are you offering that would be good enough for him to walk away from that situation?"

"A number of things." Garold withdrew a small folded transi from the interior pocket of his formal jacket. Deftly he unfolded it, scanned it, and then lowered his hand back into his lap. "As you know, Coach Crombie has been with our team for over a decade, and his contract is up at the end of this season. What you don't know – considering that you're the first people other than me to hear about it – is that he's decided that, rather than renew his contract, which we would have done without hesitation, he's ready to retire and spend more time with his grandchildren."

Daemyn smiled. "He's certainly earned it."

"Yes, he has." Garold smiled back for a moment, then grew serious again. "Your clashes with Coach Farrier, over any number of issues, are well known. As for what that means for our offer, well, we would be willing to recruit and hire the coach of your choice for the GM team."

Daemyn and Reiton shared a glace. That was definitely unexpected news. Perhaps the only angle they hadn't anticipated in preparing for the meeting. As much as he appreciated Garold's understanding of the importance of a positive working relationship between pilots and their coach, though, with all the other factors involved it was a trivial issue for Daemyn. He had been plan-ning to tolerate Farrier a bit longer while he waited for their plans to come to fruition. On the other hand, with Project Lariat suddenly compromised, his confidence in the plan was a lot lower than it had been a few weeks ago. Thoughtfully he leaned back in his chair; only Reiton would interpret it as a signal.

"I'd have a few names in mind, absolutely," Daemyn said.

"Names I could easily share with Fith," Reiton pointed out. "I think it's more than a fair question who Fith would pick if they faced a zero-sum choice between Daemyn and Farrier."

"You would know better than I," Garold conceded. "But I'm aware that your difficulties with Fith extend well beyond the coach's handling of the team."

Reiton's face gave away nothing. "Such as?"

"I speak from my perspective as an outside observer, of course. Only watching what Fith's leadership says and does where Daemyn is concerned." Undoubtedly that wasn't true; Grandell Motors had an extensive and effective corporate intelligence division. But Garold was far too savvy to even hint at the origins of their insights, whether from Fith, WI, or other sources. "I'd say it's jealousy."

"Really?" Daemyn grinned broadly. "You think they're jealous of me?"

"I do." Garold spread his hands, his gesture indicating the opulence of the room in which they sat. "Fith is a famous corporation, just as GM is. But when it comes to celebrity, a company can never compete with an individual. Everything they're doing suggests to me that they're worried Daemyn Wynde is well on his way to building a more prominent, more respected brand than Fith."

"That's rather unlikely, don't you think?" Reiton barely kept his voice from sounding like a full-on scoff. "Famous as he might be today, Daemyn has a century's worth of familiarity and marketing to catch up on."

Garold offered a sly grin. "I suppose it depends on what you think of the current status of Fith's public standing."

Reiton chuckled. "Fair enough."

"You have a number of high-profile endorsements, Daemyn," the GM executive said, facing him directly. "I can't help but notice that they all involve products and services that have nothing whatsoever to do with anything offered by Fith. I can't imagine that's a coincidence."

Reiton raised a brow. "And GM would be more willing to allow a broader range of endorsements?"

"Within reason, of course," Garold replied. "But compared to Daemyn's current slate, yes, we would be open to considerably more."

Daemyn sat forward in his chair. "And what about Wynde Industries?"

"I don't see why the relationship between GM and WI should be anything other than fully synergistic. There are many ways we can help each other."

"What do you have in mind?"

"We're prepared to install the marzite batteries in the team airblades, for one," Garold said. "They're outperforming our best ones by nearly twenty-five percent."

Daemyn didn't even try to suppress his smile. "Why wait?"

Garold chuckled. "We do that, and then sign you to our team once the offseason begins? I'd prefer to keep my tampering a *lot* more secretive."

"You're right," Daemyn said. "Afterward would be better."

"Back to the topic of corporate synergy," Reiton said, sitting forward too. "Your board would approve that?"

"I haven't presented anything to them yet, for obvious reasons." Garold motioned with a hand to indicate the subject he'd just been discussing with Daemyn. "With the immediate benefit to our Airspar team and the overall GM public profile, though, I don't foresee any problems getting a straightforward arrangement through the board."

"That's good to hear," Reiton said. "While we still have time here in person, there are a few other terms I'd like to discuss, as well."

For the rest of the meeting, Daemyn paid exactly enough attention so that he responded appropriately at the right moments. Otherwise, his thoughts were elsewhere. Elsa's assessment of GM had been accurate, but now he was confident she had underestimated the degree of desperation driving their proposal to lure him to their Airspar team. That left him even more certain that accepting their offer was the last thing he should do. For one, you didn't climb aboard a sinking ship; you jumped off. More importantly, if GM thought his name and reputation was that valuable, he had even less reason to share it with anyone. Maybe step one in their plan was closer than they'd thought after all.

Everything depended on getting the Project Lariat hack under control immediately. That had to be his top – his only – priority.

SIXTEEN

...Buneen Architectural & Engineering Corp., City of Buneen, Hyj-gon

The receptionist started to rise from his chair to show him back, but Daemyn politely declined the young man's offer. He knew the way.

After a brief winding trip past cubicles and down a hallway of wide-windowed offices, he arrived at the spacious corner room that had been his mother's workspace the last few years. He paused at the glass door, peering inside to make sure she wasn't on a comm. She stood in front of a low table with a small diorama spread out across its surface. He rapped a knuckle on the glass. She glanced up, then hurried to the door.

His mother pulled him into a tight embrace. Daemyn hugged his mother back firmly.

Ripi gave him one last squeeze, then stepped back. "I'm so glad you got my message. I was hoping I would be able to see you. Your travel schedule can be crazy sometimes."

While that was true, his mother had proven many times her ability to correctly estimate the days of his departures and arrivals for matches. It was no lucky guess that her comm had coincided with the day he ordinarily would have returned from Occanan – if it hadn't been for the detour to meet Garold in Port Vulcania first.

"I'm glad the timing worked out, too. How's Father?"

"The same as always. All this week he's been stuck in, as he so artfully put it –" She affected her comedic mimicry of his father's voice of complaint. "– another pointless meeting with the numbskulls at Okomo Aerospace."

"I bet," Daemyn said, and they both laughed. His father's impatience with what was undeniably his most obnoxious subcontractor was legendary. "You're at work today. What project is this?"

"It hasn't been announced publicly yet," his mother explained, "but the government of Hyj-gon and the leaders of the Plains Terrans have finalized an agreement to jointly fund a memorial to the Karagashi disaster. Honoring all those who died, on the plains and in the city. The goal is to have it built and opened in time for the twenty-fifth annual remembrance."

The goal made sense, but the date was barely more than two years away. "They really think they can have it ready it time?"

Ripi grinned. "Depending on the design they select, sure."

"Right." His mother hadn't achieved such success in her career without some insight into people and a hefty dose of strategic cunning to go along with her brilliance as an architect. Daemyn hoped that, in time, he could bring the same combination to bear on behalf of Wynde Industries. "Can I see what you have so far?"

"Of course," she said, and immediately launched him into a fully in-depth tour through all of the materials gathered in her office.

One entire glass wall of her office was filled with viscaps. The bigger section was labeled BEFORE. Karagashi in the days preceding the firestorm. The skyline, individual buildings, people walking across its skyways and waiting on its landing platforms. Even some pictures of their apartment back then; simple images of daily life, a happy family oblivious to the impending tragedy. Images of the Plains Terrans villages too, a simpler existence among the lush, rolling grasses. Each community, Faytan and Terran, beautiful in its own way. Both had lost so much.

Then a smaller area captioned AFTER. Karagashi in ruins, forever scarred by wind and flame. When the media showed scenes of the abandoned city today, they always used more recent footage, scoured clean by two decades of wind and rain. The immediate aftermath, black with soot and still trailing wisps of smoke, looked like a war zone. Images of the Plains Terrans villages, too, utterly annihilated. The media never showed those.

Daemyn had been too young at the time to comprehend the carnage. Seeing the images now, as an adult, shook him to his core.

He looked to his mother. "I never realized."

"I know." She touched him on the shoulder. "I haven't seen them in years, either. But for this, I thought it was important to remember."

Daemyn nodded.

"Very little video of the firestorm exists, particularly once it reached Karagashi. But we found one vidfeed that was well preserved. Do you want to see it?"

He hesitated, then said, "Yes."

She tapped a spot on the wall, bringing a small still image into fuller scale before them on the glass. She tapped again, beginning the playback.

Daemyn watched, enraptured. The storm swirled and burned its way through Karagashi, bullying past skyscrapers like twigs on a scrub bush. The clouds weren't as dark as the ones in the recesses of his memory – but the fire was brighter, angrier, whipping the skies with vicious tendrils. He leaned closer, trying to determine what part of the city the video showed. His eyes focused harder, looking for something, any hint of what he remembered. The footage ended abruptly.

He stood up straight once more. "It's a miracle we ever made it out of that."

"Yes." Ripi tapped the wall, dismissing the vidbox back to its corner. "We never even learned his name, but you revered that shuttle pilot. For months he was all you could talk about."

"Years, I think."

She smiled. "I was giving you the benefit of the doubt."

He smiled back. "I don't know if I would have become a pilot if it weren't for that day."

"Oh, you were obsessed with Airspar long before that." She moved away from the wall, leading him toward the diorama. "But perhaps it's part of what drives you to be the very best at everything you do. Including flying."

Often it seemed his mother knew him better than he knew himself. She was probably right this time, too. "So, what's your theme?"

"Our unity in our grief and remembrance, despite our differences then and now."

It was an inspired choice. Political clashes between Hyj-gon's Faytans and the Plains Terrans had led to a seven-year stagnation in dealing with the climatological and environmental circumstances that gradually had escalated into the confluence of events that made the firestorm possible. Both sides had paid a terrible price – and both governments had pledged to never let such a disaster happen on their territory again.

Daemyn listened carefully while she explained the symbolism of the various structures in the memorial, and the path visitors would follow while weaving through its elegant design. When she finished, he said simply, "It's beautiful. I love it."

"Hopefully the selection committee will think so, too."

They moved from standing beside the diorama to sit side by side on one of the sofas. Once they were settled he said, "I have an odd question, but I suspect you know the answer."

She grinned. "We'll see."

"When Father changed companies a while back, who initiated the move? Him, or them?"

"He was recruited." Ripi peered at him. "Why do you ask?"

"Just curious."

His mother raised an eyebrow.

He had to be careful how much he said, even though he trusted her discretion implicitly. "Another Airspar team made an overture recently."

"Can they afford to outbid Fith for you?"

"They can, yes. Whether they will, I'm still not sure."

"A local team, perhaps?"

"No, actually. Why?"

"At one point during the broadcast they showed a viscap of you talking to Mataki the day of the race. Your father had commented to me about it, wondering if perhaps he was acting as an intermediary for someone."

For a man who held his son's career in racing in such low esteem, Sai Kuron apparently was watching an increasingly conspicuous amount of the coverage of the races. "That would certainly be flattering," Daemyn said, and meant it. "But that wasn't the topic of conversation. Although Airspar did enter into the discussion, in a roundabout sort of way."

"How did you end up talking to him, anyway?"

It turned into a longer story than Daemyn had intended. What started as a simple account of pressuring Mataki to support the installation of Faytan alternative fuel technology in the Future Cities on Loorriri had to keep doubling back to explain why the Future Cities had come up, which led to why they'd talked about Loorriri at all, which led to why he'd inserted himself into the conversation between Mataki and Utara Fireheart in the first place. By the time he finished, Daemyn decided he would have been far better off starting at the beginning instead of rambling his way through it.

"Good luck getting Mataki to take action," his mother said. "He's useless."

That was probably a bit uncharitable to the politician, but in a few more weeks Daemyn might very well feel the same. Time would tell. "Let's hope not. Some of the Faytan companies would make a great deal of money on the project if it went through."

"It would be good for Hyj-gon," she agreed. "But would it help your company?"

"Not directly," Daemyn conceded. "We'd probably be able to subcontract on some of the component parts, though."

"That's better than nothing, I suppose." She put a hand on his knee. "Supporting our fellow Faytans is admirable, dear. But if you want your dreams to come true, your focus must remain on benefitting your company most of all. Otherwise, you will never attain the self-sufficiency you seek."

Daemyn nodded. "I'll remember that."

Ripi leaned forward and propped her elbows on her knees. "Are you planning to see Utara Fireheart again?"

Daemyn blinked. "Uh, no. Why?"

"You smiled when you first said her name."

"Mom!"

"Well, you did," she said, a little too triumphantly.

...Grandell Motors Corporate Intelligence Division

Monson strode into his office. He shut and locked the door, then slid into his chair and spun to face the array of display screens before him.

The text message from his contact at Boynton Logistics Dynamics had requested that he comm her sometime in the next hour, during her lunch break. He checked the side screen that always ran a constantly updated feed of the highest-priority news media reports from around the world. He tapped an icon and confirmed that no groundquakes or catastrophic weather events were impacting Loorriri. Another tapped icon confirmed no media bulletins about the corporation, either.

He waited for the privacy bubble to finish sealing him within its silencing confines. After he entered her comm codes, she answered only a few seconds later.

No greetings or preambles. *"Your bounty for more intel is still open, right?"*

"For the first person who provides valuable information, yes. Which, presumably, you are interested in becoming."

"Things are getting worse here every day. Sometimes every hour, it seems like. I don't know how much longer I can take this."

"I thought you weren't going to quit."

"I may have to change my mind on that. After we spoke last, I decided you were right that I shouldn't put in extra effort for the company if they don't respect me and my work in return. I told a few of my colleagues how I felt, and they agreed with me. So as a group, we've been putting in the bare minimum, nothing more, on the Loorriri AIs."

"Boynton had it coming. Good for you."

"Yeah, well. Not so good for the Future Cities."

"What's happening now?"

"People are leaving."

"Leaving?"

"As in, literally walking out the gates into the wilderness. From all twelve cities now. From some, it's been over two weeks at this point from when it started. Durnow held out the longest, but residents started fleeing there a few hours ago."

"And the AIs?"

"The server activity is off the charts. Last week's record levels look like nothing by comparison to today. It's an astounding amount of data the AIs are crunching."

"Every city?"

"Yes, each city AI on its own. And the Loorriri network as a whole. They're communicating more than ever before through the hub."

"And that's worrisome because of what occurred in Blonkas."

For a moment no response came over the comm line. *"Yes."*

Monson had to give her credit for not rushing to spill the details. To keep her talking, he'd have to offer an opening of his own. "I have many contacts in many walks of life on Prime. Including the Unified Forces. I know they sent a PARTE, and the mission failed."

"Is that the word they used? Failed?"

"Yes." Actually, he'd been told that all the soldiers sent to the Future City were dead, and the aircraft dispatched with them destroyed as well. But if frustration with corporate hierarchy was fueling her disgust with Boynton, he'd play the same angle with the Unified Forces, too. "Though I'm not entirely sure," he lied, "exactly how much my source knows."

"Annihilated is more like it," she said. *"When the PARTE showed up, the Blonkas AI analyzed the numerous possible scenarios presented and concluded that the strike was launched to disable or destroy the AI itself."*

"Why would it draw that conclusion?"

"Oh. So your source really didn't tell you everything."

"Apparently not."

"A few days ago a mob of residents went after a water-delivery pumping station. It got so bad the AI deployed security drones to secure the city's water supply from interference. About a week before that, some sort of armed raiding party from the wilderness made an incursion on the city's perimeter, and drones had to go out to drive them off, too. Put all three together, and the Blonkas AI made the determination to reclassify HUMANS from OPTIMIZE WELFARE to MODERATE THREAT."

"That's not good."

"No, it isn't."

"And the rest of the AIs know about this?"

"The Future City AIs, yes."

"But only those?"

Beyond the full-spec AIs designed to carry out the entire city-management operations of the Future Cities on Loorriri, Boynton operated hundreds of additional limited-task AIs all across the planet – including ones retrofitted for providing various subsets of logistics and administrative support in cities from New Romas to Port Vulcania to Buneen and beyond. Even a few in Grandell Valley, within shouting distance of the chair Monson occupied at this very moment. A chill ran down his spine.

"Right, only Loorriri. Because they're comprehensive, we created a separate network for them to deal with the entire scope of what they address and analyze. All the other AIs share the INMASS."

"The what?"

"Sorry, Intercontinental Network for Metropolitan Area Support Services."

"Ah, yes. Appropriate. What's its status?"

"Stable. Normal, essentially. Nothing out of the ordinary, because the situation in the Future Cities has no impact on the operations they're running elsewhere."

"Can the Loorriri AIs and the INMASS communicate with each other?"

"No, the networks aren't linked."

Monson knew exactly what to do next. "This information has been incredibly insightful. Within the hour, I will disburse triple your previous payment."

"You're serious?"

"I am. And I will send ten times the previous amount if you are willing to do something for me in exchange."

She didn't hesitate. *"What's that?"*

"Deactivate the Future City network. Shut down the central hub, so the AIs cannot communicate with one another any longer."

"We've been considering that already, actually. What's in it for you, though?"

"The payment," he said flatly, "is what's in it for you."

She laughed. *"Right. Consider it done."*

"Excellent."

"I'll have an update tomorrow."

"We'll talk then," Monson said, and ended the comm.

He could see the cascade of events in his mind's eye already. Boynton would sever the AI's communications with one another. To a rational calculator like a computer, such an action would only confirm that human actors were a threat to the AIs. The other cities would respond by reclassifying humans, agreeing with the conclusion drawn by Blonkas. Once that occurred, all of the AIs would become much more aggressive toward the residents of the cities. More security drones opening fire within city walls. Some might even pursue the fleeing humans outside the city walls. The AIs also would enact electronic countermeasures designed to ensure that their code could not be deactivated. And they would find a way to resume communication with each other. Monson didn't know how – his specialty was gathering intelligence, not coding or engineering – but he was certain they would find a method. Once that happened, the AIs would conspire together, and the situation would get even worse.

Monson smiled. Events on Loorriri were spiraling downward rapidly. The worse it got, the more desperate the government would become. Their desperation would play directly into his plans. It wouldn't take long for the PIS to need the best minds working on solving the crisis – and Monson would be right there to fill the void.

Motion in his peripheral vision caught his attention. He looked up to see Dana Bristow standing in the corridor, a transi in her hand.

He gave her a quick nod. Moments later the privacy bubble was deactivated and he rose from his chair and stepped to the door. When he opened it, she handed over the transi with a dramatic flourish. While he started reading the short text, she explained, "I was digging around on Worty, and happened across this offer of sale in the code hacker circles. I'm sure you'd have seen it soon enough, but no reason to wait."

"You're the best," he told her. "You just made my day."

She laughed. "From that grin when I showed up, it looks like you're already having a pretty good one."

"Oh, I am." His grin widened. "But a chance to buy out secrets from beneath Daemyn Wynde? That beats everything else."

...Durnow

Incomprehensible.

It was the only word Utara could think of to describe the speed at which Durnow had plummeted from agitation and disorder into complete and utter anarchy. Mere hours ago the city had teetered on the edge of chaos, yet still had held much promise for regaining stability. Now it had free-fallen into what she feared was unsalvageable panic.

Even more distressing, she doubted this kind of calamity was limited to Durnow. When she'd left last week, Blonkas already had been in much worse shape than Durnow had been this morning. If this could happen to Durnow, what horrible reality must Aidan be facing in Blonkas? She couldn't let herself imagine it.

Not that she blamed the residents. By itself, losing residential power was frustrating but manageable. The air-circulation fans had turned off too, though, and already the heat and humidity were unbearable. Shutting down the transportation systems kept everyone trapped where they were – and many people had been at work or away from home on errands when the lockdown had happened, keeping them apart from their families. In combination with the shutdown of the comdee network within the city and the communications embargo beyond its walls, panic had risen. Worst of all, water delivery apparently had been terminated at its origin points at the pumping stations; faucets and privies ran dry, and dehydration was setting in for many. On top of all the rest, the reassuring hum of daily life was gone, replaced by an eerie silence broken only by the sounds of the security drones – the roar of the engines when they passed overhead on patrol, and the occasional burst of machinegun fire.

The people had been disquieted enough before, when the city was troubled but still mostly functional. It would be unlivable if those necessary utilities weren't restored within a day or two, and nobody thought that would happen. Not anymore.

Durnow was a deathtrap. And everyone knew it.

The most natural of instincts – fight or flight – had kicked in. The few who'd tried to fight had ended up on the fatal end of a flyover from the security drones, and that word had travelled swiftly among the residents even with all electronic communications inoperable. Fleeing was the only option left, and from the look of it everyone who was in any sort of physical condition to leave the city was already on their way to the gates.

If nothing else, at least the AI's power shutdown was fully thorough. The automated security cordons had been toppled and the crowd of people streamed past the wreckage unabated. The massive steel gates had been smashed open – from a powerful blow delivered by the front end of some kind of large truck, most likely – and they teetered precariously from what remained of the hinges. Nothing blocked the egress of the throng of humanity fleeing Durnow. For a moment, Utara tried to convince herself that might be a good thing.

Standing on the rise of the side street that sloped downward to the main boulevard leading out the gate, she decided the only thing she could say was the truth of what she was thinking. "I should go with them."

Beside her, Koster put a hand on her shoulder. "You should."

"But —"

"They'll need leadership. None of the city administrators will go; they're too cowardly. And I don't think anyone would trust them at this point, regardless."

Utara gave him a look. "But they'll trust a junior counselor from the PDS?"

"You might be surprised."

"If I start with some of the tricks for finding food and water on the savannah, that should build me some credibility."

"Exactly."

"I'll see where J'ni is positioned. Maybe she can head this way and assist."

"With the humans? You think so?"

"Well, even keeping the wildlife at bay would really help."

"Yes. Use your assets each to their optimal advantage."

Koster reached into his slingbag and handed her his special-issue comms device. Powered by ultra-long-life batteries and shielded from electro-magnetic pulse interference by layers of military-grade alloy, it would be able to connect with just about any communications network on Prime. If she was willing to drain the battery a bit, it would even reach directly to the government's comms satellites in low-space orbit above the planet.

"I will." Utara started to slide it into her own slingbag alongside the one her mother had pulled out of the storage locker in their bedroom, then kept it in her hand. "How far outside the city do you think I'll need to get to be clear of the AI's comms embargo?"

"A dozen kilometers at most. Probably less."

"Not far," she affirmed. She hefted the device with its big blue PDS emblem facing upward. "Are you sure you shouldn't keep one here?"

Her father ran a hand down her arm. "I am. By the time the comms embargo is removed, it won't be necessary. It's best that you have the maximum possible battery charge with you out there. You'll need it. Far more than I."

She slipped the device into her bag. "I don't like the idea of you and Mom staying behind."

"I know." He touched her arm again. "The city needs me. I was part of Durnow before it was even born. Planning, construction, settlement. All the years of residential operation since then, the good and the bad. I can't give up on my city without doing everything I possibly can to save it. Any more than I could ever give up on my only daughter."

It was a lovely sentiment, but he was being profoundly foolish. Not only with his life, but her mother's, too. "I understand that, but —"

"You may think so. Trust me, though. You can't. Not yet. Someday when you're a mother, then you'll understand."

"Maybe you're right. But that doesn't change the fact that, as much as you love Durnow, it's too dangerous to stay here. Come with me. There's still time."

"I'm too old to hike out across the wilderness, Utara, even if I wanted to."

"That's not true."

He leaned down and kissed her forehead. "Actually, darling, it is." Then he put a finger to her lips. "And before you continue with your next point — which I am perfectly aware is that your mother is not nearly so old — let me remind you of one thing. However much it is that you think I am foolish in the extreme to be so stubborn in refusing to leave, your mother is even more stubborn than me."

It was true. Utara sighed. "Don't let her do anything stupid."

"One doesn't *let* your mother —"

"You know what I mean."

"I do. And I'll protect her to the very utmost of my ability."

"Okay."

"Be safe," her father said, and pulled her into a brief embrace.

"I will. You too." Utara stepped back and met Koster's gaze again firmly. "I'll come back for you. For you, and for everyone else who can't leave this way. Somehow I'll get you out of here. I promise."

Her father nodded. "I believe you will."

With that, Utara turned and started jogging down the sloping street toward the restless river of people flooding out the gate. She didn't look back over her shoulder. She didn't want her father to see the tears streaming down her face.

SEVENTEEN

...Wynde Industries

Filson's low whistle of approval broke the silence. "She's a beauty."

"She sure is. Great work."

"Thanks, boss," Lianna Bakerton said. The mechanic was the only other person at WI who worked on Project Lariat tech. She rapped her knuckles along the wing's edge. "We can't go full throttle in here, obviously, but the first round of integrity testing went about as well as I've ever seen it."

"How much longer for the other two rounds?"

"I'm available to help now," Filson interjected.

"Three hours, then, if we do them thoroughly."

"Perfect," Daemyn said. "I have too much on my desk this morning to do any more myself before then anyway."

Filson nodded. "And when we're done?"

"Load her up."

"You're sure?"

"I am." Daemyn couldn't bring himself to tell them about the hack. Not yet, at least. If the test flight went well, then he could explain to them the reason why he might have to accelerate their plans to push the engine to market. And if the test flight went poorly, well, it would be a much less optimistic conversation.

Bakerton grinned. "You think she looks good in here, just wait until you're taking those curves at Naper Peak."

Daemyn grinned back. "I know. Believe me. But I won't be flying."

Filson practically chortled. "You almost had me there, Daemyn."

"I'm serious."

"If you cleared your rehab enough to fly Airspar," Bakerton said, "I thought for sure you'd want to fly the engine test, too."

"Oh, I want to. But Reiton reminded me that we brought on Brutus for a reason. Partly because I got hurt, yes, but also because he's an excellent test pilot. It's his specialty. And we should let him showcase it."

"That's true," she agreed.

"Besides, I'm less worried about the handling than the performance. And I'll have much better perspective on that from the control booth."

"You will," Filson said. "You're thinking to head up this afternoon?"

Daemyn shook his head. "Tonight. We can use the darkness to our advantage."

"The vidfeed won't be as useful, though," Filson pointed out.

"That's fine." Daemyn walked the length of the airblade's wings, one end to the other. "The sensors will give us all the data we need on functionality. Besides, we can take all the vids we need when we make the first public demonstration."

"We'll ping you when she's loaded up," Bakerton said. "Once you know your schedule, an hour's lead time before takeoff is enough for me."

"For me, as well," Filson said.

Daemyn nodded. "It's a plan. See you in a few hours."

...Midland Savannahs Wildlife Sanctuary

"I'm on my way." J'ni steered her truck down the gentle slope to a flatter stretch of the rolling grasses. "Where are you now?"

On the other end of the comdee, Utara paused before reading off a set of coordinates in a slow and deliberate progression.

Driving with one hand, J'ni tapped the numbers into her compupod. The screen displayed Utara's distance from Durnow – not as far as J'ni had hoped – as well as the terrain between them. "Keep heading west for now. When you get to the river, turn south and stay along the banks."

"What about the caimans?"

"The noise of a group that large should be plenty to keep them scared off." For a second J'ni grabbed the steering wheel with both hands to maneuver around the leading edge of a swale. "To be safe, keep the children and slower people away from the waterline."

"I can do that."

J'ni checked the screen again. "I'll catch up to you in... a couple of hours."

"Right before dusk."

"Let's hope so. If you have to stop, set up as many campfires as you can around the perimeter."

"Affirmative. It's worth the risk."

"Yes, it is." The fires would keep the animals at bay. Maybe an unexpectedly hungry kinana or a particularly bold silver jackal might have the courage to charge past the flames and prey upon humans, but the odds of that were low – and J'ni would be bringing enough weapons to deal with it if it happened. The risk was that the fires and their smoke would attract the attention of the outlaw bands. If those vicious knarfers chose to attack the refugees, well... There would be nothing J'ni or Utara could do to defend them.

"How are your supplies?"

"I managed to fit more than I thought into the truck." J'ni spared a glance over her shoulder to the weapons, flares, and other various and sundry wildlife-management supplies stacked into the back seat and the straps holding down the lid of the overloaded rear storage compartment. "That will buy us some time until we'll have to resupply."

Utara didn't ask how J'ni planned to be able to do that. Which was a good thing, because right now she didn't have a plan. They'd have to think of something when the time came.

"It will be enough," Utara said. Always insistent to offer reassurance.

"Tarah willing," J'ni replied. "The escapees from the preserve might actually work in our favor. At least for a while."

In her hurried departure from Durnow, Utara had heard only secondhand reports that the animals in the city's preserve had escaped, but with the city's power shut off their freedom was inevitable. Now dozens of new animals would be scouring the nearby savannah for food. The zeraffes would probably happily amble to open land and begin to graze, but the more aggressive predators would almost immediately end up clashing with their counterparts among the savannah's current inhabitants. In that showdown for supremacy, the human refugees would be inconsequential. That was what J'ni's experience in the sanctuary predicted, anyway. The scientist in her would soon find out if her hypothesis was correct.

For a moment, J'ni smiled. Now *that* would be a dissertation to set her apart from the pack.

"*See you soon,*" Utara said.

"Copy," J'ni said, and clicked off the comdee.

Her fingers clenched the steering wheel and her eyes focused on the long drive ahead of her.

～◯

...Blonkas

"It's back on," someone shouted. "The water's back!"

A cheer rose from the residents in the street. It didn't last long, though, because everyone started rushing inside their homes to refill their canisters right away.

Aidan pushed himself up from where he'd been sitting on the front stoop of the building and walked back inside to his apartment. He snapped the end of the tube over the sink's spout and wrapped it tight with a cord, then dropped the end of the tube into his empty canister. Sure enough, after a hiss and pop cleared the pipe, the water began to pour out.

While he waited for the canister to slowly fill, he watched out the window as Hasto, Roturo, and several of their friends began lighting the bonfire they'd prepared in the middle of the street. Once the wooden slabs and other flammables had started to burn, the young men carried over the giant kettle — provided by one of the neighbors down the block, who operated a restaurant — and positioned its support legs to hang its rotund belly over the flames. Soon, all the neighbors would add their canisters to the communal share, one kettle-full at a time, until everyone had sanitized water to take back home.

For the first time in a long while, even with the effort necessary to prepare a basic necessity like drinking water, the residents of Evostown were becoming optimistic. Everyone had heard the explosions from the Unified Forces' failed attack, so there had been no point in trying to lie to them. As shocking as the drones' defeat of the RACs was, though, the news actually had given the residents of Evostown hope. Now, they believed that help was on the way. The government cared. Even if the first attempt had failed, they would try again. The prospect of rescue was no longer a fantasy, but something inevitable they simply had to wait for.

With the canister full, Aidan shut off the flow at the tap and pulled up the tube to put it back in the sink. He hefted the transpariplast container in his arms and strode outside. One of the first to reach the bonfire, he poured out his canister into the kettle, then stepped back to make room for others.

Less than ten minutes later the first kettle's worth of boiled water had been redistributed into canisters, and another full allotment was hanging over the flames to start the process anew. Aidan drank down a tall glass of water offered to him by Hasto. It was warm, but he didn't care; it was refreshing all the same. Then he snatched up his empty canister and headed back indoors.

Right as he set down the canister on the floor beside his sink, a heart-wrenching scream from outside shattered the celebratory mood on the street.

Without hesitating Aidan ran for the door.

"Help!" someone shouted.

"A medic," cried a mother. "We need a medic!"

Aidan ran up to the group gathered outside the building two doors down. "What's happening?"

They moved aside to show him. On the steps, two teenagers flailed uncontrollably. They gasped for breath, helplessly clutching at their throats.

Then one of them heaved and vomited.

A man in the crowd started to cough. The mother tried to call for help again, only to double over in agony grabbing at her own abdomen.

Aidan suddenly felt light-headed. His knees slammed into the sidewalk. He reached out for the man next to him, but his hand found nothing but empty air. He looked around. Everyone was falling down.

"The water," he managed to say before the roiling in his gut drove him face-first into the sidewalk.

The water was poisoned. He had to warn them. Warn the other neighborhoods. The other Future Cities, too.

No comdee. No comms. But he had to warn them. Somehow.

He tried to stand, but couldn't. More screams reverberated along the street.

He pushed up on one arm, looking back toward his apartment. He had to warn them. He lunged, stretching for his home, and collapsed.

Aidan was dead before his head hit the ground.

...Naper Peak Regional Aerial Complex, Hyj-gon

Daemyn watched the airblade swing around the tall spire at the far end of the track. Once Brutus cleared it he spun the wings through a full rotation, then leveled out and slowed the engines.

"How are the readings?" Daemyn asked.

"Couldn't be better," Filson replied. From the other side Bakerton added, "Better than I'd expected, to be honest."

"Works for me." He clicked the comm to Brutus and said, "Another pass."

The test pilot kept the blade steady, tracing out a long, leisurely loop around the entire facility. Daemyn was confident in the design, and in the testing results. The engines would perform to full parameters when pushed to their limits. All the data pointed squarely in that direction. But still, to know for sure they had to fly it.

"Elsa," he said into the comm. "How are we doing on observers?"

"The usual activity," came the reply from her perch somewhere in the heights of the facility. *"Nothing of note. No one paying any particular attention to you, from anything I can tell."*

Not yet, anyway. That was about to change.

"I'll take what I can get." Daemyn took a breath. "Keep the sensors active." He toggled the comm back to Brutus. "All right. Take it through a maneuverability validation pattern. Full-throttle."

"Confirm," the pilot requested, *"maneuverability validation at full throttle."*

Filson's low whistle spoke for itself. Bakerton looked at Daemyn and asked, "You're sure about this?"

"Now or never," Daemyn replied. Over the comm he told Brutus, "Confirmed. When you're ready."

The test pilot didn't hesitate.

The engines roared – with a noise that was completely foreign to Daemyn. He'd spent his life watching and flying airblades with open-system engines relying on large air intakes as crucial components of their cooling systems. The closed-system engines on this blade had no intakes; they opened only to the aft, venting exhaust. The same self-contained design that had completely altered the airflow affected the engines soundwaves just as much. It was really going to take some getting used to.

Daemyn kept his eyes on the blade. Brutus flew the validation pattern deftly, with impeccable precision measured by a pilot's intuitions. Turn. Dive. Roll. Climb. Rotate. Turn. Loop. Daemyn didn't fly these patterns much any-more, but he still remembered them clearly. Watching Brutus fly, he almost imagined himself at the yoke.

"How's it look?"

Engrossed in the data scrolling into the control booth, Filson and Bakerton responded only with affirmative gestures. Daemyn could hardly blame them. He was equally captivated by the aerial flight before him.

Daemyn toggled the comm. He would have plenty of time to review the data back at WI. What he needed now was something different.

The airblade itself needed no validation. A somewhat older model, now a bit too obsolete for Airspar racing, its maneuverability ratings had been proven over years of testing. All of them with traditional artronium engines. The experimental engines had proven out in the lab. It had taken long enough to get there, but they'd done it. The engines were efficient, fast, and wouldn't overheat. All that was left was to confirm the synergy of the two together. Would the blade still fly as true? Would the engines hold up in the twists and turns of flight, pushed to the limits?

"One more pass," he told Brutus. "This time, fly it like your life depends on it."

Bakerton glanced away from the data displays long enough to make sure Daemyn saw the look on her face. Not that he needed the reminder that pushing the blade this hard in the first test flight was going against her recommendation.

"Copy," Brutus said.

He was a pilot like Daemyn. He understood.

Daemyn set down the comm and watched. Brutus forced the next turn even sharper. Pulled the barrel roll even tighter. The next climb, higher. The loop, harsher. The dive, steeper. Speed matched with ferocity, taking each roll, turn, and loop as viciously as he could force the blade to fly.

A steep climb. The airblade swung around the spire so close Daemyn couldn't see the gap between the tower and the blade. A plunging dive, spinning as he went. Brutus pulled up, leveled off. And then, finally, slowed down.

Bakerton let out the breath she'd been holding. "That was... *amazing!*"

Daemyn snatched up the comm. "Beautiful."

"Confirm, test flight concluded."

"Confirmed. Bring her in."

Filson and Bakerton had turned to face him. The pair stared at him. "What?"

"So much for the careful, cautious approach you've been insisting on all along." Filson shook his head. "Something to prove out there I don't know about?"

"He's right," Bakerton said. "What is going on with you tonight?"

Daemyn gestured to the displays. "How's the validation data look?"

"Amazing," Bakerton repeated.

Daemyn looked at Filson and raised a brow.

"Well, I don't know that I'd go quite that far." Filson shrugged. "But sure. You couldn't have asked for better results in the first test flight."

"Excellent."

Elsa cleared her throat. Daemyn hadn't even noticed her arrival in the control booth. He met her gaze and said, "What?"

"Are you going to tell them, or do I have to?"

"How bad is it?" Bakerton asked.

"Daemyn," Filson said, waggling a finger. "What are you up to?"

He sighed. There was no good way to do this. "All right. There's something we need to talk about."

...Kyetalle River, southwest of Durnow

Considering that nearly everyone had made the trek on foot, Utara was honestly surprised the refugees had managed to make it this far from Durnow in the course of one afternoon and evening. Fear was powerful motivator, however, and the horrors they had left behind had been more than enough to keep the feet moving.

With dusk rapidly plunging over the savannah, the meandering parade of humanity had coalesced into something approximating an encampment stretching along the riverbank. With the river to the west and a steep rise shielding them from the easterly winds, it was as safe a place as they could hope for to stay the night. To the north and the south, a line of campfires dotted the swatch of land between the river and the rise as far as the eye could see. Some people had brought tents, and others had erected makeshift shelter from whatever fabric and sticks or poles they could muster.

Walking back northward, Utara paused when she caught sight of a woman she had encountered several hours earlier. "Lina?" she asked. "How are your feet?"

The young mother looked genuinely shocked that Utara had remembered her name. It took her a second to collect herself. "Better. I didn't think walking without shoes would actually make them hurt less, but it did. Thank you."

"You're welcome." Too many of the city's residents only owned footwear suitable for urban living. As refugees, that would be one of the smaller challenges they would face in the days ahead. Utara knelt down to the woman's daughter, probably seven or eight years old. "And how are you feeling, Jupie?"

"Okay," the girl said, ducking behind her mother's leg.

Utara stood up again. "Sleep as much as you can," she told Lina, even though very few of the refugees would probably be able to fall into slumber tonight. "And make sure she does, for as long as she can."

Lina nodded. Utara turned to keep walking. A few strides off, she heard Jupie's meek voice ask, "Where are we going tomorrow, Mommy?"

Utara wished she knew the answer.

A bit further up the riverbank she helped a family restart their fading campfire, and a group of teenagers stabilize their precariously leaning shelter.

Most of the refugees, though, barely noticed her walking past them. The day's trauma was simply too much.

She glanced up the rise and saw a lone figure standing atop the slope a few dozen meters ahead. Rangezoomer to her eyes, J'ni was keeping watch on the savannah beyond the slope. And probably on something else, too.

Utara stepped around another circle of refugees by a campfire and headed toward the rise. She started to traverse the slope at an angle, but that just make the walk harder. So she stayed at the bottom of the rise, skirting the edge of the encampment, until she reached the point directly beneath J'ni.

Utara compelled her legs to trudge up the steep slope of the rise. With each step her feet sank into the dirt, making every stride seem more difficult than the last. Finally she reached the top, and stopped at her old friend's side.

On the western horizon, the last scarlet glimpse of the sun barely curved above the endlessly straight line of the savannah. Its rays lit the indigo sky with brilliant hues of oranges and reds. At any other time, Utara would have found it a beautiful sight, perfectly suited for another shared sundowner. But not tonight.

The sunset gave the silhouette of Durnow in the distance the appearance of an entire city ablaze with towering flames. Utara knew that wasn't really happening, of course, but her heart still skipped a beat at the image before her. Durnow still stood. Several wide columns of smoke did rise from behind its walls, and the air above the city was blurred by a haze of dissipated soot.

Without a word, J'ni handed her the rangezoomer. Utara took it and held it up to her eyes. A flick of the toggle adjusted the focus, and Durnow came into crisp clarity. It was too dark now to distinguish the buildings or identify the neighborhoods. Still, the dark silhouette against the sky provided enough contrast for Utara to see what had captivated J'ni's attention – bursts of color, flashes of light, erupting against the darkness. They looked like torchflies. But they weren't.

"It's good you got out when you did," J'ni insisted, her voice quiet in the stiff, chill breeze of the savannah's onrushing night.

Still trying to pick out her parent's neighborhood amid the silhouette, Utara offered only a noncommittal "sure" in reply.

J'ni said nothing more until Utara lowered the rangezoomer to her waist a few minutes later. Then she waited for Utara to look at her. "You're going back, aren't you? Into... *that.*"

"I have to," Utara said. "Not just for my parents. For everyone who's trapped. We have to get them out of there."

"How?"

"I don't know yet. But I'll find a way."

J'ni put a hand on her arm. "It's not your responsibility to save them, Utara."

"If I don't," she replied, her eyes unerring from her friend's gaze, "who will?"

EIGHTEEN

...refugee convoy, southwest of Durnow

"I*'m sorry, Counselor Fireheart,*" the voice on the long-range comdee said. "*But there's really nothing I can do to help.*"

"I appreciate your time in any case," Utara replied. Somehow she compelled her voice to remain polite. "Many blessings."

"*Many blessings to you, as well. Good luck.*"

"Thank you."

Once the transmission ended, Utara immediately checked the battery indicator. Still over ninety percent power, even after her seven comms. At least something was going in her favor. Her attempts to reach Aidan and the PDS field office in Blonkas had been unable to make a connection to the receiving network. The other comms had gone through, but hadn't produced any results. She dropped the device back into her slingbag.

J'ni strode up to her. "That bad?"

"Nothing. Yet again."

"Disgusting. What excuse did this one give?"

"His agency has several transport shuttles that could fit a sizeable number of the refugees, but they're only capable of landing at the transportation hub. Which doesn't do us any good out here, obviously."

"Are you serious?"

"Unfortunately."

"Bureaucrats whose primary responsibility is disaster relief and emergency response rely on shuttles that can only land at hubs."

"So he says, anyway. But there's no reason to doubt him."

"The very kinds of places most likely to be among those knocked out of commission in a major disaster."

"Yes."

J'ni kicked a rock. Hard. "How do these people still have their jobs?"

Right now, Utara wondered that, too. "I need a break."

"Understandable," her friend said, patting her shoulder. "I'm sure you'll think of something, or someone will come through for us somehow. Another hour or two won't matter at this point."

Utara wasn't so sure they had any time to spare, for these refugees or for her parents and everyone else still left inside Durnow, but she couldn't deny that her frustration had started to get the better of her. At every turn, she kept running up against obstacles. A woman in the PDS who'd genuinely wanted to help – Utara had heard the heartbreak in her voice – but had neither funds nor vehicles at her disposal. A man who'd offered that he might be able to round up a few shuttles – five or six weeks from now. The budget officer who could allocate some funds, as long as Utara was willing to wait the two months processing time. Each one of them had a reason they couldn't help the Durnow refugees. Legitimate reasons, even, for some of them. But the end result was always the same – no one was stepping up to make a difference.

Utara looked down the long, straggling line of refugees ahead of them. "How far do you think we should try to get today?"

Shielding her eyes with her hand, J'ni checked the angle of the sun. "A few more kilometers if we can. So, maybe three more hours."

"That's enough distance?"

"It should be." J'ni kept her eyes on the sky. Early this morning, just after dawn, four separate pairs of security drones from the city had flown overhead. They hadn't deviated from their flight path or even slowed down as they passed over the refugees, so the drones probably hadn't been conducting direct surveillance. But the impact on the refugees had been immediate all the same. The people didn't trust the AI or the drones, not even a little bit, and they wanted to get away from them as quickly as possible. "They're sticking to the routine reconnaissance patrols for now."

"Let's hope so," Utara said.

"Plus, that will leave us with a good amount of daylight to get a camp set up. It won't be as rushed. I think they could use that."

"Yes. That would be good."

For a few minutes they walked side by side in silence. No longer focused on making the comms, Utara started to notice things. The sweating dripping down her back beneath her shirt. The sun beating against her skin. The ache in her feet and the dryness in her mouth. She took a long drink of water from her canteen.

"Maybe I'm approaching this wrong," Utara said. "Somewhere on Prime there has to be a young reporter who might see potential to break out of the pack with a humanitarian crisis story. If it goes big quickly enough, it might force the government to act."

"Wouldn't be the first time," J'ni agreed. "I'm not sure it'd happen fast, though. At least in terms of helping this group. But longer term, sure."

Utara nodded. "At least I could reach out and see if I can put something in motion. A parallel track to trying the government angle, too."

"No harm in that. Still, don't get your hopes up. The timing couldn't be worse right now for trying to get people to pay attention to depressing news."

"Why's that?"

J'ni gave a wry smile. "You were just at Occanan. You figure it out."

Occanan. Of course. "Airspar."

"Right." J'ni gestured toward the column of trudging refugees. "Good luck getting anyone to want to see this, when they can be watching the races."

Suddenly, Utara had her plan. "J'ni! You're a genius!"

"I know. But why, specifically?"

"Airspar." In an instant she'd snatched the long-range comdee from the slingbag. "That's the answer."

"It is?"

"Well, not Airspar itself." The hand with the bigger, heavier device gesticulating in air, she dug through her slingbag for her regular personal comdee. "The pilots, or owners, or whatever they are. You know."

"Actually, I don't. What in the Hells are you talking about?"

"The ones with all the money."

"Oh, *that* narrows it down."

"The venturists." Utara finally found it. She tapped the screen with her thumb and brought up her contacts list. "The ones I met at Occanan."

"What do they have to do with anything?"

"Here." She opened the entry she wanted and handed the comdee to J'ni. Then she readied the long-range device in both hands. "Read me the numbers."

"This is a joke, right?"

"J'ni..."

"You have Daemyn Wynde's personal comdee code? Since when?"

"Read. Me. The *numbers*."

J'ni's hands flew up defensively. "All right. I will. Calm down."

Utara tapped them in as J'ni read the digits aloud. The device chimed, opening a line to the satellite. The tone pulsed three more times as the signal connected to the CasTel network.

Heart racing, Utara held her breath and waited.

...Wynde Industries

Daemyn swiped his hand, clearing all the data displayed on the desk's surface. "Anything else we need to follow up on?"

Reiton glanced to the handwritten list on his transi. "The only other item we owe a response about is Celia's offer sheet."

"I thought she hadn't decided yet which angle to pursue first."

"She hasn't. But she did update with the three highest-priority opportunities."

"When was that?"

"Just after the race."

"Right." Daemyn made sure his stare made the point.

Reiton laughed. "In case you weren't entirely focused on it, her suggestions were the following. One, the World Parks. With New Romas so short on funding, the government is looking to unload line items that consistently produce deficits over revenue. It's unclear, at least so far, if the World Parks are on the table for sell-off, but it would be a major opportunity if they are."

"Agreed."

"Two, the Hastorian Forest Preserve in Rombovia. The last grandson of the duke recently passed away. He was the last in the line to hold title to the preserve in its entirety. Under the terms of the duke's will, the preserve must either be sold as a single unit, or each of the thirty-nine next-generation heirs —"

"Thirty-nine!" Daemyn slapped his palm on the table.

"Yes. Each of them would inherit a share."

"One-thirty-ninth shares, sold off individually, are basically worthless."

"Precisely. Celia believes we should be able to make the high offer to the heirs pretty easily. But it's a lot less land area than the World Parks, so the long-term prospects are considerably lower, too."

"Makes sense to me."

"And third, the investment in the Future City nature preserves."

Daemyn had been gazing out the conference room window, but now his eyes snapped back to Reiton's. "The what now?"

Holtspring peered at him. "You really didn't read the memo, did you?"

"I skimmed it. Well, most of it."

Reiton cleared his throat.

"Some of it."

"Finally, the honesty. When Utara Fireheart was with the rest of us on the yacht, the idea came up in the conversation." Still grinning victoriously at him, Reiton quickly summarized the proposal. "And from what Celia has heard from her preliminary inquiries to New Romas, it definitely sounds like the government would go for it."

"I can see why," Daemyn said. "The idea has a lot of potential for good publicity for us — and in making a difference for the residents of the cities. But what's the math for putting it third on the list?"

"I don't think she went into detail, but let me double-check." Reiton set down the transi and spun his chair to check his compupod. It only took him a moment. "She didn't specify. I imagine I'm wondering the same things as you."

"It just seems so... small. Relative to the other two, at least."

"Yes."

Daemyn leaned back in his chair. As a group, the venturists had committed to devoting a segment of their interests toward conservation. Some of their projects emphasized preserving land from development; others focused on wildlife habitats and endangered species. In either case, they invested in opportunities that would ultimately become profitable over time, usually through tourism revenue or tax deductions. But the nature preserves in the Future Cities seemed to fall short on both measures. Even in the aggregate, they only preserved a small amount of land and barely sustainable breeding populations of species. Tourism to the preserves was, to put it kindly, unlikely – and Daemyn didn't see another angle for future payoff, either.

Still, Celia knew what she was doing. She hadn't steered Daemyn wrong yet. He wasn't about to start second-guessing her now, at least not without a lot more information to evaluate first.

"All right," Daemyn said. In the corridor Elsa stopped at the conference room door, waiting for an indication from him. He motioned for her to join them. "Tell Celia I'm in for the full amount previously discussed. And that she has my vote on the top-three list, too, although I'd like to hear more on the Loorriri option."

"Will do. Same for me."

"Perfect." Once Elsa took a seat opposite Daemyn at the table, he asked, "What have you got?"

"Two updates. Project Lariat and Loorriri."

"Lariat first."

"I'll warn you. It's... interesting."

Daemyn looked at Reiton. "I'm not sure I like the sound of that."

"The guy who did the hack finally surfaced, offering for sale high-value trade secrets from Wynde Industries. No detail about what it is, simply that it's extremely valuable. We made contact through his requested channels, and set up a comm. Even with all the precautions we took, he still knew I was WI corporate intelligence."

Daemyn leaned back in chair. "Normally, I'd predict that ended it right there. But if it's interesting, I'm guessing not."

"Right." Elsa ran a hand across her face. "Once I was busted, there was no point to pretend. I offered to outbid everyone else, and he acknowledged that we could. But he wouldn't go for it."

"Why not? That doesn't make any sense."

"Like I said, interesting. I told him to name his price. His response – and this is verbatim – was, 'Why should I give it back to you?' I knew better than to argue the morality or legality of it with him. So I was honest. I told him I wasn't sure, beyond the money, what answer he wanted."

Daemyn nodded. "What did he say?"

"Again, verbatim – 'Contact me again if you figure it out.' And that's when the comm ended."

Reiton heaved a sigh. "This is some sort of game to him? Is this one of your old university rivals pulling a prank on us or something?"

"I don't think so," Daemyn said. "Hackers like this, the ones whose talent is so extreme they don't really know how to use it, don't think that way. And I really do believe it's not about the money for him. If he's that good, he could take whatever money he needed any time and never get caught. He wants something else."

"Any ideas?" Elsa asked. "Because my team is coming up empty."

"Not off the top of my head," Daemyn admitted. "But now that I know the context, I have some direction to focus my thinking. I'll let you know."

"We'll keep at it, too, obviously," Elsa said. "Here's what we've been able to find out about what's going on in Loorriri."

It wasn't much. Only a few media reports had surfaced, and they were very sparse on specifics. One thing was clear, though – in at least some of the Future Cities, some of the residents had fled the deteriorating conditions for the untamed wilderness of the continent. How many cities and how many refugees was impossible to glean. But it was more than one, and more than a few.

Reiton met Daemyn's gaze. "I'll loop Celia in on this right away."

"Definitely. Rustle, too."

"Reacquiring the Project Lariat data is the top priority," Elsa said, "but I have my team monitoring news and data from Loorriri every hour."

"Good," Daemyn said. He pushed off from his chair and stood. "Let's see what we can figure out. On all of this."

After he left the conference room, he went straight to his office and dropped himself into his desk chair. He closed his eyes, mulling over the inscrutable comments from the Project Lariat hacker. If he didn't want money, what did he desire instead? Clearly it wasn't fame, either, or he wouldn't be hiding in the shadows. He ran down other options, trying to find an explanation that fit.

The comdee trilling broke into his thoughts. Elsa couldn't have another update that quickly, could she? Daemyn looked at the desk comm panel and realized the alert tone was something different. He spun his chair to the small table beside his desk. It was his personal comdee. He picked it up and looked at the incoming number. "Who's that?"

For a moment he hesitated.

Then his finger moved and swiped the screen to answer it. "Daemyn Wynde."

...Sturgeon's Bounty restaurant, Cascadia

Monson had met a fair number of code hackers in his time in corporate intelligence, and each time he met another that person invariably was utterly different from the one before. They came in all heights and proportions, from all faiths and cultural affiliations, from the most prestigious universities to self-taught savants, and attired in every manner of dress and coiffed in any imaginable style of hair or headwear. Yet somehow, amid all that, they always shared one thing in common – what could only be described as a truly peculiar taste in places to hold clandestine meetings.

This particular restaurant, to Monson's eye, was trying a bit too hard to offer a little bit of everything. The soft ambient music was definitely Aquarian – Monson recognized some of the folk songs from his childhood – while the art pieces and decorative furnishings were Terran. The food being consumed by the patrons around him consisted of principally traditional Aladarian dishes; the wine and spirits list was stocked almost exclusively with Faytan brands. The dissonance was, frankly, bizarre.

Still, Monson had to credit the hacker for his selection of establishment. The main seating room was crowded, filled with a constant murmur of conversation punctuated by an occasional shout, laugh, or raucous cheer. The words exchanged in any given booth, so long as they were spoken with a modest degree of circumspection, would be almost impossible to overhear. Which was exactly what both men wanted.

Monson was about to reach for his glass when a short, gawky man slid into the bench seat opposite him. He settled into the booth, avoiding eye contact. His overgrown hair was a week away from reaching unmanageably unkempt, and the scraggly beard was only marginally more trimmed. After the other man set his comdee on the table before him, their eyes met.

"You brought the money?"

Monson used two fingers to reach up the hem of his left sleeve and withdraw a wrapped stack of hundred-dract coins. The precious metal glittered in the dim lighting, enough to make entirely clear the denomination and quantity of the coins. The other man nodded, and Monson slid the roll back up his sleeve.

He looked at the hacker. "You brought the schematics?"

The man tapped the end of his comdee, popping out a small datacard in its base to let Monson see it before returning it to the slot in the comdee. "I'll upload them onto this once our deal closes."

Smart. Any attempt to rob the hacker would only leave the thief empty-handed. Even if it was a bluff, it was a good play; it sweetened the odds in favor of a deal. "Perfect."

"So," the hacker said. The eye contact ended. "You're Marx Monson, corporate intel at Grandell Motors."

Monson hadn't revealed any of that in their brief exchange of messages, of course. But if the hacker was anything close to as skilled as he would have to be to steal engineering designs from Wynde Industries, he would've been able to figure it out no matter how hard Monson tried to prevent it. The first test of the man's veracity had been passed. Now Monson had to pass his.

"That's right." His part of the dance included not asking the man's name this early in the negotiation. "And I'd like to purchase what you're offering."

"You don't even know what it is."

"I know enough," Monson said, making sure the words came out explanatory rather than arrogant. "For one, Wynde Industries thinks it's valuable enough to make it very difficult to hack. For another, you think it's very valuable or you wouldn't be soliciting offers from competing bidders. And if both of those things are true, then Grandell Motors would front pretty much any sum of money necessary to acquire it."

"Maybe I'm bluffing."

"It's possible, I suppose. But unlikely."

"Why do you think that?"

"Because if you only cared about the money, you'd simply set up some sort of backchannel auction and hand it over to the highest bidder. The fact that you're not following that course, that you want to meet with a buyer before closing a deal, tells me that you're after something else. Or, rather, something more."

The hacker glanced down at his comdee, then up at Monson. "Let's say you're right. Why should I sell it to you?"

Monson leaned forward, and made his voice almost conspiratorial. "I think what you're really asking is, what is it that I think you really want?"

"Right. What do you offer me that none of my other bidders can?"

"A challenge."

He waited for the other man's reaction. His eyebrows rose, but he said nothing.

"A challenge even bigger than successfully hacking Wynde Industries in the first place," Monson continued. "I am well aware how difficult that feat was. I may not be much of a writer of code myself, but breaching security at Wynde Industries has been a goal of numerous corporate intelligence operatives, from all manner of competitors, for some time. No one's accomplished it before – no one until you."

The hacker smiled. "No one in corporate intel."

"Perhaps so," Monson conceded. "Still, you've achieved something many of your peers dreamt of doing, and could not. What mountain do you tackle next? What could possibly live up to this?"

"I'm listening."

"You're quite the hacker, apparently. You've beaten the very best individuals on Prime. But have you ever faced off against an AI? And to be clear, I don't mean some low-level system to keep the trains running on time or the flights at a transportation hub taking off and landing in an orderly progression. I mean the biggest AIs Prime has ever seen. Supercomputers so powerful they run city management for entire urban populations."

"The Future Cities, huh? Sure, it'd be harder than beating people. But at the end of the day, stealing data is only so difficult, no matter how fast the opponent is."

"I'm sure that's true," Monson said. "But much more than data theft would be involved. You haven't heard about it on the news – and I'm quite sure New Romas and Boynton Logistics Dynamics will do everything they can to keep it out of the news for absolutely as long as possible – but something very wrong is happening in Loorriri. Something I don't think the people at Boynton will be able to stop."

Now he had the hacker's attention, all right. "Going into the AIs to shut them down?"

"When they know you're coming and will try to stop you."

The hacker sat back until his head rested against the upright wooden back of the bench seat. He blew out a long, heavy breath. "You're right, Master Monson. No one else from your side of things could top that. Maybe only PIS."

"I'll be candid. This situation in Loorriri may end up in the Intelligence Service's portfolio before it's all over. If you work with me on this, we may find ourselves working with them to address it."

The hacker thought about it for a long moment. He took another deliberate, slow breath. Finally he said, "I'd need my expenses covered, of course. Travel, lodging, and the like."

"Naturally. And double your usual daily stipend for contract work."

The hacker nodded. "All right, Master Monson. You've got yourself a deal."

"Excellent." Monson gave a genuine smile. "Do you have time to stay for a meal? To celebrate our arrangement?"

"Sure."

Monson raised a hand in the air, indicating to the server he'd spoken to earlier that he was now ready for the menus.

"By the way," the other man said, "my name is Kirkland Oggust."

NINETEEN

...refugee convoy

"*D*aemyn Wynde.*"

It wasn't until she heard his voice that Utara realized she probably should have figured out how she planned to greet him when the comm connected. Calling him Daemyn seemed too personal; Master Wynde too formal. In an instant, she decided simply to skip the whole problem.

"This is Utara Fireheart," she said. "We met –"

"*I remember.*"

"I apologize for not contacting your office for an appointment to comm you, but with the urgency of the situation I couldn't afford the delay."

"*No need to explain.*"

She wondered if he was serious, or being polite. "I know this will probably sound presumptuous, but I commed to ask for your help."

He paused. "*Are you back in Blonkas?*"

"Actually, no."

"*Durnow?*"

"Not exactly."

"*You're off the regular comm network, aren't you?*"

"That's right. I'm on a long-range comdee via satellite direct transmission."

"*That makes sense.*" He chuckled. "*Sorry. I thought I was hearing quality degradation in the feed. Please, go ahead.*"

"As I said, I commed you to ask for your help." Quickly she explained the plight of the refugees, then circled back to summarize the crisis in Durnow that had led to their exodus from the city. "They won't last long out here. We can make do on water from the river temporarily, but we don't have food, or any method for obtaining it, much less medicines, clothing, or other necessities."

"And the government hasn't offered any prospect of relief, despite your best efforts to instigate a response, so you're reaching out to me, and my venturist friends, as an alternative of last resort."

His words weren't delivered as an accusation, just a statement of fact. Utara bit back the truth's sting and tried to laugh a bit as she said, "It's that obvious?"

"Not really. But on the government's ineptitude, it's sadly predictable."

On any other occasion, she might have argued with him. But not right now. Not when he was still on the line, still listening. "I pursued multiple angles within the PDS, of course, as well as contacting several other agencies in New Romas."

"Nobody stepped up?"

"Not with anything that would matter in the kind of timeframe these refugees are facing, unfortunately."

"The other things would probably take a few days to arrange, but an emergency food drop is easy enough. I could get started —"

"Maybe as a backup plan for the short term," she said, regretting having to interrupt him when he seemed willing not only to hear her out, but also to take action to help the refugees. "But long term, supply deliveries won't make it tenable. Between the wildlife and the outlaws, the threats are too great."

He paused. *"You're thinking of... what? An airlift? An evacuation?"*

She swallowed hard. "Yes."

"Grassland terrain, is that right? Fairly flat?"

"Low hills and rises, but yes, it's the savannah. There's a wide riverbed close by, as well, if that makes a difference."

"It might." His tapping fingers echoed over the feed. *"How many people are we talking?"*

"The refugees? Roughly six thousand at my location."

He whistled loud enough she heard it over the comm. *"I'll be honest. That's only going to happen if we can make multiple flights to the location. Even best case, with the kind of craft we'd need to use to land or hover in that terrain, it would take trips back and forth to get everyone."*

"I can keep the refugees under control, if that's what you're worried about."

"That's helpful, yes. But I'm mainly worried about resistance. Anything trying to oppose our flight in or out. These won't be military craft."

"I see. I can tell you that the security drones from the city have been maintaining patrols but not interfering in any way. The only issue might be the outlaws. I could see them trying to shoot down or steal a shuttle. From here, I have no way of knowing if any of them are in this area, though."

"Let me deal with that, then," Daemyn said. *"What about Durnow itself?"*

Utara blinked. "I'm sorry?"

"Durnow. From what you described, it sounds pretty terrible. You want to evacuate the people there, too, right?"

Her pulse started racing. "Well, I – I can't. You've already offered more than enough. I couldn't possibly ask –"

"You didn't ask. I did."

She caught herself smiling. "Right. If we're being honest, then yes. I do think the city needs to be evacuated."

"That's a much bigger endeavor, obviously. By fifty-fold or more, if we tried to get everyone out."

"Yes."

"Is there any chance that landing and takeoff at the intercontinental hub is an option? Without that, the types of transports we could deploy would be too restricted. We wouldn't be able to move even close to the numbers that we'd need."

"Best case, air traffic control is offline but the airstrips are open. Worst case, it's unusable. I have no way of knowing what we'll find when we get there, not with the comms down."

"I may have an angle to work on that, too."

"Understood."

"Not to mention, there's no way of knowing if the drones or the AI would let us even approach the city, either, much less land there and evacuate."

"Correct."

"One step at a time." Daemyn's fingers tapped again. *"How's your power charge? How long will I be able to reach you at these codes?"*

"I should be fine for several days with this one, and I have a second one that is fully charged in my bag."

"Perfect."

Utara took a deep breath. "I'm sorry I brought you into this. It's asking an awful lot from someone I barely met. You're sure you're —"

"Trust me, Utara," he said. *"I say no to people all the time."*

"All right."

"One more question."

"Anything."

"I'm sure I can find a cargo ship or shipping vessel offshore as a temporary drop for the evacuees while we're in process. But once we get the people out, where are we going to take them?"

Utara smiled. "Actually, that's the one piece of good news I managed to acquire."

～◯

... *Grandell Motors Corporate Intelligence Division*

"But this is the part that surprised me," Dana Bristow said. "Those five patents? The designs all originated with the same engineer."

"Really?"

Monson glanced down at the files displayed on the tabletop in front of him as though he were double-checking that he hadn't read them wrong. In truth, he couldn't have cared less about their topic of discussion. He needed to learn more about the current situation in Loorriri, he was overdue for checking in with Kirkland Oggust to see what the hacker had uncovered from within Boynton Logistics Dynamics, and he had considerably more progress to make before he could even think about approaching the leadership of the Prime Intelligence Service to insert himself into their crisis operations. But for both Dana Bristow right now and Grandell Motors in general, he had to keep up appearances of another ordinary day in the corporate intelligence division. At least for a few more hours.

"It's not on the applications."

"That is certainly intriguing," Monson said.

"I thought so."

It was risky, too. If the patent application was proven to be falsified, even on something as comparatively insignificant as the name of the individual engineer who had begun the design work in the Worty computational electronics division, it would become legally null and void – opening the technology up for immediate use by all of Worty's competitors. The interesting question, though, was which way would be better for Grandell Motors to play the situation. Contest the patent? Or steal away the brilliant designer whose identity Worty was obviously trying to conceal?

"How'd you figure it out?" he asked.

Bristow launched into an explanation of the technical similarities that had led her to the conclusion. By the time she finished, he had no doubt she was correct. It was a good catch. Monson was impressed.

He scanned the names on the files. "Is one of them accurate? Or are they pulling a distraction on all five?"

"All five is my guess. From what I've seen previously from the names listed on these applications, none of them is capable of generating the whole set."

"Makes sense," Monson said. "Let's see if we –"

The loud trilling of his comdee startled them both. He snatched the device and silenced it, not needing to check the screen. That alert tone – and the fact that the device had emitted a signal in audio mode at all – could only mean one thing.

"My apologies," he said. "But I need to attend to this immediately."

She waved off the explanation, as they had each done for the other many times before. "Get to it. I'll keep digging."

"Definitely," he told her. "I agree it has great potential."

"Thanks," she said, already back to focusing on her compupod.

Monson hurried to his office, shut and locked the door, and activated the privacy bubble over his desk. Taking a second to catch his breath, he tapped the comdee's screen to reconnect to the man who'd tried to contact him.

"Hybollo."

"It's Monson."

"That didn't take long."

"I've made this is a priority."

"Me, too." One of the best Senior Agents in the PIS, the Suterran had long proven himself a trusted resource. They'd met years earlier, when Birto Hybollo was still serving in the Unified Forces' special operations and Monson had barely begun working in corporate intelligence. As they'd both advanced their careers, they'd provided beneficial information or a favorable word of reference for one another on numerous occasions. In a field with so much betrayal and backstabbing, Hybollo was one of the few individuals whose loyalty Monson never doubted. That was why Monson hadn't hesitated to call in a favor this morning. *"I have your update on Blonkas."*

"And?"

"They're all dead."

"Who?"

"Everyone. Including four operatives for PIS stationed there."

Monson inhaled slowly, then exhaled equally carefully. "The drones alone couldn't possibly have done that. Not in those numbers."

"Agreed. We'd have received word from at least one of our assets. Plus, satellite reconnaissance would have detected the muzzle bursts from gunfire of that sort of intensity."

"Have you figured out what the AI did?"

"I think so. I've been looking at all the data – vidfeeds, infrared cams, everything we have pointed down there. One thing it showed, definitively, is no more human life within the city walls. Anyway, after a few hours I finally got a hit from the chemical spectrometer scans. If I'm interpreting it correctly, the AI formulated a mixture of eridanthol and vanitorine and then released it into the water supply. Highly toxic to all forms of biological life."

Monson didn't know the chemistry of it from memory, but he could pull the research and determine the implications quickly enough. If the poison could be aerialized, as well, the danger was astronomically larger. "How can I help?"

"I need a sense of the status inside Boynton's operations. As quickly as you can get it. From human assets in the company, if you have any reliable ones, plus whatever that hacker can dig up in the meantime, too."

"Of course."

"The situation is escalating quickly, Marx. More than the toxin. You might need to be on the ground in Port Vulcania for this."

"I'll leave tonight."

"Perfect."

"What else is escalating?"

"Some of the AIs are taking action to pursue the refugees outside the city walls. It started with Blonkas, which appears to be hunting down the former residents who'd fled to the hills. Satellite feeds suggest three other cities – not the closest ones to Blonkas, either – may be starting to do the same."

"Pursuing the refugees using the security drones?"

"Correct. The cannons on the city walls have a very short range. The drones are the AI's only physical weaponry capable of extending outward."

"How far?"

"Assuming a fully charged power core and optimized flight speeds to minimize the rate of depletion, twelve hours of flight time."

"Enough to wipe out everything in a hundred-kilometer radius."

"Farther," Hybollo said, *"if the drone was able to take off in one city and recharge its power core in another."*

Monson caught himself holding his breath. Given the parameters of how the AIs managed resources, they almost certainly would not launch a drone without a high level of confidence it would be able to remain in service. Consequently, a city-to-city journey was quite unlikely – unless carried out with coordination between the AIs beforehand.

"You want to make sure Boynton keeps the AIs cut off from each other."

"Exactly," Hybollo said. *"Which is why I need your eyes and ears there. PIS is obligated to build sufficient proof before we can justify seizing control of their facility, and until then I need to rely on other assets."*

"Understood. I'll let you know once I have more. Comm me if necessary sooner."

"Will do."

Monson set the comdee on his desk and rose from his chair. He had no time to waste.

...Wynde Industries

He'd been worried it might take all day to find a time when everyone would be available to discuss the operation he was planning. Instead, less than an hour had passed since the comms requests had gone out, accompanied by a hastily written executive summary and synopsis of resources needed. Reiton settled into the chair next to him, and Daemyn activated the comm microphone on the desk.

"Everyone can hear me?"

On the full-wall vidscreen, three heads in three separate vidboxes nodded.

"Did the ES and synopsis make sense?"

"For once," Sage said, grinning at him, "they actually did."

Rustle and Celia indicated their agreement, too. "In that case," Daemyn said, "let me elaborate on a few things we've been working up in the meantime."

Briefly he described his updated plan. As many transport aircraft as they could muster on short notice, either venturist-owned or rented, would be flown to Loorriri. First they would airlift the Durnow refugees gathered on the savannah kilometers distant from the city. The number of available aircraft capable of landing and taking off in open terrain was likely to be fairly small, so the plan assumed numerous repeat round trips over many hours would be necessary to complete the airlift. Then, after confirming the facts on the ground with the local observers, including their contact Utara Fireheart, they would attempt to evacuate as many of the residents remaining within in the city walls as they could. All aircraft could participate in this stage, using the intercontinental transportation hub as a landing and loading point – assuming flight into the Future City would even be possible at all.

"I've reviewed the cost estimates carefully," Reiton added. "It's not a trivial expense, particularly in the short term. On the other hand, the opportunity cost in time for the transports is not significant, only a matter of a few days, and the expenses for fuel can be recouped on future tax returns as a charitable donation."

"That's the basis," Rustle asked, "of your recommendation that we not consider the financial layout alone as a reason to reject the proposal?"

"Correct."

"The financials don't particularly trouble me," Celia said. "But the downside risks are substantial. The potential of damage to the transports or injury to pilots or crew. Possibly even losses or deaths, if events progressed more toward a worst-case scenario."

"I'm also concerned," Sage added, "that some quarters in the government may not view favorably our circumvention of what they view as their responsibilities."

"Which they're failing to fulfill, naturally," Rustle muttered. "Nonetheless, it's a consideration we can't ignore."

"On the other side of the equation," Daemyn insisted, "the prospects for substantial upsides to the operation are significant. We have been making a major effort to publicize our conservation and humanitarian efforts, and this would be a vivid demonstration of our genuine commitment to those values."

The others nodded, but no one jumped in to agree with him.

"As you all know," Rustle said, "I have been looking into the dearth of information available about conditions in the Future Cities since we spoke to Counselor Fireheart in Occanan a few days ago. I'm now convinced the government has imposed a deliberate comms blackout over the cities. Something is going on that they don't want the public to know. Gaining access to the refugees and the information they possess could be critical to understanding the truth."

"Which will bring us further heat from some within the government, no doubt," Reiton pointed out. "But reporters love a scandal. Especially an illegal cover-up. That can work in our favor significantly, I think, and undermine any attempts by governmental actors to retaliate against us."

"Maybe." Sage glanced at something on her desk. "The operation may provide some soft capital, but I think its value is quite unpredictable given how limited our information is currently."

"Celia," Daemyn said. "Your last round of investment analyses included a substantial section on the idea of subsidizing the Future City nature preserves. How should we view this operation in light of that?"

"The original impetus for that idea was quite similar to what we've been saying just now, actually," she replied. "Primarily about investing in building goodwill and furthering our conservation objectives. I had been examining a relatively small potential for direct financial gains, based around the notion that creating an ongoing relationship with the Future Cities would facilitate winning contracts down the line for retrofitting and upgrading their obsolete physical and technological infrastructures, some of which would be quite substantial. To be honest, though, I have a completely different concern now, in light of what Rustle has found. Or his lack of findings, rather."

"That they're hiding something important?" Rustle asked.

"Exactly." Celia exhaled sharply. "If Durnow is in serious trouble – and even more so if all of the Future Cities are in crisis, as your findings imply – then the *last* thing we want to be doing is making long-terms investments there."

"Yet another reason," Rustle said, "that the sooner we find out the truth the better."

Everyone nodded.

"I don't oppose the rescue operation in principle, even with the risks. It's the right thing to do," Reiton said. "My point of hesitation, however, is whether we could end up in a situation where we've not only done the airlift, but taken on the moral obligation to house, feed, and care for the refugees on an ongoing basis. *That* is the government's obligation, without question. In other words, when we airlift the refugees out of Loorriri, where are we going to take them?"

"I don't have a definitive answer on that yet," Daemyn admitted. "But we have preliminary approval to bring the refugees to the Aladarian Guard base at Steamer Point."

"That works for me," Reiton said. "A government location, particularly a military facility, will undeniably put the burden of the refugee's care in their hands."

"All right," Daemyn said. "What resources can we bring to bear?"

By the time the meeting ended a few minutes later and the three vid-boxes disappeared, he didn't know whether to laugh, cry, or punch someone. He had Reiton's support for diverting transports and money from Wynde Industries, and Rustle had agreed to use his connections to line up several dozen transports capable of evacuating from the city's transportation hub. Sage and Celia had offered to float him short-term loans to help pay any immediate expenses WI couldn't cover with dracts-on-hand, but nothing more substantial. Beyond that, though, Daemyn had come up empty.

He looked at Reiton. "I can't believe it."

"I'm sorry."

Daemyn ran a hand through his unkempt hair. "If that shuttle hadn't been there when I was a boy, I wouldn't be here. I'd be dead."

"I know."

"They're my friends. Why can't they see it? Why we have to help these people."

"Yes, they're your friends," Reiton assured him, reaching out to put a hand on his shoulder. "But you're not asking for a small favor as a friend, like sharing a bottle of Aladarian branibon after a bad breakup or making time to attend a child's recital. This is a business decision, too."

"Not for me."

"I realize that. But for the rest of us, it has to be. And I can't blame them for assessing the odds differently than I did."

"Odds? Or pity for your reckless best friend and his childhood trauma?"

Reiton offered a smile. "We'll do everything we can to save as many people as possible, Daemyn."

"Right. But will it be enough?"

TWENTY

"**Q**uadrant Three clear," Elsa confirmed from the console station directly behind the pilot's seat in the cockpit. "Take us over to Four."

"Copy," Daemyn said, steering *Stalker* into a loop arc toward the next surveillance scanning point.

So far so good on their approach to the coordinates for the refugee's encampment. The sensors and scanners had picked up a few roving herds of animals, of course, but no indications of the presence of humans, much less one of the outlaw bands. If the next set of scans came back clear, they would give the signal to the assembled aircraft waiting offshore to begin the first run of evacuations from the camp.

Less than three minutes later, the *Stalker* reached the designated spot. Daemyn slowed the shuttlecraft into a hover and said, "Go."

"Scanning Quadrant Four."

It didn't take long for Elsa to speak again. "I might have something."

"Where?"

She read off the coordinates while Daemyn accessed the scanner report on the heads-up display layered over the cockpit viewport in front of him. "Passive scans continuing. Focusing on the anomaly."

Daemyn watched as the report updated live before his eyes. "Looks to me like it could be a line of trucks."

Elsa remained quiet while the scans homed in. "Thermal. Electro-chemical. Biological." She paused. "All in. It's a line of human vehicles, all right."

"Outlaws?"

"They've got tech. And weapons. Chem check confirms it."

Daemyn reached for the yoke. "Head their way?"

"One sec." She tapped furiously on her console. "Other scans came back clear. This one's the only anomaly in the quadrant." She rotated her chair away from the console to face forward, meeting his gaze in the reflection of the viewport. "Okay. Go."

With the coordinates already in the navigation system, Daemyn swept *WyndeStalker* into an acceleration so quick it pushed them back in their seats. "How close?"

"Half a klick. Out of visual range. Even if they have scanners, they'd have no reason to be expecting anything to have them operating. We should be good."

"Do you want me to back you up with a strafing run?"

She didn't hesitate. "Only if I call you in. Until we've secured or destroyed whatever anti-aircraft weapons they have, it's too risky."

"You sure?"

She chuckled at him. "Yes, I'm sure. I'm the bodyguard in the company, remember? Not the other way around."

"I'll be ready if you need me."

"I know," she said, putting a hand on his shoulder as she rose from her seat to head for the craft's interior corridor. "But we won't." She stopped in the doorway and glanced back. "Watch the feed if you want. I'll signal when we're clear."

"Good luck," he said as she disappeared. Daemyn flew the last three minutes to the drop point alone in the cockpit. He swung *Stalker* into a hover three meters above the savannah and opened the internal comm. "We're here."

He didn't expect a response, and Elsa knew it. He tapped the console and brought up *Stalker*'s internal cams. He watched Elsa open the ventral access hatch and hold it clear for her team from Wynde Industries' security division. One by one they jumped out the hatch, arms crossed over their chests for a quick drop to the grasses below. Elsa went last, tossing something approximating a salute to the cam before she swung her legs down through the portal and pulled the hatch closed behind her.

Daemyn swiped a finger, closing the cam feed. He tapped the console again, bringing up the vidcam and audio feeds from Elsa's helmet. Her team didn't talk much, though; mostly he heard her deliberate, measured breathing while they ran toward the outlaw convoy. The vidcam feed was a bit disorienting, with the constant glances side to side and the ups and down of bounding over the rises and ebbs of the savannah.

In what seemed like no time at all, the team had covered the half-kilometer to their destination. Following Elsa's hand signals, they spread out in a line along a rise overlooking the outlaw band. Seven or eight trucks. A few dozen men and women on foot. From this close, Daemyn could see how heavily armed they were. Unconsciously his hands reached for the yoke, ready to assist.

He needn't have worried. Elsa flashed another signal, and three of her men simultaneously lobbed grenades toward the trucks. A second later the pair of women on the far ends of the line opened fire with their sniper rifles. Daemyn could tell only from the muzzle flashes on Elsa's vidcam feed. He didn't hear a sound, and neither did the outlaws. The snipers dropped three outlaws each before the others realized something was going on – just in time for their front three trucks to explode in massive detonations.

While the snipers remained in place behind the rise, Elsa and the other five members of her team surged over it at a run. In seconds they were amid the trucks, rifles seemingly firing nonstop. Daemyn lunged forward to lower the volume on the audio feed before it deafened him. Then he sat back in his chair, trying to watch Elsa's helmet cam from a bit of distance before it made him dizzy.

She spun around a truck and gunned down a pair of outlaws. Diving feet first, she slid under the truck and came up on the other side with a grenade in one hand. A flick of her wrist sent it through the open side window of the next truck's cab, but she was meters away before it exploded. She knelt and squared her rifle, shooting upward to take down a pair of men on the back of another truck a good ten meters away.

Elsa sprang forward again, cutting diagonally across the line of devastated trucks and tracking her rifle as she went. Two more shots sent a man and a woman flopping lifeless to the ground. She was still running when the first shout of "clear!" came over the audio feed. Elsa slowed, then stopped, keeping her rifle ready.

One by one, her team checked in. Two women's voices last – the snipers, Daemyn assumed – each with a "visual mark, all clear" before Elsa declared, "All clear confirmed. Mission accomplished." For just a moment, she heaved a breath. "Good job, everyone."

A loud *click* sounded over the audio feed. "You ready, Daemyn?"

Hands on the yoke he said, "On my way."

"Copy."

"Remind me," he added, "never to get on your shig list."

For the first time since they'd arrived on Loorriri, Elsa laughed.

～

…Millennium Grand Hotel, Port Vulcania

His latest comm concluded, Monson checked the comdee to see if any new messages had arrived during the conversation. This time, none had. He walked from the wide window overlooking the city to the bedroom door, and opened it. If he hadn't known better, he would have thought the suite's spacious sitting room was empty.

Despite the richly appointed furnishings surrounding him, Kirkland Oggust still sat on the floor beneath the wall-mounted vision pod. Cross-legged with his back against the base of the wall, his fingers flew across the keypad of his compupod like the madly skittering legs of an insect. The only sign of the nature of his work was two thick cables running from the back of the pod to a cubical red case on the floor next to him. Oggust had explained that the portable signal node allowed him to access any data network in the city, even the hard-wired ones. Monson didn't have any idea how the device worked, but right now the technical specs were quite irrelevant to him.

"You're sure a chair wouldn't be better?"

"I'm good."

Monson had the distinct impression that the opulence of the hotel made Oggust uncomfortable. Its proximity to Boynton Logistics Dynamic's principal server facility, though, was superior to any other readily accessible option. "If you say so."

"When you talked to the lady at Boynton, that was earlier today, wasn't it?"

"Only for a few minutes, but yes."

"Right. So the most recent status update on the INMASS she gave you, saying that it's mostly stable and under control, that was supposedly accurate as of this morning?"

"Correct."

"Yeah, it's not."

Monson wasn't surprised. "So she lied."

"Not necessarily, I guess. Looking at it superficially, quickly – sure, the system could seem fine. Maybe she hadn't checked very carefully."

"How bad is it really?"

"Well… not terrible." Oggust's fingers went still momentarily. "Not yet, at least. But network integrity is deteriorating pretty rapidly. They'd better get a handle on it soon, or the network hub will go haywire."

"If that happens?"

Oggust shrugged. "Too hard to say. Although I suppose it's a safe prediction that if the network hub goes wonky, a lot of the AIs drawing on it for data and support will malfunction to some degree, too."

"But the nature of any given malfunction isn't predictable."

"It might be. I haven't been in their system even a full day yet. With some more time, especially if I can get into their raw code, I could tell you a lot more."

"Understandable. Regardless, it's clear to you that the INMASS is on the verge of no longer being under control. Especially if they're not focused on addressing it."

"Definitely."

"How about the Loorriri AIs?" Monson asked. "Any luck there?"

"I think so. With their interconnective network offline, I can't snoop directly on what all the AIs are doing. I'm having to reconcile patterns in the data on Boynton's end instead. Give me a few more minutes?"

"Absolutely."

Monson's next course of action already was firming up in his mind. While he waited for Oggust's impending assessment, he pondered the other information he had gleaned from his sources over the past hour.

Three separate contacts at global cargo shipment firms had confirmed essentially the same thing. All delivery flights to Future Cities were suspended. Pilots had been retasked to other assignments, rather than remaining ready for anticipated departures, and clients had been told that an estimated delivery date could not be provided. More disturbing, the sources reported that their firms had been unable to make any successful comm connections into the Future Cities in at least two days. When they had asked government officials about the apparent comms blackout, no response had been forthcoming.

One of his contacts in the Unified Forces had seen a briefing memo analyzing the combat deployments of the Future City security drones. Three cities were actively using their drones to hunt down and exterminate any humans, including refugees from the city itself, within the aerial range of the drones. Three others seemingly had not ordered active pursuit, but their drones would fire upon any humans encountered during perimeter patrols of the land beyond the cities' walls. So far the other six cities had not followed the same course, but that could change at any moment.

Another Unified Forces source had revealed something Monson hadn't anticipated in the slightest. Daemyn Wynde and several of his fellow venturists had cobbled together a fleet of aircraft and were flying them to the savannahs outside Durnow, where they apparently intended to evacuate thousands of refugees who had fled the city. Outer perimeter sweeps by the Durnow AI's security drones likely would have have flown close enough for their sensors to detect the arriving aircraft, but no sign of any response from the AI had been detected. It was possible the drones' processors had dismissed the data as insignificant or erroneous and hadn't even reported it; perhaps the AI had rated the human's distant actions irrelevant when the drone's data came back. Either way, the fact that the AI was not reacting to the savannah evacuation meant nothing if the venturists tried to conduct an evacuation from within the city itself, too. The other cities' AIs had proven how negatively the algorithms reacted to any perceived interference.

Finally, his contact at Boynton. She had told Monson that Boynton had tried three times to execute the kill switch function in the Loorriri AI's code, and each time the AIs had blocked its use. She also had admitted that all eleven of the other Future City AIs had followed Blonkas' lead and reclassified humans as a threat. Though she had given him inaccurate information about the status of INMASS, sloppiness rather than deception seemed the most likely explanation for the error given her previous track record on the Loorriri AIs. Yet the cause was irrelevant. If the crisis had broken her, if he could no longer count on her providing reliable intelligence from inside Boynton, then she would be liability rather than an asset. Which made Oggust's inquiry all the more crucial.

"All right," the hacker said, as if reading Monson's mind. "I've got your answer."

"Let's hear it."

"They're communicating."

"You're certain?"

"As certain as I can be without seeing the code in action directly," Oggust said. "For one, there's too many parallels. Even with running the same base code, the cities are too different for this many things to pop out the same."

"It's not coincidence, it's coordination."

Oggust glanced up from his compupod, the first time in hours he'd actually looked Monson in the eyes. The hacker smiled. "I like that. You have a way with words."

"It's a necessity in my line of work."

"I bet." The hacker's gaze dropped back to his lap, where he turned the compupod's screen so that Monson could see the two charts displayed side by side. Monson didn't need to know the details of what the lines represented to see the obvious symmetry revealed by the charts. "Anyway, it's also the timing. If the AIs were reaching the same conclusions independently, the timing would be variable, almost random. But what I'm seeing is synced up. Teamwork, basically."

"I understand." Monson hefted his comdee. If the Future City AIs were talking to each other, then surely Blonkas already had shared its scheme for using the eridanthol-vanitorine toxin against the humans. And the longer the AIs kept talking, the more likely it became that more cities would unleash the poison. The clock was running a lot faster than Monson had expected. "Do you think you can determine what method they're using to communicate?"

"Probably. It'll take a while, I expect, working from the outside like this. But yeah, I'll see what I can figure out."

"If you get hungry, the room service menu is on the stand by the table." Oggust nodded.

"I'll be back in a few hours," Monson said. "Right now, there's someone I have to meet in person."

...near the refugee camp, southwest of Durnow

Legs churning, Utara was starting to wonder if the rise was getting steeper with every step. It wasn't, of course. But the last thing she needed now was one more obstacle.

Beside her, J'ni crested the rise first. "They're here."

"Good," Utara huffed out, powering herself the last two strides.

It had been J'ni's suggestion to have Daemyn's personal ship land at this location. A few hundred meters from the closest edge of the latest temporary camp, its approach would have been neither seen nor heard by the refugees. The less time they had to ponder the possibility of rescue before the evacuation airlift got underway, the better.

At the bottom of the descending slope, the shuttlecraft rested on its landing gear. Dust kicked up beneath the ship while the engines wound down. For a moment the nose of the ship teetered, then stabilized when the landing strut resituated on the soil with a noticeable *whump*.

Arms out to keep their balance, Utara and J'ni bounded side by side down the rise. By the time they got there, the boarding ramp had lowered and two people were walking out to meet them.

Daemyn appraised them, seemed to notice they were out of breath, and started talking. "We sent the signal to the other shuttles and transports a few minutes ago. They're traveling as a group to maintain security with the very limited number of escort craft we could obtain on short notice, so we've got almost an hour before they get here. That's not too soon, is it?"

"No," Utara said. "That's great."

"We've looked at the map you provided," he continued. "It appears we'll need to use the riverbed for a few of the bigger transports to land. What's your sense of how unstable the soil – or mud, or whatever it is – will be today?"

Utara cast a quick glance to J'ni. "It's dry season," her friend answered. "So it won't be muddy. Even if the landing struts sink a bit, it won't be anything the engines can't easily overcome."

"Even fully loaded with people?"

"As long as they don't set down in the water, definitely."

"Perfect." He extended his hand to her. "I'm Daemyn Wynde."

"I know." They clasped forearms. "J'ni Acai."

"Utara told me about you." He pointed to the tall Polar Aquarian woman at his side. "Utara, J'ni, meet Elsa Ovella. She's head of security for my company – and also former PARTE, along with the rest of the team she's brought."

"We'll try to hang back a bit, especially at first," Elsa said. "Best to keep everything as calm as possible, if we can. But if you need any assistance with crowd control, signal any member of my team. We're trained for it."

"Thank you," Utara said.

"Based on the number of aircraft we have and their respective capacities," Daemyn said, "we've worked out a rough schedule for loading at the camp. It wouldn't be efficient to load too many ships at once anyway, so we'll start a cycle going where some are loading, some departing loaded, and some inbound to load."

"How long do you think it will take to get everyone?" Utara asked.

"Best case, with maximum efficiency, maybe seven hundred people per hour," Elsa said. "More likely, based on my experience and the physical and mental exhaustion of the refugees in this situation, something closer to three hundred per hour."

"All day, and probably into the night," J'ni said.

"Yes."

J'ni nodded. Utara took a deep breath and said, "We still haven't heard anything from inside Durnow. No comms, no contact from any new refugees."

"The comms blackout is still in place," Daemyn said. "But we'll have intel from inside before we'd launch for the city."

Utara compelled her voice to stay measured. "How?"

He canted his head toward Elsa. "I've got PARTE people, remember?"

"But what about the comms blackout?"

"Nothing we can do about that." Elsa checked her wrist chrono. "He should be in the city about two hours from now. He'll gather the intel we need, particularly on whether the transportation hub is usable, and then get back outside far enough to make contact sometime during the night or early tomorrow morning."

Utara nodded. "It'll still be difficult to organize the residents with comms down. But I guess we'll do the best we can. And word of mouth will spread very quickly if it's information about how to get evacuated."

"That was my thought," Daemyn said. "We also printed up a couple of boxes of transies telling people to go to the hub for evacuation. If we know that's an option, we can airdrop those over the city on the way in."

"That would be incredible," Utara said.

At her side J'ni muttered, "If we get so lucky."

"We'll know soon enough. I also –" His comdee trilled. "Sorry," he muttered, and snatched it off the holster on his belt. "It's Reiton checking in."

Before Utara could say anything he had surged a few strides away and started talking in a hurried, low voice into the comdee. She looked at Elsa. "Thank you. You can't understand how important it is to have this kind of assistance. When I asked Daemyn for help, I had no idea."

"Very few people do." Elsa smirked at her. "I don't know how you did it, Utara, but you've really impressed him."

She blinked. "What makes you say that?"

The tall woman laughed. "Other than the fact that he discarded some very important work at Wynde Industries to fly halfway around the world to help you?"

"I didn't –"

"Didn't what?" Daemyn said, striding back to join them.

Elsa said something that sounded like "P.L."

"Oh, that?" Daemyn looked right at Utara. "Don't worry about it. We'll deal with that when we get back. It's nothing."

Utara didn't dare tell him she had no idea what in the Hells he was talking about. Instead she said, "Thank you again. Both of you. But if we're going to get this airlift running smoothly, J'ni and I should probably get back to the refugees and start organizing them into loading groups."

"Great," Daemyn said. "See you soon."

Moments later when they were powering their way back up the rise to head toward the camp, J'ni looked over at Utara. The expression on her face was all too familiar.

Utara breathed hard. "What?"

"The strangest people I've ever met in my life," J'ni replied between her own deep breaths, "have always been through you. Where do you keep finding them?"

TWENTY-ONE

...War Memorial Park, Port Vulcania

T he setting sun dipped behind the trees, plunging the glade into a purplish
gloom. With its immaculately maintained landscaping and burnished stone
walls, paths, and obelisks, the city park was actually quite stunning to behold
even in the rapidly approaching darkness. On another day, Monson would
have stayed longer and taken in the rare, man-made beauty of the place.

Tonight, though, he had too much on his mind, and the beauty wasn't
the purpose of meeting his contact here. Rather, the park was one of the few
locations in Port Vulcania free from vidcams, audio surveillance, or other
forms of observation. Ostensibly to allow anyone to mourn the fallen with
full privacy, it also permitted clandestine meetings for all manner of scandal-
ous or illicit objectives. Perfect for Monson's purposes, too, and exactly the
kind of location where his contact wanted to meet, as well.

He had a few more minutes before she would arrive, so he made one
more check of the news searches he was monitoring closely. As they had
been all day, the media feeds remained largely silent regarding the situation in
Loorriri. A few additional sources had reprinted the previous reports about
the refugees fleeing the Future Cities for the wilderness, but no new reporting
had emerged. Several items about Boynton Logistic Dynamics had popped
up here and there over the past three hours, but all of those news reports
were completely unrelated to the AIs or the Future Cities. Monson also had
begun monitoring media coverage on the activities of the venturists, in case
a reporter might stumble upon the refugee airlift and then the rest of the
crisis that way. His searches pulled a fair number of reports mentioning various venturists, of course, but nothing more numerous than ordinary. Even

the trashmags seemed oblivious to the airlift in Loorriri, and they usually
followed Daemyn Wynde's trail like a merciless scenthound.

All of this was good, as far as Monson was concerned. His best opportunity to insert himself into the PIS would exist when the crisis was still being
managed away from the prying eyes of the media and the public. The quiet
feeds worked to his advantage. The longer it took reporters to get involved
in earnest, the better.

Sheathed in the lengthening shadows, a slender figure approached along
one of the stone paths. Monson had selected a particular obelisk as their
meeting point – one topped by a tall statue of a naval admiral in full battle
regalia, in the style of the historical era when the Navy actually commanded
waterborne warships on the seas instead of military spaceships in the stars –
so that there would be no doubt of their respective identities when his contact
arrived. He kept his eye on the figure, waiting to see if the individual took the
side path that would reach the obelisk, or rather continued along the crossing
route through the park.

Moments later he received his answer. The Faytan woman walked up to
the obelisk, stopping less than a meter from where Monson stood. "You're
sure we're safe here?"

"Nowhere better in Port Vulcania, I assure you."

"All right," she said.

"You told me it's getting worse every hour. How bad is it now?"

"It's basically full blown panic. People in the AI division are losing it."
Even though they were alone in the darkness, her voice was barely louder
than a whisper. "We're trying everything we can think of to get the Future
Cities back under control, but nothing we've done has even come close to
working."

"Can you tell what's obstructing you?"

"No. Anything we do, they see it coming and have a block. It's as if
everything we try, the AIs are one step ahead."

"They must be communicating with each other, then. Cooperating to
thwart you."

She shook her head. "That's impossible without the network hub."

"You're certain?"

"Positive."

"What about the INMASS?"

"I hardly have time to pay it any attention. We're so busy scrambling to handle the Loorriri AIs, that's all we can deal with. But last time I checked a few hours ago, it seems to be functioning pretty much normally."

"That's good," Monson told her.

"Yes, it is."

He leaned closer so she could see his eyes. "What do you hope to gain by lying to me?"

"I'm not —"

"Liar," he hissed. "What's your play? How do you benefit?"

"I'm telling you the truth!"

"No," Monson said, taking a step closer. "You're not."

"But —"

"I know the Future Cities are communicating. I know the INMASS is on the brink of collapse. Why are you lying?"

She stared at him, gaping. Finally she said, "Everything's hopeless."

"Only for you."

She never saw it coming. His hands seized both sides of her head. A sharp twist, a snap, and her body slumped lifeless into his arms. Propping her against the obelisk, he checked her pockets. As expected, he found two comdees — one that was obviously her usual personal device, and the other a temporary disposable one she'd been using to contact him. He put both of them in his back pocket. After that, with her size and his strength it was easy enough to carry her body to the bridge overlooking the ravine that bordered the south edge of the park. He heaved the corpse over the railing and dropped it, making sure it would suffer a rough and vicious set of collisions with the wall of the ravine on the way to the trickling stream thirty meters below. Then he retrieved her personal comdee, powered it down, and smashed it as hard as he could on the railing with both hands. He flung the utterly wrecked device into the ravine after her.

By the time they found the body and identified it as a distraught employee of Boynton's AI division, the cause of death would be so obviously suicide the medical examiner wouldn't think to look closely enough at the precise angle of the spine injury. And even if, somehow, they did, no trace of evidence existed to link the woman to Monson. He tugged off his gloves and tucked them under his arm.

He checked his comdee. Still no update from Kirkland Oggust, though that wasn't unexpected. Monson took one last look into the black depths of the ravine and smiled. At least one thing tonight had gone smoothly.

...refugee camp

"Daemyn!"

The sound of Reiton's voice ripped his focus away from the compupod screen. For a second he wondered if this wasn't the first time his friend had called his name. Not that it mattered. His gaze found Holtspring on the far side of the command post, leaning inside through the tarp flap over the side entrance. Daemyn raised a single finger; Reiton nodded, but also gestured with a hand for him to hurry it up.

Quickly he glanced back to Elsa. "Need me to check on anything?"

"Not for now." She didn't look away from the pod, where she was updating the tallies from the two shuttlecraft that had departed minutes earlier. "Thanks."

"Sure." Daemyn scooted between the tables and headed for Reiton – who apparently had already closed the flap and gone back outside. On the way, he pondered the numbers. They weren't too far behind pace, which was good. For six hours into the evacuation operation, it was going about as well as he could have expected.

Slapping the flap aside, he emerged to find the late afternoon sun blazing right into his face. He raised a hand and squinted, blinking away the sunspots in his vision.

"Over here."

Daemyn turned and saw Reiton a few meters away, at the corner of the temporary structure. He strode over, and reveled in the lack of direct sunlight once he joined his friend along the south edge of the tent. "What is it?"

"The three transports that just landed. The pilots want to speak with you."

"What kind of problem are we facing?"

"Nothing external," Reiton assured him quickly. "Something with the ships."

"Could you be more specific?"

Holtspring scowled at him. "No, *I* can't. They lost me as soon as they launched into the technical jargon. Unless you'd prefer my mangled recap to their direct explanation?"

"I think I'll pass."

"Thought so."

Daemyn nodded. "Thanks. I'll see you later."

Holtspring muttered a noncommittal reply before he stepped around the corner and disappeared.

Chuckling to himself, Daemyn headed off toward the riverbed, where the trio of inbound transports had been scheduled to land. It didn't take him long to get there, and he found the three pilots clustered together beneath the wing of the nearest transport. "Holtspring said you wanted to see me. Something with the ships?"

"Yes," the tallest pilot said.

The placards and logos on their flight uniforms identified two from the company Rustle Tames had convinced to participate, while the third came from one of the contractors Daemyn had hired. He may not have ever met them before, but they wouldn't have had to ask which of the mission leaders was the expert on aircraft technical issues.

"What's the status?"

"Weather's fine, no rain or lightning," the tall one began. "No airborne interference or anti-aircraft fire from the ground, either. So it took a while to figure out why the engine diagnostics were giving us trouble."

The redheaded woman turned her compupod screen so Daemyn could see. "All three of us were getting similar alarms, and comparable readouts from the scans."

He leaned over to inspect the display. They waited until he looked up and said, "Particulates?"

"We're pretty sure," she replied. "We commed the other pilots to see if they're getting similar readings."

"We didn't fly through a dust storm or anything," the tall man added. "It's must be the ambient particulates in the air."

The dark-skinned Aladarian pointed to a set of lines on the screen. "My shuttle is the only one of our three that has a sensor suite aboard. It's not sophisticated by any means, but it's good enough to run some air sample analysis on our way back. Definitely a much higher quotient of particulates in the air here than back home."

"It lines up with the engine performance alarms," the redhead said, swapping displays on the pod to show him the results of diagnostic scans. "No damage yet, as far as any of us can tell, but it's degrading efficiency for sure. And if we keep it up without adjustments for another six hours or longer, we could see damage."

Daemyn nodded. "This looks right to me, so we can probably expect that the other pilots will report similar results from their craft. Which means, to prevent any problems, we'll need to build in time for engine clean-outs."

The pilots seemed surprised that he'd agreed with the necessity of that step so easily. No doubt they were used to bosses who pushed them to complete the task at hand in the short term, losing sight of the long-term ramifications. And Daemyn was a pilot himself – he understood the stakes all too well. The last thing he would do was risk a catastrophic engine failure just to maintain the pace of the evacuation flights.

"Which," he added, "we obviously can't do here. But it's something you can manage offshore, right?"

"Yes," the tall one said. "We'll have the space and tools we need there."

"And you've made three round trips each so far?"

"That's right," the Aladarian said.

"So, you perform the first clean-out when you make the dropoff. Then again after three more runs. And third clean-out after three more, if we're still going then."

"Unless something really changes," the redhead said, "that should work."

"Let's get the plan in motion," Daemyn told them. "Keep me updated if the other pilots report anything different. Otherwise, let's assume all pilots will perform clean-outs after every third run. And let me worry about the rest."

After the three of them confirmed the plan, Daemyn weaved his way back through the refugee camp on the path toward the command post. He'd made the only choice available under the circumstances – and not just for these refugees, but also if they had any hope of running an airlift out of Durnow. Now he had to find a way to break it to Utara that the pace of the evacuation flights would have to slow down to enable the pilots to clean their engines.

Then he realized he was about to wreck Elsa's carefully crafted numbers, too.

He stopped in place and sighed. Which woman was he going to disappoint first?

...refugee camp

"One more confirmation," Utara called out. She made her voice loud to ensure it carried through the cargo bay – now filled to capacity with dozens upon dozens of people rather than crates and containers – but measured enough so that it wouldn't sound like she was shouting. "Everyone is accounted for? All of your family and friends are present with you?"

The murmur in the cargo bay briefly rose in volume, then ebbed. "Last call," she said again, a little louder. When no one spoke up or signaled a problem, she finished with the only thing she could say. "Hold on tight. Many blessings to you all."

She gave the affirmative hand gesture to the crewer standing at the far end of the cargo bay. He nodded and snuck out through the portal to the vessel's fore. With that Utara turned and hustled down the ramp before it started to close.

Blinking against the sudden gloom of dusk outside the transport, she hurried toward the evacuation command post. Over half an hour remained before the next aircraft would load, and she needed to make the best use of every second she had.

It was these moments, the brief lulls between the frenetic bursts of activity in loading aircraft, when her emotions threatened to get the better of her. Still no word from Aidan or anyone in Blonkas. Worry about what her parents might be facing inside Durnow – and fear that they might be trapped there if an evacuation through the hub wasn't possible. Too much remained unknown, and the anxiety all those unanswered questions produced made her whole body tense up. But she couldn't afford to get distracted from the task at hand. People were counting on her, here and in Durnow. She had to focus on that now, and leave everything else for later.

Approaching her destination, Utara paused to collect her thoughts. The sight before her helped. The colors of its exterior tarp unblemished, held up with clean white ropes and neatly polished metal spikes, the tent was exactly the kind of temporary shelter erected to shield the catered food from the elements at any number of fancy parties for political dignitaries she had attended with her father over the years. Out of context, the sight was so utterly ordinary it wouldn't have even registered in her mind. Today, here and now, it stood out like a majestic temple amid the squalor. The venturists could fly a tent like this around the world without a second thought. As time dragged on, some of the Durnow refugees might not survive the savannah's night – literally – for lack of shelter even this basic. The contrast made her stomach drop, but it also inspired her to remember the necessity of finishing the evacuation as soon as possible.

Utara brushed open the flap and walked inside. At one of the small tables in a corner, standing over a transi map stretched over nearly its entire surface, J'ni was waiting for her. Waving a hand, her friend beckoned her over.

"I guess that's not a good sign," Utara said, indicating the map.

"Can't get anything by you." For a moment longer J'ni studied the map. "The good news, such as it is, is that the dissenters haven't been able to increase their numbers at all in the last two hours."

"That's something, at least." Utara didn't like the label *dissenters* for the refugees who were refusing to board the evacuation transports – something about the connotation just didn't feel right – but she hadn't come up with a better one, and now it had stuck among the evacuation's leadership team. "The bad news, I assume, is that we haven't been able to reduce their numbers at all, either."

"Correct."

"Honestly, I can't say that I really blame them."

J'ni met her gaze. "I know. That's the problem."

Utara nodded. Fortunately most of the refugees were so happy for rescue that they weren't thinking too hard about where they'd be taken in the short term or where they'd end up living in the long term. Of the ones who did ask questions, the majority had been satisfied with the answers. The humanitarian relief facility at Steamer Point sounded like a much better temporary home than a tent out on the savannah – and many of the refugees didn't even have one of those to sleep in. And the prospect of resettlement somewhere other than Loorriri – with essentially no specifics on when or where that might occur – was enough to reassure them that they wouldn't just end up back in the Future Cities, which was the one thing none of the refugees wanted.

The dissenters, though, hadn't accepted the best explanations Utara and J'ni could offer them. Fearful of the AI that had turned against them in Durnow, they insisted on promises that they wouldn't be resettled in other cities across Prime that also had AIs in them – promises that couldn't be made. Even the offer that they could return to Loorriri from the Aladarian Guard base if they didn't like the resettlement options later hadn't been enough. In the face of a future equally at the mercy of technological betrayal, the dissenters were refusing to even get on the transports in the first place.

After all they'd been through, the last thing Utara was going to do was forcibly compel them to board. Staying in this riverbed encampment, though, wasn't a viable solution, either.

"Any ideas where to take them?" Utara asked.

"We don't even have basics here." J'ni ticked off the points on her fingers as she spoke. "Sturdy woods for durable shelter, kindling or firewood for heat and cooking, reliable clean water either naturally or with purifiers, reliable food sources, raw materials for new clothing... If they're going to set up a place to stay, even something semi-permanent at first, those are non-negotiable. At a minimum."

"What locations have them?"

"A few within manageable trek by foot." J'ni pointed them out. "This basin might be the best one overall, but it's too far from any existing settlement. Starting entirely fresh is too risky for this group."

"Especially with none of them having any real skills for surviving in the wilderness," Utara added.

"Exactly. That's why I think it's better to head this way, toward Agoelo."

Utara saw the three locations J'ni had circled on the map. "Each of those could support a new settlement, if needed."

"Yes. For all we know, some of the refugees might like Agoelo and want to stay there. With the resources available in the vicinity, the town could certainly expand a lot and still maintain a sustainable population. And new settlements are viable at those locations, too. So it presents the best long-term potential."

Utara considered the map again. "I agree. Do you think they'll accept this plan?"

"Who knows, at this point. But yes, I think they will."

Utara nodded. "All right. Let's go present it to them."

TWENTY-TWO

...outskirts of refugee camp

Pacing down the ramp, Daemyn put a hand on one of the struts and swung himself out of the ship and onto the ground. His boots crunched on the gravel, bringing his momentum to a skittering stop. He tapped the fob and dropped it into his pocket; the ramp began to raise. Once it closed and *WyndeStalker*'s hull sealed with a sharp hiss of air, he turned and walked toward the rise that shielded the shuttlecraft from the brisk night winds.

For a minute he stood at its top, looking out over the savannah. The moon was low in the sky, so the view before him was nothing more than a single indistinguishable spread of land. At midday the tiny silhouette of Durnow on the far horizon had barely been visible to the naked eye. In the dark of night, the city was invisible.

The glittering panorama of stars, however, was as sharp and beautiful as Daemyn had ever seen it. Even in the remote areas of Hyj-gon, the black never looked this dark and the twinkling specks never looked this bright. He tilted his head, picking out a few of the familiar constellations in the sky – in completely the wrong places and totally the wrong angles. He chuckled to himself. Going halfway around the world would do that.

Not that he hadn't traversed the globe many times over at this point. Airspar raced on every other inhabited continent, and some of the prominent archipelagos between them. No track existed on Loorriri, but several were located roughly at the same longitudes. Daemyn had never bothered to stop and study the stars there before.

Shivering a bit against a gust of wind that whipped around him and plastered his clothes against his skin, Daemyn decided to reduce his profile to Fayti's icy breath. He lowered to a crouch, then settled himself down atop the rise and clasped his hands on his knees. Once again he looked up at the unfamiliar starscape.

To be honest, never before had he dropped everything and flown across the planet to rescue people he'd never met from a crisis he barely understood, either. In the frantic hours of planning the airlift, then the nonstop operation of the refugee flights once they'd arrived, Daemyn hadn't really stopped to think about why he'd been so quick to commit to the endeavor in the first place. Was it because Utara's plea had come the day after he'd visited his mother, when his newly torn open memories of his family's evacuation from the firestorm had still been so raw? That was probably part of it. What if his racing luck had fallen into place a little bit differently and Fith had qualified for the championships? Would he really be here tonight, on the savannah of Zanita, if Fith was flying in the quarterfinals tomorrow? If circumstances hadn't conspired to make him ready and willing to save these people, would he have turned his back on them, left them here to die? He was pretty sure he knew what the answer was – and he didn't like it.

A howling burst of wind almost concealed the gentle crunch of approaching footsteps. He looked up to see Utara climbing the last few strides to the top of the rise.

In the dark, he could barely see the small smile on her face. "You looked," she said, "like you could use some company."

"I'd like that."

Smoothly she lowered herself to sit cross-legged beside him. "So far it's gone about as well as could be expected, I think."

"Other than taking most of two days, instead of one. But that's fine. We accomplished what we came to do out here. That's the important thing."

"The pilots agree with you? Even though it took longer than we thought?"

"Pilots care about flying. The weather cooperated, and they didn't encounter any obstacles from people, animals, or the drones, either. To them, that's the win."

"I'm glad."

"Me too." He chuckled lightly. "Otherwise, I'm not sure how many of them would've been willing to stick around for tomorrow."

She nodded. "It's going to be a lot more difficult, isn't it?"

"Hard to say. But I expect so."

"Probably with the people, too." Utara looked off into the distance. Unlike Daemyn, she knew where exactly on the horizon Durnow was. "The ones in the camp, they were more exhausted than anything. I could see it on their faces. Whatever fear they might have felt, the sense of relief was stronger. The residents still in the city, though, that could be a different story. I haven't talked to my friends in Blonkas in almost two weeks. Or my parents since I left Durnow. A lot could have happened. It could be about the same, or… A lot worse. I try not to think about it."

"It's the only way to manage, sometimes."

She nodded. "I'm not sure what we'll find, honestly."

"Whatever it is, we'll handle it."

"I hope so."

"Hey, if nothing else, tomorrow I don't think you'll have to argue with anyone about whether it's a good idea to get on a transport to leave."

She smiled a little. "I imagine you're probably right."

"The ones who wouldn't leave – where are they going to go?"

"For now, Agoelo." She glanced over to him. "It's a town – well, more like a large village – a few days' trek on foot from here. J'ni knows the way."

"Can they absorb that many new people at once?"

"They don't have much of a choice."

"If they can't?"

Utara wrapped her arms around her chest, fighting off the chill. "There's a map. Years ago, when the Future Cities were first built, a whole set of locations were identified all across Loorriri. Sites for additional waves of Future Cities – they never got built, obviously – as well as smaller settlements. Most of those places are still wilderness, but the sites would work just as well today as they would have back then."

"Wow," Daemyn said. "Building whole new towns."

"Maybe. The ones who left with J'ni, they're never coming back to urban life. Not the high-tech, computer-driven version of it, anyway. So if they can support themselves with food and water, and get the shelters built quickly enough, why not?"

"It makes sense." He stretched his arms to ward off the stiffness setting in. "When all this is over, keep me updated whichever way it turns out for them. Generators, water purifiers, temporary shelters – those are the kinds of things that we could airlift to…"

"Agoelo."

"Right. We could airlift supplies like that pretty easily. To Agoelo, or a new location. Wherever. That's not a problem."

She faced him, but the look in her eyes was playful, not accusatory. "Another charitable deduction on the corporate tax return?"

He grinned. "I assume so. I let Holtspring handle all of that."

"I'm sure he's very good at it."

"Not very good. He's the best."

"I bet." Abruptly her face grew serious. "Thank you."

"For?"

"This. Everything." She canted her head to the camp behind them, now mostly empty. "You saved a lot of people."

"No, *we* saved them." He met her gaze. "Sure, I wrangled up the ships, with a little bit of help. But none of this would've happened if it weren't for you."

She shrugged. "Maybe you're right. I'm not so sure. If it hadn't been me, someone else would've stepped up to address the crisis."

"I suppose it's possible."

"You don't think so?"

Now it was Daemyn's turn to shrug. "I think most people only make big commitments, or take big risks, if there's something in it for them."

"Money?"

"Sometimes, sure. But it could be something intangible, too. Anything they value. Glory in battle, being remembered as a military hero. Plenty of examples of that in the history books, right? Or fame. That's practically every vidstar's motivation now."

"You see a lot of that in Airspar, too, right? The fame-seeking."

"You have no idea." He fought down a laugh. "Look, no offense, but from what I see a lot of the people in politics sure seem like they're motivated by enhancing their own personal power. Especially the ones at the top, or who are trying to get there."

For a long moment she was quiet, and he worried he'd offended her after all. She drew in a deep breath and said, "Some of them, yes. But I see every day how the people in the PDS think and act. The decisions they make. And most of them, most of the time, they really are trying to make the right decisions. To help people."

"I believe you."

"But?"

"But I don't see a lot of results." He kept talking so she wouldn't misunderstand. "Not the PDS specifically. To be honest, I've never really paid a lot of attention to the PDS and its projects before."

"It's all right. Very few people do."

"What I do know, what I pay attention to closely, is Airspar and my company. The competition side, of course. And then the technology side – aerospace engineering, computing, all the things Wynde Industries works on. In those fields, the government doesn't really seem to have any idea what it's doing."

She met his gaze and smiled a little. "I've never really paid a lot of attention to that side of things before."

He smiled back. "Right."

"It's about having the right people in the job," she said. "Our deputy minister now, PDS has been struggling under his leadership. The prior one, things were better. It matters."

"No different than business, really. A good leader can make a company thrive, a bad one can destroy it."

"Yes." She paused, looking toward Durnow again. "I wish the government could have stepped up sooner, of course. But they will. Bureaucracy is slower than it should be sometimes, but there's always a person who will want to make the right decision, and who can act on it. Like Captain Forta opening up Steamer Point for the evacuees. It's about finding the right person, getting their attention."

Daemyn didn't have the heart to tell her how slim he thought those odds really were. At least on the kind of timetable she was operating under. With everything else the government faced, Loorriri and its people were way too low on the priority list for anyone to risk their career sticking up for them. He hoped Utara would prove him wrong – but he didn't think the prospect was very realistic. Not this time.

"I hope you do," he said.

"I will." Still looking toward the city she added, "I found you, didn't I?"

He blinked. "Meaning?"

"The attention of the right person, who stepped up to make a difference."

"Oh. Right."

"We need more people like you in the government, in politics."

He couldn't help himself. Daemyn genuinely laughed. "Sorry to burst your bubble, Utara, but no. Actually, we don't. I'd be terrible at it."

She laughed too, just a little. "Well, maybe you would be. I guess I should take your word for it. I don't really know you very well, do I?"

"Nor I you," he pointed out. "Other than you're apparently a hopeless idealist."

"Idealist, yes. You've got me there. But not hopeless. Not at all."

"Maybe I'll take your word for it."

"You should."

Daemyn hadn't missed her seemingly offhand remark about not knowing him very well – and he was pretty sure it wasn't nearly as tangential as she'd tried to make it sound. He'd take her hint and run with it. Worst case, she'd stand up and walk away. Best case... He didn't honestly know what he thought the best case would be. Or what he wanted it to be.

But he knew one thing – he wanted to find out.

Daemyn leaned back, bracing his palms on the ground behind him. "Have you ever been into space?"

"Only a few times." If the sudden change in direction in the conversation fazed her, she definitely didn't let it show. "I did my service term in the Aladarian Guard."

"Really?"

"You're surprised?"

"I would have been sure you'd chosen one of the humanitarian options. Seems like more your style. With everything you experienced growing up here."

"That's just it. There was nothing I could gain from a service term in Zanita – or any other humanitarian one, for that matter – that I hadn't already seen. And I already knew I wanted to join the PDS when I was done. So I picked something that I'd almost certainly never have the chance to do again."

"I'm impressed."

"Why's that?"

"I haven't met many people who used their service term that way. Like you're supposed to. And not because their parents forced them to."

"That's probably true." She glanced at him. "I guess you took the easy route with yours, then?"

"I'd been considering a few possibilities, but in the end I didn't really have a choice. When the Navy comes calling, you don't really get to say no."

"They wanted you to be a space pilot?"

"Yeah. On the big ships."

"You turned it down to fly Airspar?"

"And start Wynde Industries, too. But yes."

"You made the right call."

Daemyn hadn't expected that. "You think so?"

"Don't get me wrong. I'm sure the Navy needs good pilots. Those ships are incredibly expensive. We wouldn't want them getting wrecked with a bad pilot behind the helm."

"No kidding."

"But something tells me that a career flying a cruiser around, just to make sure it doesn't crash, is a waste of your talents. And your brain."

"Well," he said, grinning at her, "you said it, not me."

She gazed up at the stars. "We have so many problems here on Prime. We need our best people here, focused on solving them. For most Primeans, traveling to space is just as fantastical as something out of a vid. We owe it to them to spend our money and resources on making their lives better, not on creating another opportunity for boutique tourism for the very wealthy."

"You think the space budget is too big?"

"Overall, yes. The science and exploration, I don't have a quarrel with. The discoveries we've made, the medicines. Those are important. They help everyone."

"The trade side matters, too. In some areas, it's practically keeping the economy going. And there are some prospects for technological innovations that could really make a difference here on the ground, in people's daily lives. The truth is, we don't spend enough money on space, given how much positive return it brings in so many areas."

"A service term in the Navy turned you into a venturist. I never would have expected it."

"Not only that, of course. But I suppose it was one of the first big steps in getting me there, yes."

"Interesting. And certainly, nothing's wrong with the privately financed side of space investment. I'd prefer it, actually." Utara shook her head. "It's not that I don't appreciate what the Aladarian Guard does in space. But even in my service term alone, I saw what they can accomplish here on Prime when they put their resources to it. That's where they're needed. Not running patrols that never actually find anything to protect us from."

"So far."

"Who's going to attack us? That's what the studies all show, isn't it? That trading partners don't go to war."

"I'm not so sure."

"We haven't had a war on Prime in lifetimes."

"Depends on how you define it, though." Daemyn leaned forward, clasping his hands on his knees again. "And military offensives aren't the only disaster to worry about. The Faytans and Plains Terrans had been centuries-long trading partners, very successfully in fact, when their inaction and stubbornness on other issues ended up producing the Karagashi firestorm. I think the fact that we still have a Cultural Minister, who by all accounts is very busy dealing with all sorts of disputes all around the world – that tells us something."

"But they all get resolved peacefully. That's the point of having the Ministry."

"Or maybe we've been lucky."

"It's an awfully long track record to write off as luck."

He had to admit she had a point. "For Prime's sake, I hope you're right."

"I usually am."

When he glanced at her, she laughed. He did, too. "If you're right, the place to cut the budget is the Army and the other forces that only operate on Prime. Space, that's another story. Trading is going well, but aliens are still, well, aliens. They're not us. They don't think like us."

"I've never met one. Have you?"

"Not personally. But I've studied them, and their tech."

"You think they'll turn on us?"

"We don't know enough to know. What if the next alien species we encounter isn't interested in trade? We need to be ready."

"Between the Navy and the Guards," she said, "I believe we are."

"I hope we never find out."

"Me too."

"I might have more of your confidence," he said, "if the Colonists hadn't disappeared into the stars, never to be heard from again. Nearly two hundred years, yet none of our trading partners has ever encountered other humans out in space? In all that time?"

She met his eyes. "Everyone says they didn't have the resources to mount a sustainable mission. That it was a one-way suicide trip from the start."

"I've read the actual reports. The historical documents. It was a risky proposition, I admit. But they also had a lot of brilliant minds and skilled people. I find it hard to believe that a group like that would have starved to death in the void – especially without triggering any distress beacons that one of our alien trading partners would have detected at some point, even if it was only after it was already too late."

"You think whoever found them wiped them out?"

"I think something doesn't add up." He took a breath and said it. "They had the Guardians with them."

Her gaze on his didn't waver. "You believe in the legends, too?"

"Since I was a boy."

"Most people grow out of it, or so they say. Why didn't you?"

He peered at her. "You didn't either?"

"I asked first."

"Right. So..." He closed his eyes, remembering. "When I was young, we lived in Karagashi."

"The firestorm," she said, her voice practically a whisper. "You were there."

"Yes. We were among the lucky ones. We got out." He opened his eyes and looked into hers again. "In the middle of the storm. Everyone told me it was only my imagination. Insisted it was a child's mind trying to cope with the tragedy I'd seen. But it was real. I saw it with my own eyes. I can see it now, as real as it was that day."

"A dragon," she said, as if it was the most normal statement of all in their entire conversation.

"Yes."

"I believe you."

He nodded.

"When I was a girl," she said, her voice still quiet, "I was out alone on the savannah. I'd gone for a ride on my horse. He spooked, and I fell off." She chuckled. "Not the first time that happened, or the last. Anyway, it was no big deal; I wouldn't have thought anything of it. Then I saw what spooked him. A dozen meters away, maybe less."

Daemyn caught himself holding his breath. In the wilds of Zanita, either of two legendary beasts was a possibility. The fact that Utara was still alive, though, probably told him the answer. "A pegasus?"

"Yes. I only ever saw her the one time. My parents insisted it was a hallucination from knocking my head on the ground when I'd fallen. I knew what I'd seen, though, and it was no dream. I went back so many times looking, but I never saw her again."

"Well," he said, "I guess that explains why we both believe the Guardians were real, too. Even if everyone else thinks we're crazy."

"Are we?"

"Not for what we believe in," Daemyn said. "What we're trying to pull off tomorrow, though? For this, we might be."

"Can't argue with that." The way she was looking at him, there was something in her eyes he couldn't quite place. "So... Crazy's not necessarily a bad thing?"

"Uh... No?"

"Good," she said, and kissed him.

TWENTY-THREE

...WyndeStalker, *airborne over Durnow*

Daemyn checked the mission timer on the heads-up display. Once it toggled over to the next full minute he asked Elsa, "How's it look?"

"Activity holding. Slow but steady."

Slow was probably an understatement. Based on the analysis of security drone patrols provided by the operative she'd inserted into the city, though, they had determined that flying a large number of vessels into Durnow at once would be too likely to trigger an overreaction from the city's AI. A steady pattern of arrivals posed a much lower risk. One or two ships at time would approach the city, enter its airspace, and land at the transportation hub; only after their landing was completed would the next flight begin its approach. Still, if it got the whole airlift flotilla into Durnow without conflict, Daemyn was perfectly happy to tolerate the languid pace.

"Nothing at the hub, either?"

"Reiton knows what he's doing. All clear there, too."

"Good." As part of the comms blackout over the city, the hub's air-traffic facility was offline. No commercial or government flights had arrived or departed in days. But the venturists had brought highly skilled pilots with pre-determined flight paths, and the plan for evacuation flights was equally deliberate as the insertions. With no other vessels in the air but their ships – and the AI's security drones – they didn't need the hub's controllers to avoid mid-air collisions, and Holtspring was leading a team of people tasked with directing each arriving aircraft to a designated spot on the expansive tarmac. "The longer the drones don't bother to care that we're here, the better."

"No kidding."

Daemyn spared a quick glance over his shoulder to Utara, who was seated directly behind him. "If that's our status, any reason to wait to start dropping the transies?"

"No. It will take time for people to get there, and it's not a short walk for most of them. The longer we wait to start dropping, the fewer people we'll be able to evacuate before we have to end the operation." The comms black-out had prevented her from speaking directly to her father, but Elsa's opera-tive had located him and had passed along a message from him to Utara as part of the databurst received before they'd launched. Elsa would've shown it to him if he'd asked, but Daemyn had let the full scope of the news about the status inside Durnow remain Utara's alone. She deserved that much. But she had shared the most important piece of information: that nearly a third of the city's population had already fled onto the savannah, meaning the airlift had a legitimate chance at evacuating most of the people still remaining within its walls. "While I'd hate to drop them and have residents start mass-ing at the hub, only to find out that they have to go somewhere else after all, this is our best chance to save as many people as we can. So yes, let's take the chance and start the drop."

"Elsa?"

"Agreed."

"Me too," he said. "Always nice to have unanimity."

Daemyn tapped the console, bringing up the airdrop flight pattern on the heads-up. Layered over a map of Durnow, it marked out a series of loop-ing arcs over the residential neighborhoods. They didn't have nearly enough transies for everyone – maybe one per five or six families, at best – but word would get around quickly once people read the evacuation notification. The key was distributing the transies as evenly as possible throughout the city, maximizing their coverage.

"*Stalker*," he said, "execute airdrop pattern Aladare."

The heads-up flashed green. Daemyn released the yoke, and the shuttle's robotic brain took over. Moments later a big blue dot appeared on the air-drop map, blinking as it approached the flight path line. Daemyn waited, drumming his fingers on the console. When the dot reached the path line he said, "Begin airdrop."

The console chimed. An indicator light confirmed the drop-chamber had opened. Now, all Daemyn could do was hope nothing interfered.

Behind him, Utara whispered to Elsa, "Does he always talk to the ship like this?"

"Like what?" Elsa kept up the game, whispering in reply.

"Like it understands him."

"He does," Daemyn said, turning in his seat to face her.

Utara flinched, and looked at him sheepishly. "I didn't –"

"Mean to imply that I might be out of my mind?"

"Get in line," Elsa said, shifting back to the sensor console.

"We pilots have our odd habits, I'll admit," Daemyn said. "But *Stalker* isn't just a figment of my imagination, he's real. Isn't that right, *Stalker*?"

"Correct." The artificial, synthesized voice of the ship's robot brain, deliberate and stilted in its diction as always, emerged through the same speakers in the cockpit console as any routine ship-to-ship comm. "I exist."

Utara didn't even try to hide the shock on her face. "I'm… sorry."

For her part, Elsa didn't bother to hide her short, light laugh.

"Don't worry, he's not offended," Daemyn told Utara. "You're now on a very short list of people who know he exists."

Utara said simply, "Okay."

He peered at her. Something was wrong. "Are you all right?"

She straightened in the seat, struggling to regain her composure. "I'm fine."

"You sure?"

"Yes. It's just…" She took a breath. "Why do you have one?"

"Have what?"

"An AI."

Daemyn could have slapped himself. Of course. He was an idiot. A massive, blazing idiot. "*Stalker* is a prototype," he said. "For Airspar."

"Oh. That makes sense."

"We've just started introducing voice commands. Too many of the pilots aren't used to it, though. They have a hard time distinguishing between talking to the team on the comm and talking to the blade. So I've been working on code that will help the blade be able to tell the difference on its own, so that the pilot doesn't have to think about it. The tech is simplistic so far, but in a certain sense it's a kind of AI."

Utara nodded.

"AIs aren't good or bad. They're just code. They only do what we enable them to do." He reached up and put a hand on her knee. "And if they do bad things, it's because we gave them that capability. Code didn't do this, Utara. *People* are responsible for what happened here."

For the first time since *Stalker* had spoken, she looked him squarely in the eyes. "Yes," she said. "Yes, they are."

~⌒⌒

...*Agoelo*

Her comdee trilled. Focused on the daunting task of explaining the latest change in the plans for providing temporary housing for the newly relocated refugees now encamped on the outskirts of the town, J'ni ignored the insistent tones and continued her clarifications for the half-dozen individuals gathered around her. When it trilled a second time, followed by a third, she no longer had a choice. Something was wrong. She didn't know who or what yet, but it couldn't possibly be good.

"Give me a moment," she told them, and strode over to retrieve the comdee from where she'd left it resting on the driver's seat of her truck.

The source of the incoming comm surprised her – and chilled her to the bone.

Considering how long it had been since Urttu had contacted her with the electronic device, she harbored no doubt about the gravity of whatever situation he faced. "I'll finish up with you shortly," she called out to the waiting group. "I need to take care of this first."

Before anyone could try to object, or even ask her a question about the urgency of the comm, she hurried down the dusty road and cut between two of the buildings. Within a minute she'd reached a small storage shed where she was confident no one would think to look for her. She bounded inside and shut the door behind her.

She tapped the comdee's screen, praying to Tarah that Urttu still had his comdee ready and waiting. Fortunately she didn't have to wait long.

"Acai?" came the chieftain's voice.

"Yes, it's me. What's wrong?"

"The river is sick."

"What do you mean?"

"We come to the water to sustain life. Now it brings nothing but death."

She tried to get him to elaborate, but the combination of his confusion at the sight before him and his discomfort with the comdee's technology made it difficult to gain much useful information. Nonetheless, he described the situation at the river as best he could. The water still ran clear; it wasn't runoff or pollution muddying the river's flow. Likewise no stench rose into the air to indicate some other manner of befoulment of the ordinarily pristine water. But the horrible reality was undeniable all the same. When the nomads had arrived at the river they'd immediately noticed the dead fish, dozens and dozens of them, floating down the current's path. Checking up and down the riverbanks they'd found the carcasses of the savannah's land animals and birds, in all shapes and sizes, dead along the shores where the creatures had come to drink. At first the aquatic plants in the waters had looked normal, but not long after the nomads had begun to observe the river the greenery had become wilted, discolored, and finally dead, too.

"I will come to you right away," J'ni told him. She checked the comdee's screen, confirming that it had retrieved the geographic coordinates of the incoming transmission. They were along the banks of the Morrusi River where it ran south from Luppitan. "I am in Agoelo right now. It will take me several hours to reach you, even traveling on the expressway."

"I understand," the chieftain said.

"Take the phanters to the Vintall oasis. Its water comes from deep under the land, and it has been down there for a great many years. Whatever is wrong with the river, it will not be in the water there."

"I will send the herd immediately."

"And as many of your people as can leave now, too."

"Yes, we will go swiftly."

"If anything more happens before I arrive, use the comdee to contact me again."

"I will."

She wasn't sure she would be able to determine what was wrong with the river, much less figure out a way to cure whatever had turned the life-giving waters into fatal poison. But Urttu trusted her, and he'd asked for her help. J'ni couldn't have brought herself to refuse to help the nomads even if she'd wanted to. Something told her, though, that much more was at stake than one band of nomads, and one stretch of river within their traditional phanter-grazing lands.

"I will be there soon."

"Make your path here safely," the old man said, then added, *"Acai, please hurry."*

⌒つ

...intercontinental transportation hub, Durnow

Utara ran across the tarmac toward the rear of the transportation hub. Fortunately the fences and barriers along the security perimeter of the facility continued to hold, which forced the residents to enter through the main doors at the front of the hub and file their way through the terminal before exiting on tarmac level out the back. The slowed pace was causing its fair share of agitation, to be sure, but Utara was grateful for the inherent advantages in crowd control the facility provided. Outside on the tarmac, a combination of heavy barriers and metal cordons had been moved into place to create a blockade that funneled all the people into a waiting area. From there, they were directed in small groups to the various waiting transports and shuttles. The security team Daemyn had brought would never have been enough to manage the situation, but the members of Durnow's law enforcement units had voted unanimously to support the evacuation effort. With their assistance, everything was under control. So far.

Behind her engines roared. She glanced back to watch a pair of shuttles levitate from the tarmac, turn in midair, and soar away into the sky. A few strides later she reached the tarmac side of the security cordon, where Elsa Ovella was talking to a pair of Wynde Industries security operatives with large military rifles strapped diagonally across their backs. "Ready for the next ones," Utara told them.

Elsa gave a quick nod, then a hand gesture to the two men. Effortlessly they vaulted over the cordons and began to push their way through the throng of evacuees toward the doors to the hub. "More residents are still arriving out front," she explained. "We're moving the people out to the ships as quickly as we can, but we can only go so fast. I'm doing my best to keep it from devolving into a stampede up there."

"I understand. Is there anything I can do?"

"You're more useful here. The crews keep reporting that you seem to have a way with getting people to load up in an orderly fashion." Elsa offered a bit of a smile. "Funny how PDS training comes in handy for that, compared to PARTE."

Utara smiled back. "That's probably it."

The tall woman gazed out over the tarmac, watching for the hand gestures from the crewers near the transports. "Two more ready to go." She turned to the law enforcement officers manning the exit point from the cordon. "Two-fifty in one, three hundred in the other. Let's get started."

The officers started waving people through a few at a time, keeping families together and letting lone individuals or pairs slip ahead to walk faster. The bright red paint hurriedly slapped down on the tarmac showed them the path to follow. They didn't need to be told to hurry; even the children and elderly were walking as fast as they could.

Everything went smoothly for a few minutes, until a loud burst of shouts, yells, and cries exploded within the transportation hub. The people outside behind the cordon reacted immediately. Some looked back at the hub, trying to figure out what was happening inside. Others looked at the tarmac, eyes full of fear. Everyone started talking, asking questions that had no answers.

Midway into the crowd behind the cordon, a big man surged forward. Taller than Elsa and built like a phanter, he knocked several people down as he forced his way to the edge of the cordon. "Come on!" he shouted. "Let us through!"

"Step back, sir," Elsa said, her voice loud and firm, "and wait your turn."

"So you can run out of seats and leave me here to die?"

Everyone outside heard him. As if in a coordinated dance the crowd surged forward, pressing toward the barriers. The law enforcement officers held their positions, refusing to yield. But to keep control of the cordon, they also had to stop letting people through toward the transports.

"We have plenty of seats for every one of you waiting here," Utara called out. She kept her voice as reassuring as possible, and phrased her words carefully so the fearful crowd would understand she was speaking specifically about their own lives. "But if you want to be able to evacuate, you'll have to remain calm so we can proceed in an orderly manner to ensure that not even a single available seat goes unused."

The surge in the crowd ebbed, but the big man wasn't convinced. "I don't even know who in the Hells you people are," he screamed, "or why you think you get to decide who lives and who dies."

"I said," Elsa barked, "step back!"

"I don't have to take orders from you!"

"If you want to leave on our ships, you'll follow our instructions," Elsa said. Her eyes never left the man, but her hand drew the pistol holstered at her hip. "I'm not going to ask you again, step back to your previous place in the line."

"I'm not sitting here waiting to die!" he yelled. With a sudden move he reached the cordon, placed his hands atop it, and jumped over.

By the time his feet hit the tarmac, Elsa had her pistol leveled at his head. "This is your last warning. Go back to your place in line."

"No!" The big man's face was twisted with rage. "I'm leaving *now*!"

He lunged. Elsa fired. He fell.

His body thumped to the tarmac. The man screamed in wordless agony. Utara glanced down, saw him clutching his eviscerated knee, and wished she hadn't.

The crowd gasped, almost in unison. Then, hundreds of them, they went eerily silent. One of the law enforcement officers called out, "Medic!"

Elsa's hand was still in the air, pistol still leveled toward the man. Slowly, deliberately, she holstered the weapon.

"You could have killed him," Utara gasped.

"I don't miss." Elsa looked at her. Unapologetic. "If we don't get this done, they all die. If bullies get their away, everyone else dies but them. He gave me no choice."

"You didn't have to shoot him," Utara insisted.

"Yes," Elsa said, "I did." Then she turned to the law enforcement officers and ordered, "Start it back up. Let's get them loaded."

...Midland Savannahs Wildlife Sanctuary

J'ni accelerated the truck, compelling it to take her even faster along the hole-pocked dirt path through the grasses. She was pushing the limits of the vehicle's capability to cross this terrain, but she couldn't bring herself to slow down. She couldn't afford even a minute to spare in reaching the nomads gathered at the Morrusi riverbank three kilometers ahead.

Keeping her eyes fixed to the open path before her, she replayed the conversation with the nomad chieftain over and over in her mind. Every time she did, the fear gnawing inside her only got worse.

J'ni glanced down at the map display on her compupod, set up to track her current location as she drew closer to Urttu's coordinates. She was almost there. Part of her wondered if what she would find would be better or worse than the nightmares she'd been envisioning since she'd departed Agoelo and raced up the expressway at top speed before turning off to head to her destination.

A few minutes later she had her answer. The reality was definitely worse.

The dissonance in the visuals before her was staggering. The river looked as bright and true as it always did. Everywhere around it, and within it, death made its gruesome mark. And yet for all the dead animals of all shapes and sizes – bobbing atop the eddies and whirls, dragged along beneath the surface, laying lifeless on the muddy banks – not a single drop of blood tainted the immaculately clear water. J'ni wasn't sure what she had expected, but she hadn't anticipated that particular detail. Not in the slightest. She clenched her fists, struggling to process in her mind what her eyes told her was present in front of her.

At her side, Urttu gave her time to take it all in. After she finally released all her pent up emotion in a deep sigh, he spoke.

"We have many legends," the chieftain said, "and tales from our past handed down from parents to children through the years. Some of them speak of times when the water ran brown with mud, or choked full of weeds, or smelled of rotting flesh. But I cannot recall a single one where water so normal brought such death."

Acai knew quite a few of the old stories from Zanita, too. "Same for many of the other clans. I've never heard one anything like this."

"In your travels —" That was what the chieftain always called her time away from the plains of Zanita for education, first in Durnow and then at Rampart. "— have you ever heard of events like this beyond the savannah?"

"No. Never."

"I feared not."

Acai forced herself to stop looking at the river, and turned to the chieftain. "You must warn the other clans, as quickly as possible. Not every river and stream has nearly as much animal life as this one to give warning of the danger. They must be on guard of any waters, until we can find a way to determine which are still safe."

Urttu nodded. "We will send riders at once, and each clan onward to the next. Word will spread quickly."

"Yes. My *axchay* in Agoelo will be safe, but they have reached far from Durnow already. Others may be too close to the river, and still in grave danger. If the riders see anyone who fled from Durnow who is still alive, they must warn them right away."

"I will make certain they understand. *Axchay* or not, no person deserves such a fate."

"Thank you."

No amount of warning, though, would help the residents of the Future City. On its southerly journey to the sea, the waters of the Morrusi fed into the Kyetalle River — the only viable source of potable water for Durnow. Once the toxin arrived, the only options would be poison or dehydration. For anyone who remained after the evacuation ended, death was on the way.

The old man met her gaze. "Do you believe you can figure out what has made the waters into poison?"

Acai owed him the truth. "I don't know. But I will do everything in my power, use every resource I can draw upon, to get the answers we need."

TWENTY-FOUR

...intercontinental transportation hub, Durnow

"You've helped enough," Utara insisted. "Now you need to get on the shuttle."

"If you have more aircraft to load, I have more time to continue assisting." Never one to give up easily, her father stayed where he was. "Every last minute —"

"I'm not having this argument." Utara uncrossed her arms only long enough to point with both hands toward the boarding ramp next to them. "Get on board. Now."

"Only if you join us," he replied, his own arms crossed, too.

"No."

"Then we're at an impasse."

From somewhere in another part of Durnow, an explosion rumbled. Utara had lost track of how many she'd heard, but they undeniably were becoming more frequent over the past hour. The distant sound of security drone gunfire was happening more often, too.

"It's fewer than a hundred more residents at this point," she said, gesturing across the tarmac. "Elsa and her team are nearly finished."

"Then it's time for you to board, as well."

"Listen," Utara said, staring at her father. "You've got to trust me. I have a plan, okay?"

Over the last hour the drones also had started paying more attention to the departing aircraft. Although they had yet to take any aggressive action, they certainly appeared to be monitoring the outbound flights closely, sometimes flying within meters of the cockpits. With the possibility of an attack increasing, the corresponding risk was that the drones would strike before all of the aircraft had been loaded and launched, effectively trapping them on the ground. Stuck without a good option, the evacuation mission's leaders – Utara, Elsa, Daemyn, and Reiton – had agreed that their best chance was to stop departing flights temporarily, wait as long as possible to squeeze every single evacuee they possibly could aboard the ships remaining, and then launch all of them at once.

Jasiri reached out and put a hand on each of their arms. "We don't have time for your stubbornness. Either of you. Not right now."

Koster scowled. "Staying behind to make sure everyone evacuates, even if you risk ending up stranded here without a seat to leave, doesn't count as a plan."

"That's *not* my plan!"

"To be fair," Jasiri said to her husband, "it does sound like a risk she'd take."

"Well, maybe," Utara admitted. "But not this time."

"What is it, then?" her father demanded.

"The *WyndeStalker*. It's staying to see this through. Daemyn and Elsa won't leave without me. I promise." Again Utara pointed insistently at the ramp. "End of discussion."

"She gets that from you," Jasiri told Koster, taking his hand and tugging him toward the ramp. To Utara she said, "We love you. We'll see you soon."

"You will," Utara replied. "Love you too."

She watched them until they disappeared inside the shuttle. Then she waited for the ramp to close to make sure they didn't try to sneak back out – which would be very much like them. Not that she blamed her father, especially right now. Like the captain of a seagoing vessel honor-bound to lead his crew to the bitter end even as the passengers escaped on the lifeboats, Koster would never have left Durnow behind no matter how terrible living conditions might have become for its residents. Between the evacuation and the exodus to the savannah, however, only a slim fraction of the city's former population remained. His life's work, erased in a flash. But even if the city was dying, he could still help Durnow's people. Utara had pointed out that they would need him more as refugees than they ever had as residents. That was the only reason her father had consented to boarding the shuttle. And because leaving to survive another day meant he could personally ensure that no one on Prime ever forgot what the Future Cities had accomplished – and how horribly New Romas had failed them.

Once the ramp sealed, the shuttle's engines fired up for preflight checks and Utara had to back away before the noise got too loud. Taking one last look at the shuttle, she hustled back to the cordon to rejoin Elsa. Compared to the morning when the airlift fleet had arrived, filling nearly every square meter of the landing zones, the tarmac now looked deserted. Until this point, aircraft had taken off when they were full to capacity, usually two or three at time. Only the final dozen had been held back as the single flight to leave together.

The space behind the cordon, which had been overcrowded nonstop all day, was equally empty. Only a trio of law enforcement agents approached from the hub.

Elsa noticed Utara's gaze at the open space. "That's everyone we could take."

"I know."

"No time to –"

The hub doors burst open and a group of men, maybe ten of them, charged out. The law enforcement agents didn't hesitate. They turned back to intercept.

To the pair of Wynde Industries security operatives at her side Elsa said, "I thought you sealed the front doors."

"We did," one replied. "Almost two hours ago."

The men and the agents met halfway. Utara couldn't hear what the agents told them – but she could see clearly when the Aladarian in front withdrew a pistol from his jacket and shot one of the agents in the head. The Faytan next to him lunged forward, scrambling for the fallen agent's rifle. An Aquarian pulled out a pipe from behind his back and swung it. One of the agents shot him. A Terran snatched the pipe before it hit the ground. The Faytan came up with the rifle and –

Utara wasn't sure what happened next. Except that Elsa's pistols were firing, and so were the operatives' rifles, and Utara hadn't thought to cover her ears. All she knew was that her entire head was ringing.

She didn't remember crossing the tarmac to the *WyndeStalker*, or boarding, or entering the cockpit. But she was there now, and Elsa was indicating the empty seat behind Reiton in the co-pilot's seat. Daemyn was in the pilot's seat, of course, working diligently on the console. Elsa sat behind him. Utara strapped in.

Moments later *WyndeStalker* rose into the air. Daemyn kept the shuttle-craft pointed toward the transportation hub, giving them a view of the scene beyond the building once they cleared its roof. The sight wasn't as bad as Utara had feared – no rioting in progress, no bodies on the ground – but it was depressing all the same. Utara couldn't deny the reality that the airlift hadn't been big enough. Too many people had been left behind. Some people gathered sullenly on the promenade. Most, though, made up the stragglers walking away from the hub, back into the streets of the city.

"Oh, shig," Daemyn said just before an alarm began to wail from the console.

Two more alarms joined the first, then a fourth. Utara caught herself clenching the armrests of her seat, and compelled her fingers to release their grip.

"Preparing countermeasures," Reiton said.

The words left her mouth before Utara could stop them. "Countermeasures for what?"

Elsa replied without taking her eyes from the sensor console at her seat. "The security drones. They're inbound."

"How many?" Daemyn asked.

"From the looks of this," Elsa said, "all of them."

...*Prime Intelligence Service Headquarters, New Romas*

"Normally I'd say that it's always a pleasure to see you, Marx," his old friend said as the two men gripped forearms. "But today, sadly, I think we'd both rather not be having this meeting."

"Unfortunately, that's true." He indicated his companion. "This is my associate, Kirkland Oggust."

"Ah, yes." Hybollo offered a smile. "Marx has spoken very highly of your... talents."

"Thanks," Oggust replied.

"Let's have a seat and get down to business," Hybollo said, indicating the desk on the far side of the office from the door.

Monson lowered himself into the chair directly opposite Hybollo across the wide, transparent surface. Currently the glass was completely void of content. "I'll get right to the point. We have information to share, and I am confident it will qualify both myself and Master Oggust for the automatic immunity provided by the Corporate Malfeasance Whistleblower Protection Act."

The Suterran usually did an admirable job of keeping an impassive expression on his face. Not this time. "For my own peace of mind, let me remind you that the requirements for immunity are considerably higher when the informant is not affiliated with the malfeasant corporation."

"I reviewed the regulations this morning," Monson assured him. He fully appreciated why the law's restrictions were so tight. It was one thing to protect individuals who risked their careers, reputations, and sometimes even their lives to expose wrongdoing within a company they worked for. It was another thing entirely to look the other way at corporate espionage or code hacking as long as it got lucky enough to uncover misdeeds. When the stakes were sufficiently high, though, ensuring the government could obtain the truth was more important than worrying about the methods used to acquire it. "What we have isn't even close."

"All right," Hybollo said. "Tell me what you've found."

"To begin, I'd emphasize that whatever information PIS has obtained from individuals affiliated with Boynton Logistics Dynamics, either company officials or sources within the employee ranks, has extremely dubious reliability. Based on what we have uncovered, a pervasive pattern of deception exists within Boynton regarding conditions in its AI division."

"I was beginning to suspect as much," Hybollo admitted. "Let's hear what you've found."

"Initially, Boynton followed the assumption that once the central communications hub for the Future Cities had been disabled, the AIs would not be able to interact with one another any longer. Within a matter of days, however, it became clear the AIs in fact had discovered a means to continue communicating. Boynton tried to determine what the AIs were doing, but could not. So they simply have been insisting that communications are impossible without the network hub, knowing that is not true."

"That would certainly explain the rapid escalation in anti-human activities by the AIs in cities beyond Blonkas." Hybollo leaned back in his chair. "Have you figured out what the AIs are doing?"

When Monson glanced to Oggust in the chair at his right, the hacker said, "I did. Took me a while, but some spikes in hardware usage logs gave it away."

"What method are they using?"

"It's actually pretty creative," Oggust said, leaning forward in the chair. "The same comms blackouts that knocked all of our comdee traffic out of commission into and out of the Future Cities also prevents the AIs from beaming messages to each other over those networks, and similar tech like the veepee antennae. But even spread across an entire continent, the farthest distance between two cities is about four hundred kilometers. At that range, subsonic pulse bursts can travel from one city to another in a couple of minutes, and then each city can pass it along to the next one until they've all received the same message. It's not nearly as efficient or instantaneous as an electronic data network, of course. They're trading information over the course of an hour instead of seconds."

"But it's still an interconnective communications method for sharing information."

"I don't know how they came up with it," Oggust said. "But, yeah. It works."

Hybollo nodded. "How do we stop them?"

"We can't," Oggust said.

"You mean you haven't figured it out yet?"

"No. Literally, we can't. It would be like trying to stop the ripples in the water when you throw a rock in a lake. Except subsonic tones in the air."

Hybollo ran a hand over his face. "This is… very bad."

"There's more," Monson said.

"Worse?"

"Yes."

Hybollo drummed his fingers on the edge of his desk. "I almost wish I didn't have to know. But I do."

"Boynton's second network, the INMASS, is also at risk." Quickly Monson summarized Oggust's findings about the high levels of instability in the other AI network. "If it were only the instability," he continued, "the situation might be tolerable. But the problem is that the Future City AIs now hold the capacity to potentially directly interfere with the INMASS and all the AIs within its scope."

"How so?"

"At least seven cities with Boynton AIs on the INMASS fall within the geographic range of the subsonic pulse burst method. If a Future City AI were to try to make contact by that method, and the other AI received and understood the message being sent, then the information could be instantaneously shared via the INMASS with every single AI on that network."

"And if such contact happens," Hybollo continued, "likely one of the first things the INMASS AIs would do is block the kill switch just as the Future City AIs did."

"Yes. And we cannot allow that to occur. A city-by-city manual shut-down isn't an option. Loorriri will be enough of a nightmare by itself. On the scale of the INMASS, it would be impossible. We'd have to use the network."

"Right. And if there's any chance the AIs on the INMASS might start using any of the tactics of the Future Cities, like security drone attacks or the eridanthol-vanitorine toxin, we have to shut them down before they can implement it."

"Exactly."

"I'll get the authorizations ready," Hybollo said. "There's no doubt in my mind you're well within the Whistleblower Act at this point."

"Excellent," Monson said.

"I'll be right back." Hybollo rose from his chair and headed out into the corridor.

When he returned twenty minutes later, he had two transies in his hand and a grim expression on his face. "A full-complement strike team is preparing to depart for Port Vulcania," Hybollo told them. "We're raiding Boynton headquarters the moment we arrive, so they have no time to react. With the expertise you've just shown me, we'll need you for this – both of you. Get your things from your hotel and come to the airfield; I'll send the coordinate to your comm. Flight leaves in an hour."

"We'll be there," Monson promised.

For a raid this important, Intelligence Chief Maxilla Firebird would be there, too. Which meant Monson had to find a way to get himself in front of her at some point during the raid. At least he had some time to figure out the angle. Some extra level of accomplishment to earn a meeting with the Chief.

One meeting. That was all he would need to break out of corporate intelligence and into the PIS. Where he could make a difference not merely for a company's bottom line, but for Prime. His goal was so close to achievement he could almost taste it.

…WyndeStalker

"*Stalker*," Daemyn shouted. "Activate tactical holo."

In a flash the entire layout of the heads-up display changed from the shuttlecraft's routine flight parameters to a version nearly identical to the one in his Airspar cockpit – except this time the weapons involved were entirely real. Daemyn assessed the inbound vectors most closely associated with *Stalker*, then considered the broader ramifications of a dozen airlift transports and nearly twenty security drones.

He saw options, but not many. And none of them were any good.

"Countermeasures ready," Holtspring said.

"Hold them," Daemyn replied. "Elsa?"

"Drones still inbound. Not a single shot fired."

"Yet," Daemyn muttered. He blew out a quick breath. "Let's see what they do."

Three columns of drones approached the airlift flotilla from three directions. Only when they drew close did the arrangement of drones finally split apart. Suddenly the heads-up was filled with a kinetic splatter of dots.

"Whoa," Holtspring said.

"Right?" Daemyn watched, looking for a pattern. Really, though, it just looked like a hornet swarm raging around a hive. "What in the Hells are they —"

Then his eyes found the altimeter readings along the left edge of the holo, and he figured it out. "Pinning us low." He asked Elsa, "Are we still in the comms bubble?"

"Affirmative."

"Shig." He checked the holo again. The drones were spread around the flotilla, roughly encircling it, but more of the drones were coming over the top of the evacuation aircraft. Like a net to keep them down.

A net made of engine-powered metal armed with machineguns.

"Let's hope everyone has the sense not to fly into one of them, then, at least until we can get out a warning."

At the speed the aircraft were flying, though, it wouldn't take long to reach the city walls. Little favors had to count for something.

From behind him Utara asked, "Why?"

"Not sure yet," Daemyn told her.

He rotated *Stalker* ninety degrees and accelerated, passing between two of the larger, clumsier transports. Leveling the shuttlecraft, he swung beneath a third transport before looping to port to overcome another shuttle. Along with one of WI's shuttles, *WyndeStalker* was now at the front of the flotilla's formation.

Moments later the city walls passed beneath them, and the rooftops of Durnow were replaced by the rolling grasses of the savannah. Just as abruptly the drones began to shift formation. Proximity alarms wailed on the console.

Daemyn plunged the yoke, shedding altitude fast. At least outside the city he no longer had to worry about colliding with a building or antenna. He checked the tactical holo for the status of the other ships. Sure enough, all of them were decreasing altitude too, though the less maneuverable ones were descending more gradually than *Stalker*.

A half dozen drones raced past, taking up positions ahead of the flotilla.

"Can their guns fire backwards?" Holtspring asked.

"No," Utara said. "Forward-mounted only."

Daemyn was about to breathe a sigh of relief when he realized the drones hadn't slowed down, but kept accelerating ahead of them. Simultaneously on the tactical holo, the downward pressure from the overhead drones eased when they leveled off, allowing the evacuation aircraft to maintain a steady altitude a few dozen meters above the savannah.

Holtspring continued, "Then what are they —"

The drones ahead opened fire. At the empty ground.

Utara spoke for all of them when she said, "What the —"

The drones continued to fire. The impact of their heavy bullets kicked up soil, rocks, and dirt into rising columns of brown. The more they fired, the more debris filled the air.

"Oh, no," Daemyn said.

"Comms clear," Elsa called out.

Daemyn slapped the button on the console so hard he worried he'd broken it. "All aircraft, slow down. Slow down!" He paused, jamming the pedals and yanking the yoke. "Repeat, decrease velocity. Let the debris drop out of your path. They're trying to kick it up into your engines."

With *Stalker*'s superior maneuverability, Daemyn let the shuttlecraft drop closer to the ground. The other aircraft passed over the top of them, also trying to slow. Then he pulled *Stalker* into a climb again to miss the worst of the airborne dirt.

More drones zoomed over them, joining the others ahead of the flotilla formation. Their machineguns also erupted, ejecting even more debris into their path.

One of the large transports couldn't get out of the way in time. It rocked violently side to side. Its outer starboard engine erupted in a ball of flames. The pilot managed to shut down the engine before the fire worsened, but now the transport's trajectory wobbled even worse.

To the side, another transport tried to climb higher. In response a pair of drones buzzed its cockpit so closely Daemyn thought they would actually collide. But they didn't, and the pilot brought the transport back into line.

A shout came over the comm. *"They're right on my tail! Speed up!"*

Daemyn checked the holo. The pilot was right. The drones flying at the rear of the flotilla had pushed forward, now flying within meters of the back aircraft.

"If we speed up," another pilot yelled on the comm, *"our engines will never make it through that chaff!"*

The struggling transport was only having even more trouble staying airborne, and the lead drones were still kicking up massive amounts of dust and debris directly into their trapped flight path.

"My ship can't take much more of this!" a third pilot declared.

"Mine can't either," another added.

"Why don't they just shoot us down?" Holtspring asked.

"Only one reason," Elsa said. "They want everyone alive."

"I've got one buzzing me hard," came Brutus' voice on a private comm line. The test pilot was flying the WI shuttle at the front of the formation. *"And it's getting more reckless with every new approach."*

A quick glance at the holo confirmed only the WI shuttle had its own individual harasser in the pursuit. "Why that ship," he asked, "out of all of them?"

"Because," Utara said, her voice flat, "my father's on board."

"Vindictiveness? Or desperation?" Elsa asked.

"I don't know," Utara replied. "But we're abandoning the city – and they're trying to force us to go back."

"Sure seems like it," Daemyn said.

As if on cue, the tactical holo showed exactly that. The drones on the starboard side of the formation drew closer, forcing the flotilla aircraft into a turn. To port, the drones yielded, creating room for the turn to proceed. As more of the ships started to make the turn, the forward drones reduced their rate of fire into the ground – rewarding compliance. Slowly, in a big wide arc over the savannah, the airlift was being forced back around toward Durnow.

Utara asked the million-dract question. "And if we don't?"

Daemyn didn't know the answer.

Without a landing field, nearly all of the flotilla's aircraft would crash catastrophically on the savannah. Putting down out here wasn't an option.

Going back to Durnow was, but that had to be the last resort.

The drones had set the pace of flight so far, but only because the airlift ships were flying at far from full throttle due to the drones' net entrapping them. If the shuttles and transports could get up to speed, they would leave the drones behind in seconds. The problem was the seconds before then, the time it would take the vessels to accelerate…

Daemyn toggled the comm. "If they really wanted us dead, we already would be. Time to call their bluff. Everyone, maximum acceleration on my mark." He waited only a second for the instruction to sink in. "Mark!"

The g-force of *Stalker*'s acceleration slammed them back in their seats. The large transports were close enough that the roar of their engines pushing to top speed reverberated even within the shuttlecraft's sealed cockpit. For a second the drones ahead of the formation appeared to rush backward toward the airlift ships. Then, in unison, the drones reacted.

Daemyn watched it all on the tactical holo. The drones at the rear of the formation opened fire with their machineguns. The drones over the top of them began to dive-bomb toward the transports, trying to keep them low. The drones in front stopped firing, spread out wide, and slowed.

Three of the transports rose toward the sky. One dodged a plummeting drone. Another managed to twist just enough to endure only a long scrape along its dorsal hull. A third took a direct hit on its nose, but kept flying.

The transport with the wrecked engine, though, wasn't so lucky. Unable to accelerate as fast, it couldn't zoom past the drones ahead of it. With one engine offline, the attempt to swerve wasn't quick enough, either. Two drones cut their engines and hung dead in the air – and the transport flew straight into them.

The explosion lit *Stalker*'s entire front viewport with the fiery hues. The blast wave buffeted them, but Daemyn's firm grip on the yoke rode them through it without a loss in forward momentum. He pulled them into a climb, pushing the engines harder until he caught up to Brutus's shuttle.

More maneuverable than the transports, most of the shuttles dodged the drones' gunfire. To *Stalker*'s port, one took a chain of machinegun fire to the wing, shearing the metal clear off the side of the ship. The damaged shuttle lost control, plunging into a death spiral toward the savannah below.

To starboard, bullets shredded the main engine of another shuttle. It fought for altitude, and lost. Moments later it too plummeted uncontrollably toward the ground.

Drones closed on *Stalker* and the WI shuttle. Daemyn checked the holo. They were clear of the other ships now. He slipped *Stalker* slightly to aft of Brutus. To Holtspring he called out, "Deploy countermeasures."

Clearly the drones hadn't been expecting that. They spun and spiraled, avoiding the flares and boomers ejected from *Stalker*'s rear-mounted ventral firing tubes.

Another blast wave rocked *Stalker* from aft. One of the transports had exploded, taking out one of the shuttles along with it.

Daemyn was about to tell Holtspring to eject another round of counter-measures when he realized all of the drone-dots were receding rapidly on the holo. He checked again, making sure he wasn't seeing things. But the holo was accurate.

Stalker and the remaining evacuation aircraft rose higher into the sky, free from the deadly trap of security drones.

But only half of them had made it.

DESPERATE MEASURES

"Effective Immediately — any and all Future Cities intel designated Internal Distribution Only. Forward all inquiries directly to the Office of the Chief."

Urgent Bulletin (All Staff), Prime Intelligence Service

TWENTY-FIVE

…Auxiliary Hangar Delta, Aladarian Guard Rescue & Recovery Operations Base, Steamer Point

"Utara?"

She recognized the voice before she turned around. In that instant, she didn't care about the crisis, or all the work to be done, or the formalities of the Aladarian Guard. She bounded over and pulled her friend Trace Chal into a tight embrace.

The other woman hugged her with equal fervor in return. When she stepped back she said, "I'd say it's good to see you, but…"

"Same," Utara said. She took both of Trace's hands in hers. "Thank you."

"Of course," Trace said. "But don't thank me. This was way above my pay grade. It's Captain Forta who exercised his authority to make this possible."

"Maybe so, but I doubt he would have done it only with a plea from me. You're very persuasive when you want to be."

"If you say so. Regardless, it didn't hurt that I leaned hard on the obligation to put the capabilities at Steamer Point to their best use. The Guard has housed refugees at this base several times over the past decade. Various natural disasters, hurricanes, earthquakes, and the like."

"See? I couldn't have known that, but I'm sure it resonated with the Captain."

Trace grinned. "I suppose it did."

"I doubt they've ever had to manage this many people at once, though."

"No. Never quite the same scale of human tragedy before, either."

Utara could only nod. "At this point I have many questions, and very few answers. About Durnow, much less the other Future Cities."

"The top priority for us has been getting the base ready for the refugees, of course. But Captain Forta clearly was distressed with the information I provided to him. Last I spoke to him, he'd been able to make only a few preliminary inquiries through the Guards and the Unified Forces, and he didn't seem the least bit satisfied. From what he said to me, I get the feeling he wants to get to the bottom of this, too."

"The more allies I have pushing for the truth, the better. Let me know if there's anything I can do to assist."

"I will. Though I should warn you, impressing the Captain can have its own downsides at times."

"How's that?"

Trace winked. "In the Guard, it might get a person assigned to his personal staff. For you, don't be surprised if you end up on the receiving end of a hard-sell recruitment pitch for reenlisting."

Utara smiled. "I'll keep that in mind."

"I'm sorry I can't stay longer; I'm expected back. But I wanted to be sure to see you as soon as I could."

"It's all right," Utara said, reaching out to squeeze her friend's hand one more time. "There's a great deal more left to do here, anyway."

"Many blessings," Trace said, already striding toward the exit.

"Many blessings."

Utara took a deep breath before walking the few paces back to the wall. Six oversized sheets of transi covered most of the brick. Affixed with adhesive tape, they rustled in the drafts from the overhead fans along the peak of the vaulted ceiling. She took a moment and skimmed over the lists one more time.

"That's everyone?" she asked the Guard ensign who'd been helping her.

"Confirmed," Paige said. The teenager couldn't have been more than a few months into her service term, but she had worked tirelessly at Utara's side for the past few hours without missing a beat.

"Good."

Utara finally let herself feel a little bit of relief. To maintain simplicity amid the chaos, the Guard soldiers had kept each new batch of arrivals together in the same groups that had boarded the airlift flights, however happenstance the conglomeration of individuals might have been. When Utara and Paige had moved from group to group, recording which flight's passengers were located in which of the makeshift housing locations at the base, they had appointed a single liaison for each group. Often it was a volunteer or a trusted elder, but in each case Utara had insisted that they not be called *leaders* or anything implying authority over the others; their task was simply to serve as the key point of contact between that group of evacuees and the Guard.

The liaisons' first task, already underway, was to compile a list of the members of their evacuation group. Names, ages, occupations, former address within Durnow, names of family members also living in Durnow, and anything else the individuals could provide. The more biographical data gathered, the better.

Only then would they know who had made it out of Durnow – and who hadn't.

In the coming days, once the immediate urgency of the evacuation had eased, extended families could be reunited and erstwhile neighbors housed nearby to each other again. Today, though, everyone was happy to be alive and, more importantly, away from Durnow. Their temporary new reality, tens of thousands of people huddled on the unforgiving stone floors of the base's massive hangars, would sink in soon enough. Utara would deal with that problem next. Right now, she let herself enjoy the moment's sense of accomplishment that the lists of evacuation groups and their respective liaisons was finished, double-checked, and accurate.

"You look like you could use a break," Paige said. "I think we have a pretty good handle on this for now."

"I'm fine."

"If you have other friends in the Guard here, it's okay if you want to go say hello to them, too."

"I don't, at least as far as I know. But thank you for the offer."

"You're welcome."

Utara appraised the transies a few minutes longer. The whole time, Paige kept glancing at her – and it was starting to make Utara self-conscious. Maybe she really did look that tired. She was about to say something to Paige when another thought occurred to her. There was one more person at the base she wouldn't mind tracking down.

...Aladarian Guard base

"Daemyn!"

He stepped out from beneath *WyndeStalker*'s wing, wiping his hands on the rag tucked into the back of his belt. "Over here."

Utara jogged up to him, crossing the open tarmac faster that he'd expected. "Have you been avoiding me?"

"Uh, no."

"You're sure?"

He smiled. "Yes. *Stalker* needed a thorough inspection, that's all."

"Oh, I'd assumed so." She peered at him. "For five hours?"

He wiped his hands again. "All right. Maybe there's some avoiding. But it's not you. I'm not sure I'm ready to deal with... people yet."

"You mean the pilots."

"Right. And Holtspring and Tames."

"How about the evacuees?" She motioned across the tarmac, to the main area of the base in the distance. "Have you gone over to see the refugee area yet?"

"No. I haven't."

"You should. It's really quite remarkable how much the Guard has set up for them already, in such little time. It's better than anything I let myself expect."

"Maybe later."

She reached out and touched his arm. "You need to see it for yourself, Daemyn. To understand what you did. How much of a difference you made for these people."

"*We* made."

"Maybe so," Utara said. "But you're the one dwelling on the losses."

Her tone was gentle, and the look in her eyes was kind. But the words still stung. Probably because she was right. "We watched them die."

"That's true," she conceded. "And it was awful. Terrible." She shuddered. "Not something I ever want to witness again, that's for sure."

Daemyn heard something in her tone. "However?"

Utara gave him a little smile. "*However*, I've also seen what we accomplished. All the people we saved."

"So I'm just supposed to forget about all the ones who died? Who died because of decisions I screwed up?"

"No. Not at all. I'm only asking you to try to start to accept that their deaths weren't for nothing."

He scowled. "I doubt they'd see it that way."

"Maybe, maybe not. What's the alternative? No mission at all, and everyone's still stuck back in Durnow?"

"No," he admitted. "That wasn't an option."

"Exactly," Utara said. She took one of his hands in both of hers. "I know you hold yourself responsible that those pilots died."

"Everyone on their ships, too," he insisted.

"Yes." She stared right into his eyes. "But what about all the people who died in Durnow before we got there? Over the weeks and days before we arrived. Do you blame yourself for not saving them sooner?"

Daemyn stared back, and found he couldn't lie to her. "No."

"Those pilots, you'd met them. You'd briefed them on the operation. Maybe even remember their faces. So it hits you hard that they're dead."

He could only nod.

"You're focused on what went wrong because you knew them, and you watched the ships go down. But all those people you evacuated, everyone from the hours and hours before the last flight out, they're still abstract to you. Let's change that." She squeezed his hand. "I have some instruction transies I need to distribute, and some preliminary lists of names I need to deliver. I'll be walking through a lot of the base for the next hour. Come with me. Meet them. See them. Make them real."

Daemyn took a deep breath. "I'll think about it."

"Would you sacrifice the lives of almost half the population of Durnow," Utara asked, "just to spare yourself the grief and guilt for the six ships that didn't make it out?"

"Of course not," Daemyn said before he even processed what he was saying.

"Right answer." She tugged him, gently, toward the direction of the base. "I understand what you're going through. I really do. Here's the thing – intellectually, you know you achieved something good from this operation as a whole. It's your emotions getting in the way of accepting it."

Daemyn chuckled. "You had this whole conversation planned when you came over here, didn't you? This whole little intervention?"

"Actually, no."

He wasn't sure if that made him feel better or worse about how quickly she'd been able to get him where he was now – following her across the tarmac into the base – but either way he was impressed. Besides, an hour with her, spent among the evacuees, would be an hour he wouldn't have to think about the downed aircraft. That was a good thing, even if she'd tricked him into it.

By the time they finished, an hour had turned into two – and Daemyn had accepted that Utara had been absolutely right. Seeing the refugees, witnessing first hand all the lives they had saved, made him feel a lot better. It didn't erase the feeling of blood on his hands, not by a long shot, but it reinforced that they had done the best they could under the circumstances. Entire families, whole neighborhoods, had survived to live another day. He couldn't help but acknowledge the good in that.

Especially after the last half hour. They'd both realized that they hadn't eaten since arriving at the base, and they'd joined a group of four or five families sharing a simple meal of military rations and water while congregated around a low wall that served as seats for those not limber enough to sit on the ground. One of the families, a Terran father and Aquarian mother and their son, had kept Daemyn enraptured. Not because there was anything special about them, really, but they simply reminded him so much of his own family two decades earlier.

For all these years, Daemyn had remembered the pilot who'd flown their evacuation shuttlecraft to safety. He'd never spared a second thought for the people who had found them shelter, given them food and clothing, during the few weeks it had taken for his parents to resettle the family to Buneen. But someone had helped them back then, just as Utara and the Aladarian

Guard were helping the Durnow refugees now. And the opportunities for relocation after the firestorm, for all the displaced Faytans in general and his family in particular, had been made far easier by the drastically greater wealth of Hyj-gon compared to the Future Cities like Durnow. These people were in for a much longer transition period than the Kuron-Wynde family had faced.

"Thank you," he told her. "You were right. That was good for me. But I'm sure you have to get back to work, and I need to catch up with Reiton and Rustle to make sure we're sending back the aircraft on schedule."

"I do have a lot more to do," she admitted. Before he could react she stepped forward and hugged him. Harder than he'd expected. From the quiet noise that came from her, maybe harder than she'd meant, too. "You're welcome."

He held her close.

She stepped back and looked into his eyes. "I owe you one."

He smiled. "You're a pretty good tour guide, you know that? When everything calms down, maybe I'll take you up on seeing the sights of Loorriri."

She gave a quick nod. "Deal."

～⌒

...PIS Field Office, Port Vulcania

The status update had been short and to the point. The venturist evacuation of Durnow had succeeded beyond the PIS analysts' expectations. Satellite imagery had confirmed that a few aircraft had been shot down by the AI's drones during the last flight out of the city, but otherwise many of the residents had been saved. The people who hadn't been evacuated, though, were as good as dead – and a second airlift would be impossible. It was only a matter of hours, at most, before the other Future City AIs learned of what had occurred at Durnow and readied themselves to take offensive action against any similar airlift attempt within their walls. In the meantime, the eridanthol-vanitorine toxin was spreading far and wide along the rivers of southwest Loorriri, an unstoppable march of death. Monson imagined the rest of the meeting would have to be less depressing.

"We have much to assess overall regarding the Loorriri crisis," Chief Firebird told the two dozen people gathered in the conference room, "but right now we have one and only one priority: shutting down the Future City AIs as quickly as possible. Have we made any progress in achieving that?"

"Not really," Hybollo admitted. "Most of the underlings have cooperated without hesitation. A few of the supervisors gave us a little stalling, but they've all started cooperating at this point, too. The problem is, so far none of them has any idea how to accomplish what we need to do."

"That's not surprising," Monson said. The situation wouldn't be any different if it were Grandell Motors suffering severe PIS scrutiny. "Boynton seems completely incapable of addressing this situation of their own creation."

From his seat next to Monson, Oggust put up his hand in the air with all the hesitancy of an anxious schoolboy afraid to give the teacher the incorrect answer. Monson successfully managed not to laugh. For her part, Chief Firebird smiled ever so slightly before she pointed to him and said, "Yes?"

Oggust cleared his throat. "They may not have any idea how to get these things turned off, but it wouldn't take me long to figure it out. Ripping apart other people's code... " He shrugged, almost apologetically. "No problem. It's what I do."

Though some of the PIS agents around the table murmured skeptically, Firebird didn't waver in holding Oggust's gaze. "How soon?"

"A day, probably." Oggust canted his head back and forth. "Two, maybe, if the code's a lot more complicated than I'm expecting. But I doubt it."

Firebird looked around the table. "Anyone else have any prospects for a quicker solution than that?" The murmuring fell abruptly silent. "Very well, then," the grim Aladarian declared. "We will of course continue with our other lines of inquiry, as well. But let's get Master Oggust here started right away."

"Well, that's the thing." Oggust's fingers fidgeted along the edge of the table. "I'd need to be working with the raw coding itself. I've tried accessing the backup copies onsite, but they're encrypted. Twenty-eight digit passcode, thirty-two variables per digit. A logarithm would crack it eventually, but –"

"We don't have that kind of time," Firebird said.

"Right."

"So," Firebird asked, looking around the table, "how do we go about getting this necessary passcode?"

"Actually, Chief," Hybollo said, "I think I might know."

"Go ahead."

Hybollo shuffled through the stacks of transies before him on the conference table, scanning for something. "Based on our initial approach, the individuals on the corporate org chart next up for interrogation would be the three program managers for the city-management AI program. But if we're looking to get the raw code for the entire AIs, we'd have to go higher."

Firebird nodded. "Who do you have in mind?"

"I suspect that the top-ranking officers, even the Vice President for the AI division, are number-crunchers and personnel-managers, not technical people."

"That's certainly true at Grandell Motors," Monson pointed out.

"Right. So I was thinking..." Hybollo found the transi he was looking for and snatched it up with a flourish. "This guy."

Monson leaned over to skim the page. Gorbin Canter. His title wasn't that impressive – technical assistant – but his position on the org chart was. He reported directly to the AI division's VP.

"The right combination," Monson said. "Important enough to have access to everything, competent enough to understand how the tech actually works."

"Exactly."

"Anyone disagree?" Firebird asked. When no one objected, she looked back to Hybollo. "All right, get to it. See what he'll give up."

"Yes, Chief." As Hybollo rose, he motioned for Monson to join him.

Once they were out into the corridor, Hybollo explained, "You know how these Boynton folks think a lot better than I do."

"I suppose that's true."

"Oggust will manage in there with all those agents surrounding him?"

Monson grinned. "He'll survive."

They walked quickly, and it only took a few minutes to reach their destination. "He's in here," Hybollo said, stopping in front of Room 6 in the hallway lined on both sides with interrogation rooms. "We can –"

"Actually, you try alone first," Monson said.

Hybollo considered it, then chuckled. "I'll just be my natural self. You think you can smooth-talk him if my grumpiness doesn't work?"

"Absolutely."

"All right. I'll signal for you when it's time to switch off." Hybollo tapped his identification badge on the scanner. "Here we go."

Monson strode to the next door down and walked into the unlocked observation room. He bypassed the chairs and chose to remain standing a meter from the one-way window that separated the two rooms.

He listened to Hybollo's questioning, but his eyes never left Gorbin Canter. The Terran was entirely nondescript. Nothing remarkable about him at all. Even his haircut and his clothes were utterly ordinary. His personality was equally flat, and it didn't take long for Monson to determine it wasn't an act or a symptom of fear or anger. The man was simply... boring.

But he knew the company line. By the seventeenth time Canter used the words "it's proprietary" when insisting he couldn't give Hybollo what he sought, Monson was thoroughly regretting the plan of having the Senior Agent start the interrogation alone. Even when Hybollo explained the gravity of the crisis and the necessity of deactivating the AIs with the greatest possible haste, Canter kept saying, "it's proprietary."

Forty-seven minutes into the questioning, Hybollo still hadn't given the signal. Maybe he believed he was making progress, but Monson knew better. Canter had what they needed, but he simply wasn't going to surrender it – not to someone using Hybollo's techniques, at least. Monson exited the observation room, tapped his badge on the scanner, and flung open the door to the interrogation room. Both Canter and Hybollo looked his direction in surprise.

"You had your chance to cooperate with Agent Hybollo," Monson said. "Now, we're going to finish this my way."

TWENTY-SIX

Utara considered stopping for now, then changed her mind. The comms directory for PDS headquarters in New Romas remained toggled red from top to bottom. After leaving voice messages for a few of the envoys and other mid-level officials she knew personally, she hadn't bothered doing so for the others she'd tried next. She might as well take her chances on the last two envoys with oversight roles that included Loorriri, though.

She tapped the icon for Envoy Bozeman and waited. After nearly a minute the comm finally connected – only to drop her into the voice message system. No point in that. She tapped to end the comm.

Last on the directly was Envoy Walton. Finger waiting over the icon to end the transmission when it proved futile too, Utara had to jerk her hand away from the screen when the comm line clicked open to make sure she didn't touch anything accidentally.

"Envoy Walton's office," the man's voice said.

"Yes, this is Counselor Utara Fireheart," she replied. "I am dealing with a very urgent situation regarding Durnow, and –"

"I'm sorry, Counselor, but Envoy Walton isn't available."

"As I said, this is a matter of grave urgency. I don't mind holding."

"It may... be a while."

"I've been trying to reach someone in New Romas all day, and you're the first actual person I've spoken to in over an hour. I'll wait as long as it takes."

"That's really not a good idea. And I can't tie up the line."

"I'll be reachable at this comm code for the duration of the business day, New Romas time. Can you at least give me a sense of when Envoy Walton might be able to return my comm?"

The man was silent for an inordinately long time. *"I'm sorry, Counselor, but I don't think I can give you a reliable estimate."*

"Very well," Utara said, and ended the comm.

For a moment she sat staring at the screen and the obstructionist PDS directory it displayed. Then she reached up, removed the comms headset from her ears, and set it down atop the comms station.

Beside her, Trace Chal said "thank you" into her headset and tapped her screen. She glanced to Utara and nodded. Removing her headset, she spun her chair so the two women faced each other. "Any progress?"

"Not even a little bit."

"I've been through eight of the contacts from Captain Forta. Nothing from them, either. I still have four left."

Utara nodded. As an institution, the Aladarian Guard had no reason to possess any insight into the status of the Future Cities. The Guard had a few sparsely staffed outpost bases on Loorriri, but none of its personnel were deployed in the cities. The situation was the same with the Terran Guard, and she was pretty sure the Faytan and Aquarian Guards didn't have a presence on the continent at all.

The Unified Forces was another matter. Between operational deployments, surveillance satellites, and recruiting centers in the cities, the military certainly would have at least some information on what was happening. No doubt it was all classified, but high-ranking officers in the Guards had comparable security clearances to their counterparts in the Unified Forces. Utara didn't know the regulations in detail, but she was pretty sure it wasn't even legal for Captain Forta's contacts in the military to refuse to recognize Chal's deputized inquiries under his credentials, which were tantamount to requests from the Captain himself. If they were doing it anyway, then something very untoward was taking place.

"Hopefully one of them will do the right thing," Utara said. "Forta isn't the only one with integrity in the chain of command."

"No," Trace agreed. "But fear causes people to do all kinds of things they otherwise would never dream of doing."

"Tell me about it."

"Any luck getting through to the Future Cities?"

"Not one." Utara forced herself not to think about Blonkas, and Evostown, and Aidan. "I tried all the comm codes I know or could look up. PDS field offices, personal comdees, anything. I'm not even getting through to voice messages."

"Comms blackouts over all twelve?"

"Yes."

Trace's expression grew worried. "There's no way the Unified Forces doesn't know about that. They'd have to."

"I'd certainly think so."

"Well, let me try these last few. Then we report back to the Captain and see what he says. Maybe he'll be willing to make a comm personally."

Utara didn't have any confidence that it would matter. She smiled at her friend and said, "Sounds good. I'll try a few more while you're doing that."

"It's a plan," Trace said, hefting the headset back over her ears.

Utara tugged on her own headset and looked back at the display screen. Forta had given the two of them full access to the pair of comms stations, with the assurance that neither cost nor authority was an obstacle to any comms they made. From the look in his eyes, Utara had known he wanted answers as much as they did.

She considered her options. Above the PDS into the Cultural Ministry hierarchy, perhaps? A Senator, or a delegate from the Lower Assembly? Who would want to help? Who would even care? At this point she didn't need to get information directly – she just needed someone to ask the right questions, with enough power that they couldn't be refused answers.

Her fingers drummed on the edge of the workstation. She hissed out a sigh. It was probably a good thing Trace was almost done with her list; Utara needed a break. She glanced up from the screen. Her eyes happened to fall upon the veepee mounted in the upper corner of the room. Currently it was deactivated, its screen blank.

Still, it made Utara remember something: there was more than one kind of power.

She took a breath. It was one thing to make herself a persistent, meddlesome pest from bottom to top in the PDS hierarchy until its leadership took action. Bringing the fiery heat of media attention down on their heads was something else. She would pay a high price. It might even cost her a PDS career. Utara took another breath.

She entered a comdee code on the screen. It processed the request for nearly a minute before a burst of static preceded the voice.

"This is Reiton Holtspring."

"It's Utara Fireheart." From the incoming comm code, he would have known it was someone from the Steamer Point base. "I won't keep you long, and I hate to contact you asking for another favor, but I think this one is quick and simple."

"You're safe? Did something happen to Daemyn?"

"Everyone's fine here. Thank you for your concern. Are the aircraft making their return flights successfully?"

"Without a hitch so far, fortunately. I'm quite pleased. So, what is it you need?"

"In your line of work, you must have to deal with the media quite a bit. To try to keep the coverage going your way or tell your side of the story, give a tip about something bad on a rival or something favorable on your company. Situations of that nature."

"That's right."

"Hypothetically, if I wanted to make contact with a reporter – would you have a name to recommend? Someone trustworthy?"

He didn't hesitate. *"Absolutely."*

...PIS Field Office, Port Vulcania

The good news was very good indeed. Kirkland Oggust had lived up to his boast. Less than a day from Gorbin Canter's surrender of the raw AI code, and the PIS already was well on its way to possessing a fully operational code virus that would wipe the AIs out of commission within minutes after its insertion into their systems.

The bad news, however, made Monson's blood boil. Despite Monson, Hybollo, and Oggust impressing upon Chief Firebird and all of her top lieu-tenants the necessity of devising a delivery mechanism as soon as possible, the PIS apparently had made exactly zero progress toward a viable solution. The ability to take down the AIs wouldn't make the least bit of difference without a means to exercise the power they held.

As the others filed out of the room from the status briefing, Monson stayed behind. He took a deep breath. Then another. No longer could he deny the truth – years had passed since anything had created such emotions in him. Powerlessness. Helplessness. But today, they were real. And he had to make them disappear as soon as possible.

An old trick came back to mind. Simple yet effective. He would take a walk.

Monson paced through the streets of Port Vulcania. He put only the bare minimum mental effort into his journey – avoiding collisions with other pedestrians, crossing the traffic lanes at the proper time, pausing to let an elderly couple pass in front of him – and paid no attention to his path. All of his concentration was focused upon the problem he faced. Primean civilization had to be saved, and the danger was far too massive for Monson – for anyone – to solve alone.

He blinked. Apparently his footsteps had brought him to the city park that stretched along the northern edge of the harbor. Across the waters the seaport, one of the world's busiest, hummed with an incomprehensible hive of activity. As if nothing was amiss, and this was merely another ordinary day in life on Prime. Monson knew the truth.

More than that. He feared it. The emotion he despised more than any other.

He took a series of slow, deep breaths. He removed his shoes and set them atop a boulder. He rolled up the cuffs of his pants as far as he could, not quite to the knees. Then he walked slowly, step by step, across the pebbles and into the shallows where the saltwater lapped the shore. For a moment he shivered against the chill, but quickly it passed. He shifted to face the open sea beyond the harbor. He closed his eyes.

The water's surface rose and fell in a gentle rhythm as the waves passed by him to reach the pebbles. Tiny eddies swirled around his feet when the water retreated back into the sea. Ebb and flow. Forward and back. All around him the seabirds cawed and cried, an endless extemporaneous symphony.

From the seaport a loud *fffwhonnnnk* sounded from a cargo vessel's horn. Despite himself, Monson chuckled. Technology couldn't help ruining his day, apparently.

He kept his eyes closed, surrendering to the cries of the birds and the rhythm of the waters. He cleared his thoughts of everything but the immediate dilemma.

The AIs were code. Incredibly complex and sophisticated code, but still nothing more than code. They had no emotions, no judgment, no sentience. Only algorithms. Supposedly that was their great advantage over human decision-making: they were impartial and unbiased, immune to personal weaknesses and venal corruption. Now, it posed their great danger: the inability to consider any factors beyond their programming. Ultimately, they were only code.

And that would be their undoing. Code could be rewritten, even erased. Oggust's code virus would take down the electronic AIs as effectively as a fatal disease in a biological organism.

The challenge was clear: Monson needed to figure out how to infect their systems. To sicken a person, any number of delivery mechanisms might suffice: consumption of tainted food or beverage, inhaled aerialized particles, contact toxin applied to skin, even direct injection into the veins by syringe. Options for breaching into code, though, were more limited. For one thing, the AIs would be on guard against what they now had classified as human threats, so any recognizable attempt to modify their code would be blocked long before it neared installation. Somehow they had to infect the AIs without the supercomputers recognizing what was occurring. Worse, with the Boynton Logistics Dynamics network disabled, the easy route for code delivery was unavailable. The Future Cities' AIs would have to be taken offline one by one, by some method on site in Loorriri itself – where the AIs, their drones, and their poison held sway.

Rarely did Monson ever feel so completely at a loss about how to proceed. Even with his mind clear, no productive course of action presented itself to him.

At that precise moment, something utterly unexpected happened.

The wings fluttered and the air washed over his face. The tiny feet plopped down on his shoulder, adjusting several times before coming to rest.

Monson turned his head, then opened his eyes.

The bird was staring right back at him.

He thought it might shriek in his face, but it didn't. So he said, "Hello there."

The bird canted its head, appraising him. Then it pushed off with its feet, pumped its wings, and soared off over waves.

Monson understood.

And his sign had come not from Evos, but from Fayti.

Monson laughed. To beat the AIs, it would take the very best Prime had to offer.

He had been able to breach the security parameters of every company he had tried to investigate or infiltrate – except one. Every other firm had a weakness of some kind: a disgruntled subordinate, an underpaid and therefore bribable guard, out-of-date access codes, or any number of other defects Monson could exploit to learn what he desired. But not this one. Honestly, it had been driving him crazy. Yet that signified something else in turn: this particular adversary posed a challenge like none of the others. And if that was true, then the Faytan who ran it was something Monson rarely found. An intellectual equal. A peer.

Monson spun and splashed his way toward the shore. Much as he hated the idea, he knew what he had to do.

He knew who he needed: Daemyn Wynde.

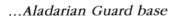

...Aladarian Guard base

Daemyn held his jacket closed across his chest. From its name, Steamer Point sounded like a nice tropical locale. Apparently it actually had been named after the seafaring vessels of a few centuries' past – the ones powered by steam engines. Because the weather here was quite unpleasant. Ironic that a Faytan would be so bothered by cold gusts of air, but the gods knew no mercy sometimes. He pulled the jacket tighter and shivered against another blast of chilly air.

The last dozen transports from the Durnow evacuation lifted off from the secondary landing field and rose into the cloud-covered sky. He stayed in place and watched them go. Reiton and Rustle had assured him that everything was going well on the arrival end, getting the various aircraft returned to their usual assignments. With the departures concluded, now Daemyn had to decide what to do. Elsa was probably right that his top priority remained getting back to Wynde Industries and figuring out what to do about the Project Lariat hack. Seeing the refugees with Utara yesterday, though, realizing how much help all of these people still needed… Maybe that was more important.

Walking slowly back into the base to begin weaving his way toward *WyndeStalker*, lost in his thoughts, it took him longer than it should have to realize something wasn't right. When his conscious mind finally caught up to the anxiety pulsing in his subconscious, he abruptly drew to a stop and looked around.

That was what gave them away. The four men tailing him made an admirable job of trying to conceal what they'd been doing, but they obviously hadn't anticipated Daemyn's sudden stop. Not that he blamed them, considering he hadn't anticipated it, either. He didn't bother to hide that he was inspecting his surroundings while he made sure they were the only four here. Everyone else was clearly refugees or PDS, though. Which told him something else, too – whoever these men were, they'd rushed their preparations so much they hadn't brought any attire to help them blend in.

He didn't know what was going on, but whatever it was, it couldn't be good. Daemyn reached into his pocket and pressed the panic button on his comdee.

Then he started to run.

He ran down the central street first, then cut between two buildings to head toward a side street. Glancing behind for his pursuers, he tried to remember the layout of the base as best he could. He'd never bothered to memorize it. Why would he have, only ever intending to be here a few days at most? But he knew where *WyndeStalker* waited, and the general direction to get him there was good enough.

Reaching an intersection, he turned left. Feet pounding the stone tiles as fast as he could go, he cut between another pair of buildings on a more direct route toward *Stalker*. He emerged on another street – to find himself with only a couple of meters' lead on a pair of black-clad men who'd come this way to cut him off.

He ran harder, barely staying ahead of them. He judged his distance to *Stalker*, waited past another structure, and then slipped between that building and its adjacent peer. It was a narrow alley between them, and his pursuer had to go single file after him. He burst out onto the tarmac, where *Stalker* waited a dozen meters ahead.

Behind him he heard a shriek, and spun to see the first pursuer flailing through the air after Elsa had slammed him full across the chest with her arm as he'd come chasing Daemyn around the corner of the building. The second pursuer ran out a moment later, hands up and ready from seeing what had happened to his comrade. Elsa threw a punch, the man dodged – and her leg swept his feet out from under him. He hit the ground, hard, and Elsa took a long stride to put her boot cleanly down on his neck.

"Who are you?" she demanded.

The man glared at her but wouldn't answer.

She motioned toward the other pursuer. "He's out cold. Check him."

Still heaving air into his lungs, Daemyn walked over and kneeled beside the unconscious one. Carefully he lifted open the man's coat, checking the pocket where agents from the government's various law enforcement divisions usually kept their identification credentials. Sure enough, he found one.

When he pulled it out and read it, he said, "Oh, shig."

"What?"

"They're PIS."

"Is that true?" she asked the man under her boot.

He scowled and gurgled something Daemyn couldn't hear.

"Let me see," Elsa said.

Daemyn stood up and tossed it to her. She caught it cleanly in one hand. "Doesn't look fake."

"It's not," came a man's voice, loud and angry.

Daemyn and Elsa turned to see two more black-clad PIS agents step out from around a building behind them – with guns drawn. The second one said, "Let him up."

Elsa stepped back, releasing her boot. The formerly pinned agent sprang to his feet, rubbing at his neck. "Your other buddy hasn't finished his nap quite yet."

"You think this is funny?" the agent on the left demanded.

"Until I see an arrest authorization," she said, "I think what you're doing is so comically illegal that I'm going to have a lot of fun watching your trial."

"I don't think so," the agent spat.

"We'll see."

"Authorization or not," Daemyn said, "they have guns and we don't. And they're PIS and we're not. Let's be smart about this."

"Too late for that," said the man still rubbing his neck.

Daemyn looked at the other two. "Can you at least tell me why you're here? Kidnapping a civilian off a military base doesn't seem like your usual style."

The agent on the right holstered his gun. "We've been instructed to take you into PIS custody and bring you to another location for further debriefing."

"Where?" Elsa asked.

"I can tell him," the agent said, indicating Daemyn, "but only once we're in the air."

Elsa scowled. Daemyn could tell she was still seriously considering fighting back. If she did, she would probably win. But that wouldn't do either of them any good in the long term. "It's all right," he assured her. "We'll figure something out."

After a moment, she nodded. Then she glared at the agents. "I assume you're expecting me to come up with a cover story about why Daemyn Wynde has suddenly vanished from the refugee location and his company?"

"That would be wise, yes," said the agent on the left, finally holstering his pistol, too. The other two went over and hefted up their fallen peer, who blinked groggily and muttered under his breath.

"You guys are a real bunch of asshats, you know that?" Elsa made an obscene gesture, then stormed away.

The agent shrugged, then looked at Daemyn. "You're coming voluntarily, then?"

Daemyn laughed. "I wouldn't exactly call this voluntary."

"Right. Well, conscious and unrestrained counts for something."

"If you say so," Daemyn said.

"Let's move," the agent said. Daemyn went with them.

TWENTY-SEVEN

...headquarters communications suite, Aladarian Guard base

When Paige had run up to her with the message, Utara almost hadn't believed it. Finally, after a day and a half, someone from the PDS had made contact with the comms officers at the base to follow up on her many entreaties. It wasn't clear who would be on the other end of the comm, but the incoming transmission was now only minutes away.

Utara hurried into the room. One of the ensigns waved her onward. Forta had ordered the comms station be kept reserved for her.

She slid into the seat. Out of breath from running full bore the whole way here, she clutched the edge of the workstation and forced her lungs to inhale and exhale rhythmically. Pulse racing, hands wobbly from the exertion, she reached for the headset. Unsteadily she lowered it into place. Again she concentrated on breathing. Slower. Methodically. Inhale and exhale.

The chime sounded in her ears.

Utara's eyes shot to the display screen. She recognized the name immediately: Burlong Mintex, an Assistant Deputy Minister. An Aquarian, he was two steps down the hierarchy from the Deputy Minister; too low to wield much political power personally, but high enough to interact with Foson Solaris on a daily basis. She genuinely hadn't expected someone of that rank as her first point of contact from the PDS.

Fighting back expectations, she tapped the icon. "This is Utara Fireheart."

"Counselor, it's Burlong Mintex. I'm pleased I was able to reach you."

"Not as pleased as I am to hear from you, sir."

"I suppose not."

"I realize your time is valuable. I don't want to waste it explaining what you already know about the dire situation here."

"That's very little, I'm afraid," Mintex said. *"I've listened to your message, and read the bulletin you submitted to the Emergency Incidents logline, but I have no additional information beyond that."*

That wasn't good. But the immediate future was more important than the past, so Utara got right to it. "The Guard base will be able to manage for a few more days, but after that we'll need a major infusion of resources to keep the refugee camp functional. Food and water most of all, of course. Many of them also need medicines of various sorts, and some require treatment by healers in fairly short order. More clothing will be necessary soon, too, along with blankets and basic supplies for personal grooming and quality of life. The other Guards have agreed to provide some assistance, but we need considerably more."

"Emergency relief assistance is not the primary responsibility of the PDS," Mintex said, almost as if quoting some governmental regulation by rote, *"and certainly not in the numbers involved in the Steamer Point situation. Nonetheless, given that these refugees had been living in a PDS-assisted community, I imagine we should be able to contribute to some portion of the necessary aid."*

"Thank you, sir. The Guard is reaching out to other agencies to contribute. It would help the cause greatly if the PDS would lend its voice to the plea, as well."

"I don't see why not."

"Once we address the imminent humanitarian emergency here at the base, we'll need to identify a long-term solution for these people. I know that's weeks away, possibly longer, but —"

"I understand that's a very real concern to you, Counselor, there on the ground at the base with the refugees. The Cultural Ministry might play a role in some capacity, perhaps negotiating with cities or regions regarding opportunities for resettlement, but what you're talking about is far beyond the authority of the PDS."

"I understand," Utara said, clenching her fists. "If I provide a more thorough briefing paper, would you be able to ensure it reaches the desk of Deputy Minister Solaris and Cultural Minister Cirrus?"

"Certainly, Counselor."

"I do have one other matter I wish to speak to you about," Utara said. "It's now been more than ten days since I've been able to make contact with anyone in Blonkas. Governmental or residential, I can't seem to get through."

"I don't know why that would be."

"You've seen updates from the city more recent than that?"

The line was silent for several seconds. *"No, not personally."* Another, briefer pause. *"But PDS operations in Blonkas – in any of the Future Cities, to be precise – aren't within my direct supervision."*

"I'm sorry, sir, I do realize that. I was only hoping that perhaps you had heard something. After what we experienced in Durnow, the silence from Blonkas is… distressing, to say the least."

"I imagine so."

"From within Durnow before we left, and since arriving here at Steamer Point, I've been unable to raise any of the other Future Cities on the comm, either."

"I… did not realize that."

"That's why I've become so worried. I hope you can understand."

Again Mintex went quiet for a few seconds. *"I'm sorry I don't have more information for you, Counselor Fireheart."*

The tone of his voice didn't give away whether he was lying or telling the truth. At this point, Utara wasn't sure it mattered. She only had another minute or two, at best, with Mintex on the line. She had no way of knowing when she'd hear from someone in New Romas again. This very well might be her only chance. So she took it.

"I don't know what's going on, sir, but I'm not giving up until I find out. If the PDS is impotent to render the necessary assistance, the government needs to know. And if the government is trying to hide this tragedy, the world needs to know."

"Be careful what you imply, Counselor, or you may be putting your young career on the line."

His response told her all she needed to know. "I'm not implying anything, sir. I'm ready to contact my friend Allyton Granitine right now, if that's what it takes."

She hadn't reached out to Holtspring's contact yet, and the Terran reporter certainly didn't qualify as a friend, but Mintex had no way of knowing that.

"You're bluffing," the Assistant Deputy Minister said.

"I assure you I'm not. I want information – real, specific information – about Blonkas and the other Future Cities by the end of the day. You'll be able to reach me here at the Guard base, at the same code."

"You're serious," Mintex said, his flabbergasted tone audible on the comm.

"These people have nothing to lose," Utara said, "and neither do I."

Before he could respond, she cut the transmission.

$$\sim\!\circlearrowright$$

...*PIS Field Office, Port Vulcania*

The young man who'd been sitting in the interrogation room with Daemyn canted his head to the side. The kid was probably a university intern, or maybe doing his service term, but he was new at this. Among other things, he still hadn't figured out not to give away when someone was speaking into his earbud.

"They'll be here momentarily," the kid said. "I apologize for the delay."

"Right."

They hadn't treated Daemyn like a prisoner, exactly, but they certainly hadn't given him the full scope of privileges he would've been entitled to as an individual voluntarily cooperating with the government, either. They probably weren't used to dealing with people who knew their rights – and who had multiple, very expensive lawyers available to vindicate them. Unless his situation suddenly got a whole lot better in a hurry, PIS was going to have a real publicity – and litigation – problem on its hands once Daemyn got out of here. No amount of shrieking "top secret" or "planetary security" would keep the media and the trashmags from reporting on the forcible abduction and incommunicado detention of a world-famous Airspar racer without lawful basis.

This time, though, someone finally had given the kid good information. The door to the room opened. Two men entered, and the kid hurried out. Only the Suterran introduced himself.

"Master Wynde, my name is Birto Hybollo, PIS Senior Agent. I'm here –"

"You know," Daemyn interrupted, "I always thought those vids were exaggerating all the cloak-and-dagger stuff with you intelligence types. Guess

I learned my lesson. I keep hearing PIS say they want to improve the agency's reputation with the public, and then you pull a stunt like this. Maybe you could start by not having your people act like one massive group stereotype."

Taken aback, Hybollo hesitated.

Daemyn pressed on. "If I'm detained because I'm under investigation, you're obligated to tell me the nature of the inquiry before I answer any questions. And I'm well aware that there is no exception for PIS to that requirement."

"You're not a suspect in any matter that I'm aware of, Master Wynde," the Suterran said. "If that wasn't made clear earlier, I apologize."

"Why am I here, then?"

"PIS has jurisdiction over certain aspects of the crisis currently unfolding on Loorriri."

"Is this about the Durnow airlift? I'm willing to –"

"Actually, Master Wynde, it's much bigger than that." Hybollo paused, considering something. "Forgive me. First I must commend you on the lives you saved in Durnow. I pray that we are able to save many hundreds of thousands more before this is all over."

"Well, that's a pretty grim way to begin."

"I tend not to sugar-coat the truth, Master Wynde."

"Good. Neither do I." He motioned with a hand. "Who's the other guy?"

"Marx Monson," the Aquarian replied. "Special Consultant to the PIS on the Loorriri crisis. I don't believe we've met."

"I think that's right. I may be familiar with the name, though."

"I doubt that."

"There's a Monson in corporate intel at Grandell Motors."

"Ah, yes. I stand corrected, then. That would be me."

Daemyn looked back to the Senior Agent. "All right, gentlemen. I'll give you the benefit of the doubt that you didn't kidnap me and haul me halfway around the world for no reason. So let's hear it."

For a few minutes Hybollo and Monson provided a high-level summary of the rapidly escalating use of violence and toxins by the Future City AIs. It was far worse than Daemyn had ever imagined. He asked a few questions along the way, but mostly he listened. Then Monson explained the two core problems – writing AI shut-down coding and figuring out a way to deliver it into the AIs – and the very short timetable that remained for coming up with a solution.

"So," Hybollo said. "Can you help?"

"I can." Daemyn held the agent's gaze. "But you could have *asked*."

Hybollo nodded a concession. "I'll make a note for next time."

Daemyn was pretty sure the agent was trying to make a joke. He ignored it. "Who else are you bringing in?"

"I'm sorry?"

"Besides the PIS team you have already, and me. Depending on who else you've brought in, I might have suggestions on ways to maximize our approach."

Hybollo and Monson shared a glance.

"What?" Daemyn asked.

Monson went to the door, opened it, and stepped out into the corridor. Hybollo told Daemyn, "We're keeping this very small. In addition to PIS resources, it's only you and one other individual."

"Really?"

"Yes. We need the best minds on this."

"I appreciate the flattery, of course, but I'm not sure two people will be enough to make a difference."

"It's not the quantity of resources that concerns me," Hybollo said. "As I said, it's the quality of insight that we need. That's what will tip the balance."

The door opened again, and Monson returned. Another man came in right behind him. With hair and beard utterly unkempt, the new arrival looked like the kind of guy who would get himself thrown out of a casino for trying to use expertise in math to increase his winnings, not some sort of super-sleuth.

"This is our coding asset, Kirkland Oggust," Monson said.

The euphemism explained it. PIS had brought in a corporate espionage specialist to deal with Boynton Logistics Dynamics, and a hacker to take on the AI code. Which probably meant Daemyn was the expert for delivery mechanisms. "Good call."

Oggust gestured toward Daemyn. "Who's he?"

Hybollo blinked. "You haven't figured it out?"

Oggust rolled his eyes. "Would I have asked if I had?"

Monson laughed. "He's Daemyn Wynde."

"No he's not. Come on."

Momentarily, Monson's face flashed with confusion. "Yes, he is."

"You don't think I'd recognize him?"

Hybollo glanced to Daemyn, indicating he should do something. Daemyn tried his best to put on his celebrity smile, and offered a small wave of a hand. "Hello."

Oggust peered at him.

"I, uh… really am Daemyn Wynde," he added.

"Wow," the other man said.

"Pleasure to meet you, too." Daemyn returned his attention to Hybollo. "I'll help the PIS, and when this is all over you can do a favor for me."

"Within reason," the agent said.

"My company was hacked recently. Some important trade secret information was stolen. We've been trying to track down who did it, but no luck yet."

"It wasn't GM," Monson said.

Daemyn gave him a look. "I know. They're not that good."

"I don't foresee any obstacles to assisting with identifying the perpetrator," Hybollo said. "Between PIS and Master Oggust, we'll crack the case in no time."

"Right," Oggust said. "Sure."

"Now that we have that out of the way," Hybollo said, "do you have any other questions?"

Daemyn pushed up from his chair. "No. Let's get to work."

...Aladarian Guard base

Utara stood at the edge of the tarmac, arms crossed against the brisk wind blowing inland from the sea. Three large cargo carriers descended toward the ground, setting down side by side in a row at the far edge of the landing zone. Closer, a single shuttlecraft landed cleanly in the passenger debarking area. All four aircraft bore government insignia, but only the shuttle was from the PDS.

She waited for the shuttle's engines to wind down, then strode quickly across the crete while its ramp lowered. A half dozen young men and women in PDS jackets hustled down the ramp. With the cargo carriers' engines still roaring, she couldn't say much. She pointed to Trace Chal, standing tall in uniform back at the tarmac's edge.

"Follow her," Utara shouted.

The others made affirmative gestures and jogged off toward Trace. Last down the ramp was a Terran man, probably in his mid-thirties, wearing a similar PDS jacket.

"Counselor Fireheart?" he said, voice raised against the noise.

Utara nodded.

"I'm Envoy Carter Platinost. I don't believe we've met."

She shook her head. "This way."

He tucked a compupod inside his jacket and kept pace with her as they hurried across the crete. When they reached the edge she glanced back at the cargo carriers. "Anything we need to discuss out here?"

Platinost swiped hair out of his face. "No."

"Good."

She led him to one of the administrative buildings nearby. Once the door slid shut behind them and they were out of the wind in the building's main corridor, she offered her hand. "Good to meet you."

He clasped forearms. "Likewise."

"I wasn't sure what kind of response I'd get from headquarters, to be honest."

"I'm not fully clear myself on what's going on within the leadership, actually." He used a hand to bring some order to his unkempt locks. "I wasn't even told what designation my operation has, or what authorization I'm operating under."

"That's... unusual."

"Unprecedented, as far as I'm aware. All I know is that everyone available at headquarters was called into an emergency briefing. We heard a short explanation about the situation here at Steamer Point, followed by a request for volunteers. That's who came on the shuttle."

"How much did they tell you?"

"The numbers, and the origination point in Durnow. That's about it. I was able to read a few additional documents on the flight."

"I see." She met his gaze. "They sent you to take over the lead on this?"

"No." He chuckled. "At least I don't think so. I was instructed to undertake a full needs-assessment inventory and file my report in a week."

"Well, that's progress, I suppose. Less likely they'll abandon these people entirely."

"I think so. Honestly, I'm not even sure how long I'll be staying. The junior counselors who came with me, they appear to have been assigned here indefinitely in assist-and-support capacity. Some of them have familiarity with Loorriri, even speak a couple of the languages between them. Me, I've hardly ever been in this hemisphere before, much less the Future Cities or anything."

"Why'd you volunteer, then?" Quickly she added, "No offense."

He laughed. "None taken. I've been wondering the same thing. Mostly, I was the senior-most person available on short notice, and it was the right thing to do."

"Sorry you got the pointy end of the stick." She smiled. Maybe the leadership had let her down, but there were still plenty of good people in the PDS. "But I am very grateful that you volunteered. The refugees will be, too."

"I'll do as much as I can to help. It's been a while, but I did management for disaster relief interventions twice before. That earthquake in the Redstone Buttes province a few years back, and a hurricane on the Voluni Peninsula what, maybe five years ago? Both of those were large scale, like this. There, though, we were able to execute some quick infrastructure repairs and get life back to normal for many of the people within a week or two. This… it's going to be pretty different."

"I don't think New Romas, PDS or otherwise, has ever dealt with anything like this before."

"I agree." He seemed to suddenly remember about the compupod, and drew it out from within his jacket. "And that would be true even if it's just Durnow in trouble. If it gets bigger than that…"

Utara nodded. She was also trying not to think about that. "Three cargo carriers is more than I expected on the first day."

"I was kind of surprised myself, too. Mostly water tanks and nonperishable food supplies. Warehoused military surplus would be my guess."

"At this point, any food is better than no food."

"True. There's some temporary living supplies, as well. Tents, bedding, blankets, and the like. No medicines yet, unfortunately. Supposedly they're working on getting a healer team here soon, but it'll be at least a few days, I'd imagine."

"We'll do the best we can."

"Anyway, I've got the full manifest on here," he said, hefting the pod. "Whoever needs a copy, I'll get them one."

"Thank you."

"One more thing," Platinost said. "I have a message for you from Deputy Minister Solaris. It's… eyes-only."

Utara did a poor job concealing her surprise, and didn't care. "All right."

He activate the compupod and tapped the screen a few times. "Okay," he said, passing it to her. "It's ready."

She accepted the device, shifting the angle to avoid the glare from the bright overhead lums in the corridor. The message was displayed, but its contents were still illegible. A warning icon flashed on the screen, demanding her official PDS passcode.

Utara tapped it in. An indicator line spun a circle on the screen three times before the warning icon vanished and the message appeared.

In the corner, a countdown timer had begun. Thirty seconds.

She ignored the timer and read the message. It wasn't lengthy.

Solaris skipped any salutation and went straight to the point: the PDS had no idea what was happening in the Future Cities. The agency's communications had been cut off right along with personal comdees and the rest. Other than Utara and two PDS counselors who had fled upriver from Zimbar with a band of refugees from that city, headquarters in New Romas had not heard from anyone in the Future Cities in a week. There was nothing else he could tell her.

His final sentence was not his own. The line of bold, red text warned her that any dissemination of classified information without authorization was a felony punishable by imprisonment and a fine.

She had ten seconds left. Utara read the message again, committing it to memory.

The timer ran down. The message scrambled, then disappeared. The compupod returned to its default home screen, as though the message had never existed.

Carter Platinost was looking at her. "How bad is it?"

"I don't know," she said. "But I know what I have to do next."

TWENTY-EIGHT

...PIS Field Office, Port Vulcania

"That's what I've got so far," Oggust said. "I think it should work."

"I agree." Daemyn shifted the angle of his compupod screen so the other man could see. "Here's what I came up with for beating the comms bubble."

Pointing with his finger on the diagram, he explained his idea. The signal-jamming parameters the Future City AIs were using to blackout comdees, veepees, and other common forms of Primean communications technology also inhibited the comm systems installed in aircraft. Inspired by the AI's own use of subsonic pulse bursts, Daemyn had worked from the premise that the radio-wave spectrum wasn't the only method available for transmitting data.

"Ultraviolet, huh?" Oggust ran his fingers through his beard. "I like it."

"Beating the blackout was key, no matter what we did." The comm devices to pull off tight-beam transmission via satellite were extremely expensive and military-grade, but Hybollo had assured Daemyn that any Unified Forces tech they needed to execute the operation successfully would be obtained by PIS, no matter what strings had to be pulled to make it happen. "Having pilots able to communicate with each other, and a central control room, in real time is even more important."

"Oh, for sure. And they're small enough to fit in a cockpit?"

"I saw one this morning. It's bigger than a regular comdee, but not by a lot. Worst case, we'll use some powerful adhesive to stick it somewhere and string the wires into the main console comm."

Oggust nodded. "Easy enough."

"You agree it'll work?"

"Oh yeah. It's a great idea."

"Thanks."

The other man shook his head. "I still can't believe they're going to do this with Airspar pilots instead of Unified Forces. I mean, isn't dealing with this sort of thing supposed to be UF's *job*?"

"You'd think so," Daemyn said. It hadn't taken him more than a few hours of working with the PIS team and their data to determine that only two viable options existed for delivering an AI kill-code once they had it: either a databurst from an aircraft or operatives on the ground making a physical insertion. Almost immediately, it had been made eminently clear that the Unified Forces had been decreed off limits – when and by whom, Hybollo had refused to reveal – for carrying out the mission, regardless of which one they picked. At that moment, Daemyn had finally understood why they had really grabbed him. "But it's the reality we're stuck with. And in the long term, Air Branch is probably going to regret conceding the point that they're not the only combat-capable pilots on Prime."

"I hadn't thought of that. I guess they didn't, either." Oggust chuckled to himself, then said, "This time around, it isn't going to be as simple as that airlift you did, even before it shigged out. It's way more than a landing-and-takeoff mission. We're talking about going up against AIs and drones that will be fighting back."

"I know. The good thing is, all but eight teams are eliminated now. That's dozens of pilots, and we only need a small number of them. I know how they think. Whether it's a financial reward or a medal or glory, some of them will take the opportunity."

"Assuming the PIS lets you tell them what you're actually recruiting for."

"They'll have to, at least to some extent. Still, it might be better if they don't know up front." Daemyn forced himself to stop tapping the edge of the desk with his fingers. "It's a fair concern, though. But I think we can make it work."

"If you get Airspar aces to fly, the only other issue is getting the airblades."

"Right."

"What's your plan?"

"For starters, there's not a chance the teams will agree to use the competition-spec blades, especially not after all the engine problems during the airlift. Word is already getting around, I'm sure. Pilots talk. They can't help themselves. So I have to assume that'll be a known quantity for anyone I approach, either before or after I talk to them about going to Loorriri."

"Makes sense. Plenty of non-competition airblades around, though. I bet a lot of those Airspar jockeys have a couple of blades in a hangar at home, just to fly for fun."

"Exactly."

"Except for the engine problem. No one's going to sign up to wreck a blade and crash out in the wilderness of Loorriri somewhere."

"Fortunately, I have a solution in mind for that, too."

"Oh, right. The Lariat design."

Daemyn froze. "What did you say?"

Oggust blanched. "Uh, nothing."

Before he even realized what he was doing, Daemyn was out of his chair and looming over the hacker, fists clenched. "How do you know that designation?"

Oggust gripped the arms of his chair so hard his knuckles went pale. "Oops."

"Tell. Me. *Now.*"

The hacker raised his hands defensively – and told Daemyn everything. By the time he finished, Daemyn knew the other man was telling the truth. The theft wasn't something he could forgive, and the ongoing deception since they'd met only compounded it with betrayal. Yet he found his immediate fury had dissipated. For Oggust, it had never been about malice or profit, only the challenge; whatever motives Monson or GM might follow after they'd bought it from him hadn't really been his concern. Daemyn took a deep breath and sat back down.

"You know," he told the hacker, "you're the only one who's ever breached that far into my security barriers."

Oggust didn't miss a thing. "You mean, Wynde Industries' security."

"No. I mean *my* security."

"You wrote it yourself?"

"Not every single line, admittedly," Daemyn said. "I have to delegate some of the backend writing. I don't have that kind of time. But the core of it? Yes. I wrote it."

Oggust leaned forward. "Well, it's good. *Really* good."

Daemyn scowled. "Apparently not good enough."

"No, it's top notch. Believe me. I would know."

Despite himself, Daemyn chuckled. "I suppose so."

"You should sell it. Through the company. It's better than pretty much anything else on the market. By a lot."

"I've thought about it. But then the code would be out there. Other people would learn from it. I'd lose my advantage."

"Smart." Oggust sat up straight in his chair. "I'm going to make this right. Those files will vanish before anyone sees them."

"What?"

"Look, I know you have no reason to trust me. I can never undo what I did to you. But I do have the power to guarantee that's the only harm that comes from my actions."

"Are you worried about the operation? I'm not going to abandon –"

"No, it's not that. I know you wouldn't. That's why I need to make this up to you. You're a good person."

"Seriously?" He felt bad about the way it sounded coming out of his mouth, but Daemyn couldn't help it.

Oggust nodded with great sincerity. "Honestly, I've never really thought about it before. My targets, I mean. Take from one corporation, sell to another, what's the difference? That's how it always felt before."

With his knowledge of Fith, Grandell Motors, and most of the other companies he or the other venturists had worked for, investigated, or invested in, Daemyn wasn't sure how much he could even disagree with the sentiment. "And it's different now because you've met me."

"Yes."

"Well, that's lucky."

"It's not only meeting you, though," the hacker insisted. "You must have a sense of the kind of people I usually deal with. Then I end up working with this Monson guy. He's a real genuine –" He swallowed whatever curse had reached the tip of his tongue. "Well, he's *not* a good person, let's call it that. You did an airlift for people on another continent you'd never met and will never see again. You're here, saving the PIS's rear end even though they've treated you like a pile of phanter dung. And now you're going to put your company on the line by handing over an unproven new engine tech for a mission that might get you killed."

Daemyn shook his head. "When you put it like that, I sound pretty stupid."

"No. You sound like someone worth respecting. Which why I'm going to delete those copies before Monson can do anything with them."

"But how —"

"I put a trace in the data files before I handed them over. With this crisis getting worse all the time, he hasn't opened them yet. They'll be gone before he does."

"It's that easy?"

Oggust shrugged. "Like you said. GM's security's not that good."

For the first time since the PIS had showed up at Steamer Point, Daemyn laughed.

～⌒⌒

...Aladarian Guard base

After an hour checking in with Trace Chal and Carter Platinost for the latest updates on the status of the refugees, Utara walked out onto the tarmac toward the smaller shuttlecraft that had set down in the landing zone next to the PDS craft. In the frenzy of the morning's distribution of a new supply of water, she hadn't seen the CenterPrime News Network aircraft arrive. Its passenger, though, had followed her every move for three hours, then interviewed her for twenty minutes before scurrying away. Utara had no idea what Allyton Granitine had been up to since then. Approaching the shuttlecraft, she tamped down the fear that this whole idea had been one big waste of time.

She stopped at the closed boarding door along the aircraft's side, a meter aft of the cockpit viewport. Unsure what else to do, she pounded on the metal with a bare fist. "Miss Granitine?" she shouted. "It's Utara Fireheart."

From inside a muffled voice said, "It's open. Come on in."

The inset handle yielded to Utara's grasp, and she swung the door inward. Stretching up the long step into the ship, she cross the threshold and entered. Once the door was shut behind her, she realized how narrow the corridor really was.

"Back here," Granitine's voice called.

A few steps toward aft brought Utara through an open portal and into a small room in the back of the ship. Actually, the room itself wasn't that small – but it was crammed so full of display screens, workstations, and other electronics that only a small amount of floor space was left for a pair of chairs. The near one was empty; Granitine sat in the other, working diligently at one of the consoles.

"You said to come by when I finished the meetings," Utara said.

"Yes, thank you." The brunette Terran took a moment finishing something at the workstation, then spun the chair to face Utara. "The report is going to broadcast any time now. They didn't tell exactly when it would be, but it'll be soon."

"Really?"

"The editorial director didn't even hesitate. It's going out right away, without any changes from what I submitted."

"I… honestly didn't expect that."

Granitine shrugged. "Always hard to predict what they'll like and what they won't. Would you like to see it?"

"Oh, yes. Definitely."

Granitine indicated the other chair, and Utara slid into it. A few seconds later the report began to play on the largest, central screen. Watching it took some getting used to. Granitine had spliced some of their conversation atop video recorded at other times, and parts when both of them appeared onscreen were included out of order, too. After she got past the disconnect, though, Utara was impressed. The reporter had condensed a morning's investigation into less than five minutes while still hitting all of the crucial points: a crisis in Durnow, the refugees' flight onto the savannah, the airlift to Steamer Point, the unknown fate of the many thousands of other residents who'd fled the city but hadn't been part of the airlift, and the urgency of the unsustainable living conditions of the people at the base despite the very best commitments of the Aladarian Guard.

"So," Granitine said, "what do you think?"

"It's on point." Utara took a breath to keep her composure. "I hope enough people see it to make a difference."

"We'll find out. But sometimes it's not about the number of people who watch the report – it's about the right people seeing it."

"Whatever works, I'll take it."

"I'm sure you –" A loud trilling from a comdee echoed in the small room. "Hold on," the other woman said, snatching the device from atop the workstation. Lowering her head and cupping a hand to her other ear she said, "Allyton Granitine."

For nearly a minute she held a hushed conversation with the person on the other end of the comm. Utara didn't try to eavesdrop, but kept her eyes fixed on the still image from the end of the report. It showed one of the base's massive hangars, empty of aircraft so that every square meter of floor could be filled with the refugees and their meager belongings. She prayed that this, finally, might turn things around.

"All right," Granitine said, sitting up straight again. "They want me to do a live report. Since you're with me, I said we're a go in five minutes."

"What?"

"The viewer response rate is off the charts, apparently. They want more, and we don't have time to cut together additional video. So we'll go live."

Utara took a breath. "Me, too?"

"Of course." Granitine looked at her like she'd abruptly transformed into a jorkat. "I'm just the reporter. You're the expert."

"Right."

"Come on, we have to hurry."

Utara let Granitine hustle her out of the shuttlecraft and across the tarmac. They hadn't made it far into the buildings, though, when the reporter stopped.

"We had some good shots inside the hangars before. Let's stop here. It'll show the wind and the weather, and it gives a better impression of how big those hangars really are."

"Sure," Utara said. The wind whipped around her, and she tugged tighter at the PDS jacket Platinost had found for her right before they'd started recording this morning.

Granitine tucked in a small earbud, then pulled her palm-sized hovercam from her pocket, activated it, and tossed it into the air. She pointed with a finger, adjusting its position, while appraising the cam view on her handheld pod. "Perfect," she said to herself, then clipped one lapel microphone to her jacket and another to Utara's. "Ready?"

"Do I have a choice?"

"Not really," the reporter said, grinning. Right at that moment, she canted her head. "They're ready for us."

She counted down three, two, one on her fingers and said, "This is Allyton Granitine, reporting live from the Aladarian Guard base at Steamer Point. With me is Utara Fireheart, the counselor with the Prime Diplomatic Service responsible for the successful evacuation of the refugees from Durnow, one of the Future Cities on Loorriri. Utara, after our first report, one of the things our viewers are wondering is why the people became so desperate that they were willing to flee the city and take their chances on the savannah. What would lead people to do something like that? Tell us more about that."

"For most Primeans," Utara began, "it's probably even hard to imagine what life would be like without reliable power. But that's only part of what these people had faced." She described some of the worst aspects of what the residents of Evostown had suffered.

After letting her talk for over a minute, Granitine said, "And as a PDS counselor assigned to assist the residents, you experienced all of this first hand."

"I did. My assignment is Blonkas, but the situations in the cities are very much the same. In the neighborhood where I live, the residents —"

"Hold on a moment," Granitine interrupted, reacting to something in her earbud. "You haven't been in Durnow all along?"

Momentary panic gripped Utara. She hadn't even thought about what her reference to Blonkas might mean from the reporter's perspective. She prayed she hadn't accidentally ruined everything. "No."

"What about the residents of Blonkas?" Granitine asked. "How are they doing? Are people from your neighborhood fleeing their city, as well?"

"I don't know," Utara said, forcing her expression to remain calm. "I haven't been able to get through to anyone there on the comm in over a week."

The reporter's eyes flew wide and the candor crossed her lips before she could catch herself. "What? How is that possible?"

"I don't know that answer either," Utara said, looking straight into the hovercam. "But I would certainly like to find out."

"Well, we most definitely will have to follow up on that angle to this story for our viewers, won't we?" Granitine said to the cam, too. Then she looked back to Utara with a grin that Utara couldn't possibly mistake. If Granitine had been pleased before, now she was practically giddy with exhilaration. "While we still have the chance to speak to you live, Utara, tell us some more about what you personally experienced in one of the Future Cities as it descended into chaos."

... *PIS Field Office, Port Vulcania*

Displayed on the enormous central screen in the facility's primary surveillance chamber, the map of Loorriri marked the staggering toll in a few simple symbols and numerals. Filling the entire rest of the wall, numerous smaller screens showed satellite imagery, aerial reconnaissance, live-updating datafeeds, and the latest assessments from the several dozen PIS analysts frenetically working at their consoles in the tiered auditorium. Monson took a deep breath and forced himself to review the updates.

In four of the Future Cities – Blonkas, Luppitan, Manjaro, and Cirro – the AIs had administered the Blonkas-inspired toxin to the local population, killing everyone within the cities' walls. Now the poison was spreading across the adjacent areas of the untamed wilderness of the continent, after the other three cities had followed Luppitan's lead in dumping massive additional quantities of the toxin into their respective rivers. At three more cities – Tagron, Zimbar, and Gastoa – the AIs had deployed the security drones to exterminate refugees fleeing into the wilds of the continent, though the residents who'd stayed behind remained unharmed, at least since the initial carnage caused by the animals released from the nature preserves. Durnow had allowed refugees to escape unimpeded prior to the venturist's airlift; afterward, those who hadn't been able to leave for either the savannah or the skies apparently had chosen simply to stay in the city – only to be wiped out by the poisoned waters of the Kyetalle River once the toxin dumped by Luppitan reached them. The remaining four Future Cities faced varying levels of disarray among their human inhabitants, with large refugee exoduses from two and comparative stability in the other two. How their AIs would react continued to be unpredictable, no matter how many simulations the PIS analysts ran. Based on the pattern so far, though, Monson didn't like the odds.

And that was only the current toll. The locations of the poisoned cities, drenched with the toxin, would be uninhabitable for decades at least. Hundreds of square kilometers impacted by the toxic rivers and their drainage basins would be similarly annihilated, killing off innumerable wildlife and flora. Anyone who survived the immediate crisis would find life on Loorriri more inhospitable than it had ever been. If additional cities released the poison into more rivers, the impact would increase exponentially. Even now, the very future of sustainable human settlement on the continent was in doubt.

He turned to Hybollo. "I'm reading that correctly? Still no indications of any additional Eri-Van being produced by the AIs."

"The what?"

"Sorry. The eridanthol-vanitorine toxin. The analysts have started calling it that to –"

"Right. Much easier to say," Hybollo said, chuckling. "Anyway, yes, you're correct. Although we have to assume all of the others have access to the chemical formula and manufacturing protocols."

"Which puts us hours away from another implementation, should one or more of them choose to do so."

"That's right."

Likewise, perhaps only days away from a far worse catastrophe on the rest of Prime, should the formulas and protocols reach the other Boynton AIs along with communications and supporting data recommending their implementation. That contingency had to be prevented, no matter the cost.

"What's the latest from the Chief on the INMASS?"

Casting his eyes to where Firebird stood at the front of the room, talking to a pair of Senior Agents at the central command podium, Hybollo could only shake his head.

"Seriously?"

Motioning with a hand, Hybollo indicated they should move away from the workstation where they'd been standing to check on some data not displayed on the wall screens. A few seconds later they reached an alcove along the rear wall of the chamber, away from the eyes and ears of the analysts and agents. Hybollo glanced around, making sure they were alone, then nodded once.

"The Chief took it to the Prime Minister herself, in person, late yesterday. She wouldn't share a verbatim account of the conversation, of course, but the bottom line was very clear. Tamorchin won't authorize a deactivation."

"Preemptively?"

"Ever."

"No matter what?"

"Sounds like it."

Monson clenched a fist. "That's unacceptable. There has to be a way to convey the gravity of the stakes to him."

"Oh, that's not the problem. The Chief practiced the briefing with a few of us beforehand. The intel he received was plenty stark."

"Then how in the –"

"You have to remember, Marx. For Tamorchin, everything is politics. If he shuts down the INMASS but nothing bad ever happens outside of Loorriri, he pays a massive electoral price. One he'd never recover from. And not only him – his entire party. They wouldn't win a PM election again for years. Maybe ever. He's simply not willing to risk it."

Monson couldn't dispute the gravity of the political stakes. Simultaneously deactivating every single AI operated by Boynton Logistics Dynamics everywhere on the planet would cause major turmoil worldwide. For months at a minimum, until work-arounds could be put in place, it would negatively impact daily life for hundreds of millions of Primeans in wealthy urban centers accustomed to a disruption-free existence of expected facilities like transportation systems or comdee networks. In certain cities, where delivery of basic services like water or power was more deeply dependent on the AIs, the ramifications would be severe and last for years.

But politics wasn't the most important consideration in play. "And if he doesn't shut it down in time, and the AIs go rogue beyond Loorriri, hundreds of millions of people will die. Billions, possibly. He's willing to risk *that*?"

Hybollo gave a grim chuckle. "Dead people don't vote against you. Living people whose lives were disrupted for no reason? They do."

"You can't be serious."

"Well, to be fair, I assume he didn't say it quite that bluntly. But the Chief clearly believes the INMASS deactivation is off the table. Completely."

"That's insane."

"I know. If I understood the Chief's implication, Tamorchin made an oblique reference to another solution besides what the PIS is working on."

"Any idea what it could be?"

"None at all."

Monson took a deep breath. "So there's only one move in play for us – taking the Future City AIs offline before the INMASS is compromised."

"Right."

"I suppose that means we have our decision made for us, then," Monson said. "Time to find out if Daemyn Wynde has come up with something brilliant enough to save the world."

TWENTY-NINE

"Hey, Daemyn," the hacker said. "How busy are you?"

Daemyn looked up from his compupod. In the two days they'd spent together, he hadn't heard that sense of urgency in the other man's voice before. His list of Airspar pilots who would make good potential recruits for the Loorriri mission could wait. He tapped the screen and stood.

"Nothing I can't put off a few minutes. Need help with something?"

"No. I think I finally have the solution put together."

Daemyn stepped over to stand behind Oggust. Unlike Daemyn, who preferred working on a single compupod screen, the hacker had his workstation set up with an array of five different screens. Daemyn wasn't sure which one to look at. "Let's hear it."

"So, thinking about it, I kept coming back to first principles. Never make the action-process complicated if you can keep it simple. Especially on something like this. The more stages in the process, the more code that has to run, equals more places where something can go wrong. So the goal is, minimize the opportunity for failure."

Daemyn nodded.

"Great," Oggust said, glancing back over his shoulder. "So the people at Boynton who created the AI, they had the kill-switch in there from the very beginning. I mean, I checked all the way back, even into the prototypes. It's been tweaked and modified a little, here and there, but it's never been missing, throughout all the versions."

"The simplest kill of all," Daemyn said, "is the kill-switch fundamental to the code itself."

"It's practically organic to the AI. Metaphorically speaking. So, for a minute, let's put delivery to the side and do implementation." The hacker's fingers flew at the workstation, and one of the screens changed to display a straightforward block of code. He pointed to it. "Now, in theory if we've spoofed the AI on delivery, then we could just put in the code to trigger the kill-switch and be done with it. But I don't want to count on that."

"I agree."

"But again, avoid complexity. I buried it three layers down. Enough to hide it, not enough for anything to mess up."

Daemyn leaned down and read the code. "Looks good to me."

"And here's what makes the trickery better – and ties into what I've got next for delivery. The first two layers look like an upgrade patch to guard against manipulation of the code from outside. It'll read like exactly the kind of upgrade the AI will prioritize to run. By the time it gets to the third layer, and the kill switch triggers…"

"Boom," Daemyn said. "Game over."

"Exactly."

"I like it. I like it a lot."

"Thanks. I had it pretty much ready yesterday, actually, but I didn't want to say anything until I had a way to deliver it."

"Makes sense."

"For delivery, I went back to first principles, too. Basically, the goal is to trick the AI. So to figure out how to trick someone, I need to know how they think. For the AI, that's partly from the drudgery of reading the code, seeing the algorithms, reviewing the PIS reports on how the AI acted in response to various inputs."

"That," Daemyn said, "is a pretty clinical way of describing it."

Oggust glanced up. "Sorry. I didn't mean anything by it." He looked back at the screens. "You spend so much time inside the brain of the AI, I guess you start to talk like it, too."

Elsa said that *WyndeStalker* sounded like a childish version of adult Daemyn. He'd always assumed she was joking, but maybe not. "Don't worry about it."

"The other part," the hacker continued, "isn't specific to this AI. Code is code, and it runs with impeccable logic."

"Beat logic by being illogical," Daemyn said.

"And tailor it to what Boynton actually wrote, and what these Future City AIs have actually experienced."

"Good concept. What's the gambit?"

"One or more airblades at the city. The AI's going to log that as, humans are being a threat again. Any data sent from the airblade is going to be logged as, here comes the threat. On the flip side, the airblades are hitting all the cities at the same time, right?"

"As close to simultaneous as we can, yes."

"It's perfect. The AIs have experienced coordinated moves from Boynton and other humans before. They'll be expecting it. And they'll check for confirmation that it's occurring again this time."

"So we let them know that it is?"

"Correct. Which is illogical, because it's not how humans behave. Humans try to hide when they're attacking the AIs. If we tell them the truth, they'll react incorrectly because they'll be assuming deception and reacting to that instead."

"I thought you said this was supposed to be simple."

"On an AI's level, it is," Oggust said. "What the airblades do first is emit signals and transmissions that match up with a simultaneous coordinated airblade operation in all of the Future Cities. Which is easy to do, because that's what'll actually be happening. And with the AIs communicating by subsonic burst, the lag time only works in our favor to confirm it."

Daemyn chuckled. "Trick them with the truth."

"Then, when the AIs are running the response algorithms, another data burst pops in through their antenna. Data from another AI. Saying, watch out for those humans, they're probably attacking you too, here's a quick patch to block against what they just tried against me."

"You can do that? Make it read like it's from another AI?"

"Absolutely. I've got a little side program running over here —" He pointed to the screen on the far left. "— that's been doing nothing but analyzing the existing data packets the AIs have sent, mimicking them, learning from them."

"It has to match," Daemyn insisted. "It has to be perfect."

"It will be. AI code, one-hundred-percent."

"So the AI gets the message, logs it, and runs the code."

"Boom." Oggust spun in his chair and met Daemyn's gaze. "Game over."

...headquarters communications suite, Aladarian Guard base

"Thank you, Governor," Utara said into the headset. "Your support means a great deal to me, and it will mean even more to the people you're resettling."

"I am honored to be of service," the elderly leader of the Plains Terrans said. *"Perhaps not many of your refugees will wish to join in our nomadic way of life, but we would be humbled to welcome anyone who chooses that path, whether of Terran ancestry or any other."*

"I will be sure to convey your openness to all."

"Thank you, Counselor. I will await your follow-up in a few days' time."

"You'll have it, Governor. Your generosity will be long remembered."

"Many blessings, Miss Fireheart."

"Many blessings."

The comm line clicked off in her ears. She kept the headset on. Over the past day, four different cultural governors had contacted the base to offer support to the Durnow refugees. Each one had asked to speak to Utara specifically. After three more interviews with reporters from a trio of other media channels, plus a lengthy meeting with Captain Forta and Carter Platinost to review the next few days' allocations of food, water, and supplies for the refugees, only now had she finally found the time to reach out to them.

The comms had gone even better than she had expected. The Crown Prince of the Obsidian Ridge Suterrans had pledged a significant delivery of grains and vegetables beginning within days. The agricultural harvest in his region was exceeding predictions by a large margin, and after seeing Granitine's reports his government had quickly voted in support of sending part of the surplus to the refugees immediately. The Governor of the Plains Terrans had made an even bolder offer of resettlement. In quickly researching the Cultural Ministry's basic briefing points on the cultural group before contacting him, Utara had learned of the low birth rates that had befallen the Plains Terrans in the last decades. Likely the Governor did not have purely altruistic motives in allowing an influx to his population, but it would hardly be the first time a good result had been obtained through opportunistic use of self-interest.

If the next two comms – another Terran governor, and an Aladarian – went equally well, the situation of the refugees would have improved more quickly than she had let herself hope. Still, she knew better than to count on the trend continuing. She took a deep breath and readied herself for the next comm.

Before she could check her list for the code she needed to enter, though, an incoming comm chimed in her ears. She thought about letting it pass through to the voice messages – until she saw the name on the screen. Her finger flew to tap the icon.

"Daemyn? It's Utara."

"Oh, good. I'm glad I caught you directly."

That didn't bode well. "What's going on?"

"We need to go back to Zanita."

His word choice didn't escape her notice. He could have said Durnow, or Loorriri. He hadn't. "Why?"

"I can't explain over the comm. Reiton is already on his way to get you."

"Get me? But I have to –"

"Trust me, Utara. Whatever you're doing there, it's not as important as this."

"Okay," she said. "I trust you."

"Reiton will Put *everything* In *better terms* So *you'll understand."* He waited only a second, then said, *"Did you get that?"*

His odd diction had caught her attention, all right. Put in so. Putinso? That wasn't a name or term she recognized. Nor was it a homonym that made any sense, either. An acronym? The realization sent a chill down her spine. If the PIS was involved, she couldn't imagine how bad things must be.

"Probably, I suppose," she said.

"Great." His muffled voice said something to someone on his end of the comm, then spoke clearly to her. *"Reiton should be there in two hours, give or take."*

"I'll be ready."

...Airspar Governing Authority Headquarters, Hyj-gon

Standing behind the podium at the front of the auditorium, his compu-pod ready to display a series of graphics on the room's central screen, Daemyn appraised the individuals taking their seats among the sloping rows. More pilots than he'd expected had accepted the invitation to attend on short notice. Many of the teams were conducting their end-of-season debriefing meetings with the sport's governing authority, though, so the timing had worked out well for their presence in Hyj-gon. The invitation's implication of the possibility of financial remuneration for a couple of days' work probably had triggered a lot of the interest, too. Mere curiosity at the deliberately vague description of the topic of the briefing might have appealed to others. Whatever their reasons were, Daemyn would take it. Without people in the seats, his pitch had no chance for success.

He waited a moment longer for the interns at the back of the room to finish taking their seats. Most wore logos from the various teams, although some were assigned to the Airspar headquarters staff itself. Apparently the invitation had reached them, too.

"Thank you, everyone, for attending this morning," Daemyn said.

He displayed the first graphic and began his presentation. Every word of it had been thoroughly vetted by the PIS to ensure he didn't reveal any classified information. He described the need for highly skilled pilots to fly a brief but risky mission to assist the government in a crisis-management capacity. In fact, nothing in this initial recruiting pitch to the pilots even mentioned Loorriri, much less the Future Cities, the AIs, or the drones. If anyone made the connection to the few reports that had circulated on the news about the Future Cities, or the more recent bulletins about the refugees at Steamer Point, he had scripted answers ready. Only after pilots expressed interest, and agreed to sign a confidentiality decree to learn the specifics, would they find out the truth.

After appealing to their patriotism to help the government, Daemyn told them the compensation the pilots would receive for participating. It wasn't much, but the PIS had offered to front the funds. Without it, Daemyn had told them, they wouldn't get anyone. Hopefully it would be enough.

"Any questions?" he asked. He waited, but no one spoke up.

The room was eerily quiet. Someone coughed. Another person shifted in their seat, and it squeaked. Nobody said a word.

"All right, then," Daemyn said. "If you're interested in participating, come over and let me know. Everyone else, I appreciate your time. Thank you."

The pilots rose from their seats and headed toward the exits. Not a single one of them headed in his direction. He looked out over the group, but none of them would even make eye contact with him. So he stopped looking.

Surprisingly, the heavy weight in Daemyn's gut came far more from disappointment than fury. Not that he wasn't angry. But no amount of rage would change their minds. They'd made their choices. He would have to find another way.

Daemyn pretended to make some notes in his compupod while the last of the Airspar pilots filed out the doors at the front of the auditorium. When he glanced up, he realized one remained.

Corin Rockreikes walked over, her pace careful and deliberate. She put her hand on the table beside the podium, fingers splayed. She looked him right in the eyes and said, "I'm sorry."

"Thanks." He shrugged. "It's not your fault."

"A few of them are good people, only they're too afraid to do the right thing." She shook her head. "The rest of them… Entirely too predictable in their narcissism."

He chuckled. "I think I might resemble that remark."

"Neither part of it, actually. Even if you sometimes do put on the self-centered act for the trashmags."

"You're so sure it's an act?"

Her eyes twinkled. "I do one, too."

Had he really been judging her wrong the past few years? Maybe so. "Which part is the real you, then?"

Her gaze bored into him again. "I'm with you. I'll fly. Even if none of those other knarfers will."

"Seriously?"

"Yes."

"Wow." He blinked. "Sorry. I didn't mean it how it sounded."

"It's all right." She smiled. "I have my reasons."

"Well, thank you. Sincerely." He blew out a sigh. He put one of the confidentiality decrees on the table, and she signed the transi in one stroke of the inker without reading it. "Unfortunately, we still need a lot more than the two of us. After this, though, I can't imagine it's worthwhile even to bother talking to anyone else from Airspar. I really didn't want to go back empty-handed. The only other option is to force this on the Air Branch, and they've already made it perfectly clear they want absolutely no part of any of this."

She nodded. "Can't say I'm surprised, unfortunately. But I guess we're out of other options at this point."

"Master Wynde?" came an unfamiliar voice.

Startled, Daemyn glanced out into the auditorium. In the center aisle, a few steps up from the front, stood two of the interns. A young Aquarian man and a Faytan young woman, side by side. "I apologize for disturbing you," the man said. "I'm Xane and this is Karina. The others asked us to speak to you."

"The other interns?" He looked up to the back of the room. Where they previously had been spread out in single file taking up the back row of seats, now they all stood gathered in a group at the top of the center aisle. The exit door at the end of the aisle was still closed.

"Yes, sir," Karina said.

"Sure thing," Daemyn said, stepping around the podium toward them. "I have a few minutes. What do you need?"

"Well, we were talking about it as a group," Xane said, "and we voted —"

"It was unanimous," Karina added.

"Right," Xane continued. "We want to help. We'll fly the blades."

Daemyn knew he was staring, but he couldn't stop himself. "I'm sorry?"

"We're all from the academies," Karina said. "We all fly for the Airspar teams there. I know it's not the same as the professionals, but we're good."

"Good enough to fly what you're asking," Xane insisted. "If your colleagues from the pro circuit won't meet the challenge, we will." Before Daemyn could say anything he added, "And it's not about the money. We know it wasn't meant for us, only them. We realize that."

"There's more than thirty of us total," Karina said quickly. "We'll all help out any way you need us to. Including as many of us as you need to fly."

Daemyn took a deep breath. "I appreciate this, I really do. It means a great deal to me, more than you realize." He looked at the two young people in front of him. "But you heard the presentation. The truth is… Well, if you heard the full mission briefing, you'd know this is going to be incredibly dangerous. I can't possibly ask you – any of you – to put your lives on the line."

"We understand," Karina said. "But you didn't ask."

Xane nodded. "That's why we volunteered."

THIRTY

...WyndeStalker, in flight on approach to Agoelo

The closer they got to Agoelo, the more scans Daemyn asked Elsa to run from the consoles behind him. So far, though, *WyndeStalker*'s sensors hadn't detected anything of note. No new groups of Durnow refugees fleeing across the savannah. More importantly, no bands of outlaws on the prowl for defenseless victims. All manner of local wildlife, of course, but nothing of human origin. Exactly how they wanted it.

"We're near enough now," he told the others in the cockpit with him. "Start looking for somewhere to unload the blades."

Without any threats to manage, that was going to be their biggest challenge. Given Utara's description of the area near Agoelo, he'd already made the decision to not even bother looking for a landing area for the transport aircraft. Instead, the transports would slow down and fly a wide holding pattern while the airblades, one by one, dropped into the sky and flew themselves down to the ground. Taking off again wouldn't be an issue. If a competition airblade could launch from a standstill on a landing platform at a racetrack, these blades could manage it from the ground. As long as they found somewhere relatively flat, anyway.

"Three locations on the terrain map look promising," Reiton said from the co-pilot's seat. "Sending to your heads-up."

The map flashed up on the left side of the graphics on the interior of the viewport. Three yellow dots indicated the potential landing areas, with the *Stalker* and Agoelo marked by green and blue icons, respectively. "Let's take a look."

He flew them to the closest yellow dot, bringing *Stalker* within thirty meters of the ground. Slanting the wings at a forty-five-degree angle, he took the ship in a long, slow pass over the area. The ground was flat enough, but several stands of short scrub trees would get in the way. "We can make it work if we have to," he said. "One of the others might be better."

The next location, a few kilometers to the north, was better. A dried-up riverbed, it was wide and clear. Not a tree or shrub to be seen, nor any large rocks. It wasn't quite as flat, but the gradient was sufficiently shallow a simple thruster adjustment would level out the blades' takeoffs without any difficulty. "This one I like. Don't you think?"

"Definitely an improvement on the first one," Elsa agreed.

"Still, worth checking the last one."

The closest to Agoelo, the third spot on the map was flatter like the first. Also like the first, it had a few too many trees to Daemyn's liking. No reason to clear the vegetation when the riverbed would serve their purpose just fine. "Second spot it is," he declared. "Flag the coordinates and get them to the transports."

"On it," Reiton said.

Daemyn put a bit more altitude under *WyndeStalker* for the short flight the rest of the way to Agoelo. Without any other aircraft in the sky, it was about as uneventful of a flight as he had ever made. Considering what would happen tomorrow, he relished the moment when he had it. Two minutes later, he saw the speck on the horizon.

"Should we try to land in the town?" he asked Utara.

"I'm not sure we'll find any room," she replied. "But it's worth a look. That would probably be better if we can."

"Will do."

He slowed *Stalker* and tilted a bit to starboard, giving them a visual on Agoelo as they passed overhead. A rough layout of buildings and streets formed on the heads-up as the scanners ran progressions over the ground. He didn't see many prospects, and those looked like they might be markets. The others in the cockpit were peering out the viewport, too.

"Anything?"

"Nothing worth the risk," Reiton said.

"Outskirts it is," Daemyn said, not waiting for the others.

"Less crowded to the southeast," Elsa said. "I noticed earlier."

"Works for me."

He took *Stalker* in a wide loop to bring them around to that heading. He kept the ship's nose tilted downward, giving them all a better view ahead. Sure enough, the encampment was less compact than the others, with a broad field of dirt somewhat off center from the middle. "That'll do."

The closer they got, though, the more refugees noticed their approach. By the time Daemyn had swung *Stalker* around to line up for landing, the dirt field was half full of people, with more on the way. Hands on the yoke, he didn't change his landing vector.

From behind, Utara's voice was urgent. "What are you doing?"

"Landing."

"You wouldn't!"

"Why not?"

"You can't possibly –"

"They'll get out of the way in time."

"Daemyn!"

"If there's one thing we know about these people," he told her without ever taking his eyes from the heads-up and the viewport, "it's that their survival instinct is particularly keen. Trust me, they'll move."

"I can't believe you!"

"I wish I could say this is abnormal," Reiton said, glancing back to her. "The truth is, he gets this way sometimes. Best not to argue."

Utara muttered something Daemyn couldn't quite hear. Probably for the best.

Ten meters from the ground he kicked up the intensity of the downward thrusters. A cloud of dust bloomed beneath them, quickly obscuring the viewport entirely. He modulated their descent carefully, keeping the pace measured. Five meters. He slowed the descent again, just to be sure. Three meters. Still the proximity alarms remained silent. They set down with a *whump* and a soft bounce.

The dust in the air dissipated, and they all looked out. The gathered crowd stood near, but not too close. No one looked agitated; no one was screaming.

"See?" Daemyn said. "I knew they wouldn't get themselves crushed."

"You're something else," Utara said.

Minutes later they stood at the top of the boarding ramp while it lowered to the dirt. A pair of large pistols strapped openly to her belt, Elsa strode down first. Daemyn and Utara walked after her. Reiton followed, a holstered pistol on his belt, too. Daemyn couldn't remember the last time he'd seen Holtspring armed – but that didn't mean his friend wasn't a skilled shot if a situation required it. Hopefully, it wouldn't.

They'd only gone a few paces on the ground when J'ni Acai emerged from between two tall men in the throng of refugees and rushed forward to meet them closer to the ship than the crowd. "I got your message," she told Utara. "How bad is it?"

"Worse than we feared," Utara answered. She reached into her slingbag for the transi map they'd marked up on the flight to Loorriri. "The poison is coming from more cities than Luppitan."

"You're sure?" The fear was written on Acai's face.

At this point the last thing Daemyn cared about was what some bureaucrat thousands of kilometers away would want him to say. So he told her the truth. "The information is straight from the Prime Intelligence Service. It's as good as we'll get."

Acai met his gaze. He couldn't read her expression, but she gave him a quick nod before she held out her hand to Utara and said, "Show me the map."

...outskirts of Agoelo

The tattered, much-used map of the Midland Savannahs Wildlife Sanctuary was spread out across the front hood of the truck, prevented from blowing away in the breeze by four large stones at the corners and a few smaller rocks along the edges. Utara held the one she'd brought in her hands for comparison.

J'ni pointed to the small river nearby, tracing her finger around the map as she talked. "This is our primary source of water for Agoelo. The Kyetalle is down here, coming off the Morrusi, then passing through Durnow from the northwest at the point where the river turns southwestward again. Combined, their waters will impact a wide area between Luppitan and Durnow, but none of the offshoots will bring the poison in this direction."

"So the water supply here should be safe for now."

"Yes. Long term, we'd have to consider the possibility that the poison could leach its way into the aquifers, gradually reaching in this direction. Fortunately that's years away as a danger, meaning years of rainy seasons between now and then. There's a good chance it would become too diluted by that point to be dangerous, but we'll have to figure out a way to monitor for it."

Utara nodded. "What about from other directions? With additional rivers involved, could the poison still make its way here now?"

"I thought about that, too." J'ni pointed to several locations. "It's bad for other areas of the continent, of course, but for Agoelo's future I confirmed it against the topographical maps. The flow patterns all head away from here."

"That's lucky."

"It is."

"Have you figured out anything about the poison?"

J'ni reached into her back pocket and retrieved a small, handwritten journal. She flipped it open to the pages where a small strip of fabric served as a bookmark. "Chemistry is years ago in my coursework, and even biochemistry isn't exactly my specialty, but all my old textbooks are still backed up on my compupod. I'll need at least a few hours to look into it more, now that we know the exact chemical formula. Given how fatal it's proving to all forms of life, though, I'd already pretty much determined that we won't be able to generate any kind of quick antidote from resources available here in Loorriri. We have to assume the only way to deal with the poison is to avoid it entirely."

"That's bad."

"Yes. If there's a positive aspect to any of this, though, it's that the current high level of toxicity means the human population won't need a laboratory or chemical test to be able to figure out if the poison's coming." J'ni scanned the page for a moment, then closed the journal and tucked it back in her pocket. "Keeping watch a few days upstream is the key. Fish, frogs, reeds and algae, anything living in the water will be dead. Maybe even the insects. And of course any land animal that comes for a drink wouldn't last long, either."

"Post lookouts to make sure nothing like that is happening, with enough lead time to warn the people living downstream to stop drinking from the river."

"Exactly."

"Easy enough to do, and simple for the lookouts to understand, too."

"Yes. It's a very basic warning: if the animals and plants at the river aren't normal, don't drink the water."

Utara nodded. "The nomads have been following that guidance as a matter of received wisdom for generations. Only people who grew up in a city wouldn't know better."

"Right," J'ni said. "The Turtu clan already had figured out that plan when they contacted me. Still, it's one thing to know what you're supposed to do, and another thing to recognize the situation when it's actually happening. Understanding they need to be extra vigilant of the rivers could save lives."

"Very true. What about the wildlife?"

"Catastrophic, most likely. We'll have to wait and see." J'ni shook her head. "Long term, the ecosystem's only chance is that either we find some sort of chemical counteragent to disperse that can render the poison inert, or we hope the combination of the poison spreading out quickly along the rivers, plus all the new water from the rainy season, will dilute its toxicity fairly quickly."

"And until we know more about the chemistry, we can't know whether either of those might possibly come true."

"Short term, we have to hope that the same clues that warn humans of the threat will trigger many of the animals' danger instincts, too. If we can get past the immediate risk of mass casualties at the rivers, and the animals begin drinking from smaller sources of water replenished by the rains and the aquifers rather than the rivers... Well, then it's possible sustainable populations might be able to make it through."

"Let's hope so," Utara said. "For the people, what can I do to help?"

"On the warnings, several families keep modest farms upstream, and every few weeks they bring their surplus to the town to trade. They're at the river multiple times a day. Once we get word out to them, that's our early-warning system for Agoelo."

"And the nomads?"

"The Turtu already sent out riders to warn the clans near the Morrusi and Kyetalle. What you've brought, though, means we have a lot more clans to warn, too. Once things are a little more stable here, I may take a couple of days and go out myself. Between the speed I can make in the truck, especially along the expressways, and the nomads sending a scout to meet me once they see the flares, I should be able to warn three or four of the clans to the north and east in pretty short order. They'll be able to pass the word on to most of the others in the greatest danger within days. The rest, we can handle with riders from here."

Utara appraised the map, and realized how much land area they now had to cover. "Will you have enough riders?"

"I'm going to ask for volunteers. We have to be careful how we do it, though. We need to manage how word of the potential poison threat in other places gets out, so that we don't end up with a panic here in Agoelo, where it's safe."

"I'd offer to ride," Utara said. "But I'm afraid I'm considerably out of practice, especially for a trek like that."

She missed riding, of course, but more than that she wished she was able to do more to contribute. If she couldn't warn the nomads, though, she could certainly do something to help the people of Agoelo – and the massive unexpected influx of Durnow refugees encamped on the outskirts.

"Working hard to avoid a panic is something I've had a lot of practice at lately, unfortunately," Utara continued. She locked down her fear about the fate of Blonkas before it had a chance to rise up inside her. "Including keeping information contained to only the right people who need to know. So, let's go meet these riders and see what I can do."

...PIS Headquarters, outskirts of New Romas

The door to the briefing room slid open. The men were on their feet before anyone entered. The first person through was a burly security agent who took up a post right inside the portal. Idly Monson wondered why the

Intelligence Chief would need a bodyguard within the walls of PIS head-quarters. The slender Aladarian woman entered next.

"Gentlemen," Maxilla Firebird said. "Let's get down to business."

"Of course, Chief," Hybollo said. He waited for the door to slide closed, and then the three of them sat down in unison. "There's very little to supplement beyond the most recent briefing memo. Fortunately the AIs have remained stable over the last few hours."

"Good. And the operation with the airblades?"

Monson sat forward in his chair and faced her. "All status markers indicate that they will meet their timetable to launch in the morning, as planned. The airblades have arrived on Loorriri. They're in the process of loading the artronium fuel now, before the pilots make their preflight inspections."

"And you're confident in your updates?"

"I am." He gestured to his compupod. "Daemyn Wynde personally instructed his head of security to provide me with hourly notifications of their progress. She has been very diligent and thorough, and under the circumstances I don't believe she would have any incentive to provide me with anything but the truth."

"Even to make her boss look good?"

"I've considered that," Monson said. "To this point, the updates have included information even when it is not entirely favorable, such as a slight delay in the delivery of some of the airblades due to a band of silver jackals running across the landing zone until they were chased off, so I believe in their accuracy."

Chief Firebird nodded. "Hopefully they'll remain that way. But I'm instructing you to keep a keen eye on what you're receiving. It's human nature to avoid an unfavorable reality on the overconfidence that the situation will turn for the better in time."

"Yes, sir." Monson held her gaze. "No different, I imagine, than the objective perspective you take when reviewing the memoranda and documentation from myself or the members of the PIS team handling this crisis."

She smiled, but there was no warmth in it. "Indeed."

"I can assure you," he told her, "that we have been fully candid about our evaluation of the options and the results of the simulations, and the odds of success which are set out in the briefing memos."

"Even so, we all know that this operation cannot be the only option. If it fails – and that remains a real possibility, even under the odds as currently calculated – we simply cannot leave Prime undefended against whatever the AIs might do next."

Monson didn't disagree with the sentiment. Those were politician's words, though, not an intelligence analyst's. The thought made his blood run cold. Ideas from politicians and bureaucrats were in large part responsible for creating the circumstances that had produced the very crisis the PIS now found itself fighting to solve. The notion of turning to the same kind of thinking for solutions was madness.

Hybollo knew it, too. He said, "The Prime Minister insisted on another strategy. One beyond the PIS."

"The Unified Forces."

Monson shivered. He had a pretty good idea where the conversation was going to be headed. And he didn't like it one bit.

"I take no offense at the idea of alternatives," Hybollo said, "but with all due respect, Chief, what can the Unified Forces do to stop this?"

"Believe me," she said. For only a moment, her voice had the slightest hint of fatalistic levity in it. "I said the same thing to the Prime Minister myself. Nearly verbatim, in fact."

Monson gripped the edge of the table to keep himself from saying anything.

"Of course his first idea was simply to blow up the entire Boynton Logistics Dynamic facility in Port Vulcania. It took us a few minutes to get him to realize that doing so wouldn't make a single bit of difference."

"You can't be serious!" Hybollo exclaimed before he could stop himself. When he started to verbalize the chagrined apology written all over his face, Chief Firebird waved it off.

"I assume," he said, "that he remains unwilling to use the INMASS to deactivate all of the other Boynton AIs across the planet?"

"Correct."

Monson understood the reason, but couldn't figure out the alternative solution. Wiping out the INMASS AIs would forever stain Tamorchin's legacy with the infamy of presiding over a steep, enduring decline in quality of life across the world. Much better, from the seat behind the Prime Minister's desk, to let the rest of Prime continue their lives in blissful ignorance, and make the continent no one cared about anyway pay the price.

Just like that, Monson deduced Tamorchin's move. "If he can't hit them in Port Vulcania, he's going to blow up the AIs where they are. In the Future Cities."

"Yes." Firebird's voice went flat. "If the code can't be shut down, the alternative plan is to physically annihilate the AIs by destroying the hardware and infrastructure in which they exist."

"That would work," Hybollo said. "If they have a way to do it."

"The last time the Unified Forces tried to take action, it didn't succeed in the least," Monson said. "What's different with this plan?"

"Air Branch alone," Firebird said. "High altitude bombers, to ensure the strike is above the range of their sensors to detect on approach. And the bombs will be falling too fast. By the time the AIs detect them, it will be too late to do anything about it."

"We have bombs that precise? To hit the AIs from such altitudes?"

Firebird shook her head. "Not the AIs. It will be macro-fusion bombs."

Hybollo gasped. Monson slumped back in his chair.

"He's willing to wipe the Future Cities off the face of Prime," Monson finally said. "Erase them from existence, to destroy a handful of buildings housing the AIs."

"No other distance weaponry," Firebird said, "can provide a one-hundred-percent guarantee that the AIs could not possibly survive the attack intact."

That was probably true. But the macro-fusion bombs wouldn't merely level the Future Cities to piles of rubble. The blast wave would devastate the terrain in a hundred-kilometer radius. The radioactive residues would poison the land for decades. Along with the humans, entire generations of animals would be wiped out, too. Species would never recover. With twelve bombs, located roughly evenly around the continent's land area, Loorriri itself would essentially become extinct. Not to mention the collateral consequences, radiation and otherwise, for the rest of Prime.

Monson looked at Chief Firebird. "We can't let him do it."

THIRTY-ONE

...Agoelo

T he *WyndeStalker*, at rest atop the dirt with its boarding ramp lowered, came into Utara's view at the same time she saw her friend hurrying in that direction. She called out to her.

J'ni looked over, consternation on her face. She slowed at first, then drew to a stop. She waited for Utara to catch up.

"What's wrong?"

"I heard from Urttu again. On the comm."

Utara's heart skipped a beat. "More refugees from Durnow?"

"No."

At this point, Utara wasn't sure if that was good news or bad news. "Did the drones go after the nomads?"

"Nothing about the city, and no additional poisoned rivers, either."

"What is it, then?"

J'ni took one more deep breath, exhaling sharply. "One of the outlaw bands."

"Coming this way?" Utara compelled her fists to unclench. "With the weapons –"

"They're dead."

"What?"

"The whole band," J'ni said. "They're all dead."

"How?"

"One of the riders Urttu sent out after we discovered the poisoned rivers. I spoke to him personally. On his way back from warning the nearby clans, he came across the scene basically through sheer luck."

"Was it the drones? Maybe somehow this band learned that Durnow was in trouble? The city would make a very tempting target to plunder as long as they believed its defenses were compromised along with everything else failing."

"I thought that was probably it, too, and the location he described might be within the outer perimeter of their range, but…" J'ni took another deep breath. "Drones would be able to gun them down, but they couldn't have buried the bodies."

"Do you —"

Utara cut herself off when J'ni abruptly glanced away, her face drawn into a scowl. Utara followed her gaze and realized Daemyn was striding over briskly to join them.

"Is something the matter?" he asked.

"Honestly, I'm still sorting through everything," Utara said. Quickly she recapped the situation for him. "It happened much closer to where we did the airlift, not in the immediate vicinity of Agoelo, which is good."

Daemyn glanced between the two women. "One less gang of thugs making everyone's life more dangerous is a good thing, too."

"Maybe, if we knew who did this," J'ni replied, crossing her arms. "But we don't. Anyone strong enough to wipe out an outlaw band also endangers everyone here if they come this way."

"You're the expert on life out on the savannah." Daemyn crossed his arms, as well. "I have to say, though, it sounds to me like some human predators found out the hard way how easy it can be to end up as prey. That's how it always goes for bullies."

Nearly everywhere else on the planet, Primeans believed their technology, sophistication, and quality of life had moved beyond the primal instincts of the animal world. Food and water barely at subsistence levels, the possibility that the next day might be your last, the implacable march of survival where the fittest lived and the weak perished – for the rest of Prime, these were little more than notions to be studied in school. Utara had seen the mentality in practice, had heard those overconfident declarations expressed, more times than she could count. On the savannahs of Loorriri, they were the realities of existence – and undeniable truths. Even for the human inhabitants of Zanita.

Utara suppressed a shudder. "Compared to a Future City, Agoelo is about as easy a target as outlaws could dream up. If the refugees are a little bit safer now, I think I'll sleep a little easier tonight."

"Vigilante vengeance isn't justice," J'ni insisted.

Utara believed that, too, and J'ni knew it. Right now, though, she couldn't bring herself to feel any guilt for the slain outlaws. "At least they received a proper burial. More than was granted to those refugees from Luppitan."

"Even out here," Daemyn said, "only the worst of the worst fail to honor the gods by respecting their teachings in the correct way."

"Murder is murder, even when the dead are bad people," J'ni retorted. "The gods teach that, too. We don't get to obey selectively."

"When this is all over, we can sit down over some branibon and debate theology," Daemyn said. He waved to Elsa, who had descended *WyndeStalker*'s ramp with several members of her security team. "All set?"

The Polar Aquarian jogged over to join them. "Scanners appear to be functioning well from this spot. Mainly a validation patrol," she told him. She looked at the two women. "Anything else we should know about before we head out?"

Before Utara could form a response, J'ni spat out, "No. Do your job."

Daemyn looked to Utara. She gave a nod, and he told Elsa, "Good to go."

Elsa hustled back to her team – and J'ni already had started marching off the way she'd come, too. Utara bounded after her.

"Where are you going?"

"I have something I need to take care of."

Utara reached for her arm, tugging her to a halt. "If you need Daemyn's help with something, we can still –"

"He learned what he needs to know," J'ni said. "It's fine."

"You're sure?"

"I am."

"All right." Utara wasn't convinced, but it was clear J'ni was unwilling to discuss the matter any further. "See you soon."

J'ni looked away, then back at Utara. "Right. See you soon."

Utara walked back to Daemyn, who had waited for her. "I'd better get started making those comms to Steamer Point."

"Hopefully you'll get more good news."

"That's the plan."

They were halfway to the *WyndeStalker* when Utara noticed he had a strange expression on his face. One she found she couldn't read.

"What is it?"

"Hmm?"

She looked up at him. "You look like you have something to say."

"It's nothing." He shook his head. "I'm thinking I should've known your friends would be idealistic, too."

Utara smiled. "I have that effect on people."

He smiled back. "We'll see."

...airblade staging area, near Agoelo

The pilots stood in a rough circle. Each pair had a handheld compupod with the unique data for their respective Future Cities. All of them had reviewed the maps and flight routes for hours on their journey to Loorriri. Some of them would review it again tonight, probably. This session now, though, would be their one and only chance to review the mission together.

"We're synced up?" Daemyn asked.

Beside him, Kirkland Oggust was the only one in the circle who wasn't a pilot. Daemyn doubted there were more than a handful of individuals on the planet who could have designed and cobbled together the elaborate system of compupods Oggust had set up in the *WyndeStalker*'s galley to oversee the mission real-time. Daemyn didn't count himself on that list.

"Ready," Oggust said.

"Begin." While the other man advanced the progress of the mission preview on every pod simultaneously, Daemyn reviewed the key points from the pilot prep memo. "We begin launches shortly after dawn, in three waves based on distances from our location to the Future Cities. Slight differentials in the flight speeds assigned to each team will enable all of us to reach our respective target cities over the span of about three minutes."

"Close in time," Oggust chimed in. "But not too close. Remember, the AIs expect humans to make mistakes, and we want their observations to match predictions."

"The approach vectors are designed to ensure the AIs detect our arrival without also presenting an attack trajectory. At this point in the mission, your airblades will be emitting signals consistent with a scouting run by reconnaissance aircraft. That will continue as you reach the city walls and begin your path over the city. Again, each team's particular route accounts for the street layout and topography of your target city. Continue with the dummy reconnaissance route as long as the AI lets you."

Oggust chuckled. "My sims suggest a ten percent chance the AIs may allow recon uncontested. So, maybe one or two of you will get lucky."

"Sure," Daemyn said. "For the rest of us, once the drones start coming, break off the dummy route and go for it. No more mission clock at that point, take your shot at the receiver antenna as soon as you have it."

Rockreikes grinned. "Treat it like free-fire phases. No coach in your ear, take whatever points come open. Except this time, there's only one shot to take."

"Exactly." Daemyn looked around and saw the other pilots – it was hard to think of them as interns anymore – nodding to each other. "Your city specs provide several suggested routes, but fly whatever you can get. You have the list of countermeasures loaded in the blades. That's like a match, too – use what you need to keep flying, while managing your usage rate, if you can, so you don't run out too fast."

"That's plenty familiar, definitely," one of the pilots, a short Aladarian man, said.

Daemyn had tried hard to learn all their names. He'd failed. "Once you've fired your shot to the antenna," he continued, "you're clear to fly maximum thrust to get out the city as fast as you can. With these engines, you'll outrun the drones within six or seven seconds at most when you're no longer moderating speed for maneuverability. Keep that in mind as you're allocating countermeasures, especially once you're in close proximity to taking the shot."

"Throughout the mission we'll have real-time coordination through the command center," Oggust reminded them. "In addition to comms, we've modified the uplinks so that all the blades will be sending vidfeeds from the cams mounted on your headrest. I'll see what you see, literally. In addition to monitoring each blade's sensor data and engine performance, of course."

"Currently the plan for audio is to have each pilot team paired together, but only the command center connected to all twenty-four blades. If necessary, we'll patch through anyone who needs to comm." Daemyn checked the faces around the circle. "Does that work for everyone?"

The consensus was quick. "Great. Any last questions?"

A few of the pilots had technical questions that Oggust answered easily. After that, there was no reason to keep everyone gathered. "If anything comes up, we can always address it in the morning," Daemyn said. "That's all for tonight. Now, everyone get some sleep and be ready to fly in the morning."

The circle gradually lost its shape as the pilots wandered back toward the two shuttlecraft that had flown them here, where temporary beds had been set up for them for the night. They all stayed in their flight pairs even though no one had told them they should. Daemyn barely knew these interns, and he was proud of them.

"I need something to eat," Brutus said. He was Daemyn's flight partner for the mission, and he hadn't left yet. "You want me to get you anything?"

"No, thank you," Daemyn said. "Anything you want to go over for Durnow tomorrow?"

Brutus grinned. "I'm wingman for the very best pilot in the group. I'm feeling all right about our chances."

Daemyn laughed and gave him a firm pat on the shoulder. "I'll do my best to live up to expectations."

"You will," the test pilot said, then strode off for the shuttle with the food supplies.

"I hope they're ready," Oggust said.

Daemyn turned to him. "I do, too."

...near Agoelo

On the back side of the ridgeline, it was almost as dark as nighttime. Only the sky overhead, the rays of sunlight still draping orange banners across the darkening blue, made it clear the sun hadn't set. Utara peered ahead, watching for the distinctive tree J'ni had described.

From the passenger seat Daemyn asked, "Where are we going?"

She laughed. "Wondering what excursion could possibly be interesting enough to tear you away the night before your big mission?"

"I didn't mean it like that."

"I know." She smiled at him. "And it is a fair question."

When he realized she wasn't going to elaborate, he exhaled an unimpressed huff. She wondered if he'd press further, but he didn't. Then she recognized the tree, slowed the truck, and made the turn onto the secondary slope that brought them smoothly right up to the top of the ridgeline. Taking another moment to line up the hood of the truck toward the setting sun, she locked the brakes and shut off the engine.

"We're here," she announced.

"Okay…"

"Out of the truck." She reached behind her seat for her slingbag. "And hop up onto the hood."

In the fading light he gave her a skeptical look. Unlatching his restraints, he opened the door and bounded down to the soil. Utara did the same. When she clambered atop the truck's hood, he was already there. Scooting up next to him – there wasn't much room to spare, anyway – she opened her slingbag and handed him a pair of metal cups.

"What are these for?" he asked.

She pulled the flask out next. "This."

"Excellent."

She poured a generous quantity into each up. Once she'd secured the flask, he handed her one of the cups. She hefted it toward the scene before them. "We call this a sundowner."

"We?"

"Me and J'ni. It's sort of a tradition of ours, I guess." She held up the cup, and he clinked his with hers. They each took a long sip.

"Oh, good."

"Good?"

"Well, for a minute there I was worried that this was one of those *final farewell before I never see you again* kind of things. But apparently you only do this with people you actually like."

Utara laughed. "You're a smart one, Wynde."

"I like to think so."

"Humble, too."

"Very."

Even in the short time they'd been here, the sun already had lowered further. Now partway obscured by the horizon, it lit the indigo sky with hues that were quickly deepening from oranges to reds. Daemyn took her hand in his. They sat in silence, side by side. Utara took another drink from her cup.

"Look," Daemyn said, releasing her hand to point. "Over there."

It took her a moment, but she spotted the animal. "I see."

From this distance, the wide wings appeared barely three centimeters from tip to tip. Rising on the air currents, soaring with only a rare beat of its wings, the pegasus inspected its domain below. In the daylight it would have sparkled in a brilliant, almost blinding, shade of white. Instead, the sundowner's rays had painted it a shimmering red from nose to tail, wingtip to wingtip.

"You knew he'd be here?" Daemyn asked.

"No." She took back his hand now that he was no longer pointing. "I mean, I knew that he could be. But this time of year, his range is enormous. Anywhere within a hundred kilometers. Maybe more."

"I guess tonight is my lucky night, then."

And it wasn't over yet. "You're ahead of me now."

"Hmm?"

"You've seen two. A dragon before this. I've only seen the pegasus."

"Right. But you've seen two separate ones. So that still counts as two."

She laughed. "You really are a scorekeeper, aren't you?"

He shrugged. "Being a competitive racer will do that to you."

"I think that's why you enjoy the racing so much."

"You're probably right. Either way, it's not a win. That can only come tomorrow. Let's call it a victory, even if it's a small one."

"Works for me."

The sun made a red dome against the horizon. Still the pegasus glided on the air. A bit closer to them now, but not much.

"We're saving him too, you know," Daemyn said.

She squeezed his hand.

"Sure, saving the people is the main goal," he continued. "But the land matters too. The animals, the plants. The ecosystem. We can't let it be wiped out any more than the cities, or the nomads. Prime can't afford to lose a continent."

"Even one most Primeans hardly ever think about."

"*Especially* that one."

"At least the refugees are finally starting to get some assistance, now that I've embarrassed New Romas about it in the media."

He chuckled. "Nice work on that, by the way."

"The best part is, if the PDS fires me, all I have to do is file for my unemployment coverage. The government will still have to pay me one way or the other."

"Careful hanging around with venturists, Utara. You might start thinking like them."

"I could do worse."

"Yes, you could." He took a long sip from his cup, finishing it off. "Keep your focus on the refugees. I think the conservation of the land will work itself out."

She had a suspicion that was the venturist talking, working another angle. Right now, though, she wasn't going to ask. She didn't want anything to wreck this moment.

The top edge of the sun was about to dip below the horizon. In the sky, the pegasus made a wide turn over the savannah, one last surveillance before nightfall. For a moment it faced straight toward them. Wings drawn high to take a downbeat. Legs pulled up, almost as if making a leap in midair. Head held high. The entire beast a dark, glimmering hue of red.

"There's my logo," Daemyn said under his breath.

"Your what?"

"For Wynde Industries. Reiton's been pestering me for weeks. The company name is fine, but we need a logo. And that –" He waved his hand toward where the pegasus had been, except now it was nowhere to be seen. "Well, anyway, the way he had his wings up and all that."

"Red, too?"

"Yes." He turned to look at her. "What do you think?"

"It's perfect."

THIRTY-TWO

...airblade staging area

Even in the confines of the airblade cockpit with his flight helmet covering his ears, Daemyn heard the roar of the engines from the four blades rocketing away into the cloudless sky. On his heads-up display, the countdown timer in the upper right corner at last began to run.

Seven minutes until the last blades launched. Daemyn and his wingman, Brutus, had the shortest distance to travel of any flight team. At the blades' top speed on a straight line, they could reach Durnow in a matter of minutes. Instead they would fly a broader arc around the savannah to approach from the opposite direction of Agoelo. Combined with a relatively leisurely flight speed, at least by airblade standards, they would arrive at their Future City at the appointed time, in sync with the other blade pairs at their respective target cities.

Into his comm he asked, "How's your blade look?"

"Purring like a kitten," Brutus replied.

"Thrusters at sixty seconds," Daemyn reminded him. Not that the other pilot needed it. In their last mission review before climbing into their blades, Brutus had proven himself eminently prepared.

"Copy."

Until the last possible moment, Daemyn had been considering having Oggust put the mission status of all twelve pairs in a running datastream on his heads-up. Now, though, prepping his own blade for takeoff, he was very glad he'd decided against the idea. Whether the other pilots flew well or poorly, succeeded or failed, even lived or died, he needed to keep his focus on his own part in the mission. Besides, after the mission was over he'd learn the truth soon enough anyway. Assuming he lived through the mission himself, of course. Which he planned to.

He tapped the button on his yoke, toggling the comm to a dedicated feed directly with Oggust alone. "How's the status so far?"

"All clear on the first eight to this point. Blades are sound, flights are unimpeded."

"How do the vidfeeds look?"

"Better than I expected, to be honest. The image stabilizers clean it up more than I thought they would. Of course, we'll see how it handles the aggressive stuff later, but for now it's top notch."

"Excellent." Daemyn already had visions of using the vid footage of airblades racing over the Loorriri terrain in advertisements. The technical specs would be impressive in their own right, but these kinds of visuals would set Wynde Industries apart from anything its competitors had shown the people of Prime. The WI ads wouldn't be able to show the Future Cities or the drones or anything specific from the AI mission, of course – no doubt the PIS and its innumerable cohort of lawyers would insist on it – but simple terrain vid wouldn't have any government-secrecy significance. "Can't wait to take a look when I'm back."

"You got it."

"Feeds are open with PIS, too?"

"Affirmative. Functioning as planned. They haven't said much, but they're on with me via the uplink."

"Copy." His timer was running down, and Oggust would see it, too. "Comm if there's anything I need to know."

"Will do. Anything else you need before launch?"

"Just that favor we talked about."

"Already on it."

"Perfect. Wynde out."

He toggled the comm back to his feed with Brutus. "Ready to fly?"

"You know it."

"Let's do this."

The countdown reached one minute remaining. Daemyn tapped the console buttons and activated the airblade's vertical-lift thrusters. The yoke vibrated in his hands and the wings wobbled before the forceful *whoosh* of downward air levitated the airblade straight up from the ground into the air.

He glanced out the cockpit viewport to confirm that all four airblades still at the staging area had made their liftoff successfully.

They kept their ascent measured. Compared to typical airblade flights, the altimeter readings were almost comically low. More like birds than human aircraft.

At thirty seconds and twenty-five meters off the ground, the other pair of airblades engaged their engines and raced away over the savannah. In the blink of an eye, Rockreikes and Karina were mere specks on the horizon – then gone.

Daemyn readied his grip on the yoke. With time to spare, he and Brutus rose to forty meters, then leveled off.

He released and clenched his fingers one more time. The timer spun down the last few seconds. The countdown timer flashed. Daemyn fired the engines.

The force of the acceleration drove him back in the seat. The savannah whipped past beneath him. The engine hummed and the blade assumed its equilibrium vibration of flight. Daemyn held the yoke and watched their progress on the heads-up map as their blades raced toward their fateful rendezvous with the AI and its drones in Durnow.

~⌒

...WyndeStalker *groundside, outskirts of Agoelo*

Once the airblades had launched, Utara had quickly realized she needed to keep herself distracted. Despite her hurried packing of her slingbag at Steamer Point after Daemyn had commed to tell her Reiton was on his way, somehow she had remembered to include the heavy-duty, satellite-direct comms device her father had insisted on giving her when she'd first left Durnow with the residents fleeing to the savannah. Its powerful transmitter was plenty strong enough to make contact with the Aladarian Guard base to check on the status of the refugees there.

Equally quickly, she also had realized that nowhere in Agoelo was nearly quiet enough for her to be able to make the comms with any chance of clearly hearing the audio coming from the other end of the feed. That had brought her back to the *WyndeStalker*, away from the cacophony of the townspeople and the refugees. Toward the back of the shuttlecraft, Holtspring and several others were engaged in frenzied monitoring of the airblades and their mission.

In the cockpit, though, it was quiet. She'd been here nearly half an hour, but still she hadn't activated the comdee. She would soon. She just wasn't ready yet.

"Utara? Am I interrupting anything?"

She looked up and realized Elsa Ovella was standing at the entry to the cockpit. She hadn't heard the other woman approaching up the corridor, but that wasn't really a surprise. Between PARTE and being Daemyn's chief of security for Wynde Industries, sneaking up on people came with the territory.

"No," Utara told her. "I'm between comms."

Ovella nodded. She took two steps forward and offered a folded-up scrap of transi between two fingers. "This is for you. From... the back."

"All right."

Utara took the transi and started to unfold it. Ovella stepped back to the entryway but didn't leave. Something about her pose made Utara not want to lift open the last fold to read the words. She did anyway.

The note was short. Written in simple, precise lettering. Almost like a child trying a little too hard to make the letters perfect.

Miss Fireheart,

Master Wynde instructed me to report to you what I found, no matter what it is. I wish the answer was different.

Blonkas was the first AI to use the poison. Everyone in the city is dead.

I am truly sorry.

K.O.

The first time she read it, the words weren't real. Utara read it again. Then a third time, and a fourth.

Carefully she refolded the note exactly as she'd received it. For a minute she held it, unsure if she could release her grasp. Finally she looked up at Ovella, held out the transi, and said, "Please destroy this."

"I will." The tall woman stretched down and took the note. "Can I do anything for you?"

"No."

"If you change your mind, any time, it's –"

"How does he know?" The pilots couldn't possibly have reached the city yet, much less made any kind of thorough inspection to determine the gruesome reality. It had to be something else. And Utara needed to understand.

If Ovella had any doubts about revealing the answer to someone she'd barely met, and who didn't work for Wynde Industries, she didn't let it show. "From the PIS."

"What?"

"From their server data, more specifically."

Utara took a breath. "They didn't tell you?"

"Hardly."

Utara breathed again. She had to force her lungs to work. "He… hacked it from them?"

"Daemyn asked him to," Ovella said, as though that explained everything.

"How?"

"Now that the airblades are underway, we have a real-time connection to the PIS control room. They want our updates from the blades to track against the AI server activity, and we need to know any changes on the AI end instantly so the pilots can make adjustments. I don't have the slightest idea how the hack was formulated, and I suspect Oggust would have no desire to explain it to me, but he sent some code down the feed that traced its way through the PIS systems to find out the information he wanted, then surreptitiously got it back to him."

Utara nodded.

"I'm sorry."

"Thank you." It looked like Ovella was turning to go, so Utara said, "Daemyn asked him to do this? To find this out?"

"Yes."

"If he gets caught…"

Ovella smiled. "He won't."

"Daemyn would go to prison."

"I would, too, probably," Ovella said, her words as mundane as telling a friend the final result of an Airspar match.

"Why?"

"Why what?"

"Just to find out the truth sooner rather than later? It's not like the government would be able to hide this for long. It's risking *everything*."

"I suppose it is."

Utara looked at her. "Isn't it your job to keep him out of trouble? Stop him from making stupid decisions like this?"

"It is. But ultimately, he's the boss."

Utara wasn't convinced. "Why would he do it?"

Ovella looked at her and smiled. "I think you know."

Maybe she did. "I'm sorry I've kept you here so long," Utara said. "You probably need to get back there and help with the mission."

"It's fine." Ovella paused in the entryway. "Like I said, if there's anything I can do for you, let me know."

"Daemyn ordered that, too?"

"He didn't need to," the striking blonde said.

Then she was gone, and Utara was alone.

"Well," she said quietly to herself, "time to get back to work."

First, though, she had a comm she needed to make.

Before that, Utara let herself slump back in the seat. Tears streaming down her face, she clutched the long-range comdee to her chest and sobbed.

...airblade WI-DW-01B, on approach to Durnow

The countdown timer ticked through the minutes and seconds again. This time it marked the duration remaining until the airblades would cross the city walls and enter the Future Cities. Unlike the staggered launch, now everyone's timer was the same.

Six-and-a-half minutes to go.

Oddly, Daemyn didn't find the moment particularly disconcerting. And that, itself, was a bit disconcerting. He'd forced himself into an unbreakable mental focus countless times in the last minutes before a crucial phase of an Airspar match, of course, so it shouldn't have surprised him that his mind had locked down again now. Still, the stakes were so different this time – so much more important – that it bothered him that his brain didn't seem to care. He'd have to figure it all out later, though. Right now, the focus was a very good thing. He couldn't afford any mistakes. Not today.

Their pair of blades approached Durnow on a curving path so shallow it looked like a straight line on the small map on the heads-up. Daemyn checked the indicator on the left side and confirmed that the blade's scanners were already emitting the signals that mimicked a routine surveillance run. He doubted the Future City AI's sensors reached out this far, but there was no reason to take the chance.

He opened the comm to his wingman. "How are you feeling, Brutus?"

"I'm ready."

The young man was nervous, too. Daemyn could hear it in his voice. He could hardly blame him. "Me too. Remember, fly it like a match. Nothing we haven't done before."

The laughter in his headset was genuine. *"You a lot more than me, though."*

"True, but you'd be one of the best young aces out there, if you'd chosen that instead of test piloting."

"Thanks. Really. It means a lot, coming from you."

"Don't let it go to your head," Daemyn said, making sure his voice conveyed the joking intention of the words. "Focus in. We're almost there."

Quickly he toggled the comm over to Oggust. "It's Wynde," he said, in case the other man wasn't looking at the comm screen when the voice came through. "How are the cities looking on approach?"

"Nothing but a few routine drone patrols outside the walls at a couple of locations."

"Inside the walls?"

"Can't tell from the blades' sensors. PIS control room is scrolling me updates direct from their AI monitoring team. They've not warned about drones scrambled, and least not yet."

"It'll happen soon enough," Daemyn said. "But if it's after we arrive, so much the better. One step further toward the goal without having to avoid getting killed."

"No kidding."

"I'll check back."

"Copy."

The seconds weren't actually ticking off faster on the countdown now that the blades had almost reached the city, but it sure felt like it. Daemyn took a deep breath. The heads-up map showed the two green triangles getting closer and closer to Durnow – until the terrain map vanished. A second later, a basic map of the city appeared on the heads-up in its place. Out the viewport, on the horizon, a small dark dot rose above the otherwise very flat savannah.

Daemyn opened the comm to Brutus. "See it?"

"Yep. Straight ahead."

The tallest buildings in Durnow weren't very tall. For Loorriri, sure. The Future Cities were massive compared to the local communities. He doubted the highest building in Agoelo even had three stories. But compared to the towering skyscrapers of Hyj-gon, with their majestic spires soaring to the clouds and skyways a thousand meters or more above the ground, the central city buildings in Durnow hardly merited notice.

For that reason the Future City seemed to crawl toward Daemyn. He was used to seeing a cityscape rapidly grow before him. Instead, Durnow was more like a lump growing larger and larger on the land.

At their speed, they closed the distance in the matter of a few measured breaths. The final seconds wound down on the timer.

"All right," Daemyn said into the comm, "here we go."

Side by side, the pair of airblades rushed over the city wall at moderate speed, their altitude a few dozen meters above the highest rooftops in the outer neighborhoods. Then they split apart for their southerly trajectories, Brutus to the west and Daemyn to the east. Two scouting aircraft making their reconnaissance passes – at least until the AI's reaction changed the plan. Daemyn doubted it would take long. But he would take every second he could get.

His first pass took him around the outer neighborhoods. He didn't have to adjust altitude or course very much until he reached the far end of his flight path. He pulled the yoke to take the airblade into a leisurely barrel-roll that brought him around to head back northward over the next inward group of neighborhoods.

Coming out of the roll and leveling out, he checked the sensors. Six drones in the air over the city, the same number as when they'd arrived. He reviewed the number on the datafeed and the red dots on the heads-up city map just to double-check. Surely the AI had detected their presence by now. But for whatever reason, it wasn't moving the drones to engage them.

The mission couldn't possibly keep going this easily, could it?

Of course not.

Right before he reached the northern end of his path, as he readied the blade for another barrel-roll for the next pass to take him that much closer to the city center – and the receiver antenna that was their ultimate target – the threat-assessment alarms began to wail on the console. The heads-up showed half of the drones already in the air heading his way, while others went toward Brutus on the other side of the city. More red dots popped onto the map, too, as the AI launched the rest of its drones.

"Incoming," Daemyn told Brutus. "Break off."

"Affirmative."

In sync, the two blades abandoned their pretense of the surveillance run and implemented the next stage of their plan: head in the direction of the city center without making an obvious charge toward the antenna. Oggust's four suggested flight routes flashed onto the map, each highlighted in a different color. Daemyn was closer to the blue one, so he took it. Brutus' green triangle moved toward the yellow path.

"Countermeasures only after they start shooting," Daemyn reminded him. Not that he really expected patience from the AI. But one less thing they did to provoke the drones could still make a difference in how much time they had.

"Copy."

A second later two drones approached Daemyn head-on. They flew right toward him, unyielding. When they reached him, one flew high and the other low, passing him at what had to be close to the machines' top speed. He couldn't see directly to aft out the viewport, but he checked their red dots on the heads-up.

Sure enough, they had looped around to pursue.

Their machineguns opened fire.

THIRTY-THREE

...PIS Headquarters

With the operation underway, the surveillance chamber had been cleared of everyone except essential personnel. Compared to previous days, the large space all around them was now eerily quiet. To Monson, it only made the mood that much more bleak. He tamped down the emotion and focused.

A handful of the most trusted agents and analysts sat at their workstations, monitoring every detail of the incoming data and sending any updates of measurable significance to the map of Loorriri that dominated the room's central display screen. Monson and Hybollo stood at the primary station in the middle of the room, where they were able to view any data they needed. The Intelligence Chief stood with them. Beside her, barely an arm's length away, Firebird's personal aide sat in the closest chair. The young Faytan, Athena, kept her eyes fixed not to the screen at the workstation, but on the heavy-duty compupod giving them a secured, real-time link to both the Prime Minister's office and the Unified Forces regional command center with jurisdiction over Loorriri.

Otherwise, the room was empty. Much like the continent soon would be, if their mission failed.

Hybollo checked one of the secondary display screens to the right of the map. Loud enough for all of them to hear but seemingly engulfed by the barren room around them, he said, "The airblades have reached the Future Cities."

"Monitoring," one of the analysts called out.

Firebird glanced to her aide. "Air Branch?"

"Bombers in the air. Thirty minutes out."

"That's too soon," Monson told the Chief.

"Not if things are going poorly," Firebird said, looking him straight in the eyes. "If by that point it's clear a significant number of the blades won't succeed in delivering the code, the bombs will drop."

Hybollo spun toward them. "But the pilots will still be in the blast radius!"

"The Prime Minister is aware of that."

"And what if it's going well?" Monson demanded. "If the code has been delivered, we'll barely be able to see the result by then."

"Then the altitude will work in our favor." If the Chief was offended by his tone, she didn't show it. "The bombers can fly a holding pattern if confirmation of success seems likely to be pending, while still being in position to drop the bombs on a moment's notice if failure occurs."

The idea was reasonable enough in principle. Reality was a different proposition entirely. Monson asked, "How will that decision be made?"

"We'll provide our analysis from the data we have," Firebird said, "and the Prime Minister will make the call."

Exactly as Monson had feared. No matter how well Wynde and his airblade pilots flew, everything might be thrown away on the whims of a politician more concerned about the next election than the centuries-long consequences of dropping twelve macro-fusion bombs on an electorally insignificant continent.

For a moment Monson closed his eyes and offered a missive to his favored god, Evos, and another to Wynde's patron goddess, Fayti. The airblades and their mission needed to succeed. No matter what it took, he couldn't allow the alternative to happen.

...airblade WI-DW-01B, over Durnow

"Ha!" Daemyn shouted to himself, wrenching the blade into a sharp turn to avoid the looming brick government building dead ahead.

The drones' bullets chewed into the structure's front face, spitting out chunks of stone and crete in a spray of red and gray mineral. In a flash the airblade soared past the building and swung around, its wingtips level with the residential rooftops while he continued onward straight down the deserted thoroughfare.

The airblade was handling well, but Daemyn was really starting to wish that it had been armed with some actual *weapons*. The Airspar countermeasures helped keep the drones far enough off his tail that the machines couldn't quite take the perfect shot at his blade, and gave him an advantage in controlling the path and tempo of their predator/prey aerial dance. On the other hand, none of the drones had crashed yet, or otherwise been taken out of the sky. Being able to eliminate some of them – even just a few – would be really helpful right about now.

At least their first plan to take him down had failed, too.

He waited another second, then arced off the thoroughfare and into a narrower side street. The four red dots on the heads-up maintained their path following him, while three more dots to starboard took on intercept trajectories.

The airblade burst between the buildings to soar out over the swath of open land that had served as Durnow's animal preserve. It gave Daemyn a chance to glance past the heads-up at the sights beyond the viewport.

Thick black smoke choked much of the air over Durnow. Initially Daemyn and Brutus had been confused why the drones weren't shooting at them more – until they'd realized the drones had been shooting at other things instead. Fuel depots, electrical stations, anything that would burn had been set ablaze. The drones' motors and rotors were unimpeded, but the AI had clearly expected the smoke and soot to clog the airblades' engines and bring the threat out of the sky.

If they'd been flying with normal airblade engines, the AI's plan would have worked.

But they weren't, and the two blades repeatedly had zoomed through the noxious plumes without so much as a hiccup in their flight paths. Now that the AI had figured it out, the drones were becoming more aggressive.

He couldn't afford to stay without cover for long, so he cut across the preserve and zipped into another narrow side street. He banked to port first, then to starboard after a few more city blocks had passed by him. His pursuers hadn't relented, mimicking his every move in trying to keep up. The remaining drones, though, had other plans. The three that had been cutting to intercept him at the preserve had given up that course and now headed toward Brutus instead. Two others came toward him, then turned away.

Like any computer, the Durnow AI had mastered logic and strategy. The problem was, Daemyn wasn't flying with any logic or strategy. His flight path was too random, too unpredictable. As hard at it might try, the AI couldn't make sense of it.

He needed to keep it that way for a few more minutes. Long enough to get close to the receiver antenna and take the shot without the AI catching on.

Daemyn swung the blade to the east – away from the city center. Hopefully adding a new wrinkle to the AI's analysis of humans.

…WyndeStalker *groundside*

Listening to Carter Platinost's summary of the latest developments at the Steamer Point base, Utara had to admit things were going better there than she'd expected. Already three transports had departed the base with refugees bound for resettlement. Though many more flights would be required, even her most optimistic predictions hadn't foreseen them beginning so soon. More encouraging, increasing numbers of the refugees were becoming open to the idea of permanent relocation. Not that they were ungrateful for the Aladarian Guard's hospitality, Platinost had assured her, but the longer they were away from the tragedy at Durnow, the easier it was to imagine not going back to Loorriri to live. Platinost was convinced the PDS would have plenty of people ready to fill the seats by the time the resettlement flights would begin in earnest.

"I'm grateful for the updates," she told him. "And I cannot express how much I appreciate your leadership. I'll return as soon as I'm able."

"Don't worry about it. That's what I'm here for, remember. Besides, trust me – there's plenty left for you to do when you're back."

"I'm sure there is."

"Did you have any – Oh, hello." Over the satellite relay feed to the long-range comdee, Utara could only hear a garbled, static-filled exchange of words.

Then Platinost's voice returned, audible once more. *"Your father's arrived. I'll pass you along to him, unless you have any questions for me before I go?"*

"No, I don't," Utara said. It was the truth, but she would have given Platinost the same answer no matter what. "Thank you again."

"You're welcome," he said. *"Until next time."*

A moment later her father's voice sounded crisp and clear in her earbud. *"Utara?"*

"Hi, Dad."

"How are you?"

"I'm safe," she assured him. If she said anything more specific than that, she might not be able to keep herself together. "It's great to hear your voice."

"Yours, too."

She'd managed to say a quick farewell to her parents before she'd departed Steamer Point, but had only been able to tell them that she was headed to Zanita. It wasn't until they were in flight across the ocean that Reiton Holtspring had told her the reasons for their emergency return trip. Her father had no clue how dire the situation was, and it wouldn't do any good to tell him – even if it wouldn't be breaching all kinds of classified-information laws to do so.

"How are you and Mom holding up?"

He laughed. *"Your mother, naturally, insists on making herself useful in all manner of ways. At this point she is helping some of the women prepare food in the morning, organizing a series of slapball games for the teenagers in the afternoon, and reading stories to the younger children at night."*

"I never doubted that she'd find a way to keep busy. I imagine you're getting roped into helping with much of that, as well."

"You know how it is. Not that I mind in the least, of course. Here and there, I've stepped in to help mediate with a few of the more, shall we say, surly of the elders. They were far more open to talking things out with a familiar face."

"I doubt you've lost any of your edge as a mediator, either."

"I've tried to stay out of the way. The time will come when it's appropriate for me to make my voice heard in New Romas about everything that's occurred, but right now the well-being of these refugees is paramount. My involvement would only be a distraction. Fortunately, this team the PDS dispatched here has done very well. Once

the immediate crisis situation is resolved, I'll send favorable commendations for their personnel files."

Utara smiled. Her father didn't take steps like that lightly. Not in the slightest. "It sounds like they have it well in hand, Dad. Have you thought about taking one of the flights out?"

"To go where?" he asked, his voice full of mirth, not anger or despair. *"Not New Romas, I can tell you that much. There's a lengthy list of people there who, right now, I'd very much like to punch right in the face."*

"In that case," Utara said, not even trying to contain her laughter, "I agree it's for the best to avoid the capital for a while."

"Your mother thinks so, too." He coughed. *"We've talked a bit about where we might go next, but it's too early to say. Durnow was our home for so long…"*

"It's hard to imagine being anywhere else."

"Yes."

"I understand." She took a deep breath to keep her emotions in check. "I always thought I would end up back in Loorriri, once I reached the point where my life was going to settle down. Whether it was a long-term PDS post, or another agency in the Cultural Ministry or one of the others, or something else – I always pictured it would be Durnow, or one of the other Future Cities, or maybe somewhere further out, like Agoelo. Now, though, I'm not sure the Zanita I've dreamed about will ever exist anymore."

"I hope it does," her father said.

"Me too." Utara took a slow breath. "It was great to talk to you, Dad. Take care of Mom, okay?"

"I will," he said. *"Stay safe, Utara."*

"I promise. I love you."

"We love you, too."

Utara tapped the comm device's screen, ending the transmission. She leaned back in the cockpit seat and smiled. Talking to her father always brightened her mood, even on the worst of days. Fortunately, today was no exception.

The trilling of the comdee jolted her. When she saw the incoming code, she answered right away. "Utara Fireheart."

"It's Allyton Granitine. We have a breaking story that's about to go live on the planetwide feed. I realize we're not set up to have video, but are you available to hold the line for a real-time audio interview?"

Utara sat up straight in the seat. "Yes, I am. Absolutely."

〜◯

...airblade WI-DW-01B

The airblade tipped on its wings, almost exactly perpendicular to the street below. Daemyn held the position long enough to cut diagonally across the city park and slide between a pair of residential rowhouses and onto another side street. He leveled out, preparing for his next turn ahead.

"Oh shig!" Brutus shouted over the comm.

They'd flown nearly in comm silence since reaching Durnow. Between the fact that Brutus had spoken at all and the content of what he'd said, Daemyn knew the dots on the heads-up wouldn't be good.

"Hang on," Daemyn told him, keeping his voice calm. He abandoned his intended turn and swung back around to the west. He couldn't risk rising above the rooftops – that would give a pair of drones a clean shot at him – but one of the thoroughfares would get him most of the way there. "Come toward me, best you can."

"Copy."

One eye on the air lane between the buildings and another on the heads-up, Daemyn tried to figure out what to do. Somehow the AI had managed to stitch together a net of drones around the other pilot. Only two drones actively chased Brutus, but six others held positions that would head him off no matter which path on the map he flew. The city grid had become a maze, and now Brutus was trapped in it.

The other green triangle turned eastward. The two pursuing red dots followed, but the other six simply waited. Even the pair most directly between the airblades didn't move toward Brutus, instead holding position. The AI was confident now. Daemyn didn't like the idea of that one bit.

"Forget about the ones behind you," Daemyn told Brutus. "I'll deal with them. You get past the two ahead. That's all. Got it?"

"Copy."

It was a counterintuitive strategy for many novice pilots, but Brutus had enough experience to understand the value of the tactic. Now they had to make it work.

Ten seconds later Daemyn arrived at the AI's drone trap. At the far end of the thoroughfare he could see Brutus heading toward him. The two drones chasing him were too small to see at this distance, or maybe they were obscured by the smoke. But he saw their red dots on the heads-up just fine. Meanwhile the two drones forming the eastern edge of the net finally adopted intercept vectors.

Daemyn readied a pair of flares. The drones didn't have eyes, so the blindingly bright flashes of iridescent light wouldn't bother them nearly as much as it would a human pilot. At close range, though, the machines had to rely on laser-sighted targeting more than sensors for precision aim, and the flares would create enough interference to buy Brutus the seconds he needed to get clear.

"Get ready," Daemyn said.

"Copy."

Brutus raced toward him. Daemyn aimed the pair of flares and fired. The intercepting drones closed in, one from the north and the other from the south. The flares ignited when they were aft of Brutus, erupting in brilliant sprays of color that illuminated the buildings and the street. The southerly drone arced toward Daemyn. He gripped the yoke, ready to yank the blade into evasive maneuvers.

The drone from the north swung toward Brutus. It came into sight out the viewport going top speed.

Too late, Daemyn's brain made the connection to the evacuation flights. The drones weren't Airspar pilots – they had no individual survival instinct. To the AI, one drone was a small sacrifice to pay to wipe out half of the human threat in one strike.

"Collision!" he shouted. "Evade!"

Brutus' reply was a wordless shout of fury and strength. The other airblade heaved into a starboard turn, wings banking.

The drone never slowed down. But instead of plowing into the airblade head-on, as it had planned, it only clipped the end of the blade's wing and sheared off most of one of the vertical stabilizers. The drone's own wing severed with the force of the collision, sending the machine spiraling out of control.

The detonation from drone's impact with the nearest building filled the street with a raging sphere of smoke and fire. Daemyn's blade sailed through the flaming cloud, airborne debris banging off his wings. The two drones that had been chasing Brutus zipped below him, aim still too scrambled by the flares to make a move at Daemyn. The oncoming drone passed by to aft.

"I'm flyable," Brutus said, grunting hard.

The green dot showed the other pilot maintaining altitude, but there was no way his maneuverability was anything close to what they needed it to be.

"Not enough," Daemyn insisted. "Get out of here."

"I can —"

"No!" He looked at the map and its red dots, confirming Brutus had a chance if he made a straight run away from the city. "One-ten degrees, top speed."

"You're sure?"

"Dump all the countermeasures you need to keep them off your tail until you're clear of the city," Daemyn told him. "Do it now!"

"Copy," Brutus said.

The other airblade turned to the heading, rose above the rooftops, and rocketed away with engines pushed to maximum.

It was up to Daemyn now.

He swung the airblade into a side street. Then another, and another. Keeping out of the thoroughfares, he toggled the comm to Oggust. "Mission status."

"Code delivered in six cities. Several more imminent."

"How many pilots down?"

"Nine, now. We're still in the air at all of the undelivered cities, though."

"So there's a chance."

"Getting slimmer, but yes."

"Copy that." He clenched the yoke. "Thanks. I'll get this done."

"Try not to die," the other man said.

"Right," Daemyn said, and braced himself for the sharp turn toward the city center and Durnow's receiver antenna.

...PIS Headquarters

"The Prime Minister will be on the comm in three minutes," Chief Firebird declared. She stood up straight from where she had been leaned over her aide's shoulder in preparation for the video comm on Athena's compu-pod screen. "Where are we?"

"Code transmitted in seven cities," Monson told her.

"No definitive indication it's working," Hybollo added. "But that's expected at this point. More importantly, no indicators of failure have arisen, either. We'll keep monitoring closely, of course."

Firebird nodded. She asked Monson, "Full delivery is still possible in the other five?"

"Yes. At least one airblade still flying at each one."

"No guarantee they'll have the code transmitted in the next ten minutes, though."

"They will," Monson insisted.

Firebird shot him a look. "You don't know that."

Monson strode around the console to stand right in front of the Intelligence Chief. "It might not be the Prime Minister's timetable, but we're still within the parameters we need for this mission to succeed."

"That's not the point."

"Where did his timetable even come from? Certainly not from the data we provided when we briefed the op."

"I don't know," Firebird conceded. "But it doesn't matter. It's the PM's call."

"Our plan will work. We need to let the pilots fly."

"I'll do my best when I speak to him. Maybe he'll give us more time."

He wouldn't. Monson knew it. He looked Firebird right in the eyes. "You can't let the PM annihilate a continent based on a deadline he pulled out of his behind."

The Intelligence Chief blinked. Barely audible, she whispered, "It's not right."

"They'll get it done," Monson insisted, his gaze remaining locked to hers. The pilots would succeed. They had to. "The airblades just need a little longer."

Athena's compupod chimed. Still looking at Monson, the Intelligence Chief swallowed hard. Then she leaned down toward the pod.

"Put him on," she told Athena.

The aide nodded. From where he stood, Monson couldn't see the screen. But the audio was plenty clear.

"Chief Firebird," Prime Minister Tamorchin said. *"What's the status?"*

"We're on schedule, sir," she told him. "The plan is working."

"It's over?"

"It will be, sir. The AIs aren't offline yet, as would be expected at this point in the mission's execution. But it won't be long now until the shutdowns are completed."

"I'm taking a big risk telling the bombers to hold back," the politician said, anxiety obvious in his words. *"You're certain about this?"*

"I am, sir."

"Very well. I'll hold the bombers. Fifteen more minutes." He paused. *"You'd better be right about this, Chief."*

The compupod warbled a tone indicating the transmission had ended. Firebird rose from her leaned-over posture.

Hybollo gaped at her. "I can't believe you did that."

Firebird blinked. "I... can't either."

"You did the right thing." Monson momentarily touched her arm, a reassuring gesture.

The Chief offered a small smile of gratitude. Her balance wavered before she righted herself on the back of Athena's chair. "I hope so."

When Firebird turned away to ask a question to Hybollo, Monson smiled.

THIRTY-FOUR

…airblade WI-DW-01B

He didn't have much time left.

Most of all, the longer it took to deliver the code into the receiver antenna, the more likely it would be that the AI would figure out the humans' plan and find a way to block it. Particularly now that other Future City AIs had the code in place, and their shutdowns could occur at any moment. If the Durnow AI realized its counterparts were offline, it wouldn't take any chances – and Daemyn didn't want to consider how viciously it might retaliate, considering what it had already done.

His opposition in the air was only growing tougher, too. Now that the AI no longer faced Brutus in its tactical considerations, it could focus the drones solely on eliminating Daemyn. He could keep his flying illogical and unpredictable, but the AI's advantage was catching up to him. Outnumbered like this, he wouldn't be able to evade their machineguns much longer.

Not to mention, he didn't have unlimited fuel. He might not have a countdown timer running on his heads-up anymore, but Daemyn didn't need one. He didn't have a choice. He had to execute the mission and get out.

The drones had tried to herd him into the southwestern neighborhoods of the city, where the street grid provided a good location for pinning him into a net like the one they'd used on Brutus. He needed to bust open that possibility before it got any closer to success, then head toward the city center as quickly as he could make it there.

He checked the location of the red dots on the heads-up map. He couldn't afford to try anything too risky, but something bold might be just unpredictable enough to the AI at this point that he could get away with it.

Daemyn swung the airblade around the corner of a building and zoomed along the street a few meters below the rooftops. He needed to close the distance to the city center fast, and to do that required a shortcut. On the street map, there wasn't one. But airblades flew in three dimensions, not two.

He pushed the engines to more acceleration and curved his path up and over the buildings. A few meters higher in altitude made the difference between being right below the rooftops and barely above them. On the heads-up map he sliced across streets like they weren't there – because for him, right now, they didn't matter.

He dodged to port, zipping around an antenna, then tipped to starboard to arc around a water tank. Most of the rooftops were barren, though. He only needed to make it a little farther…

The drones finally reacted. Like buzzing insects leaping into view from some unseen spot among wildflowers, four of the machines popped above the multicolored rooftops of the rowhouses. The more distant ones raced toward him. The closer ones opened fire.

Daemyn was just far enough out of their range that the bullets didn't hit him. He couldn't wait, though. He pushed the yoke and dipped back below the rooftops into the empty street between the rowhouses.

He spared a glance to the heads-up map again. He'd made it closer than he'd hoped. He still had a ways to go, but not far.

Daemyn considered comming Oggust for an update, then thought the better of it. Only one thing mattered now. He had to take his shot.

$$\sim\!\!\circlearrowleft$$

…WyndeStalker *groundside*

"The refugees gathered at this town where you are now," Granitine asked, *"do you think they will ultimately want to participate in resettlement, too, as many of the Steamer Point refugees have now begun to do?"*

Utara still hadn't become accustomed to the audio interview via comdee. The process was much easier when she could see the other woman's face and gauge her body language. Even tone of voice wasn't particularly clear over the satellite relay. But she did the best she could.

"It's difficult to say, really," she replied, reminding herself to speak a little slower than usual to account for the sound quality. "Some of them are already realizing that life here will be a lot more difficult on a daily basis than anything they've experienced before. For those people, the prospect of resuming an urban residence may become very tempting, particularly with the assurance of far more stability than Durnow had offered recently."

"That's certainly understandable. What about others? What would lead them to choose to stay?"

"A combination of factors, I imagine. Fear, to some extent. That what happened in Durnow could happen again in another city, too. Tradition carries great weight. Although many of the refugees were born in the Future Cities, their ancestors have been in Loorriri for generations. The values, beliefs, even languages of their ancestral clans still carry through in the teachings of the elders. So they simply may not want to leave Loorriri, even if it means a harsher, subsistence existence. And mistrust, as well. If the government could allow the promise of the Future Cities to be broken, as it has been, how can they trust that new pledges won't also be broken?"

"Who could blame them for wondering that, after what they've been through?"

"We will have to work to reassure them. It is possible. As you mentioned, many of the refugees at Steamer Point, who've seen what the Aladarian Guard has been able to do for them in a short period of time, are already starting to –"

"Hold on," Granitine said abruptly. It was almost ten seconds before she came back. *"Sorry about that. Utara, we're now on a private line."*

"That's fine."

"Apparently Prime Minister Tamorchin will be making an address to Prime sometime very soon. Officially confirmed. The producers are telling me they're going to full preparatory coverage, so I'll have to let you go for now."

"I certainly understand that."

"Do you have a veepee you'll be able to watch? Or an audiocaster? Otherwise I can put you through to our audio feed so you can listen."

"That's very kind of you, but I should have what I need here."

"Great. Thank you again, Utara. You've been amazing."

"I'm glad I could help."

"You have no idea. Let's stay in touch, all right?"

"Of course."

"Many blessings."

"Many blessings."

Utara put the long-range comdee in standby mode and stood up. Only when her legs expressed their riotous grievance against the action did she realize how stiff she'd become sitting in the cockpit seat for so long. She set down the device and stretched, forcing the ache from her muscles. On the third attempt, the coiled agony finally released.

Then she snatched up the comms device once more and headed out of the cockpit. Hopefully she had enough time to figure out how to get one of *WyndeStalker*'s veepees working before the Prime Minister's address started.

$$\sim\!\!\circ$$

...airblade WI-DW-01B

The option of a circuitous route toward the city center no longer fit the timetable. Daemyn weaved through the streets, following the map on the heads-up to make the most progress north and east along the shortest path he could manage. Only a couple of kilometers to go.

To aft, four drones chased him. They fired their machineguns when they could, but he had maintained a slim margin ahead of them in speed. Amid the turns through the streets, they only had split-seconds of a clear line of fire before he zoomed away into the next street. The drones coming toward him on intercept vectors were much more of a problem. He'd used bursts of unpredictable acceleration and deceleration to mess up the AI's timing just enough that the intersecting drones hadn't been able to take a clear shot either, much less ram into him. As more drones reached his proximity, though, the numbers would catch up to him.

On the heads-up map, his target flashed big and bright. Almost there...

He couldn't take any chances. With only one airblade broadcasting the code instead of two, distance was too much of a risk. He needed to be right on top of it to be absolutely sure the receiver antenna would gobble up the signal.

One street took him northward. He banked around a corner. Eastward for five seconds. Behind him, gunfire blazed. He spun the blade through a full rotation, refusing to give the drones a stable target. Coming out of the rotation he braced for the sharp turn to port, once again northward. Three seconds… Four… He turned back east. Then north.

The console beeped the proximity alert. Not for a threat, but for the target.

His airblade climbed above the rooftops and raced straight for the government complex. Several stories taller than the surrounding buildings in the city center, the four glimmering white stone towers loomed before him. On their roofs sat the antenna, its enormous receiver dish pointed skyward.

Daemyn slammed the buttons on the console. The heads-up flashed, confirming the signals were being transmitted.

He cut the blade's speed in half. The more time he gave the transmitters, the better chance the code would make it through.

And the faster the drones would catch up to him.

It didn't matter.

Almost parallel to the vertical face of the government buildings, the airblade rose toward the antenna. The moment he reached its altitude, he pulled into a looping arc over the tops of all four buildings. Practically in a heartbeat he was already past them.

He wrenched the yoke with all his strength, compelling the blade into the tightest barrel-roll he could extract from it. His breath left his lungs and his arms trembled from the effort. Still he overpowered the airblade, bending it to his will.

He leveled out and flew over the antenna once more, back the way he'd come. Almost the same instant he passed the last building's edge, the heads-up flashed green three times and the console emitted the confirmation tone.

The code was delivered. He'd done it.

Now he had to deal with the nine drones heading right for him.

...PIS Headquarters

"It's in!" Hybollo practically leaped in the air before composing himself enough to simply gesture frantically at the wall screen. "The code's in Durnow."

The last of the twelve. The pilots at Blonkas and Luppitan had kept them waiting, too, but Daemyn Wynde's own flight had taken the longest. It would have been no small irony if the entire mission had collapsed because the indisputably best pilot in the bunch had failed. But Monson understood why Wynde had insisted on flying Durnow himself, even with those stakes. From the beginning, the Airspar jockey had told them that Durnow was the most difficult flight to make. So if he had nearly failed, then none of the other pilots would even have had a chance. Wynde, somehow, had pulled it off.

"How many down?" Monson called out to the analyst tracking the status of the AIs.

"Five," she replied. A second later the Aquarian woman added, "No, six!"

"Get Admiral Ponofarre on the comm," Chief Firebird told her aide.

"One moment," Athena replied quietly.

Monson checked the map of Loorriri on the central screen. The six Future Cities where the AIs had shut down were marked with large green circles. The others had large yellow circles, denoting that the code had been delivered but its successful functioning was still pending. It was a great relief to no longer see any red triangles on the map.

"Seven," the Aquarian analyst announced. Hybollo strode over to join her in watching the tally change as more of the AIs processed the code virus into their systems.

The secure compupod chimed. Without hesitation the Intelligence Chief leaned down to speak to the screen. "Admiral, it's Chief Firebird. I have a mission-critical update for you."

"Copy, Chief. Go ahead."

"I have direct confirmation that the code has been deployed successfully into all of the Future Cities. As we speak, most of the AIs are already incapacitated."

For a few seconds, Monson heard no reply. He wondered if the admiral was speaking too quietly for him to hear. Then Ponofarre said, *"That's a relief to hear, Chief."*

"Chief," Hybollo said, raising his voice slightly to ensure she heard him, "we're at eight."

Firebird remained leaning down, but she shifted her face to look at the map. "Here's the real-time status. Gastoa, Blonkas, Luppitan, and Durnow. Those are the only ones still in process."

"Repeat for confirmation: Gastoa, Blonkas, Luppitan, Durnow."

"Copy, Admiral. That's correct."

"You're confident those AIs will shut down, as well?"

"We're eight for eight so far. That's as confident as we can be."

"Understood, Chief. Give me a moment." A few seconds later the Unified Forces leader's voice returned. *"I've recalled the bombers for the eight. Confirmation codes acknowledged and received."*

"And the last four?"

"Officially, their ready-to-strike orders remain active. But we sent the callback code telling them to end the holding pattern and fly toward base."

"Copy, Admiral."

"Should I comm the PM, or will you?"

"I'll do it. Celebrate with your team, Admiral. We didn't need to use them."

"Copy, Chief. Thank you."

The warbling tone signaled the end of the comm. Firebird braced her hands on the workstation and let out a deep sigh.

"Gastoa is offline," Hybollo said, pumping a fist in the air.

For the first time since the airblades had launched, Monson allowed himself to step away from the primary station and walk to a nearby workstation. Eyes fixed to the map of Loorriri, he lowered into the chair.

Finally, he could sit down.

~

...airblade WI-DW-01B

Three of the drones came in high, machineguns blazing. The vicious trails of bullets cut off the quickest escape route from Durnow – straight up – at least for now.

The other six were spread in a semi-circle around him, and closing fast. They hadn't opened fire yet, but they were a little farther away than the high ones. It wouldn't be long.

Daemyn plunged his airblade in a steep dive toward the street. Seconds later he yanked the yoke again, pulling the blade to level barely a meter above the crete. He added a bit more altitude to be safe – the last thing he needed was his escape ended by something stupid like smashing into inert debris that had fallen to the ground – and returned to his earlier tactic of weaving through the streets.

This time, though, more drones were coming after him. The map on the heads-up looked like a bored child's piece of art: a single green triangle surrounded by red dots seemingly scattered randomly around it. Except the pattern wasn't random. Not to the AI, anyway. But Daemyn hadn't figured it out yet, and he doubted he had the seconds to spare to try. He ignored most of the dots and focused on the ones that appeared to be making imminent intercept vectors.

One drone hovered in place at a spot ahead at the next major thoroughfare, waiting for Daemyn to emerge from the side streets and gun him down. Another cut toward him diagonally over the rooftops. The third was coming up fast four streets over, playing the odds Daemyn would have to cross that way on his path toward the city wall.

Daemyn turned at the second street, buying enough seconds to make the speeding drone overshoot his location and keeping his airblade away from the thoroughfare a few minutes longer, too. But the rooftop flier was almost there, and no route in the streets could deal with that threat.

He toggled a button on the yoke, readying a boomer. More countermeasures remained than he'd originally expected, and he had to double-check the tallies on the heads-up to make sure he was reading them correctly. It made sense, though. His initial run toward the antenna had depended a lot more on skillful flying in the streets and not much on the countermeasures. Maybe he could turn the tide by flipping his tactics for his exit flight.

Sometimes the most effective way to win wasn't to rely on pure talent, but to exploit the assets you had to work with better than the other team could do with theirs. The drones had machineguns – which, admittedly, was a pretty good asset. But the guns, and the option of a direct collision like they'd tried on Brutus, were also the *only* assets they had. Daemyn's airblade had a lot more options at his disposal – and he didn't get any benefit for leaving them unused.

He toggled the yoke buttons repeatedly, getting all the countermeasures primed and ready to fire. The drone above the rooftops was two seconds away.

He aimed a boomer and fired. The drone cleared the rooftop. The boomer detonated directly beneath it. The concussion wave knocked the drone into an uncontrolled spin. By the time it smashed into a building and exploded, Daemyn was already blocks away down the street.

He checked the heads-up and saw three more headed his way.

"All right, you shiggers," Daemyn growled, "let's play."

...WyndeStalker *groundside*

With seemingly innumerable compupods and other electronic equipment crammed into the galley to serve as Kirkland Oggust's control center for the airblade operation, and the large visionpod in the room repurposed as a live video feed from Daemyn's cockpit, it simply wasn't possible for them to watch the Prime Minister's speech in what otherwise would have been the most suitable location on the *WyndeStalker*. Instead, Reiton Holtspring, Elsa Ovella, and Utara stood in Daemyn's bedroom, gathered close to the wall opposite the bed to get a better look at the small veepee mounted near the ceiling. While the trio of newscasters blathered about what their viewers might expect to hear in the upcoming address, Utara kept fighting the compulsion to glance toward the bed. So far her mental fortitude was winning – but not by much.

Her inner battle ended when Holtspring muttered "finally!" and used the remote fob to increase the veepee's audio volume. The Prime Minister's seal had overtaken the screen. It held for only a few seconds before the image of Tamorchin, seated at the glimmering wooden desk in the Prime Minister's ornately appointed formal office in the official residence in New Romas, took its place.

"People of Prime," the graying Aquarian began. "On this day, sadly, I must carry out one of the solemn duties of this office: to deliver word of a great tragedy on our planet. Nearly a half century ago, New Romas launched one of the boldest initiatives in our history. In the subsequent years the Future Cities were designed, constructed, and inhabited by the proud citizens who have called Loorriri home. Faytans and Aquarians, Terrans and Aladarians, so many individuals with roots in so many of our cultures shared in the better lives the Future Cities promised."

Tamorchin glanced at the single sheet of transi between his hands on the desk, then looked back into the camera. "Although even I do not yet have many of the details, the core truth of the matter is clear. The Future Cities have failed. All twelve, each and every one of them. Some of their residents have fled to the savannahs, the river deltas, the jungle, even the desert. Many thousands more, tragically, have perished. The full extent of this disaster will only become clear in the weeks and months ahead, but I believe that even today we must begin to accept the reality that the Future Cities will never again be home for Primeans."

Reiton whistled low. "Here comes the other fist."

"For weeks," the Prime Minister continued, "I personally have been deceived about the full extent of the burgeoning crisis in the Future Cities. An hour ago I demanded and received the resignation of Cultural Minister Cirrus, Deputy Minister Solaris of the Prime Diplomatic Service, and fifteen other officials whose supervisory authority over the Future Cities has allowed this horrific catastrophe to occur."

"Typical," Elsa grumbled. "Accountability for everyone in New Romas – except the PM himself."

"I cannot say what the future will bring to Loorriri," Tamorchin said. "Today, however, I pledge this much to the people of Prime: the survivors of the Future Cities, whether within the city walls or beyond, will be rescued without delay. Minutes ago, I signed an executive order authorizing the Unified Forces to deploy any and all resources necessary for a full, complete, and immediate evacuation of all survivors and refugees."

The Prime Minister made a few additional remarks reinforcing his commitment to a swift and thorough investigation of the disaster, but Utara was only half listening. Rescue was coming. After all this, help was finally on the way.

But it was too little, too late. So many – too many – were already dead.

Holtspring touched her shoulder. When she met his gaze he said simply, "I'm so sorry."

~⌒

...airblade WI-DW-01B

He'd depleted his allotment of countermeasures pretty quickly, which was bad, but Daemyn wasn't exactly going to complain about the results, either. He'd used three of his flares to aim-blind drones at opportune moments. Two more boomers had knocked two additional drones out of the sky. He had one boomer and one flare left, and at least six more red dots on the heads-up.

He still had to get the last kilometer to the city wall. Escape was close, but he wasn't there yet.

He surveyed the map on the heads-up. The drones in the streets were moving to pin him in a net again. This time, they might succeed. Over the rooftops, a pair of drones zipped toward him, one from the east and the other from the northwest. Another above the city flew farther out, looping back around to make a new run to try to catch the pesky unpredictable human.

That was his opening. He had to take it. The trick was getting the timing exactly right.

He turned down a street, waited for three blocks to race past, and then turned to starboard. He watched the drones adapt to his path, then pulled the yoke and climbed.

When he popped above the buildings into the sky, the easterly drone adjusted to a head-on intercept path. Daemyn didn't flinch. He held his course, too, fingers poised over the trigger. He waited one second, then another.

He fired the flare. Unlike his previous shots, this one didn't wait until it was near the drone to ignite. Instead it burst to life almost immediately, zipping toward the drone on a sparkling trail of light.

When bullets didn't rip his blade apart, Daemyn figured the blinding trick had worked. He pulled the blade into an arc, looping around to head toward the oncoming drone from the northwest. The AI would be expecting him to engage this one, too, especially now that he was heading away from the city wall. But that wasn't his plan. Those knarfing unpredictable humans.

He lined up the targeting reticle on the approaching drone and tapped the button to time the detonation two seconds shy of collision. Then he fired, letting the boomer sail toward the drone. He held his intersecting course for the moment, though, letting the drone and the AI think he had another attack coming.

When the boomer detonated, the drone had to swerve into a high climb to avoid the concussion wave and the debris. Exactly the distraction he needed.

Daemyn wrenched the blade around in a direct line for the city wall. Other drones flew toward him, but they were far enough away that their bullets wouldn't be able to reach him for a few more seconds – and only if he maintained this speed. Which he didn't.

He slammed the engines to maximum. They whined against the sudden acceleration, but complied. Flung back in his seat so hard he couldn't breathe, Daemyn held onto the yoke with all his strength. The rooftops sped below him in an indistinguishable blob of colors. Durnow's city wall raced toward the blade, then zoomed beneath him. The savannah beyond the walls was nothing but a light-green hazy blur.

Then the engines kicked into their highest gear and the airblade ripped over the grassland at nearly supersonic speed, leaving the once-grand Future City far behind.

BOUND

"Tamorchin can say whatever he wants. His days as Prime Minister are numbered and he knows it. A motion for a vote of no-confidence is inevitable at this point. His only choice is resignation."

Senator Brady Marias, live interview on CenterPrime News Network

THIRTY-FIVE

...Prime Intelligence Service Headquarters, outskirts of New Romas

Monson spun his chair away from the pair of display screens set up on the right side of his desk. If only for a moment, he needed to take a break. Idly his eyes found the small chrono on the left corner of his desk.

A month ago today, exactly, the artificial intelligences that had spawned the Future Cities crisis had been deactivated. Much work remained to be done, of course, and Boynton Logistics Dynamics still had much to answer for. Even with the immediate emergency resolved, the PIS had been granted primary authority over the investigation and aftermath to follow.

That day also had been his last as an employee of Grandell Motors' corporate intelligence division. Due to his indispensable role in addressing the AI crisis, the Intelligence Chief had granted Monson an immediate appointment as a permanent Agent in the PIS, with a desk at Headquarters. Although the Prime Minister had yet to say a single word publicly about the PIS or its Chief, unlike the steep and very public consequences within the Cultural Ministry and Diplomatic Service, the gossip in the hallways made clear that Firebird's days in her position were numbered. Not only had the PIS failed to anticipate and identify the threat before it had erupted, but it hadn't even been a PIS employee who had made the biggest difference in saving the day. Those facts were known within the PIS and by Tamorchin and his staff, and very few others. But no Prime Minister, no matter his or her political acumen or incompetence, could tolerate such failure.

For his part, Monson would not accept another such tragedy for Prime, either. Now that he had achieved his goal, he was in position to keep that pledge to himself. With the resources and access of the PIS at his fingertips, he would be able to do everything he could to keep the planet safe. It was his responsibility.

Someone rapped a knuckle on the glass pane of his office door. Monson looked up. Without hesitation he waved a hand to motion the other man to come inside.

Birto Hybollo shut the door behind him before he paced over and lowered himself into one of the chairs across the desk. Like Monson, his leadership in the Boynton crisis had earned him a substantial promotion. "Are you still getting pushback from Wynde on the vids?"

"Not in the past week."

Within hours of the completion of the airblade flights to the Future Cities, the PIS had confiscated all of the hardware and data used in the operation, including all of the pilot audio and everything recorded from the cockpit vidcams. The surviving pilots had been compelled to execute additional confidentiality decrees which precluded them from ever speaking to anyone about anything they had seen, heard, observed, or otherwise been told about the events on Loorriri before, during, or after their mission. So had all of the employees of Wynde Industries who had worked with Daemyn on the preparations, or who had accompanied him to Loorriri – among them the inveterate criminal hacker Kirkland Oggust, who somehow had managed both to delete the files he had sold to Monson and post the amount of dracts he had been paid into Monson's personal bank account without leaving so much as a ghost of an electronic footprint.

"I'm surprised," Hybollo said. "As hard as he fought on it."

"Oh, it was all negotiating ploys from the start. He never wanted the full recordings from the entire operation, and he knew there was no way we'd release them. All that technical gibberish about engine and airblade performance was a cover. His only chance was the very preliminary segment, the part that could be any generic airblade flight over Loorriri. It's a lot prettier to look at than whatever backdrop he'll get in Hyj-gon."

"You think he wanted it for advertisements?"

"Not a doubt in my mind."

Hybollo shook his head. "Amazing."

A thought occurred to Monson. "Any problematic questions being asked on your end lately?"

"Not recently, no."

While Monson had dealt with Wynde Industries, Hybollo had taken the lead in crafting the cover story for the deaths of the nine young Airspar interns. A crash of a shuttlecraft in a Hyj-gon mountain ravine during an ill-advised flight in bad weather wasn't the best cover-up PIS had ever mustered, but it had bought them the time to recover the bodies, made a decent fit with the autopsy reports, and explained why no images of the crash site had been available. With the political aftermath of the Future Cities catastrophe dominating all of the reporting on the veepee and in the trashmags, only one or two reporters had asked any questions about a situation that, for all outward appearances, presented every element of a routine tragedy of young lives lost too soon. If things changed down the line, the PIS would find a way to quash any media investigation looking too closely at the facts, whether through bribery, intimidation, or otherwise. All the better, though, if it simply went away.

"Good," Monson said.

"Agreed." Hybollo started to hold out the single transi he'd brought with him, then kept it back. "Anyway, I came to see you about something else. You remember those rumors about a major infusion of capital into Grandell Motors?"

Monson nodded.

"It seemed weird to me, so I followed up. For once, the corporate gossip was actually pretty close to the truth."

"Oh, really?"

"The deal went through back-channel. A combination of corporate bonds, purchases of land and other assets, and acquisition of debt from existing corporate creditors. It won't show up on the official reports any time soon, but the controlling ownership interest in Grandell Motors now resides in new hands."

Monson had a sneaking suspicion he knew exactly what was on the transi. "Let's see it."

Hybollo passed him the transi, then kept talking while Monson scanned the page. "Your favorite Faytan and his venturist pals, indeed. But yes, his share is the largest among their portfolio of investors." Hybollo chuckled. "It seems you got out of corporate intelligence there just in time, my friend."

"No kidding." He met the other man's gaze. "Thank you. This made my day."

"I thought it might." Grinning, Hybollo shoved off the armrests, stood up, and walked to the door. "Back to work."

"Yes. I'll see you later."

When Hybollo shut the door and disappeared down the corridor, Monson read the transi in his hands one more time. Then he tore it in half, spun around his chair to look out the window toward New Romas, and laughed harder than he had in many years.

~⌒

...CenterPrime News Network, New Romas

The interview had been underway for ten minutes, and Utara still wasn't used to it. Compared to standing in the wind at Steamer Point or speaking into a comdee in *WyndeStalker*'s cockpit, the antiseptic sterility of the recording studio was surreal. Almost unreal. With her hair coiffed and the professionally applied makeup on her face, she had an appearance worthy of attending a formal gala. She wore an immaculately clean business suit; so did Allyton Granitine. They sat at a small table with Utara on one side and the reporter on the other. A few meters away, on the other side of the blinding lights shining on them, a dozen assistants worked diligently.

Granitine had begun with questions about the original group of refugees at Steamer Point. How were they doing? How many had been resettled, and where? Utara had answered as best she could. From her body language and eager tone of voice, the reporter seemed pleased. Utara couldn't help thinking it seemed dry and boring.

"You mentioned that a few more locations have offered to resettle refugees over the past week," Granitine said. "Where might those be?"

"The Equatorial Archipelago has a number of currently uninhabited islands which they graciously agreed to make available, and their fellow Aquarians from the Atlantean League stepped forward with supplies and funds to assist. The Rotarian Desert Aladarians have proposed an expansion in their second-largest city, Garrabah, that could house up to ten thousand refugees."

"Incredible," Granitine breathed, genuinely impressed.

"Yes. After a lengthy negotiation with New Romas, including support from the Prime Minister's office, Boynton Logistics Dynamics has agreed to fund a similar expansion of housing in the outlying neighborhoods of Port Vulcania. The final total is yet to be determined, but it could reach near thirty thousand, as well."

Granitine nodded. "That certainly seems appropriate."

"To me, also. And yet the resettlement of the refugees is, I believe, something to mourn."

"Why is that?"

"For too many decades, Loorriri constantly suffered under strife, poverty, and even war. For all its turbulent history, however, its people still developed rich and worthy cultures of their own, unlike any other on Prime. In addition to the remarkable cultural contributions of the nomad clans, Loorriri long has been the home of our truest melding of Prime's principal cultures. Aladarians and Terrans, Faytans and Aquarians, not only side by side but intermingled and conjoined across the decades. When the Future Cities came into existence, the face of Loorriri changed, but its unique cultural imprint did not disappear. Rather, it adapted to new circumstances, changing with the times as it did with each new influx of migrants over the centuries."

"But now, the refugees will never return there."

"Exactly," Utara said. "Although I am sure some of their culture will endure in their new locations even as time passes, the future of their culture has been cut off. While Faytan and Aladarian cultures, for example, continue to evolve, Loorriri's unique contribution to Prime now is forever frozen in time."

Granitine nodded sadly. "The population of Loorriri has diminished greatly, through both death and evacuation. But what you're saying is that an irreplaceable part of our planet's cultural heritage has been devastated, as well."

"That's right. For most significant purposes, I fear that as time passes we will find that Loorriri will have been all but erased from Primean society. A continent lost, perhaps irreversibly."

"Lost continent. Indeed, it is truly tragic," Granitine said. "Returning to the topic of Boynton Logistics Dynamics, if I may, there's another subject

I've wanted to ask you about, as well. We all know how difficult it can be to get legislation enacted, how long it can take even when the policy objectives have support from many constituencies. Our research department tells me it's not actually a record, but nonetheless – I imagine you must be pleased at how quickly the Lower Assembly and Senate acted in passing these new prohibitions on dangerous uses of artificial intelligence technology."

"I am," Utara admitted. "Of course, with my background the computer coding jargon contained within the law is a bit beyond the scope of my comprehension."

Granitine smiled. "Mine, too."

"Fortunately, it's my understanding that the Justice Ministry, the Unified Forces, and other agencies will be consulting with a wide range of experts in the process of drafting the regulations and technical specifications necessary to implement the law effectively." Utara remembered to look toward the vidcam. "No one takes any issue with the kinds of simplistic AIs that can make our daily lives easier. Preparing food just the way we like it, monitoring weather to adjust the temperature inside a building, avoiding collisions on the roadways, helping a family plan a yearly budget. None of that endangers anyone, and this law won't do anything to interfere with them."

"Certain kinds of AIs are dangerous, though."

"Yes. What we cannot allow is AIs to control weapons, or critical infrastructure, or the basics of survival. When our leaders make errors of judgment, the people of Prime can hold them accountable. When an AI makes the decision between life and death, what means do we have to hold an algorithm responsible? We must never permit this kind of tragedy to happen again. Human lives must be in our own hands, not a computer's."

Granitine nodded solemnly. "Well said, Counselor Fireheart."

The interview concluded with a few nondescript pleasantries. Once the live vidfeed ended, an aide rushed over to remove the tiny microphone from the collar of Utara's shirt. Granitine removed her own and handed it to the young man.

"That went great," the reporter told her.

Utara smiled. "If you say so."

"I do. Trust me."

"You have to remember," Utara said, "the first few times I spoke with you, I was literally begging to save the lives of the refugees. And what we did mattered. It had an immediate impact. This… isn't quite the same."

"That's true." Granitine leaned over and put a hand on Utara's arm for a moment. "That did set a pretty high bar. But don't lose sight of what reports like this one today can accomplish. Major incidents, shocking revelations, stunning scandals – they usually burn brightly in the moment, then fade away into the haze of forgotten memories. Sometimes it's the gradual pressure, keeping an issue on the public's mind over a longer span of time, that changes the world."

"I hope you're right. We can't let what happened to the Future Cities be for nothing."

"With your help, it won't be."

"We'll see."

"Don't count yourself out, Utara. You're a natural at this. Why do you think we keep having you back?"

…Wynde Industries, Hyj-gon

Daemyn stood at the window, looking out across the cityscape and then the plains that stretched all the way to the horizon. "Everything's done on the Grandell Motors acquisition?"

"Every last document signed and filed," Reiton said from his seat at the head of the table. "Celia confirmed the transaction is finished."

"How soon until we could get one of their factories to work manufacturing the engines? We still have a lot of ground to make up."

"Based on Filson's preliminary analysis, the facility in Dockington has all of the necessary machinery. It would take a few weeks to repurpose everything, then retrain the technicians what to do for this product. So, a month? Maybe a bit longer."

Daemyn nodded. "That's fine."

From her seat next to Reiton, Elsa whispered, "He took that better than I expected."

"I heard that."

"Celia also sent an update on the land purchases," Reiton said.

Daemyn turned away from the window. "So soon?"

"New Romas is pretty desperate." Reiton flicked his fingers, sending the chart onto the table for Daemyn to see. "They were already pretty deep in the hole. Now they're looking at a budgetary outlay with the potential to be fiscally disastrous on a massive scale. Not the human toll of the Future Cities, but comparable in scope. To bureaucrats and bean-counters? It's like the looming end of the world as they know it."

"Looks like it," Daemyn said.

Even a cursory read of the chart showed him that. Once the airblade mission to the Future Cities had ended, the PIS had cut them off from any further information on what was happening on Loorriri. They could only guess at what the government was facing now. Would the Future Cities be left standing, or razed? Who would collect all the technology, infrastructure components, raw materials, and currency abandoned there? The security drones and their weapons couldn't be left for the claiming, either. The expense of closing down the Future Cities to human habitation might cost as much as building them had in the first place. On top of that, the inevitable attempt to cleanse the rivers and land of the AI's deadly toxin would surpass any previous environmental rehabilitation in Prime's history. Either cost separately was enormous; together, they were inconceivable.

But the fiscal impact of the human tragedy on Loorriri alone might be enough to bankrupt the Treasury. If the nonstop media coverage in the last weeks had done nothing else, it meant the government would have no choice but to rescue every last possible surviving resident of the Future Cities, and resettle them either elsewhere on Loorriri or in a new location thousands of kilometers away. Even Reiton's conservative estimate, based on worst-case low number of survivors and least-expensive resettlement plans, put New Romas on the precipice of losing the legitimacy to govern.

That was why Celia Lancer had told the venturists that now was the perfect time to make the government an offer it couldn't refuse: the promise of infusions of both short-term and long-term funds to stabilize the budget, in exchange for as many of the things the venturists wanted as they could convince the government to part with in order to ensure its own survival. One of the highest-priority items on the venturists' want-list was certain tracts of land around the world, underutilized by the government but holding the prospect of immense future profits.

"In her preliminary meeting, everything stayed on the table as a potential acquisition. Even the sectors in Grand Coulee and Grandell Valley." Reiton met Daemyn's gaze. "You're sure you want to keep part of the Wynde segment in the portfolio dedicated to that wildlife sanctuary on Loorriri? It won't cost you much, but you're losing out on a share in something else by allocating for it."

"Yes, I want it."

"You're crazy," Elsa muttered. "If I ever go back there, it'll be too soon."

Daemyn chuckled. "You'll get over it."

Reiton shrugged. "It's your money. Don't say I didn't question you."

"I won't. And I'm sure."

"Noted." Reiton checked the compupod screen. "Only two more items on the agenda for today. First, which Airspar team will you fly for next season?"

Daemyn laughed out loud. "Oh, just a little insignificant question."

"Sorry. Next time I'll phrase it differently for your delicate sensibilities."

"Well, I think we can agree on one thing. The answer isn't *the Wynde Industries team*. We're still not in a position to make that leap."

"I agree," Reiton said.

"Quick question," Elsa said.

"Yes?"

"Does Fith know you purchased GM? They may... have issues."

"Oh," Daemyn said. "Right."

"We agreed to be silent majority owners for a while," Reiton pointed out. "But we definitely saved Reese Garold's job. Safe to say that offer's still open."

"I have that meeting at Kedu the day after tomorrow," Daemyn said. "Maybe we can check in with Garold before we head back."

"That works," Reiton said. "I'll get us on his calendar."

"And the last item," Daemyn said, "is the engines."

Elsa sat forward in her chair, finally not looking utterly bored. "I talked to Filson and Bakerton right before we started. They've finished inventorying all the wreckage PIS provided from the recovery operations."

Daemyn could only imagine how painstaking that process must have been. They'd been accomplishing other tasks too, especially keeping the manufacturing line running smoothly for the next batch of engines being assembled, but it still had taken them weeks. "Bottom line?"

"Lots of pieces still out in the wild. Some of them, of course, might be destroyed or totally unrecognizable. Others probably not. Overall, their best assessment is that the design probably is secure. Even if a single person somehow got their hands on everything that's missing, it shouldn't be enough to reverse engineer the specs."

"Let's hope so." Daemyn looked to Reiton. "How is the feedback from the demonstration?"

"I have Oggust compiling that. One minute, I'll get him."

While Reiton summoned the other man over the compupod, Daemyn glanced back out the window. It would take some time to gather new vidcam footage as impressive as what they'd recorded in Loorriri, but the PIS hadn't budged. On the other hand, sometimes nothing served quite as effectively as an in-person demonstration. Representatives of a dozen Airspar teams had come to Naper Peak last week to see Brutus' repeat performance of the first test flight. Daemyn thought it had gone well, but nothing was sure until the purchase orders came in.

The conference room door opened and Kirkland Oggust stepped gingerly inside. He carried a handheld pod with him. "Good timing. I was just off the comm with the last team."

"Inquiries?" Daemyn asked. "Or making an order?"

"An order," Oggust said. "Same as the others."

"How many others?"

"Everyone."

Daemyn looked at him. "Every team from the demo? Already?"

"No, not only those," Oggust said. "*All* of them."

Daemyn's legs trembled, and he reached for the edge of the table before anyone noticed. "Well, that's… unexpected. Make sure you tell Filson and

Bakerton right away. We're going to need to increase production significantly. Immediately."

"You got it, boss," Oggust said, then zipped out the door and down the hallway.

Elsa looked at Daemyn. "Boss?"

Daemyn looked at Reiton. "Well," he said, "I guess we're keeping him."

THIRTY-SIX

...*Kedu Academy*

The two men strode side by side into the ornate formal office. If their three hour stroll around the entire campus of the academy had tired the older man, he didn't let it show. He made no move to sit at his desk, but remained standing in the expansive receiving area inside the main doors.

"Kedu certainly has impressive facilities," Daemyn said. "But I have to imagine its president usually has better things to do than lead a guided tour personally."

Windwalker smiled. "Ordinarily."

"You do realize it'll be years before I have a child old enough to attend?"

"I'm a patient man, Daemyn, and I'm confident we'll be more than eager to pursue your offspring when that time arrives. Today, though, it's you I'm recruiting."

After the first hour, Daemyn had started to suspect as much. With as eager as the president had been to show him around, and as entertaining and insightful as their conversation had been, he'd never found the right moment to ask. "I'm flattered. But I'll be honest. I'm not sure what, exactly, you're recruiting me *for*."

"Not a donation," Windwalker said, almost dismissively. "I imagine venturists must receive pitches, if not pleas, on a regular basis. If that had been my plan, I would have had the courtesy to tell you from the start."

"Most people do."

Windwalker chuckled. "I suppose so. No, my offer is something much bolder. And, truth be told, part of a much larger plan for Kedu's future."

Daemyn decided to meet candor with candor. "You've got my attention."

"I thought I might." For a moment he paused. "I'll get to your offer, specifically, in a moment. First, indulge me on something else, though intimately related. No doubt the lawyers on retainer for Wynde Industries have fully briefed you on all the parameters of the newly enacted bans on artificial intelligence?"

"Yes, though we're still assessing the implications."

"As is everyone else. I imagine they called your attention to the exceptions to the ban included in the language, as well."

"They did." Daemyn tried to recall them. "Though we were focusing on the ones most directly related to Wynde Industries."

"Understandably." Windwalker lowered his voice. "I'll let you in on a little secret. One of those exceptions, if you happened to be reading along without any particular ideas in mind, makes reference to uses of artificial intelligence for pedagogical and vocational purposes at the university and academy institutions. Various purposes are listed, as one would expect. Including flight training."

Daemyn stared at him. "Airspar."

"With the tragic deaths of those young men and women affiliated with professional racing, it is now more necessary than ever before to do everything we can to assure their safety in the cockpit, wouldn't you say?"

"That's… devious."

Windwalker shrugged. "Our lobbyists – Kedu's, in coordination with those acting on behalf of Hillside and several of the other academies, too, of course – found it very persuasive to delegates in the Lower Assembly."

"You think you'll get away with it? Reading the law to allow use of AIs in Airspar at the academy level?"

"I doubt anyone will think twice of it, actually. For one, too many entities on Prime are dependent on the existence of a pool of pilots of superior skill. The Unified Forces, naturally, both the Air Branch and the Navy's space fleet. But also various companies in the commercial sector, from shipping to transportation and beyond. Those pilots have to be trained somehow. Without Airspar at the academy level, where else would they come from?"

It was a good point. Daemyn nodded.

"And surely you have felt the pressure building against professional racing. The crashes, the poor role models for youth, all the rest."

"Yes."

"But the public will never let Airspar go so easily. The people are simply too captivated by it. As the professional circuit fades, the academies will rise to take their place. Some will lose money, others will gain. Airspar will win." Windwalker paced over to the framed continental map hanging on the wall. He pointed near Kedu. "We're right on the cusp of the Grand Coulee. Neighbors to the Thunder Valley track. Yet we have failed to exploit this opportunity to maximum benefit. In fact, just last week the Board of Trustees authorized a capital expenditure exceeding three million dracts to upgrade all of our team's facilities, equipment, airblades, and tuition scholarships."

Daemyn looked from the map to the other man. "Your team is pretty good, though. Nothing to be ashamed of."

"The best," Windwalker said. "We will be the best."

"An admirable goal. But you'll need some better pilots, then."

Windwalker looked him right in the eyes. "And the best coach."

It took Daemyn a second. "Me?"

"Your salary, purely in contractual terms, would have to be commensurate with the current state of the coaching market at this level, though we'd list your compensation at the high end of the spectrum. In addition, I am authorized to offer you terms which will allow you to continue to earn income from endorsements, as well as remain fully involved in the management and ownership of Wynde Industries. I think you'll find that the short term pay cut in nominal salary will be insignificant over the long term."

Daemyn's brain wasn't calculating money. "No offense to your generous offer, but doesn't Kedu, you know, already *have* a coach?"

"We do, though he's been ready to retire for several years now."

"Oh."

The older man smiled. "I wouldn't have expected you to know. In any event, he's prepared to wait an additional season, possibly two, until you're ready to replace him. Beyond that, well, then we'd have to pursue another candidate. But I don't think it's going to come to that."

The only thing Daemyn could do was laugh. "You're a confident man, President Windwalker."

"I realize this offer has come as a surprise to you. The timing of it, at least."

"Honestly, yes." Daemyn looked back at the map. "Running a team when I'm no longer racing – sure, I've thought about it. But right now…"

"Maybe win one more championship trophy first?"

He looked back at Windwalker and grinned. "I don't like to lose."

"Neither do I." The academy president started to lead the two of them toward the door. "I won't take any more of your time today, Daemyn. You've indulged my pitch, and now I'll indulge your thoughtful consideration of it. I don't expect an answer on the spot. Not even this week. Take some time to think about it. When you do, I believe you'll see what I see. What the future could hold for Kedu Academy and Wynde Industries when they're teamed up together. What that future promises for Coach Wynde."

…*refugee resettlement village, near Agoelo*

Utara pounded her fist against the tree trunk driven like a pylon deep into the dusty soil. Close to a meter in diameter, the wooden obelisk didn't even think about budging. Nor would any of the adjacent trunks, equally unyielding in their positions. Together, they formed a stockade fortification around the perimeter of the newly forming human settlement on the savannah.

"This will hold up for years," she told her friend. "And it's sturdy enough to keep out the big animals, tall enough to keep out the predators."

"And intimidating enough to keep raiders at bay," J'ni said. "Not something they could knock down or climb over without taking a serious beating from defenders first."

"That, too. Where'd the trunks come from?"

"About thirty kilometers southeast. It's a big stand of trees there. The smaller ones will actually grow a lot bigger now that we weeded out the largest ones to bring here. About half went into the stockade; the rest they're cutting up into segments for the buildings. Some of the closer spots have trees we can cull for smaller structures, too."

"That's great."

"Yes, we lucked out. A few of the trucks have enough engine power to make the haul with that kind of cargo. I don't know if someone sent specs to Sage Gaiser or what, but those two shipments that came in her transports really moved everything along. The trucks, the power-saws, generators, hand-tools, and all that. It made a whole lot more possible than what the villagers would've been able to accomplish otherwise."

"I'll be sure to let her know."

"Thank you." J'ni laughed. "Tell her she's always welcome to send more."

Utara laughed too. "I bet. Seriously, though – I'm impressed with how much has already been done here."

"It still needs some work." J'ni stepped back, waving her hand at the stockade. "We'll have to even out the tops to a uniform height, peel off the bark, maybe even paint it. We'll get around to it eventually. The construction on the houses and storage buildings is the top priority."

Utara looked at her. "We?"

J'ni shrugged. "No point in writing a dissertation on migration patterns that won't exist anymore."

"I hadn't thought of that."

"You had some pretty important things on your mind recently, Utara. It's a few years of my life down the drain, no big deal."

"I'm –"

"I'm joking," J'ni insisted. "Science is all about new discoveries, right? Well, I get to discover how to prevent migratory animals from drinking from a poisoned river when they get back to this part of their habitat in four months. Then I get to discover how they adapt and form new migration patterns when they can't use their old ones any more. Terrible for the animals, but the new research abounds."

Utara smiled. "That does sound like the kind of project that would make a pretty impressive grant proposal."

"Exactly. In the meantime, I can help the people here. The nomads know the land better, but I've been out here long enough to add a lot, too."

"And you've lived both worlds. From city life to the savannah, and succeeded."

"Careful," J'ni said, "or you might ruin my humility."

"I doubt that very much."

"And what about you?" her friend asked. "What's next for Utara Fireheart?"

"Honestly, I'm not sure."

"I assume one option is to stay in PDS?"

"Yes. In the short term, I'll probably help at Steamer Point until all of the refugees have been relocated."

"How long is that? Six months? A year?"

"Hard to say, but the resettlement initiatives have moved faster than I expected. Maybe closer to six months than a year, if I had to guess."

"And after that?"

"Who knows, while the leadership vacuum is still there. The Governor of the Plains Terrans mentioned that they need a new PDS intermediary for their ongoing relationship with the leaders of Hyj-gon, and a substantial number of the refugees are choosing to resettle with his people, so that's one possibility once Steamer Point is concluded. Even if that particular position is filled with someone else with more seniority, I suspect that if I want to keep working with Future Cities refugees, either back in Loorriri or somewhere else, I don't think anyone would try to stop me."

J'ni chuckled. "That does seem unlikely. But you're not sure you want to do that?"

"I don't know. I haven't ruled it out."

"But you haven't leapt at the chance to do it, either."

"Right."

"That says something right there." J'ni swatted an insect off her arm. "And let's say you're ready to move on from PDS. What else is on the table?"

"Two different offers in the Cultural Ministry. An invitation to reenlist in the Aladarian Guard. And an offer to consult full-time with CenterPrime News Network."

"Please tell me —"

"I'm not."

"Good."

Utara sighed. "I'm not sure what I want to do."

"I think you should take the time to figure it out," J'ni said. "For all you've done for the refugees, you've suffered as much as they have. You lost your home, your job, your friends. You should give yourself space to grieve, before you decide how you'll move on."

As usual, her friend was right. Utara nodded. "That might help."

"And don't forget, even though you're not going to take it, that offer from CenterPrime proves something."

Utara peered at her. "What do you mean?"

"You've got public visibility. Recognition. It may be a small amount compared to the big people in New Romas, but it's political capital all the same. Whether it's PDS, or Cultural Ministry, or Guard, or another option – use it while you have it."

Utara smiled. "You're full of good ideas."

"Aren't I always?"

"I thought you were saving your humility?"

"Too late."

Utara laughed. Then an idea struck her. "If you'll be staying here a while, then I'll need a way to think of this place. *Where J'ni is* doesn't have the right ring to it."

Her friend smiled. "I suppose not. The villagers have started feeling the same way, that it needs a name. I've heard a few different ones kicked around. I'm not even sure what process we'd use to formalize something. The village barely has elders, much less a functioning leadership or municipal government."

"Maybe wait a while and see which one sticks."

"That's how things tend to happen, isn't it?"

"By accident, or collective consciousness." Utara looked around at the makeshift lumber buildings and early traces of worn footpaths starting to form in the dirt. "What's your favorite? If you had to pick."

J'ni didn't hesitate. "Araroosh."

"That's not familiar to me."

"It's from one of the nomad dialects. One of the scouts used it a couple of weeks ago, and some people took a liking to it."

"What's it mean?"

"Hard to translate, precisely. I guess the closest approximation would be, *the place for starting over.*"

...Grandell Valley

The hooves pounded a staccato drumbeat, muted in its harshness by the verdant grasses and lush soil. They rode briskly, side by side, until they reached the edge of the ridge overlooking the magnificent valley below. The vista was spectacular. One of the true natural wonders on the planet Prime.

Utara glanced over when she heard the thump of Daemyn's boots hitting the ground. He walked to her and held up a hand. She took it, and eased out of the saddle and dropped to the grass beside him. He released his grasp and walked over in front of the horses. He said something to them, each in turn, but she couldn't quite hear it.

Then he turned to her. "Come take a look."

She wondered how he planned to restrain the horses from going anywhere – then realized both massive equine heads already were firmly planted face-first in the grass, mowing down the greenery with reckless abandon. Apparently their mounts weren't interested in going anywhere. She scooted between the horses and met him a few meters ahead, right at the cusp of the valley.

"That was fun," she said. "I needed that."

"I thought you'd like it."

"You guessed right."

He grinned. "It wasn't a guess."

She laughed. "It's been a while since I had the chance to ride like this. I'm glad I didn't embarrass myself."

"Not even close."

"You didn't do so bad yourself."

"I'm out of practice, too. It's been years since I had the time to ride regularly. Hard to fit it into the schedule of an Airspar racer. Fortunately, old habits come back quickly."

She looked at him. "I didn't realize you rode horses."

He winked. "There's a lot you still don't know about me."

"I suppose so." Utara knew one thing, though. Whatever else there was to discover about Daemyn Wynde, she wanted to learn more. "I'm certain you're full of fascinating secrets and thrilling adventures."

"You might be surprised. The life of a work-obsessed, detail-focused, hyper-competitive speed freak may not be as interesting as outward appearances let on."

Utara caught his eyes. "I never called you that."

"You're far too polite." He smiled. "Holtspring did, though. He meant it in the most supportive possible way."

"I'll take your word for it."

For a few minutes they stood quietly, gazing out over the valley. The gentle wind rustled the trees, and birds soared on the rising air currents. Several unseen animals rattled the grasses as they scurried their paths toward their mysterious destinations. A lone canine splashed in the stream trickling down the slope a hundred meters away.

"It's beautiful," Utara finally said.

"It is." He paused. "We own it now, by the way."

She couldn't possibly have heard him right. "What? Who? How?"

He chuckled. "It's... complicated. Grandell Motors needed a major infusion of capital, and Wynde Industries got to the table first."

"You bought them?"

"Well, not the whole thing. A controlling interest. Which includes a lot of land around here, including parts of the valley itself."

Utara laughed. "You can do that? Plop down some dracts and take control of one of the most famous brands on Prime?"

He shrugged. "They were pretty desperate, so it was the right price."

"I don't even want to know the amount, do I?"

"Probably not."

"At least you're honest. What about the rest? I can't imagine New Romas would ever put the World Parks up for sale."

"Oh, not officially, of course. Let's just say, the government needed the dracts in a hurry, and we acquired a stable, long-term investment for the portfolio."

"We, meaning the venturists."

"Everyone contributed. Different parcels all around the planet. Including here. Holtspring and Tames have the biggest shares in the valley, but I made sure to get part of the allocation too."

"That's... amazing."

"Honestly? I was kind of surprised we were able to pull it off, too."

"What are your plans for it? You personally, I mean."

He didn't answer right away. "I'm thinking about moving Wynde Industries here."

Of all the things he might have said, she never would have predicted that. "Really?"

"There's good synergy with all the Grandell Motors facilities. I could advance things a lot faster at WI piggybacking on their infrastructure."

"You wouldn't have to move your headquarters to do that, though."

"True." He watched a bird swoop in the air. "Based on our financial projections for WI, Reiton's already planning his retirement party. And no, I am *not* joking. He's going to build a home here. Rustle is, too. It's hard to think of anywhere on Prime that's better to raise a family."

"And it wouldn't hurt to have the office right down the road."

"Exactly."

"What do your parents think about you moving halfway around the world?"

"I haven't told them yet. But they'll get over it."

Utara chuckled. "I'm not sure I'd be so lucky, keeping plans like that a secret."

He smiled. "I'll take my chances."

"Won't relocating out of Hyj-gon make logistics a lot more difficult for your Airspar? So much of it is based there."

"About that…"

She looked him the eyes. "What is it?"

"I think I might retire from racing."

She laughed. "Funny. You had me going there for a second."

"I'm serious."

"Oh."

"I just have a feeling the time is right."

"You're only thirty, and one of the best pilots in the sport. Surely you've got a half-dozen years left at that level, maybe more."

He smiled. "Oh, it's not age. Not physically, anyway."

"What, then?"

"It's not even Airspar itself, really."

Suddenly Utara knew. "Zanita."

Daemyn nodded. "After what happened there... I don't know how I could go out and fly an Airspar match again."

That, she understood. All too well. She reached out and took his hand. "A lot of people would probably think you're crazy. But I wouldn't."

"I believe you."

"I'm thinking of leaving the PDS once the refugee relocation is complete."

He squeezed her hand. "Something tells me you're not joking, either."

"No."

"I know you haven't given up on helping people. It's too much a part of who you are." He smiled a little. "Plus, you're really good at it."

"Thanks. But right now, at least, I'm not sure I can separate the PDS from everything that happened. Even an assignment in a completely different part of Prime."

"What options do you have on the table?"

Quickly she summarized them for him. His eyes perked up at her mention of the potential PDS position mediating between Hyj-gon's Faytans and the Plains Terrans, but he didn't interrupt. "I'm still making up my mind. Just like you."

"Not easy decisions."

"No."

He looked out over the valley. "I have another factor in play, too. Kedu Academy isn't too far from here. I had a meeting with their president the other day. They want me to become their team's Airspar coach."

"You're going to take it, right?"

"It's a good offer, if I can make it work with everything else."

She leaned against him. "It's one thing to not want to fly competitively anymore. To not want to shoot at other pilots, be shot at, all of that. It's something else to walk away from the sport that's been the center of your entire adult life."

"Before that, even."

"See?"

He looked at her. "You can be very persuasive, you know that?"

She smiled. "I may have heard that before."

"I'm thinking about it. I have a little more time to decide."

"Same for me. No reason to rush it."

"Unless…"

She thought he was going to say more, but he didn't. "Tell me."

"New Romas isn't far from here. Timewise, traveling by air."

"If I took a post in the Cultural Ministry, you mean."

"Right."

"But I don't have anything to fly, certainly nothing that fast."

He looked into her eyes. "I know a guy who can solve that problem for you."

Utara's heart was pounding, but she didn't break his gaze. "I don't have anywhere to stay, either. Where would I –"

"What if you did?"

"Well…" She took a deep breath. "Then that would be a very tempting proposition."

"I thought it might be."

For all the time she had spent pondering which path to pursue next with her career, for all the hours she had worried which choice was the correct one, right now Utara didn't need any time at all.

"Tally this as your first victory, Coach," she said. "I'm in."

THE FIREHEART SERIES

WYNDE
Book One of the Fireheart Series by Tricia Barr

MISSION ACCOMPLISHED
A short story set during *Wynde*, included in the anthology *Athena's Daughters* published by Silence in the Library

ZANITA
A prequel to the Fireheart Series by B.J. Priester

FORTHCOMING

SKY FALL DOWN
Book Two of the Fireheart Series by Tricia Barr

IN BETWEEN
A series of short stories set between *Wynde* and *Sky Fall Down*

For details check:
www.triciabarr.com
www.twitter.com/fangirlcantina
www.facebook.com/FireheartSeries

About the Author

B.J. Priester has been the executive editor of FANgirl Blog, and a contributor on a variety of topics, since its inception in 2010. His series on the Heroine's Journey has been referenced by storytelling and academic discussions across the internet, as well as selected for inclusion in a college composition textbook and high school course teaching materials. He has organized and moderated standing-room only panels on the Heroine's Journey at the annual GeekGirlCon convention in Seattle, Washington. He also co-hosts the monthly podcast Hyperspace Theories, which discusses storytelling and speculation through the perspective of *Star Wars*.

B.J. is a tenured law professor whose teaching portfolio and scholarly publications include subjects such as criminal law, constitutional criminal procedure, white collar crime, and national security law. A graduate of Harvard University and Duke Law School, his career includes previous positions as a law school associate dean, a practicing lawyer in Washington, D.C., a law clerk to a federal appeals court judge, and a law journal editor-in-chief.

About Tricia Barr

Tricia Barr applied her understanding of brand management, social media, and fandom interactions to create FANgirl Blog, which has grown into a prominent and respected genre-focused website. She is co-author of the definitive official encyclopedia *Ultimate Star Wars* (DK Publishing, 2015) and a regular contributor to the *Star Wars Insider* print magazine with an ongoing series analyzing the Hero's Journey and *Star Wars* characters. Tricia is co-host of the monthly podcast Fangirls Going Rogue, celebrating *Star Wars* from the fangirl perspective, as well as Hyperspace Theories. She has organized and moderated *Star Wars* panels at the last four annual GeekGirlCon conventions, along with panels at the *Star Wars* Celebration conventions Anaheim 2015 and London 2016.

A graduate of Duke University with a degree in civil engineering and a licensed Professional Engineer, Tricia has worked as a transportation engineer for over twenty years. She is also an accomplished equestrian, earning a Winter Equestrian Festival Circuit Championship and three top-ten finishes in the Ariat Adult Medal Finals in Washington, D.C.

ACKNOWLEDGEMENTS

Many times when talking about working on *Zanita*, I have been asked whether it is daunting to write a novel in someone else's storytelling universe. Perhaps it can be, but not with *Zanita*. Most importantly, as Tricia mentions in her Foreword, I didn't embark upon *Zanita* from a blank slate; all the work we had done on *Wynde* from inception to completion gave me a deep grounding in the world-building, themes, and goals of the Fireheart Series. In addition, the process of brainstorming, designing, and outlining *Zanita* was a two-person enterprise, with her input and insight at every stage. And certainly, our experiences from previous years working together as beta-readers and co-authors in the fanfiction realm made the transition to teamwork on the Fireheart Series a smooth one.

When the time arrived to begin writing *Zanita*, Tricia gave invaluable input on all aspects of the story, from feedback on characterization and plotting to scene flow and dialogue, and at every stage of the process, from the rough drafts to the final manuscript. Perhaps the rewrites she suggested delivered karmic justice for my red-pen line-edits on *Wynde*, but I am certain they have improved *Zanita* immeasurably. After so many years collaborating in writing, storytelling analysis, blogging, podcasting, and more, the creative process for *Zanita* could not have been more effortless and rewarding. It probably comes as no surprise, then, that ideas for my next contribution to the Fireheart Series already are in development.

Kay, our co-host at Hyperspace Theories, and Linda, loyal FANgirl inquisitor, provided excellent and helpful feedback on the manuscript. I am grateful for their time and insight. The perspectives eloquently advocated by our GeekGirlCon co-panelists Jennifer K. Stuller and Alan Kistler were never far from my mind in preparing and writing *Zanita*, and the book undoubtedly is much better for it. My colleagues Lucille Ponte, Tony Kolenc, and Scott DeVito offered encouragement and enthusiasm throughout the writing process.

Jeff Carlisle's fantastic cover art for *Zanita* speaks for itself. I remain delighted by his willingness to collaborate on and produce such great artwork for what must, compared to much of his other endeavors, be a small project.

Like Tricia in writing *Wynde*, I have been inspired by many great storytellers who came before me. For *Zanita*, particular gratitude is due to George Lucas, Dave Filoni, Aaron Allston, Joss Whedon, and Suzanne Collins.

Finally, for my entire life my parents always have wholeheartedly supported my creativity. From the make-believe of a young child, to toys and action figures, to spinning out tales on the school bus ride home, to roleplaying games, throughout my formative years they encouraged my imagination to run wild. When my passion for a return to storytelling awoke with a flourish years later from the inspiration of the *Star Wars* prequel films and New Jedi Order book series, their encouragement also resumed with equal dedication. So did their patience, as the writing of *Zanita* had to fit in among all my other commitments. Their questions about its progress came accompanied with excitement to read the finished product. Now it has arrived, and I can say without qualification that it never would have sprung into being without their lifetime of love and support.

Made in the USA
San Bernardino, CA
11 December 2017